Voyage
to
Nightfall

Tim Hansmann

Amniti Press

ISBN 978-0-615-45068-1

For Amy and Nick

Voyage
to
Nightfall

1

THE WORLD ENDS a quarter mile ahead, of this he is certain. All evening the fog has swirled and eddied, thickening to an unheard-of density and flattening earth and sky into one single being. Anton Eischen drives hunched over, forehead inches from the windshield, chin brushing the top of the steering wheel. He tries to focus on the few constantly changing yards ahead of him, yet cannot help but ponder how people would have evolved if the air was always as dense; ethereal translucent shapes, he imagines, all tentacles and antennae fumbling around in a murky, starless soup. No dreams of distance, of an edge, or horizon. He begins to see those creatures out there, floating in the mist, dancing mockingly at the edge of his vision, begging for direction.

Hands rebelling from their tight clench on the wheel, Anton takes a second to stretch his gaunt fingers. He has driven this road and fog before, but never as thick. On a clear day the trip is startlingly beautiful, a surprise of tropical vegetation and stunted palm trees. When the sun is just right, Anton would swear it is Caribbean paradise. But this is Ireland, and if you wait fifteen minutes the sun and clouds will change until the light feels unmistakably arctic, and then languidly move on to some other extreme. A land painted in greens and browns, changing dramatically in disconcertingly short amounts of time as you move through, its flat lowlands leading to sensuous rolling hills, abruptly cut by sheer cliffs plunging into the sea.

Anton is leaving the lowlands now, passing the last stucco house on the R559 out of Ventry and driving southwest around the Slieve Mish mountains. Unable to see any of it, he nonetheless feels the low void of Ventry Beach to his left and the looming presence of windswept Mount Eagle ahead. The road barely twelve feet wide, he is thankful no one else is crazy enough to be driving tonight.

Alone in the murky reflectance of headlights, curiosity again takes flight. Opening his window a crack he tries drawing some fog into the car. It smells damp and sweet, Anton thinks, like someone's used towel. In his mouth it is more cream than water. All this is imagination, he knows; as soon as the fog is contained it loses substance.

Disappointed, he rolls up the window, still an awkward movement with his right hand, and then switches his grip on the wheel letting his left fall back to the gear shift. The car pitches slightly and engine lowers in tone as it ascends toward Slea Head and Dunquin. The narrow blacktop rises, reflective gray of fog dissipates, giving way to extensive blackness. Empty dark sea on his left is a perfect foil to the sheer cliff of highly unproductive rock rising from his driver side. Anton suddenly misses the enveloping haze, finding this dark vastness more disconcerting. A white arrow-shaped sign appears for a brief moment: *Dún Chaoin, Dunquin, 8 km.*

The void has a strange pull, a vertigo urging him to drive in to fill its emptiness. Anton shakes his head, breathes deeply and focuses on how he got to this point, right here, right now on this end-of-the-world highway. He does not fully recall how he became the architect to this underworld, but supposes that, like most business plans, it began with one job and spread word-of-mouth. He has already lived much longer than his predecessors, a common career-ending injury being eyes or tongues cut out so that they could not reveal what they have done. *If you're lucky*, he considers. Some people have things to hide, and he helps them. Anton senses the end, and his only way out. *One last job*, he reminds himself. He just hopes his successor will not mind the referrals. Anton is uncertain if he is doing that person a favor, or condemning him to the same existence he has led. There really is a fine line between good intentions and revenge.

He can admit to himself the comfort of living in shadows; always there, infinitely varied and offering protection from the relentless glare of reality. Sometimes he regrets that none of his work will ever receive acclaim, no works ever published in magazines or singled out for awards. He is a good architect, Anton is convinced, though there really is no one similar to compare himself. At least no one he knows of. The sudden thought of someone else out there like him offers a flash of comfort. He has designed some amazing structures, beyond which he has also used his knowledge and expertise, his "cover", to run errands for clients. Sometimes it involved archeology, sometimes psychology, and often thievery. Always it had to do with the one area he knows best: the things people build and leave behind. He considers himself a detective and translator of sorts, someone who sees the forms of the world, rearranges them and reads their meaning. In his job, as he suspects is true of many other jobs, so many aspects become a part of the same whole: history, clients, laws, money, materials, nature. They become the Project.

This Project did not, at first, even appear to be in his specialty: a museum shelter for one of the many stone "beehive" huts built by Christian monks who came to this lonely part of Ireland, to what was the edge of the known world, in the sixth century. The museum was to be modest, enclosing one of the better-preserved remains and offering a comprehensive history and tour. On his first visit, wind and rain forced him to stay in his car, and Anton conceded a shelter to be a good idea but hardly worth his gifts. This referral, however, came from a longtime client who would be quite dangerous to disappoint. No one, not even Anton, knew what his Client was really after, but he rightly doubted it had anything to do with historic preservation or tourism.

At first the local farmers did not seem to care. Quite a few neighbors already have their own makeshift visitor centers attracting tourist money for piles of stone they formerly used to shelter sheep. There were, as always, townsfolk who thought what he was doing would ruin the landscape and defile their monuments. It was more likely they did not like some Yank charging admission on their history, wishing they had thought of it first.

Anton's suspicions were confirmed by the men who would arrive for second shift each evening and scour the site, rather than doing any work, often tearing apart work that was done by the earlier shift. His client could have cared less about the building: there was something hidden here. After a few months of fruitless excavation and stalling tactics, Anton was finally approached for the kind of help he could give.

Like most historic events there is no real record, he was warned, and what tales have been told are distorted to serve the teller's purpose. There would be no magical Vatican archive account here, no hard evidence other than what he could deduct from remnants. Anton chuckled at this: if there was a record, there would be no reason for someone with his talents. He understands too well how history is written, and what is left out. He listened to his Client's story about Saint Brendan and searching for proof of his voyage, or at least what was edited for him. Anyone else would assume they were chasing a myth, but Anton recognized something in his words, had seen too many myths become real, and became certain he could help.

A bank of low clouds moving in off the Atlantic sweeps over, even thicker than the previous fog. A murky claustrophobia returns, comforting, banishing the sense of unending darkness. He resumes his hunched driving position, straining to see until–SHEEP!!! He slams on the brakes, skidding with a jerk and a thud, wiry white curls disappearing under the front of his hood. Other sheep turn to observe, a flock completely surrounding him, highly disinterested in the plight of one of their own while Anton rolls down his window to have a discussion with the damn things and possibly stick his boot somewhere shaggy. He thinks better of it and opens his door, thankful that if another car comes along they would provide a protective barrier. His tense muscles force a walking version of his hunched driving posture as he stands and shuffles to the front of the stalled vehicle.

"Damn it!" he screams in frustration, assessing damage to his bumper and headlight. A few wooly monsters back away disapprovingly. The unlucky sheep who took the brunt of impact is alive at his feet, but lying on its side breathing in short, quick heaves. He sees no blood, leaving Anton uncertain if he should finish the job or give the cursed animal time to recover. He is still pondering this, and how far he will still need to drive the damaged car to its destination, when he looks up and seeing the construction fence realizes he is there.

2

528, Southwest of Newfoundland

FEAR AND COLD. The young monk shivers under a deerskin, uncertain which one of the two is causing him to shake more. He has felt this way for so long, even in the warmer climates they had ventured through. A test of Faith, the good abbot would say: *Fear is only in the mind, and cold is only the body. Neither matter,* the abbot had taught him, *only the Spirit matters.* Ciaran reflects on these words, calming for a moment. Suddenly the shaking returns, even worse than before. *My spirit is also shivering,* the monk thinks.

They are in the currach, a small vessel they have been towing behind the ship for three years now. Ciaran knows this kind of boat well; tanned ox-hides with oak bark, stretched across an ash wood frame and sewed together with leather thread, the hides smeared with animal fat for water resistance. He had built and cared for one with his father, and his father had done the same with his father before. It is the boat of his homeland so very, very far away.

The two other monks paddling refuse to look at him. The mast for the square sail was not added for this trip in order to make room for a few supplies and their cargo, the lack of anything between them making their avoidance more pronounced. The two men look more natively wild than learned monk, as does he. Years ago they shed their original clothes and had taken to wearing animal skins for warmth and protection. A few still have woolen overshirts, but most had been torn or irretrievably soiled from constant wear and are now holding parts of the ship together, or traded to natives.

He looks back towards the main vessel, which had sailed as close to land as it dare. This ship, the likes he had never seen before though now after three years knows every inch of, still overwhelms every time he looks at it from afar. Based on a Spanish or Roman design he was told, its craftsmen were sent by Pope Hormisdas himself to the monastery at Ardfert many years before this journey began. It does not have a proper boat shape, he has always thought, it is only about half as wide as it is long, but the high bow and high keel have protected them from many storms. Angled with its keel pointed inland and bow out to sea he can see both steering oars lifted just out of the water, its single square leather sail down. They were ready to depart on a moment's notice, whether from storm or native attack: a posture learned the hard way.

How the gods have a sense of irony, Ciaran thinks. *One God*, he immediately corrects. Joining the new Christian monks was to be his escape from his father's fate, a life at sea. His father had not been happy, both because Ciaran had shown more talent for the boats than his brother, but also because he feared the real gods would be angry. Ciaran was quick to learn, but had never liked the water. Neither was he very spirit-minded, yet the abbot of the Ardfert Monastery was happy to accept a recruit eager to learn; about philosophy, writing and illustration that Ciaran found he did have a passion and talent for. He was happy there, peaceful even, well inland away from the sea. However, because Ciaran had been raised helping his father fish and working boats, the good Abbot

Brennain considered him a prime candidate for this Most Important Adventure. He had merely swapped one father for another, pushing Ciaran into a life he thought he had escaped.

The boat heaves, waves increasing as they near the shore. At the low point they scrape sand beach. Their heavy cargo, this damn Holy Stone, helped to keep them steady, but as they step out into cold water the added weight makes it difficult to pull the currach along the bottom.

Ciaran looks back again, his home ship now small on the water about fifty lengths out. He is still cold–the late days of spring and they were far north–but the fear has completely left his mind. There should be much to worry about, many of the same things he had fear of during the journey: storm, hunger, thirst, sea, sky, and going off the edge of the world. He knows he does not belong here, as much as this land looks like his home. It will be a test of faith.

From their survey, this land seems to be an isolated group of five islands stretching north to south, four of the larger ones connected by long thin sandbars into an archipelago: one could actually walk from the north island to the south island without getting his feet wet. The one island that stands alone to the east is small, not offering much except for a possible escape should natives come to the main islands.

Ciaran and his brothers had gone ashore in a number of places, and are now anchored in a natural harbor on the southeast side between the two center islands. They have been parked off the coast for two weeks, watching and sending reconnaissance parties much as had done many times, many places, before. Where they are landing now seems a perfect spot; the land feels like their Irish home, though a bit less rocky, and is protected by a big island to the northeast and a peninsula to the southeast. They had missed this place the first time as they sailed south, having only marked the gap north of here as a possible entrance to a large river. The natives did not seem to settle this land, though there is food, wildlife and water. It is, the Abbot now believes, the perfect new Edge of the World.

Over the past year they had traveled very far south. However, the further south, the more natives encountered. They had thought to have found the Perfect Place a number of times, only to be confronted by mostly curious but sometimes hostile tribes. Running out of options they felt fortunate to have landed here, a place that may be used by the native tribes, but does not appear to be inhabited permanently. Unlike the big island to the north they had passed on their earlier southward trek, this group of small islands has sandbanks and good passages, and better land. There are great trees and meadows, fields of wild wheat just beginning to grow. The fishing is good, as is the hunting, especially for seals. They have stocked the main boat well in just one week.

This place also feels more like his home, his Ireland, than any other place they have come across. The cliff walls give way to rolling hills, and the sky is the northern sea sky of his youth. It is, he concedes, if not perfect, at least an Acceptable Place.

They pull the boat to the edge of tidewater. The two other monks, still avoiding Ciaran, reach in and begin removing supplies from the bottom of the boat: salt, a few extra tanned hides, a length of leather rope and one of the precious extra iron spikes they had brought with them to fix the hull cross beams. They walk them to the edge where the sand meets wild grasses.

Like his family, Ciaran is stocky, certainly shorter and rounder than the two accompanying him. He is helping, but only seems to match one trip for every two of theirs. Always a bit short of temper–something he had been working on in his studies–Ciaran finally stops and confronts the men who once were his brothers. "Thou not see me?" he asks.

"The Stone," the monk on his right said, pointing in the boat. It was all that was left. Ciaran stands a moment while the other two positioned themselves on either side of the boat to lift it. They stop, frozen in a half motion waiting for him, Ciaran wanting just a little recognition after all they have been through together. Finally, the monk who had spoken looks at him. Ciaran steps into the boat and helps them lift it out. It is not even the entire Stone, almost half of it having been broken off and kept on board the main boat for record or souvenir or proof, or simply so the currach would not sink under its weight. As they strain to pick it up high enough to clear the side of the boat, Ciaran steps out and the three of them move it up just past the pile of supplies.

They rest for a moment, side by side, on the edge of the sand, staring out to sea and the boat that has brought them here. It is a pensive moment, the noon sun providing some warmth which is quickly carried away by wind. Silence, except for the wind. Ciaran knows that before the sun sets, he and the other two will need to move all the supplies and the Stones up to the spot the Abbot has chosen.

Upon arrival, the Abbot described once more to the hunting parties what he was looking for. They came back with two or three possibilities, more than any previous landings. He came ashore and proceeded like he was choosing land for a new monastery, walking deliberately to each site and then praying there for what seemed like, even to a monk, a frustratingly long time. After two days on shore he returned to the boat.

The exact place the Abbot chose is up high among the rolling hills on the east side of the small middle island. Ciaran loves the spot, the high cliffs perfectly reminding him those near his home. Yet from here it would be a full day's hike, and then back for supplies. It will be an especially long trip with his silent, stoic companions.

Ciaran stands first, the other two following his lead. They would still not look at him, out of jealousy or out of concern. They all knew the return sea journey would be harder and longer than the trip here. They would have to leave soon, perhaps even this week, heading north and east to the land and sea of ice and then back to the land of fire where the nearest outpost of fellow monks could be found. They had left one of their own, his friend, there; was it two years ago already? They will need to leave very soon, Ciaran knows, for any chance to make it home.

At this moment, despite the avoidance of his companions, all he feels is pride and concern for his brothers. Ciaran is reconciled he would not make that trip with them. For him, and him alone, this would be the end of the journey.

3

NATHAN BANG KNOWS HE IS WRONG, and is, therefore, all the more defensive. "You don't ask clients to meet you at your 'club'," his business partner Johanna Nikolai speaks these words very slowly, jaw firmly clenched, as if speaking to her three-year-old. It is certainly not her first instance in this room scolding someone, though this time the calmness of her voice reveals exactly how upset she is. As principal and co-founder of Nikolai Bang Architects it is her name, and reputation, first. Even though discipline is part of her responsibility, she thinks having to reprimand her longtime friend, her partner, is just not fair. Johanna is feeling the strain of being the poised and charming professional, the one bringing in clients and managing staff. This situation, just another incidence in the slow erosion of her 'creative' partner, makes her more angry than worried.

"Oh, come on Jo, it's a 'gentleman's club', and he is, by definition of being a learned kind of man, a 'gentleman'," Nathan counters. His lanky frame barely holds a black on gray striped dress shirt and blue jeans. He leans to take a discrete whiff, confirming that his outfit still smells like the said club he is being reprimanded about.

"Well, Reverend Weiland was not amused." Johanna, in contrast, looks her spectacular and put-together self. She is wearing her long brown hair loosely today, and it sways with her head in disappointment.

The clubs are a new thing, an addiction he picked up to replace the smoking habit he quit some months before. Quitting anything cold turkey has never been successful; only replacing one addiction with another seems to stick. It has not always worked out for the best. Nathan finds himself fascinated by the dancers, the crowd, the predictable music, everything. Young women, girls really, moving in a practiced way to men who want something from them they know they have no chance of getting. A setting where everyone plays their part; the men feign overexcitement, and the dancers, with expressions of complete boredom, portray a completely unique blend of awareness and distance. Nathan finds it more intriguing than erotic. There is a sad beauty to the whole thing; his favorite.

Beauty, he thinks, *now there is the base addiction. It always comes back to that.*

"I honestly didn't know he was a minister," Nathan explains, "you just told me 'a client interested in building a Fellowship Hall'. Seemed kind of sexist or Masonic or something, so I picked a place I thought he might like and has great food. By the way, it wasn't very professional of him to just stand me up, either."

"Ugh," Johanna grunts, exasperated.

"What's with these night meetings, anyway?" Nathan continues, "He could have at least called. I didn't enjoy myself at all that evening." He is not sure why he added the last bit. Would it make her feel better in some way? Does he give the slightest God-damn? Even as he thinks it, he realizes he is quite hung-over, perhaps even still slightly drunk.

Johanna drops her head on the conference table. With the door closed, the thud of her skull hitting wood seems to echo. Nathan winces and thinks it must have really hurt. She raises her head to look up at him again, directly into his eyes. For a moment he thinks she achieved that same knowingly distant look his favorite dancer, Krystal with a K, has perfected. He tries to meet her gaze, but his eyes keep darting up to the red welt on her forehead. *Damn that must have hurt*, he thinks again.

"If anyone had recognized him in that parking lot, we might be in a lot of trouble. DO NOT LET THIS HAPPEN AGAIN," she says finally. Standing up and turning, she opens the door and steps out into the main office. The sound of ringing telephones and noise of working and talking and laughing in the big open office intrude into the small conference room.

"The food is really good," Nathan says quietly, reassuring himself with a sigh. He pushes back his chair. Stopping at the door, he composes himself and puts his Fearless-Leader look back on before stepping out into the abyss. Nathan anticipates that as soon as he does so, the questions will start coming, the problems will need to be solved. *The Beast must be fed*, he thinks. He is tired, and he resents the responsibility. He bristles at the work ethic expected, the one he used to have. *Work ethic is only important to society*, Nathan reasons, *if only to keep people from having time to question the meaning of it all.*

Having just turned forty, a young age in his field, he knows he should be ecstatic with his success and that he really has very little responsibility; no wife, no children, no mortgage, not even a girlfriend since Alex left. All he has is here, he realizes, looking around. It is not that he does not want more: he knows he is good, but not good enough to achieve immortality, leaving monuments behind that would cause people to marvel a hundred years from now. He has nothing against marriage or kids; he really envies Johanna and her family. Nathan has just never found someone to put up with the needs that drive him. A singular need really; an appreciation and appetite for beauty that manifests itself in women, cars, places, and all manner of things. It really is not his problem, as he sees it, any more than someone who compulsively feels the need to exercise every day. *And those bastards can find wives, raise families,* he notes. Early on he had tried to manage it, but soon realized that repression just made things worse. Chicago is a big small town; big enough that you think you can go unseen, at least get away with things, but small enough that could never happen. Someone always seems to know.

So he focuses on work, making beautiful things for other people. The office he and Johanna have built is a result of his design skills and her business sense. They could switch places–they both ran the business and both had design input–yet they had fallen into their respective roles, and this is how the world knows them.

They were friends in school, two of the most promising designers always pushing each other to be better. There was always more of a sibling rivalry rather than romantic tension. Johanna was smart, funny and very attractive, yet the thought of the two of them ever having more than their current partnership is unnatural. In a way, their lives are even more entwined than if they had been lovers. She was always more balanced than he, both professionally and personally. Although central to Nathan, this office and career is not her primary legacy. Her family is far more important. Johanna may feel the same drive to leave something solid in the world, but Nathan thinks she has hedged her bets far better.

Johanna, he thinks as he watches her walk away, is easy and charming. More wise than insightful. She is an extrovert who knows when to speak and when not to. She can talk and listen and put people at ease. People are impressed with her immediately, thereby bringing in a lot of business and a lot of talented employees. Johanna inspires confidence. If she does not inspire you right away, she will eventually talk you into it.

Nathan, on the other hand, always considered himself the thoughtful introverted type; quiet and deep. *At least I hope I'm deep*, he muses, *or I've wasted a lot of time being quiet.* In any case, it makes for a good persona to clients, especially when he could transition into marketing mode; smiling, shaking hands and giving flowing presentations. For those who saw both sides, the quiet part of him was often misread as egotistical design architect. It was a useful character, and he did nothing to discourage it. If you do not have an opinion, he found that others were more than willing to make it for you. He does not want that, especially when it pays decent money to have an opinion in the first place.

He passes Sharon, the receptionist. The conference room is located directly across from her, separated by the front entry and small lobby. A high counter in front makes her look like a floating head with a telephone attached. Sharon has been with them for years, and is far more valuable than half their architectural staff.

"Hey Nathan, while you're here, I'm typing up this letter you gave me. Did you really mean to write 'you suck' here?' Sharon holds a handwritten page over the counter, pointing to a spot near the bottom.

"No, that was supposed to be an 'f'." Nathan continues walking a few paces then stops, reconsidering. He looks up at the wood ceiling high above and, not turning around, simply says "why don't you strike that part."

"Already done, I was just humoring you," Sharon replies. "You look like hell, by the way."

Nathan waves and continues around the corner of the bookcase into the main drafting area: a huge open space, forty feet wide, a hundred feet long and at least twenty feet high surrounded on four sides with brick and fifteen foot industrial-sash windows. The space was formerly part of an old brewery in Lincoln Park, just north and west of the downtown. Surprisingly, no one seems to notice him, much less come running up looking for confirmation on one of their design decisions. He is able to cross the floor without being hassled.

Sitting down in his office, Nathan looks at the side door and considers using it, even though it is only 9:00 am and there really is nowhere to go. When they were first starting out, this room was their entire office, he and Johanna sharing the space with a single desk, a copier and two drafting boards. Now it is his alone; a perk of success, he supposes. The phone on his desk is impatiently blinking a red warning, as if it would explode any minute. He picks up the handset. Before he can dial a number Sharon peeks around the doorframe.

"There's a call for you on line five. He says it's a referral, and you would want to take it," she informs him.

"What's the name?" Nathan asks.

"I asked, he wouldn't say, only that it's important. He refused voicemail when he called earlier," Sharon states, turning to leave.

He looks down at the blinking light on line five. Nathan considers the hypnotic flashing for a moment before pressing the line. "Good morning, this is Nathan Bang," he says, finding it difficult to sound cheery with the rasp of a long night's lecherousness in his throat.

"I was referred to you by Anton Eischen," the man says. "He said you could finish the job if something happened." The voice on the other side sounds as raspy as his own, but more from years of talking and smoking. A man in his fifties, Nathan guesses. There is a snap to it, a directness of someone accustomed to giving orders.

Anton Eischen, Nathan pauses, *now there is a name from the past.* A classmate of his and Johanna's, Anton was there when Johanna and Nathan formed their friendship. Anton had always kept to himself at school, yet somehow the three of them had spent a lot of time together when they took a semester to study and travel abroad in Germany, France and Italy. With only twenty students in their group, the three of them just clicked. The dream formed that year, that together they would run an office like Nathan sits in now. However, Anton drifted away once they returned for their final year of school and thesis.

"I appreciate the reference, but I have a huge resort hotel development going up in Lake Geneva. Takes a lot of my time. I would be really happy to have one of my project managers meet with you," Nathan offers, "if you could just give me your name, number and what the project is about?"

"No," the voice states sternly, "that is now how it works. Not the firm, only you."

The last sentence piqued his interest, but whatever commitment problems he has in his personal life Nathan does not have with his professional life. A good fee and an interesting project he could spend some time on by himself gave him a very calm feeling. The idea of coming in to work knowing exactly what needs to be done, and not have to talk to anyone, is a damn happy feeling. Today, however, he feels swamped.

"Sorry," Nathan reiterates, "I would be happy to oversee it, but one of my project managers could best take care of the day-to-day work."

"Perhaps one of your project managers could take over the resort in . . . where did you say?" the man asks.

"Lake Geneva. In Wisconsin," Nathan adds, not knowing where the voice on the other end emanates from. "The Grand Hotel

Menaggio. First class rooms, spas, restaurants, everything. It's going to be fantastic: modern design, Italianate luxury. Close to Chicago, and what Chicagoan doesn't love Wisconsin, eh? It's at a critical stage of construction, and really needs my full attention for every detail." Just talking about it, Nathan feels the weight of all the decisions and conflicts waiting for him in his voicemails. Suddenly his thought is redirected. "Wait, did you say something happened to Anton?"

There is a pause, during which Nathan grows more curious about his old friend, but at the same time hopes the man would just say thank you and hang up. The mystery man instead asks, "If, when, you free up, is there anything else pressing, or would you consider my project next on your list?"

As curious as the vagary from the other end of the line has been, Nathan is feeling ready to attack his postponed messages. Besides, it would be almost a year away, so he answers with the cavalier attitude of someone thinking it will never happen. "Sure, I'm all yours," he says and with a goodbye hangs up the phone. As soon as the line goes dead, he regrets not finding out what happened to his old friend.

Shit, Nathan thinks, *didn't to get his name.* He presses his message button, dismissing the thought, resigned he would have forgotten it anyway. He was never very good with names.

4

ANTON EISCHEN STANDS, wincing against the wind-driven rain, cursing the low cloud fog that just moved out. He buttons the top of his jacket, pulls up his rain hood, and looks over at the construction fencing. A metal gate lay tipped on the ground, much like the sheep still breathing in gasps in front of his car. He had almost driven right past. Something knocked it over, but he doubts it was the wind despite its considerable force. Whatever it was had scared the sheep on to the road.

Picking up the gate with some effort, Eischen leans it against an adjacent stone fence, feeling unnerved as waves crash loudly below the sheer cliff opposite the road. Returning to his car, he grabs the sheep by its hind legs and drags it to the side. That seemed to be the resuscitation it needed; it begins to kick wildly, startling Anton and causing him to lose his grip and fall backwards into the muddy roadside.

"Damn it!!" he screams again, more loudly this time. He watches the sheep disappear across the road and, he hopes, off the side of the cliff and two hundred feet down into the pounding surf. *I'd like to see you survive that, you mangy bastard*, he ventures, knowing it unlikely.

Standing up, he realizes the muddy fall did little extra damage to his already soaking clothes. He opens the car door, wincing at the dome light. Without bothering to wipe the mud off his jeans–after all, it is just a rental car he has no intention of returning–he gets back in and moves it off the road and onto the freshly cleared entry drive. He turns off the engine, debating whether to keep the headlights on. He worries it will draw attention from the local farmer, whose yard light is now the sole point of light about a half mile further west along the road. At one o'clock in the morning, someone pulling into the construction site and parking with lights on would surely arouse enough suspicion to alert the Garda. Anton grabs a flashlight from the passenger seat with his left hand and opens the door.

Stepping carefully across the rocky terrain, he walks past the half-completed structure of the museum he designed. Currently it is just a simple rectangular structure of concrete block, about halfway up the first story. The window and door openings are spanned with steel, and the whole thing will have a stucco finish to look like a traditional Irish farmhouse. Off the back are a few concrete footings ready to receive steel and glass, extending a canopy to enclose the tight grouping of beehive huts. Anton doubts the steel structure will fare well in this climate, but is comfortable that it will become someone else's problem.

Anton had found what he was looking for earlier in the day, and now just needed the time and privacy to remove it. As far as he is concerned, this ends his involvement in the project, the only reason to finish it would be to provide cover. Frankly, he could care less; simply step away and let a local architect finish it.

The story he told his Client, however, was much different. Had he woken up this morning knowing it would be his last day? That he would tell his patron it was hopeless to find the Relic he was hired to search for, and then go back and steal it for his own use? He does not remember such an epiphany: it was just spur of the moment. To his Client, Anton Eischen has already disappeared. He is certain his old friend Nathan had probably received a call a few minutes later.

Stepping up to the low stone huts, Anton smiles at the thought of Nathan hearing his name again, wondering if he still remembers. He is certain he always considered Nathan a much better friend than Nathan had considered him. Then again, Anton did not let himself have many friends. The semester overseas with Nathan and Johanna and his beloved mentor, Professor Moynihan, was perhaps the happiest time of his life.

The beehive huts–*clochán* Anton had heard them called–on the southwest edge of the peninsula are peculiar. Mounds of stone that are remarkably similar in shape and size, with small square doors, usually in groups and surrounded by stone fences, they were either prehistoric or built by the monks who isolated themselves from the dark forces in Europe when this land was the edge of civilization. He stoops inside the one nearest his new museum, marveling and relieved that it is still as watertight as when first built.

This particular group of *clochán* is special, different in its grouping than others in the area. However, that was not why it was chosen for the museum. His Client had a map of some kind, leading them to this spot. It had taken months, maybe years, for the Client to figure out what he were looking for and where it was. All he told Anton initially it was made of stone, the most plentiful thing around here, and that it was part of an old tablet with some writing on it. He did not know how big it was, what was on it, or where exactly it would be.

At first the Client had tried digging, which had been frustrating in the rocky soil. It aroused suspicion, and ultimately yielded nothing. When he contacted Anton, he warned his client it could become expensive, especially with the suggestion of a museum as cover so that they could work in peace. Money, it became clear, was no object.

This had been the most visible project Anton had undertaken in a long time, and he was surprised at how uncomfortable it had made him feel. He thought about using a false name, but that is much easier to do when the project is not so public. When projects start showing up in the papers or on the web, just one recognized photo or misused name might start a cascade of events. It is better, he found out, to use your real name when doing something secret in public.

His real name had become just another guise anyway, he thinks. Anton Eischen muses that his whole life is a lie. But because it is all he knows, and because he had told the story of his made-up past so many times in just the right way and actually came to build his life on it, it had become the truth. Anton thinks he has reached the point, however, when being clever, witty, charming and ruthless does not seem to matter much: life has a way of forcing true meaning upon us. True meaning is exactly what he had been avoiding, and when it demanded his attention it was not what he expected.

He had neither met the Client, nor found out his real name. Anton had only worked through the Client's representative: Audrey Mays. She was disarming; not only smart and beautiful, but if you were carrying a weapon he has no doubt she could quite physically disarm you, probably breaking your arm in the process. Of course, that was why the Client had picked her for this job: the silly architect and contractors would bend over backwards trying to impress her. Human nature. Male nature. Anton did not know much about his Client, but it was clear he knew how to use people.

The rain lets up. Anton ventures out to find the spot he had been searching earlier in the day, turning his flashlight off once he reaches it. The clouds have broken, and enough moonlight is coming through to make his work visible once his eyes adjust. Balancing on hands and knees atop the rain-slicked structure, he carefully removes a stone near the top and works his way down, removing a section just above and to the right of the small, almost square, entry. Anton is careful as he works, afraid the wrong stone will make the entire dome of structure cave in. He cannot help but feel what he is doing is sacrilege, taking apart something built over a thousand years ago. In a perverse way, it bothers him more than seeing a human life taken.

Anyone else might not have noticed the difference, one stone different than the hundreds around it: more regular in shape and a slightly different color. He feels he is getting close. Anton picks up his flashlight, and as he moves a few more stones there is one that unveils a few deep etchings inscribed onto its top. This is it! Eischen clears around and carefully lifts it out. It is only about eighteen inches wide and two feet long, about four inches thick and heavy. The long edge is smooth on one side, but jagged on the other with some of the characters sliced off. This stone was quite obviously part of a larger piece, and most certainly what the Client had him searching for. Most likely from his own excitement, Anton could swear he senses a deep vibration coming off of the remnant as he holds it in his hands.

He turns off the flashlight and wraps the stone in a piece of canvas he had been keeping under his jacket. Walking back towards the museum structure and his car, Anton guesses he has been out here for about two hours. He is beginning to shake from the cold, the wind and the rain. Setting the package down for a second on a slab of concrete foundation, he shakes off as much damp from his jacket as he can.

By the time he hears the footsteps it is too late. He turns only to see the dark line of a shovel handle, obliterated by a bright flash behind his eyes and deep thud as it connects with his head, an involuntary guttural sound emanating from his throat. He is conscious only a moment as he lay in the mud, his right cheek on the ground, rain pooling and seeping into the corner of his mouth. At the moment everything goes black, Anton Eischen is thinking about that damn sheep.

5

527, The Great Bay (Chesapeake Bay)

THOUGH HIS VISIONS are less frequent, they have nonetheless become more violent: today's episode left Ciaran feeling his head had been split in half. He has had this Gift since childhood. He and his father had considered it good instincts, knowing when a big storm was coming or where the best fishing would be, but his mother had seen it as a blessing from Ecne and a sign of divine destiny. When he had entered the abbey, and his mind was no longer preoccupied with the demands of day-to-day survival, the visions took on a new power and frequency. The Abbot had recognized his gift, and Ciaran felt secure confiding in him. Ever since they embarked on this Adventure, and his mind was once again focused almost solely on survival, the visions had diminished. They had in fact all but vanished until today, on this wooded hill in a strange land.

Much of what Ciaran had envisioned about this trip has come true, though rarely in the exact way he had seen. His visions were more parables–the way things would be written down should anyone survive this journey–rather than truth. At times he thought he was reading too much into events and simply projecting his visions where they would fit. About a year into his studies, however, he saw their departure; the Abbot and about twenty monks and crew heading north in a ship the likes never seen before. They were seeking something, or somewhere.

The trip had not started out well. Bad weather arose immediately, testing the crew. Most of the monks were chosen for their seafaring ability, rather than their faith or piety. Somehow the Abbot had tested them, many of the early recruits leaving sick from his cell at Ardfert. It was clear to everyone that this was going to be an ocean adventure rather than just a search for a place to found a new monastery, and that it would be much longer than the fortnight many had been told. The provisions in the hold of the ship meant either they were traveling far, or they were off to supply a village.

They came across a few monasteries along the way, islands whose distance from home was inconceivable. The first had thankfully come just two weeks at sea, the monks needing to rest and repair from storms ravaging the ship. After this first stop it would be many more months before they set foot on land again, where they were fortunate enough to find islands populated by birds and sheep and fresh water with trout, replenishing their supplies. The monks, having grown accustomed to their foreign ship, had become more galley crew than pious order, even though the Abbot continued instruction. When they reached the Community of Ailbe, the monks who inhabited this farthest-known outpost were shocked by the arrival of this sea-roughened crew.

Though wary their isolation was broken, the Community nevertheless welcomed them as brothers. They traded stories of the giant sea sows that were curious but friendly, blowing towers of water into the sky. After spending the winter, many of his shipmates believed this to be their destination. Ciaran, knowing this was not the end, was surprised that only one monk decided to stay when the Abbot declared they would continue sailing west in Spring.

It was always cold at sea, but as they sailed and rowed on they encountered mountains of floating ice, freezing fogs and a land they had heard of from their recent hosts edged by deep fjords. They stopped at its southwestern tip, but finding little to hunt other than birds they restocked on fresh water and began to head west once more. They took to wearing skin flasks next to their bodies to keep their drinking water from freezing, and as the frequency of the floating ice increased they began to angle south in hope of warmer climates.

They reached a long land. Following its coast south, the concern for food and fresh water lessened even as the threat from strange peoples grew. The further south they ventured, the more natives they seemed to encounter. Ciaran saw the disappointment in the Abbot, though he thought he should be pleased with all the new potential converts to spread the Word. In general these natives were not hostile, but language was a problem since the longest they would remain anywhere was a few months. Some of the other monks were much more aggressive in trying to teach the ones curious enough to make contact. The Abbot's disinterest in evangelism puzzled Ciaran.

The Long Coast, as they came to call it, seemed as far a sail as their sea crossing. They followed it for a full cycle of seasons, though as the land turned west again there was continuous warmth of only summer. The Abbot, after much prayer and isolation during a hermitage inland, returned to make a decision: they would stop, and return the way they had come.

Many of the monks were confused. Had they found what they were looking for? Was the point of the journey a long retreat: an Adventure for its own sake? Or was it an exercise in futility and time to give up? No one knew, and the Abbot was not saying. The crew, for a time, forgot their vows of obedience and was on the verge of mutiny. Ciaran and a few others, however, were relieved to be heading home.

About a month after they began the return north along the Long Coast, Ciaran discovered the stones. Short in stature, he was often sent into places others could not fit. He thought after all this time he knew every inch of the ship, but this was in a section of the Abbot's private sleeping cell. At first they seemed a part of the floor along one side, five pieces laid flat taking up an area about eight feet by four feet, or almost half of the Abbot's quarters. Lying flat and sticking up just a few inches, the Abbot had unceremoniously covered them with supplies and garments. Ciaran knew them to be significant through earlier visions, but no other monk would give them a second thought, dismissing them as ballast. If they were meant to be hidden it was perfect, private enough to not illicit questions but open enough to not cause wonder.

The monks had shifted almost everything during this pause to stockpile provisions, having been especially lucky in the hunt of the white-tailed deer surrounding the bay. The Abbot had asked Ciaran to store some cured hides in his cell. He thought he was perhaps the first, other than the Abbot, to enter here. Had these stones been here the whole journey, or were they discovered on one of the Abbot's inland hermitages? Did one of the scouting parties find them? Were they a gift from one of the native tribes, or simply the Abbot's personal log? As many questions as he had, his earlier visions had taught him to remain silent.

The etchings on the piece closest to him were strange, not anything in the language or writing he had been taught. Touching a piece, he felt a strange cold and then a familiar flash behind his eyes. He jerked his hand back quickly, laid the hides over them, and left.

Though he said nothing, the Abbot knew Ciaran well enough to sense his awareness.

When they reached the Great Bay, about halfway along the Long Coast, they stopped to winter: hunting, foraging and praying during the holy days. They left their own inscriptions in stone, and Ciaran seeing a parallel finally worked up the nerve to quietly ask the Abbot about the stones in his cell. From these questions, and the ones not asked, the Abbot sensed Ciaran knew much about what they were, and what they were not.

The Abbot gave Ciaran a new Test of Faith. They rowed in the currach back to the boat, retrieving a single stone. Returning to shore, a distance away from their temporary settlement, the Abbot sent him on alone with the piece to meditate and pray. Ciaran sensed a new lightness in his leader, the constantly stern and commanding presence seeming far less burdened. Perhaps, Ciaran thought, the Abbot was finally able to share this secret and trust that something was unfolding as it should.

Ciaran prayed, touched the stone, and stared at its inscription. Nothing came; no insight, no vision. He had once seen far into the future, and knew how all these pieces would be scattered: something he did not share with the Abbot. What he did not know was where they had come from, or why. He prayed to God, and at one point prayed to the gods of his childhood.

He fell asleep, thinking he would awaken with the answers. When morning came he still had nothing. He picked through the meager supplies he had been left with, finding some rabbit freshly trapped the day before. This bay had been very well populated with all manner of deer, rabbits, turtles, and bass; they have been eating well, and curing meats for the next leg of their journey.

Chewing on some stringy flesh, Ciaran ran his fingers across the images carved a half inch into the surface. A light blinded him so suddenly that he dropped his food in the dirt and collapsed, chest first, onto the stone.

Men had long searched, even killed for this cargo. Its nature was to be hidden, to be guarded, and to never be whole again. The further scattered, the better. There was one piece more important than the others, and it had chosen him.

In the vision he saw them, his leader and his friends, going back through the islands of ice and fire and back home past familiar Rockall to Donegal Bay. He saw some pieces travel with them, but not all of those he had seen in the Abbot's cabin. In a flurry of images he saw the pieces scatter even further, protected either as holy relic or souvenir.

Once recovered, Ciaran begins to assess what he has seen and what to tell the Abbot. The vision of his monks returning home was a happy one, yet something is troubling; something was missing. Suddenly Ciaran realizes what it is: he was not with them.

6

June 28, Chicago

ENTERING THE SIDE DOOR to his office, Nathan Bang glances at his watch. It is already past eleven in the morning, and since he had his mobile phone switched off he knows there are probably a few impatient messages waiting.

He had gotten up early this morning, off to a meeting with a young rich couple who were interested in building a cutting edge home: cubist forms, glass, steel, flat roofs, the best finishes, sustainability, all the things that make a young urban architect salivate. The meeting had energized him, Nathan dangerously sketching ideas down on a scrap piece of paper over the steering wheel while driving through traffic. After a few near misses he reduced it to quick bursts of notes and lines at stoplights.

Sure enough, the red light on his phone is blinking. He lays his jacket over the chair and sets his brown leather satchel on top the desk. Even though it is Thursday and he is coming from a meeting, Nathan is dressed in blue jeans and a simple solid black button shirt. Earlier conversations with the young rich couple had led him to believe they were casual, and he wanted to make a fitting impression rather than being overly polished or professional. Nathan feels he

32

has to fake polished and professional, but good clients can see right through the ruse. Besides, he likes being in the field where construction is happening and nice shoes and pants look ridiculous.

Johanna walks past. Doing a double-take, she backs up to stand in the doorway. "What are you doing here?" she asks him, a puzzled look on her face. "I thought you were on your way to Lake Geneva."

"No, I had a meeting over in Bucktown with the Henleys."

"You're looking a lot better today," she smiles.

As she begins to leave, Nathan is reminded of the telephone call from the day before. "Jo, do you remember Anton Eischen?"

She pauses a moment, searching. "Wow, I haven't thought about him forever. Did you hear from him?"

"Not exactly," Nathan replies. "He must be practicing, since we might be getting a referral. A client called, and he seemed to suggest something happened to Anton."

"I'll try a quick search online," she offers. With a short laugh Johanna reminisces, "You remember that time we were on the overnight train from Prague? I hooked up with that Swedish guy and started fooling around in the overnight cabin we were sharing? Anton left in a huff and traded all his souvenir money to the conductor for about ten bottles of beer. Then he drank it all in the hallway until he was pissed out of his mind and almost got kicked off the train in the middle of the night near the border checkpoint. I guess he really liked me and I didn't have a clue. I felt bad for awhile, even though by the time we pulled back into Paris he was acting like nothing happened."

"Yes, I remember what a slut you were with everyone but me," Nathan teases. "Thanks for the reminder. His name was Sven by the way."

She smiles, shaking her head and turning to go. "You're an

ass," followed a bit louder as she rounds the corner by, "I'll be in a meeting."

Meetings, Nathan defines, *an action leading to inaction.* Sitting down, he sees no harm in procrastinating a bit longer. He brings up the search engine on his computer, and types the name in. A few pages of hits, but they all seem to be genealogical. *Genealogy and porn*, he huffs, *the two main reasons of the World Wide Web.* He scrolls through the first few pages: nothing. He types the word "architect" with Anton's name, narrowing the search, but still not a single reference, which is odder still. Any architect tends to show up either as alumni, or spokesperson for a project in a newspaper article, or representative at a plan commission meeting, or somewhere. *Curious*, Nathan notes, *but at least no obituary.*

Sharon walks past, and in an almost comical echo of Johanna does a double-take and returns to stand in his door. Her expression is far more concern than puzzlement. "What are you doing here? I thought you would be in Lake Geneva."

"Everybody's saying that," Nathan says with a laugh.

"You haven't checked your messages, have you?" she enters his space, looking at him disapprovingly. "You don't know? Don't you ever watch the news? They've been calling for you all morning."

"Why, what's going on?" Nathan feels her tense concern; it is palpable, and contagious.

"I'm not totally sure," she shakes her head, "but the site superintendent called for you first thing. I asked him what's up, and he said it's all gone."

"What's all gone?"

"The Menaggio," Sharon says softly, "It's gone."

"What?" Nathan furrows his brow, "you don't lose a building that size. You tend not to lose any size building."

"No," she almost whispers, "it burned to the ground. Last night." It was, in architecture, like being told you have cancer. People tend to use the same low voice to convey awful news.

"What!" Nathan draws out the "t", giving himself an extra moment to process. He spins around and turns on the television in the bookcase behind. He flips through the channels, hoping a local news program might be on and that the story is a big enough to get coverage. No luck, only talk shows.

He dials Rick's number from memory. It rings twice and then picks up. "Nathan," the voice says on the other side, "it's a total loss."

"Do you want me to come up there?"

"Only if it would make you feel better. You should give Mike a call. He's up here, and has already told me we'll start again as soon as the smoke settles and insurance is cleared. We can salvage some of the stone, but otherwise it's going to be a while before we get back to where we were yesterday."

"I'm sorry, Rick. You guys have been busting your balls to meet Mike's deadline."

"Yeah, it sucks, but that's what insurance is for, right? It goes faster the second time, I hear. Besides, consider it job security."

"Anything I can do?" Nathan asks, feeling helpless.

"Like I said, it's going to take a while to get back to where we were. We have everything on record and all the permits still good. I'll call if the lawyers get involved."

"All right, keep me in the loop. I'll see you," Nathan sighs, hanging up. He dials the client, Michael Sorensen. He realizes Rick is probably standing right next to him, and Nathan should have called him first. Michael picks up.

"Hi Mike, it's Nate." He hates the name "Nate", but with certain clients you go along when they make a choice of what to call you. Michael Sorensen is a powerful developer, and the Menaggio is their third job together. More will follow, as long as they do well. Michael is loyal, more-so than other developers the firm had worked for, and he likes to do good work that he holds on to for a long time, rather sell off for a quick profit.

"Natey," Michael answers. Nathan cringes, hating this name even more. "What a fucking mess. No one hurt, though. We're covered. My opening is screwed, but it should be fine in the long run."

Michael is an optimist, Nathan thinks, always marketing. "I'm sorry Mike. It might give us a chance to make a few changes, though," Nathan offers. "I've had a few ideas."

"I don't think so," the voice on the other end replies, muffled by the sounds of being outside at a busy site. "I don't think insurance would go for that. You just sit tight, and I'll let you know if we need anything. I loved it the way it was."

"What does it look like?" Fires are not uncommon for projects during construction, but are usually contained. Dust, scrap material, and workers with torches are not always a good mix, no matter how careful.

"They'll investigate for a while before the official report, but the fire department is already saying it looks like arson. Look, I've gotta go, but we're gonna build it again, exactly the same," he hangs up a bit abruptly. It sounds to Nathan as if he had been walking the whole time, and was probably talking to about three other people simultaneously.

Arson is more frustrating; meaningless yet personal, difficult to track down. It could have been kids, a disgruntled neighbor, a serial arsonist, or even the owner himself. This is the second project Nathan has had burn down, but the first deliberate.

Nathan Bang sits numbly for a moment, thinking he is taking all this way too personally. He had been in such a good mood today, and now it all seems lost. Is he even in the right career, Nathan wonders? He had always been good at a lot of things, but never great in one thing, which is a pretty good combination for an architect. In his mind, his obsessions and weaknesses as a human being were also what make him better than average at this job, although without Johanna they would not be nearly as successful. Even with his design skills. She is the people person, and he knows that is why her name is first on the sign. Once again he has become far too lost in the worlds in his head, not recognizing the realities all around; always the same, as some of his fantasy worlds become visceral, he starts to believe all the worlds in his head are reality until something happens to snap him back. He tries to remain focused, dealing in physical things in a physical world, yet it is too easy to envy what you cannot have, miss what you once had, and criticize what you cannot do.

Nathan is surprised that Johanna, and the entire office for that matter, had not known about this disaster. He supposes that is thanks to Sharon, who would keep her silence until Nathan was informed. The word now out, he can hear murmurs flying around the office. In no time people will be stopping in, wanting to talk.

"Nathan, you have a call on line 2," Sharon breaks into his ruminations. "Sounds like the same Mr. No-Name who called you yesterday."

"Put it in voicemail," Nathan says, deciding he does not want to be bothered after all.

"He said you might say that," she counters. "He said to tell you that he has the answers."

"Answers to what?" Nathan is confused and irritated. The ploy had worked, however, and he picks up the phone. "This is Nathan Bang."

37

"Hi Nathan, we spoke yesterday, and I just saw the horrible news. I recognized the name and just had to call. I know it's terrible and opportunistic," the gruff voice apologizes.

"You told my receptionist that you have some answers. About the fire?" his tone comes off a bit more accusatory than he means.

"No, nothing so dramatic. I was hoping I have the answer to how you might be feeling. Sometimes things happen for divine reasons."

"Divine reason?" Nathan repeats. "Don't tell me this is Rev. Weiland playing mind games with me."

"Hardly," the voice on the other side sounds very calm, very soothing, "as I said yesterday your old friend Anton referred me to you. He started a project for me, and because of some unforeseen circumstances needs your help. You are the only person he recommended, so I can only assume you're good at what you do."

"Look, I appreciate it but you haven't told me what the project is, and you haven't even told me your name."

"I have a museum. I am a collector of things, and need a place to put them. This project is both a new building for a community and an excavation of sorts; an architectural excavation that may benefit from your expertise, as Anton describes it. The new building is very exciting, and I will leave it up to you if there are any changes you want to make to the design. It's short term, I'll pay you well, and you should be back in no time to start anything else you need or manage the reconstruction of your poor resort."

Museums are usually good work, often high profile, giving Nathan pause to consider. The strain on his relationship with Johanna might be eased a bit if he brings in a nice, visible, profitable job.

"So will you accept it?" the voice on the other end of the line follows up.

"Sure," Nathan answers after his pause, "what the hell. Like you said, I've suddenly freed up." Nathan begins to tick down the checklist of items he would need to begin. "Would you like to meet? For a proposal I'll need a bit more information."

"That makes me very happy, I look forward to working with you but I'm not that formal. Look for a package with some drawings, project details, down payment and your ticket arriving by courier tomorrow morning. Return name will be Daniel Moyne. I need to say that I like to work discretely, because of the sensitivity of my collection. Nothing illegal, of course, I'm just not interested in attracting the envy of other collectors who may be less scrupulous. I assume you have a valid passport?"

"Passport? Where am I going?" Nathan is caught off guard, not considering the project may be outside the country.

"Have you ever been to Ireland?" the man asks.

7

June 30, Dingle, Dingle Peninsula, Ireland

NATHAN SETS HIS OVERNIGHT BAG on the bed, exhausted from the flight and drive. Particularly the drive. He was prepared for being on the left side of the road, but after passing Tralee the road had narrowed to where he could not tell if there even was a left or right. Nathan chose the middle, at least until the inevitable delivery trucks came hurtling towards him at a high rate of speed. After pulling over, pretending to sightsee and let people pass, he decided for everyone's safety the Irish should mandate a red "L" learner's card on all rental cars.

A scarlet letter would also certainly help the locals realize to whom they are giving directions. The first time he needed help was in Limerick, to which he received a flurry of lefts and rights and street names always followed by the phrase "you can't miss it." However, since there seems to be no rhyme or reason where the street signs are located, he had missed it repeatedly, requiring him to repeat the process.

Nathan arrived at Shannon mid-morning, the flight from O'Hare first dropping off a majority of its passengers in Dublin before backtracking west. The highway leaving south from Shannon's airport was reassuringly modern, and the land lush and rolling; all the shades of green one reads in books or hears in song. However, he found the gentle rolling lasts only past Tralee, at the edge of the Dingle Peninsula. His map showed the most direct route through Connor Pass, which turned out to be somewhat misnamed: a "pass" implies a path between ranges, but this road simply heads up and over. Climbing between the Brandon and central Dingle groups of mountains, the drive proved to be spectacular if not unnerving to a flatlander like Nathan; vast panoramas of mountains, sea, lakes and valleys unfolded, the sky a mix of clouds and sun. The narrow road wound upward, great cliffs dropping off below. He paused at the summit, taking in the small lakes in the deep valley, the wide sweeping bays of Brandon and Tralee to the north from where he had just come, and to the south Dingle Bay and Dingle town: his destination. It is rare when one is able to travel like this for work—work travel usually involves budget hotels in anonymous cities you never get to see—and it certainly beat sitting in his Chicago office mourning over a charred structure, unable to do anything but wait.

The packet Nathan received from Daniel Moyne the day before did not have as much information as hoped, but had booked flight, car and lodgings along with preliminary directions. A note taped to the top of the couriered box stated that some drawings and background would be sent to Nathan at the hotel.

Arriving late afternoon, he had little trouble finding his way around the small town of Dingle, though he was faced with contemplating the brutal horrors of life in a world without specialty coffees at every turn. There was a very evident main street, named just that, with his hotel perfectly in the middle of it. Nathan was pleased with the hotel choice; unused to giving up control and letting someone else make arrangements for him. Connor's Hotel has a front door directly on Main Street, its three story salmon-colored façade nestled snugly between bars and shops. Although the largest hotel in Dingle, it still retains the Irish character of the many bed and breakfasts he had seen. As a bonus, this one has its own bar and restaurant.

He had, just in case, stopped at a store on his way out of Tralee, picking up some supplies including the beer he was now unsure about opening. His stomach rumbles, and he decides instead to step out for some dinner. The menu at the hotel looks good, but there would be time for that; now it is time to see what the town has to offer.

Putting his keys in his pocket, Nathan steps out the front door of Connor's just as a tractor goes down Main Street and turns left at the intersection. The narrow street runs only a few blocks before it disappears over hills at either end, dipping in the middle. Cars are parked end to end its entire length, and the modest sidewalks are lively with people walking. Most of them seem to be heading down the street to his right; east, he thinks, trying to establish his bearings. Nathan closes his light jacket against the chill and turns left into the crowd of tourists coming his way.

He barely makes it to the end of his block before spotting a nice-looking restaurant on the corner. Unconcerned about the fact it is completely empty–it is still a bit early, after all–he checks the menu posted out front and then enters. It is well dark, and the restaurant full, when he stands up to pay his bill and leave.

The meal and accompanying beers are rejuvenating, and Nathan heads further up the street. A small pub, Patrick's Hardware Store & Bar, catches his eye and he enters to a surreal scene: the right half of the open store is, exactly as advertised, a hardware store now sitting dark; its left half a bar with about twenty people ranging from some dangerous looking men drinking quietly to two families with their children running around the bar stools. Nathan claims an empty seat at the bar and orders.

Everyone except the children are speaking Irish, and for a moment Nathan thinks they all might be locals paid to inhabit the bar for character to keep the tourists coming. It is too perfect, too stereotypical: the older men sitting in the corner, where the bar turns back towards the wall, are fishermen; the families, friendly and loud, were getting ready to leave long before any tourists arrived; and the woman sitting closest to him would stop to chat every now and then, usually right before pulling a cigarette out of the pack on the bar and walking outside.

The music is traditional Irish, or at least the kind packaged for Americans. At this moment it is certainly effective: a foreign bar, foreign language and not knowing what tomorrow will bring, make it poignant to Nathan he is indeed far from home. He had been secretly dreading this opportunity, removed from his normal situation, alone, his real life becomes far more objective and too easy to assess. Nathan is already beginning to feel those holes he had been avoiding. All epiphanies tend to be personal, but he hesitates to call what he is now feeling an actual epiphany. That would imply some kind of answer. *Life must have turned when I went straight*, he thinks, *the important things are clearer, but never further from reach.*

At one point the woman was outside enjoying a smoke, the kids playing in the large open area between the bar seating and counter for the hardware store, and the two men were speaking heatedly side by side with their backs slightly turned towards him. He found himself eyeing the cigarette pack on the bar, assessing his chance of nonchalantly opening it up and stealing one without notice. Nathan found he could think of nothing else, finally deciding to do it when the door opens. Without looking he knows it is her, missing his chance. He smiles innocently as she passes, downing the last of his

43

stout and paying. Nathan steps out the door into the cool night air, thankful the walk is downhill this time.

Nathan is back in his room only a few minutes when there is a knock. He sets down his newly-opened beer and walks across the room. At the door stands a young man with glasses dressed in a black rain jacket and dark pants, a roll of drawings under one arm and a plain wrapped box the size of a ream of paper between his hands.

"Mr. Bang?"

"That's me," Nathan smiles, impressed with such attentive service after eleven.

"Identification?"

Pleasantly buzzed and overtired from travel, Nathan pulls out his passport from the side pocket of his travel bag. The young courier studies it intently. Nathan, thinking the man is reaching towards his shirt pocket for reading glasses, peeks in his jacket to where his hand was resting and notices what looks like a leather holster and something black. A pistol grip? What the hell? Probably just a flashlight or for some reason they sent security, he reassures himself, or maybe FedEx always packs heat after dark. The courier, satisfied, hands the passport back, lowers his other hand nonchalantly from inside his jacket, and at last offers the roll and package to Nathan.

Attempting small talk, Nathan asks him if he knows the town, some suggestions of where to visit the next few evenings. "Sorry, not from around here," the courier replies brusquely.

"I thought you were with the hotel," Nathan searches, to which he receives a disapproving look. The courier's eyes scan the room then dart back to the beer on the nightstand, finally settling on Nathan with another disapproving look. Nathan misreads the hesitation as a ploy for a tip, and begins to reach for his wallet.

"You're not like him, are you?" the courier asks.

"Like who?"

"Mr. Eischen."

"Do you know where he is?" Nathan is somewhat relieved that this person might be able to explain what happened to his old friend.

"If I did, neither of us would be here, now would we?" the courier scoffs. "I'll return in an hour for the signed contract, once you've had a chance to read it."

"What, tonight?" Nathan is stunned.

The courier turns and leaves, abruptly closing the door behind him. Nathan does not hear him walk down the long hallway as he stands quietly for a moment, processing what he is supposed to do. He sets the roll of drawings on the chair out of the way, sits on the bed, and rips open the paper of the package. Inside are some additional drawings, a map to the site, a few pictures, and on top is the contract he is supposed to sign. There is a half size letter on plain paper clipped to its edge:

Dear Mr. Bang,

I appreciate your help on such short notice. Your colleague Mr. Eischen spoke quite highly of you. In effect, yours was the only name given who could carry on this line of work should he become unavailable. I hope this information will clarify what I need from you along with the terms of your employment on this project, and will assume through your work with Anton that you understand the language of the contract. It should also be clear that any information provided is confidential. Rest assured, there is no interest by the police or other legal issues that I am aware of, but all the usual precautions should be taken.

After your visit to the site tomorrow, I suggest you telephone with any questions. When you have found the item I am looking for, please contact me at the same number included and I will send my representative to you to pick it up.

I have included a sample photo. I am not sure of the size of the piece you are looking for, or exactly where it may be located. Having tried archeological means of finding it, Anton had suggested that it may be something integrated into the built form, or that the careful study of the layout of structures may suggest a more precise location. The museum structure is both an excuse to be digging around out there, as well as a valid project to interpret the history and meaning of the beehive huts. However, my own personal interest lies mostly with finding the stone remnant. Once you do, I will leave the completion of the museum at your discretion, the funds for which will be at your disposal.
Sincerely,
Daniel Moyne

Nathan thinks his new client must believe he and Anton work more closely than they ever have. The letter suggests something more akin to the academic work they had done with their professor while studying overseas. Though Nathan considered himself a stronger designer, Anton had actually been better at research, possessing a natural patience for the rigor required. Back then Nathan possessed the intellect and the instincts, but very little focus. He was sure he could fake it now, though. Even if Anton is not here to fill him in, there is an underlying assumption from his new and obviously wealthy client that he knows what he is doing. Nathan considers himself a quick learner, and from a professional and marketing standpoint it is usually better to let people believe you know what you are doing. So far, he has always been able to figure it out once he gets started.

He sets down the letter to take a closer look at the photos. The one on top is of a series of domed huts, looking like stone igloos but with a simple square door in the main volume. The next print is a poorly lit shot of a stone, roughly square, with a few dimensions in metric written in red pen over its perspective image. It looked like a broken stone tablet with characters etched on the top flat surface. A series of lines and crosses, the etchings look more like someone marking days in captivity rather than a language. The stone itself, Nathan judges, is lighter in color, more marbled than the stone of the huts, certainly coming from a different quarry.

Nathan ponders the contract, feeling alternately excited and wary. He reads it over, and then once again, since it is anything but the standard he is familiar with. The parts regarding Disclosure echo the things his client had said on the phone regarding his privacy, but the part regarding no photography except of completed structure from exterior and no references to Owner would mean some lack of marketing opportunities. A first foreign commission, and he could not advertise it?   And then there is the primary objective of finding this stone. What the hell, Nathan thinks; he had run errands for clients before. Often it is expected. Nathan thinks he would like his lawyer to look it over. With the time change his counsel would even be in his office, but there was language in the contract forbidding that, which is another troubling part. What kind of legal document excludes lawyers?

He would feel guilty coming all this way and then cause more delay. Knowing the Friendly Courier would be back any time, Nathan takes the pen from his coat pocket and signs it. He sets down the pen, picks up the beer and downs it in a long gulp. As he sets the empty bottle down on the nightstand and sets the pen next to it, there is a knock on his door.

8

NATHAN AWAKES EXHAUSTED, reeling from dreams unlike any he has ever had before. After a heavy breakfast in the hotel's dining room, he packs a few items into the small black rental Ford and sets out for the job site. He decides to travel light, taking only drawings and a map, writing his client's phone number on back and storing everything else in the room's safe with his passport.

At the outskirts of Dingle, Nathan passes the harbor and aims his car west. Though tired, he finds the narrow road less daunting, and once out of Dingle the traffic becomes nonexistent. The large tour buses he had dodged since leaving Shannon airport appear to be banned from the narrow roads here, opting for the comforts of the Ring of Kerry one peninsula south. Nathan takes a deep breath and decides to enjoy the drive.

About an hour later, he thinks that he may have passed right by the site, distracted by the land and sea all around. In recent miles, there have been a few crudely made signs pointing to the aforementioned beehive huts. Entrance seems based on an honor system: drop a few Euros in a box and proceed at your own risk, the farmer whose property they occupy assuming no responsibility if you fall off a cliff. Nathan is approaching another such sign, this one with a "closed" notice and a cyclone construction fence surrounding the small field inside its stone fence perimeter. There are a few pieces of equipment–a tractor with backhoe and a front end loader, a forklift holding a pallet of concrete block suspended about halfway up, next to a cement mixer–scattered around a one-story raw concrete block structure about the size and proportion of a farmhouse. No windows had yet been set in this shell of a rather plain box.

Nathan has been driving slowly, making an easy turn to enter the site's narrow driveway. He follows some muddy tracks through the open gate and pulls his car off to the side. There are no other vehicles here or across the road in the small guest parking area overlooking the cliff down to the sea. Nevertheless, he pulls out of the way to avoid blocking access if a dump truck or delivery comes.

Getting out of his car, Nathan is a bit startled to see a row of eight men sitting silently on the edge of a concrete walk. *How the hell did they get here?* he wonders, looking around again for any other vehicles. One of the men gets up and approaches, extending his hand in greeting. He is severely leaning to one side, limping and dangling his left arm as he moves. Although his nose and everything else about him looks crooked, his smile shows perfect teeth. Nathan finds the dichotomy jarring.

"*Failte,*" the crooked man says, with what Nathan believes is a wink, "welcome. You must be Mr. Bang." The man pronounces Nathan's last name as if there is an additional 'y' in the middle, in an accent not specifically Irish. "I'm Padraigh, the first general foreman. Mr. Moyne said you were coming." His hand, Nathan judges, has the rough dry texture of a mason.

"Thank you," replies Nathan, "I'm a bit new, so please have

patience if I have a lot of questions."

"No problem. I may not be able to answer all; you may also have to ask Tomas, the second foreman. He usually arrives later in the day."

"Two foremen?" Nathan asks.

"Nothing is usual here: there's two of each, even architects now that you've arrived. Seems a bit inefficient, no one knowing what the other is doing. Everything was coordinated by Mr. Ayshun," the craggy foreman adds the same emphasis to Anton's name, "and so it has taken us longer, with less progress." He pauses, a sideways glance that brings his head to an almost normal angle. "He keeps paying us, so I can't complain," he shrugs with one shoulder, "even if a bit on the boring side, what with all the waiting."

Nathan nods at the line of men sitting silently, "What are you waiting on now?"

"Your instructions," the foreman states. "Everything goes day by day. We wait like this every morning, though I've sent lads home the last few days without Mr. Ayshun around."

"Why don't you show me around; explain a bit," Nathan offers. "Then we'll decide if you should send them home again today."

The foreman, prepared for this, turns to his side and gestures up the side of the rocky incline with his good right arm. "The *clochán* here are a group of nine, most connected. If you're not familiar, they're called 'beehive huts' for their shape. Dry stone, corbelled roof, and watertight after all these centuries for no mortar, due to the way they laid the stones to shed water. Them walls are over a meter thick. Ruins of these dot the hillsides all over, but this group has been maintained and the farmer used them to shelter his sheep and pigs up until the tourists started coming fifteen or twenty years ago. It's already been excavated by archeologists. They found a cross of some significance that's now in the National Museum, but that's about it. Truth be told, not sure what the big deal is." He starts limping towards the half-constructed building. "You can get a better look up here."

Nathan steps up on a concrete walk; probably a porch for the new structure, he thinks, on the southwest side of the grouping where visitors would pay before going inside or out to the huts. He looks over the arrangement; three parallel rows running east-west. The largest of the circular structures–about eighteen feet in diameter–lies in the middle of the southern row and is connected to the huts either side and the one behind with low passages. The other huts are slightly smaller, perhaps fourteen to fifteen feet in diameter. All of them have a roughly square opening as an entry. The structures are constructed of hundreds of dark gray stones similar in shape, each stone about the size of a man's chest.

As he makes a mental plan view, something strikes him about the compound. First he is surprised by the grid-like nature, expecting a more rambling arrangement. But then he narrows it down to the layout itself. The nine-square grid arrangement is ancient, mystical even, but never so ordinary. There is usually a hierarchy, one of the squares that would stand out. The slightly larger hut does not seem special enough. Nathan expects something more communal; a shared space, or a clearly larger structure slightly off the plan grid.

"Now this here," the foreman points behind Nathan, flashing his perfect grin in pride, "is our new addition."

Certainly no award-winning design, Nathan decides *not even half-assed design.* If he was going to be involved, some things would need to change. He understands the farmhouse model, but this is a museum and the site too spectacular; the thing should make people want to stop, physically pulling them off the road. Nathan is certain that Anton's design would cause confusion, leaving visitors to wonder if this is someone's home.

Nathan had discussed his approach to design–a sort of Wholism but not in a solely spiritual sense–with Anton back in college. Rather than creating an isolated object on the landscape, which was Anton's instinct, Nathan saw everything in the world emanating from an existing wholeness. This allowed him to analyze a place and then use specific principles to extend and make it better. Anton thought this too limiting, but over the years Nathan saw a great freedom of creativity within the principles. Additionally, since he saw beauty as objective with specific guides, Nathan was usually successful at creating something that was unique and wonderful to experience. Not having a specific style, which Anton had spent a great deal of time in school looking for, also gave Nathan the latitude to create anything; although he felt he lost some clients who preferred the style-driven approach, as if they were going shopping out of a catalog. There is extra work to do things the way he does, but after years of practice he feels far more adept at seeing the world in the way he needs to.

Nathan turns back to the huts, remembering his primary objective. "Did you find chambers of any kind?"

"There's an L-shaped, um, "souterrain" I think he called it, under the entrance stones to that big middle hut in the front row. Ayshun said it has a passage of about 3 meters ending in a chamber about 3 meters. I haven't seen it myself."

"Anton was already in there?" Nathan stops for a second, debating whether to ask the question or if it was too obvious. "You haven't by chance come across a stone, a bit squarer and lighter than the rest?"

The foreman laughs at the idea of finding a stone out here. "Take your pick, the whole parish is stone. We did find one wrapped up over here," Padraigh points with his good arm towards where the men are still sitting. "I picked it up out of the mud and moved it," he gestures at a lump just below Nathan.

Nathan steps down and picks up the canvas-covered bundle with some effort. He unwraps and studies it carefully. It looks close, but not the same as the picture. This piece is light in color, a bit more regular square in shape where everything else he has seen is tapered to one side, but not marbled enough nor the same edges. There are some markings on it, but not the same pattern of engraving he had seen in the picture, nor deep enough.

Something catches Nathan's eye on the canvas. "Are you painting already, or is this blood?"

"Must be blood," Padraigh shrugs. "Could be from Mr. Ayshun, we found his car over there. Could have been from a sheep, since there was some damage on the front of his car and the things are always going out into the road. The rain would have washed away any blood on the ground or road, but the canvas must have protected that."

"Did you report this to the police?"

"Sure," the foreman nods.

Nathan considers the options of what might have happened. His heart sinks at the thought of his old friend injured and going over the steep cliff on the other side of the road. Maybe he hit his head and was wandering around, hopefully taken in by one of the local farmers. The police are probably looking around right now.

The emotional swing continues as Nathan considers the uninteresting design, and the prospect of looking for one stone in a field of thousands. On top of that, there is the double work of having two construction crews, neither of which knows what the other is doing unless someone fills them in at the change of each shift. Previously that someone was Anton. Nathan is unsure of his readiness to act as superintendent, controlling and timing all the trades. Assuming that role, he will be tied to the project until it is finished. While the extra pay might be good, he knows Johanna would have his head if he is away longer than the couple weeks agreed upon. The double setup makes no sense, but he knows sometimes a client may have a good reason. Nathan decides to stall until he can find out more from Moyne. He also needs to broach the subject of changing the museum's overall design. *That should go over well*, he thinks.

"What're your orders?" the foreman asks. The seven other men look up in his direction.

"I think I need some time here to look over the files. You might as well send everyone home today, and come back tomorrow when I've got a better handle on it." Nathan looks around, realizing there is no office. "Where would I find the files?"

"Your partner took them home at night. There seems to be plenty of money, but not a penny for a decent job trailer."

"Okay. All right then", Nathan pauses, "you have a cell number I can reach you at?" He writes it down on the back of the map with the rest of the notes and sketches he has been taking. It is almost noon now, and the sea air had given him an appetite. "Any place to eat around here?" he asks.

"You can drive a bit further west to Dunquin, there's a good pub there," the foreman offers.

"I'll come back after, and get up to speed." Nathan turns, eyeing the biggest of the huts. "What's the feeling about taking one of these apart a bit, just to see how it's put together? I'll put it right back."

"Just like Mr. Ayshun. He said the same thing when we first started. He took apart that one over there." He points to the one Nathan is considering. "I don't think it's too big a deal, but some of the local history nuts might get touchy. As far as I know they be rugged and none too precious if the farmers used to keep their sheep in 'em. They've probably been taken apart and rebuilt a few times."

Reconsidering, Nathan scans the group and the plan stored in his memory. "I might try that one," he points to the southeastern-most hut, the direction all doors of the other huts are facing. So many stones, it would take him forever unless he could narrow it down.

"Well, if there's any equipment you need, I was authorized to get it for you," Padraigh offers. "Anything you need."

The foreman's appearance is deceptive, Nathan believes, hiding the capacity to be very sharp and very brutal. None of this seems right, or real. He waves goodbye to the foreman and his group, walking through the mud to his car. Once inside, Nathan dials a preset number on the phone provided by the Friendly Courier. It rings twice.

"How does it look?" Moyne sounds cheerful, optimistic through his gruff voice.

"It's fantastic out here," it is always good to start cheerful, Nathan thinks, before delving into reality, "but I do have some issues." He describes the strange setup, his finding a stone that looks similar and had obviously been moved. The blood. The changes needed in the design. The need to get the records Anton is keeping somewhere.

"Anton was staying at an apartment I set up for him on John Street, which is basically the same street you are staying on but further east. The place belongs to Mrs. O'Malley, who runs the B & B across the street. I'll call, and you can pick up a key."

"You're sure you want me to go forward?" Nathan asks. "This thing has to change substantially, and I'm really not sure I'm the best guy to find some kind of artifact out here. I mean, professionals have already searched." Nathan is hopeful about getting his changes to the building. It is the primary project he is less enthused about;

finding one rock in damn quarry.

"In my experience, and no offense I mean it as a compliment, architects don't think like normal people. I tend to get results, but usually ones I never expect. That's what I need here. From what I understand, you and your partner provide a unique service."

Both Padraigh and his client have referred to his partner. Nathan realizes they mean Anton, and not Johanna. He thinks Anton must have misled them for a reason, perhaps to appear larger or more diverse than he really was.

"I hope you can pull this off," Moyne finishes, "I've got a second commission waiting, and I would love to just hand it to someone. Contact me if you find anything at his apartment," he orders and hangs up. Nathan sets the phone on the passenger seat and starts the car. Pulling out of the drive he again waves to the hunched foreman, and the seven workers now standing in the spot they had been sitting.

The drive west is all a sweep of land and sea, cliffs and climax in the broad sweep of the Blasket Islands. He used to fantasize about work like this: foreign projects taking him to exotic locales. Being here now, the fantasy is more palpable yet more perverse. Was he in any danger of actually experiencing his dream, or is this just a sidetrack? So far, it is only partially as glamorous as he had hoped. He is muddy, hungry, cold in June, and about as far from the kind of night life he is used to as one could get.

After lunch and a beer–*but only because everyone else is having one*, Nathan justifies–he backtracks to the site. The gate is closed, so he parks on the sea side of the road and waits to cross as a car passes. Even from here he can see they left it unlocked, the chain swaying back and forth in the wind. Prying open the gate just enough to squeeze through he realizes he is alone, the foreman and workers having disappeared as unobtrusively as they had arrived.

9

July 1, Dingle, Dingle Peninsula

A N AFTERNOON AT THE SITE had not, quite literally, unearthed anything. Nathan removed maybe a dozen stones before putting them back with a sense of futility, opting instead to take measurements and sketch the site; procrastinating in the semi-useful way architects do while trying to come up with a new approach. He also convinced himself that Anton had been through all this before, and unless he finds some notes at Anton's apartment he may simply be following a dead end.

For the new museum, however, he came up with a few exciting possibilities to explore once he returns to town; where many designers require quiet to concentrate, Nathan is the opposite, needing the noise of a pub or coffee shop to think creatively. Even in his car–a great place for insight–he likes the stereo cranked to ear-splitting levels.

Nathan returns to his hotel and changes clothes, which had somehow become damp even though it had not been raining. Craving an early dinner he exits through the hotel's front door, dodging numerous vacationing couples coming in, and turns right. He melds with the crowd heading down Main Street, stopping at its first intersection, the Spa Road, where the tractor had turned the day before heading back towards the Connor Pass. The rest of the crowd is turning right, southwest on the Mall towards the harbor. Going straight, Main Street becomes John Street in name only as it begins to rise up towards the countryside only two blocks further. The white arrow signs at the corner say "An Sráid Mhór" in the direction he had come from, "Bóthar An Spá" heading up to the Connor Pass, and "Sráid Eoin" where he is going. Nathan shakes his head in confusion and hopes he is heading the right way, thinking it would not matter too much if he is wrong; the edge of town is only a couple blocks in any direction.

Near the end of John Street is O'Malley's Bed & Breakfast, where he immediately finds Mrs. O'Malley in the lobby. She is a short oval of a woman, all pinks and whites with a piercing gray gaze, simultaneously dowdy and intimidating. Even though Moyne had arranged for Anton's key, he turns on the charm hoping to coax additional information. It begins with small talk: she asks where he is from and where he is staying. Mrs. O'Malley offers the other apartment, the one next to Anton's, as it is unoccupied and much better suited to a long stay. Nathan considers, but explains that he will be in town two weeks at most. Despite his protests, he leaves with a copy of the lease for review along with two sets of keys: one for Anton's apartment, and one to look at the neighboring unit.

As he crosses the street, Nathan is unsure how he lost that conversation. He senses there is a disconnection between his own logical and verbal precision, combined with being in a land where language is more art than strict communication. A land of Joyce and Wilde is a place where words are broad brush-strokes, running and dripping and able to mean many things at once or nothing at all. His own ability to detect distinctions, inconsistencies, contradictions and frame arguments holds little advantage here. In a logical debate,

Nathan could be devastating. In Ireland he would simply be a boor.

There is a large key on each set that unlocks the heavy wood plank outer door. Inside is a small dark landing, with a set of narrow steps leading to two doors at the top. He shuts the door and climbs the carpeted stair. The top landing is slightly larger with a single window for light. Putting the extra set of keys in his pocket for later, he unlocks the door to his old friend's apartment, half-concerned that a rotting corpse would be lying on the bed; the morbid story in the newspaper you cannot help but read.

The apartment is large, and thankfully corpse-free. To the left is a perfectly made double bed. It is doubtful Mrs. O'Malley maintains the apartments as she would her guest rooms–probably only after a renter vacates–so Nathan is reasonably certain the room is exactly as Anton left it. Hopeful that he could read a lot about his old friend from his space, even if it has been his for only a short time, Nathan begins to study the layout. The files could wait a bit longer.

The bed is, as he initially noted, perfectly made. Around the room there is a shredder, a file cabinet, two balsa wood models on the table near the wall on the right, one on the floor where the second chair across from the lone chair would normally be. Nathan tries to pull the top off one of the models to look inside, but it is glued tight.

He opens the curtains to let in some more light and turns the television on for company. There is a six o'clock "Call To Prayer" on, which Nathan finds charming yet disturbing; probably no chance he would find a gentleman's club around here.

He is beginning to get a sense from the room, its pattern, leading him to believe Anton spent a lot of time alone in here. The single chair positioned at the clear spot on the table tells him Anton worked exclusively alone. The intimate tight setting of all his work, compared to the location of the television remote, shows he preferred to concentrate rather than use the space as a refuge to relax. All the construction information is filed perfectly if someone else would need to cover for him. There are no appointment books or notes to meet anyone suggesting that he only directs others when he has to. Nathan finds it strange that he would keep such a tight control over construction scheduling and trades when it would not be necessary. If it was his nature, Nathan would expect haphazard piles, more the suggestion of someone who hoards information to make his role invaluable.

There is a picture on the nightstand: Anton standing alone, much older but recognizable. He looks the part of Rand's character Howard Roark, the Rationalist architect, all high cheekbones, gaunt face, sunken cheeks and cold steady gray eyes staring at the raw stone deciding what shape he will force it to become. It is the picture of arrogance and vanity, a commanding voice molding the structure of civilization. Of course Nathan knows how naïve this image is, and his memory of Anton as a timid young man makes it almost comical. The picture is recent, the rocks some of the larger ones on the site he had just come from. It was simply a moment caught where in some fantasy he finally looked like the architect he was in his imagination.

As the only personal picture in the room, it must have meant a great deal to him that he could be seen this way, even if his true motivation and his true character were something very different. The power to shape stone, raise steel, join wood is a means to an end, not the end itself. Anton's look was not one of power, but desperation. Nathan sees the need to mold a thing that would last, etch a stone that will remain long after he is gone. The stare was not to judge the stone's fitness for use, but its ability to convey his memory.

Inside the nightstand's top drawer, on a slightly wrinkled piece of paper, is the same number for Moyne that Nathan has. There are two more similar pieces of paper; one the name and number for Building Control Kerry, which must be the local building inspector, and the other a number for the Heritage Council, which Nathan assumes has some control over historic preservation. They look carelessly crumpled in his pocket at one point, Nathan assuming Anton is still not impressed with authority. Anton had always been combative at critiques, dismissive of grades and the university structure. He was there to learn, and he paid good money for these people to teach him. There was only the one professor, the one they had gone overseas with, who he seemed to treat with respect and perhaps even some awe.

Sitting on the bed, Nathan puts the numbers back and closes the drawer. He looks up and notices the chair next to the entry, its top worn where it would slip under the handle of the door. *Paranoid, and a loner. This could get interesting*, Nathan thinks.

He continues through the apartment. The kitchenette has some dishes in the dryer, nothing dirty. A small refrigerator is sparse with some milk, cheese and bread but no beer or wine. In the bathroom three towels, perfectly straight. Just outside the bathroom door a small stand with a row of compact discs, classical and jazz, in alphabetical order. *Paranoid, a loner, and anal*, Nathan revises.

Nathan checks the closet and finds mostly jeans and casual button shirts. He is relieved to find Anton reinforcing his earlier judgment, that he was not fitting the stereotypical architect: no sign of the expected black clothes, artsy glasses, pictures of an Asian girlfriend or hints of modernist furniture. On the floor of the closet is the same kind of safe Nathan has in his room.

After glancing through the project files in the cabinet, he sits back down on the bed eyeing the safe. Nothing had grabbed his attention within the files; mostly orders, correspondence and schedules. Nathan knows how he programs his own travel safes, and thinks maybe Anton is as predictable. It would have to be in the places Anton manipulated. The models have a specific proportion: windows in groups of threes, three towels in the bathroom, and compact discs in groups of nine. Windows in the model are the familiar Golden Section, the proportion of one to one-point-six-one-eight. While many architects dismiss the almost mystical, traditionalistic approach to numerology they receive in school, some hold on and use those proportions and numbers with an almost obsessive-compulsive need.

Nathan tries the numbers one, six, one, eight and three. He tries them again in reverse order. Then he tries them with the year they graduated, instead of the six one. Nine huts at the site. Nine? The safe clicks open.

Inside are relatively few items, just a few papers and pictures lying curled over a larger object underneath. Nathan removes the papers from the top and looks them over: a few plans and sections of the site, some notes on the side and some markings where Anton has already looked. Mathematical formulas scribbled on the side. The numbers do not match up to measurements Nathan has taken, either in metric with the tape he had found at the site or in English feet and inches. They seem to be all proportional: the center hut at 1 high to 2.49 wide, the passage at 1 high to 1.41 long, another hut at 1 high to 3.5 wide. He looks back in the safe at the two objects now exposed: a gun and a small stone cup. The gun is a shock; Nathan may not find it unusual in Chicago, but Ireland does not seem like the place people carry guns.

He picks up the cup. It is roughly hewn; ancient-looking, which he supposes any stone cup would look like, and relatively undecorated except for a carving of a leaf on one side near the handle. Perhaps a treasure found at the site, or simply bought at a local store. Some people collect snow globes when they travel, why not this? He places it back next to the gun and removes the photos which had fallen upright against the side wall of the safe. A matchbook falls out from between them with the name of a local pub, a Gaelic name he recognizes from his walk here. Inside is written 'am'. The letters are offset, so he doubts it means "in the morning". He sets it on the bottom of the safe next to the other two objects.

Nathan focuses on the two four by six glossy prints. The first is a picture of another stone, similar to the one in Moyne's photo, sitting on a table in a wood paneled room with tall arch-top windows beyond. The stone is similar, but not the same as the one Moyne had shown him; the breaks along the sides are different, the inscription the same types of markings but in a different rhythm. The second picture is of the side of a large house, the windows in one section matching the proportion, number and detail of the windows in the first photo.

Nathan turns the photos over, but nothing is written on the back. He turns the picture of the house face up again, studying it closely. There is something familiar about the red brickwork in the background beyond the house. Nathan thinks he has been there before, many years ago. The red brick gothic arches could be anywhere in the world, but the coincidence of someplace he and Anton had been together makes more sense. He would not know for sure until he can access the internet.

This last thought leads to Nathan wondering why there is no computer here. Perhaps he took it with him?

Nathan curls up the papers and photos, tucking them in his jacket pocket. He closes the safe and looks around the room for anything else he needs. Deciding all the building files were too numerous to move, he plans to convince Mrs. O'Malley that he should hold on to the key to reference them, knowing her rebuttal will be that he should just move next door. Nathan does not predict he would win this conversation either, and may very well end up renting the whole building before he knows it.

Closing the door and locking it behind him, he feels like he had just had a long conversation catching up with his old friend. He probably learned more from the room than he would have through a real conversation. His suspicious side imagines the room has been staged, clues left in a language that another of his kind could read. It has been too easy, and people are far more complex.

He unlocks the door next to Anton's and peers inside. It is perfectly lovely and comfortable: light, airy, homey in a shabby chic kind of way. Nathan instantly feels his resolve strengthen that he would not end up here.

10

July 1, Chorin, Germany

T HE EVENING IS YOUNG, early moments of a dawn that will last four more hours in this north German flatland. Peter Ruppin sits at his desk in the comfortable old library of his home, staring at a bottle of whiskey and the pistol lying next to it. He had not eaten much for dinner, has not eaten much at all recently, and Peter is certain the whiskey will not sit well in his empty stomach. Pouring a glass three fingers high, he eases back in the worn leather chair, looking out across the lake to the old monastery on the opposite shore.

Peter Ruppin is approaching his seventieth birthday, a milestone of what, he is not sure. Survival, perhaps? Alone in this large house, surrounded by the trappings of an entitled life, Ruppin senses that he has led himself backwards, despite all his superficial achievements, ultimately offering nothing new to the world. His obsession is history. It is the root of all his habits and all his actions. Unfortunately, like the history he focused on, his life has become more about the death and violence it should warn of, rather than the achievements and life it should inspire.

He has always lived in the past, relishing stories of his

previously noble family. The East German government, in a freak accident of competence, had sent him to university to study language and antiquities. He had been on a number of archeological digs in Bulgaria, Hungary, even far away Tunisia once: a privilege for those living behind the Iron Curtain. During his time in the field Ruppin discovered he was best at assessing the worth of objects dug up by others, having neither the patience nor instinct to be on the front lines digging and documenting. He was happy behind the scenes. Before his retirement, he had briefly served as curator for the Museum of the Ancient Near East, a collection in the southern wing of the Pergamon Museum in East Berlin. It was merely a political posting, reward for years of loyalty, and though providing access it meant nothing at first. German history, the history of his family, was what he wanted to study; yet had done everything except that.

Years traveling had been hard on him and his wife Marie. Before they knew it, they had passed the time to start a family. His fault. His ambition. Peter does not pretend that anyone will be there to mourn his passing when he dies.

He had lost his own sweet Marie so many years ago. The thought of her still brings a quick skip in his heartbeat. After her death he had started a new life, one he is certain she would not be proud of under the DDR's watchful eye, making a better than average income trading in antiquities. His wife's relatives in the West joined him on occasion, however, taking many chances crossing the frontier

His chance to move west had come and gone. Content with life under Party rule, he had even thrived as some nobles quietly do during populist rule. It is difficult to break out of class distinctions, even under socialism. One thing his studies had proven is that so many years of history cannot be overcome by political theory.

The noble family, at least my branch of it, he snorts, *what a fucking mess*. Another aspect of history difficult to break out of is the quiet murmurs of an ancestor's supposed misdeeds. All the wars, heroic actions, and generosity on behalf of their subjects will be forgotten due to an unfounded reputation for ruthlessness. Peter seems the only one obsessed by this aspect of his family's stigma, guessing it may partly be a figment of his imagination and partly his cultivation; such a reputation has worked to his advantage. Nonetheless, he has directed much of his existence, from his choice of profession to his current place of residence, on pinpointing where the family reputation came from, and vindicating whichever ancestor's immortality had been tarnished through rumor or imputation.

He finishes the first whiskey and pours another. His chance is dying with him now, he thinks, his ability to clear his family name quietly slipping away.

Ruppin pinpoints the pivotal offense to a moment seven hundred years ago. There was a story passed down in his family that one of his ancestors, along with Georg von Kerkow and the Markgrafen brothers Konrad and Johann, had arranged a relic for the new monastery at Mariensee, but something had gone terribly wrong. It is common knowledge the monks had been building at Mariensee for almost ten years when they suddenly stopped, abandoned it, and began work at a new location. That new monastery stands in a much modified state as the red brick gothic pile he can see across the lake. No one knows for certain the reasons behind the relocation, but his grandfather's tale led Peter to his own theory.

The story, he first thought, was just that: the kind of fantasy elders tell the younger generation to impress upon them the great history of their family. His grandfather had indeed been specific, even pinpointing the year 1272. The full story began a bit earlier with a group of influential men, a number of margraves and nobles including a Ruppin ancestor who worked to found the monastery at Mariensee. They arranged for a number of monks from the parent monastery in Lehnin, and began the search for a holy relic to help consecrate the altar and establish its stature as a destination for religious pilgrimage. They finally found some success through a connection to an Italian, John, who had become Bishop of Clonfert in Ireland. This Bishop arranged for something significant–they were not sure what–to be brought to the Cistercians at Mariensee by these well-traveled and well-connected monks. However, when the three monks from Clonfert arrived in 1272, they carried only a few meager items: a golden chalice and two stones, one large and one small. The margrave and noblemen benefactors, expecting the bones of a saint or piece of the True Cross for the large sum they had sent, were furious.

The messenger monks made camp, resting before the return journey, at the site just across the lake where Ruppin is now looking. Within a few days of their ill-received presentation, the monks were killed in an apparent ambush or robbery of the items they were carrying. The rumors began to fly that it was not just a robbery, but rather a vengeance killing for the slight of stealing payment and embarrassment of delivering such valueless trifles. There were never any charges, but locals in need of a scapegoat singled out Ruppin's ancestor as the most likely henchman. He was the only former soldier among the noble group, the only one young enough and physical enough to overcome three men.

The monks of Mariensee, aghast at the slaughter of their brothers, and the rumors of their own benefactor's hand in it, stopped all work. They petitioned that the monastery be moved to the spot near the lake where their brothers had been killed and unceremoniously buried, considering this now a holy place of martyrdom.

While building at Chorin, the monks rediscovered the three relics, proving they had not been stolen but more likely buried by the Irish monks for safety while they had rested and planned for their long journey home. Peter Ruppin's grandfather said the monks of Chorin placed the stone under the altar, using it as a base for the reliquary. The chalice was lost after the monastery's decline in the 1400's and its subsequent, and repeated, plundering. The reliquary itself was removed during the Reformation, as many considered it idolatrous. The damage to the Ruppin family, however, never waned.

A young Peter Ruppin believed the story's moral was the power of rumor, of being associated with a bad crowd and how either can affect the future and a family's reputation; that the official written history is only a small part of a culture that forms in a place through time. Back then he fantasized about his ancestors being Crusaders or something more glamorous than a monk-murdering politician, yet the seeds for his love of history had begun to take hold. His family, after all, had helped shape history, and an heir's job is to keep the memory alive. He was fascinated by the allure of getting lost in another time.

The specifics of the story were forgotten until he was a bit older, feeling the disdain from other kids and recalling this history as a possible reason behind it. Of course he was projecting; for all he knew, his grandfather had made the story up and he was the only one who had heard it. The disdain he felt may have come from the fact his family was wealthy and fairly intact after the War, eliciting the envy and distrust of his fellow classmates. The socialist views of the new government and East German culture also left little stature for a formerly noble family, subjecting them to an even higher degree of suspicion.

Ruppin refills his glass, takes a larger than usual drink, and winces at the warming pain. He looks up again through the arched windows of his home at the arches of the ruin across the lake, echoing in shape yet filled with far more meaning. The structure he is looking at now is not the monastery his ancestor helped build: this was built later, surviving until today because of its Romantic aura. The complex was almost destroyed by fire and plunder, lasting only to be used as stables and warehouses. Some of the buildings were once used as a quarry, their brick and stone taken for structures and furnaces as industry moved to replace nature and spirit. It was not until the architect Schinkel arrived in the beginning of the 1800's that efforts were made to stabilize and improve what was still left.

For decades the memory of his grandfather's story remained an interesting side note in Ruppin's life. Then one day in 1998, during a wall stabilization project by the Landesbauamt, a few items were uncovered near foundations of the first monastery. Being the expert, they had called on Ruppin.

There were a number of items he quickly dismissed. However, three that had somehow escaped earlier excavations had been laid out before him, and they shook up his world: a large stone and a small stone, both with inscriptions on them, as well as a small stone cup with an imprint design. Seeing these, holding them in his hands, he was stunned. Was it really true? Would they be evidence that his ancestor was guilty, at least by association?

Luckily, he had the resources to remove any objects before others may study them. Having expanded his business and unloaded a number of big-ticket items after Reunification, he now had a small army of men, inexpensive and loyal due to high unemployment here in the East. He bought this house across the lake from the Cloister, and arranged to have the items quietly removed and brought here.

Who would suspect someone of keeping the stolen items so close? Besides, he had a plausible reason for possessing them.

The sun is finally disappearing on the horizon, setting the red brick of the Cloister aglow and deepening the contrast of its silhouette. Westerly winds cool across the surface of the small lake before reaching his window. Ruppin can smell nightfall.

Suspicion never arose; indeed, no mention of the missing items ever came to light. It seemed his professional dismissal of them as meaningless was adequate to alleviate any concern over a worker or vagabond removing them from the site. He studied these artifacts for some time, searching for clues. The few other experts he trusted, and had shared limited pictures of them with, concluded the relics may have general historical importance regarding early settlement of the area and should be offered to a museum. Nothing specific, however, came forth. He had not shared the markings on the larger stone, which were, in his opinion, certainly a language and not random etchings. It may be significant for that alone, although he could find nothing with which to compare it except certain Ogham scripts and some ancient Middle Eastern inscription. These did not, however, match up with any degree of believable regularity. If this larger stone was indeed ancient and foreign, perhaps they were worth much more than the ancient nobles or anyone else believed.

Ruppin could not bring himself to place it in his vault. He felt it his penance to keep it in view as a reminder. It lay there now, taunting him from the table across from his desk.

In a last ditch effort he had sent photos of this artifact to his nephew in America, wanting the story to carry on, and a chance for it to have closure, peace for the family since he felt he had neither the time nor energy left to do more himself. He had heard nothing back.

Ruppin feels very drunk now, the bottle half empty and his

stomach growling in protest. He pours himself another, and sets the bottle back down in its position next to the pistol. However he is not so drunk, he is certain, that should anyone come through the door he could still put him down with one shot.

Ruppin knows he has many to fear. There are priceless valuables in the house, most of which sit safely in his vault. He had learned capitalism well, and because he had been practicing it even before the fall of the Wall he excelled when his business interests became less illegal, and could invest some of his accumulated wealth without arousing suspicion. He has crossed many people, even became a bit of a mob boss in the American fashion. Sometimes his employees took matters into their own hands, which he understands is the nature of his youthful workers. He has comforted himself that his men had sometimes misinterpreted his orders. Even if his own family would be forgiving, if any were left to judge him, his dear Marie would be most disappointed.

Sunday: a day of rest. Tomorrow, or the day after, would bring his men looking for something to do, seeking to direct their aggression. Ruppin had nothing for them, had indeed given up a few years ago, and has just been feeding them errands so they would not turn on him for his weakness. *They could take it all, what do I care?* he mutters, setting the glass down harder than he means to, its vibration traveling through his hand. *Let them break into the vault, scavenge the place.*

Crests of nausea on a sea of pain roll over him. His vision continues to spin even after he stops the quarter turn of his chair. Ruppin hunches his old body down, elbows on his thighs. He stays in this position for a few moments until his stomach and chest settle, until the scream of overindulgence dissipates in his ears. The wave passes, and he sits back up and turns to pour another glass of the amber liquid.

Though earlier it had been a hot July day, the evening has brought a cool wind. It creeps slowly, leaving footprints in the scattered petals on the lawn and delivering jumbled life and death smells from the lake through his open window. It is fully dark now, and he is too drunk and too tired to get up to turn a light on. He feels a chill, certain a storm is heading his way.

Ruppin laughs to himself at all these things he is certain of. So many, many things he is certain of yet none that matter. The one conviction he has, the one final certainty that may actually mean something, is that when the whiskey is gone, that he, Peter Georg Ruppin, is going to use that pistol lying aside the bottle to blow his brains out.

11

July 2, Dingle, Dingle Peninsula

W HEN NATHAN GLANCED at the clock at three in the morning, still sitting at the small table drawing out plans and sections, he knew he was either invigorated by the possibilities of this project or anxious to get the hell out. He managed a few hours sleep before breakfast, dosing himself with coffee before commuting to the site. Sufficiently awake, but lacking any places to stop along the way, his greeting of foreman Padraigh consisted of asking where he could take a piss. Despite the absence of a job trailer, there was thankfully a portable toilet sitting in the upper corner of the site.

The second order of business was to sit down with Padraigh and form a plan. Work had progressed too far to change the building location, so using existing foundations and partial walls Nathan has come up with a solution to make the Visitor Center far more exciting in form and material, distinguishing itself so people would know this is a public place. A sweep of steel and glass would capture one of the huts to make it accessible, allowing the others to remain in their current setting. Nathan's estimation is that despite a few delays there would be little change in cost, but more importantly he would feel comfortable, perhaps even proud, of putting his name on it. The big question is how a change in design will be received by the governing agencies that grant permits. He convinced himself in the early morning hours that his design would be hailed as what should have been done in the first place.

Padraigh is alone this morning, listening as Nathan describes his vision and how they would change little of what is already built. A few times he snorts and winks, leaving Nathan unable to tell if it is in response to his ideas or simply a nervous tic. After the presentation, the bent foreman flashes his perfect smile, rolls up Nathan's sketches, and leaves to talk with the head of his construction company. Nathan offers to go with him, but Padraigh declines and promises to call him in the afternoon if needed.

"You're not affecting the footprint, and doing even less over the *clochán*, I think they may be favorable and give you administrative approval rather than having to start feckin' over" Padraigh estimated before he left. "The bigger sell is to the historic preservation people at the Heritage Council. They'll either love it or hate it. Either way, no offense, but it be better if someone from around here present it. They don't want some Yank telling them how to treat our history. They didn't like Mr. Ayshun much, but you're a bit prettier." This time the wink and smile seemed to be on purpose, causing a shiver through Nathan.

One part of the project covered, Nathan turns his attention to locating the stone. After Padraigh leaves he is again completely alone, something rarely experienced at a construction site. Uncomfortable with the feeling, he sits in the car for a long while organizing the notes and sketches borrowed from Anton's room.

Before leaving this morning, he decided to put the pictures in his safe, if for no other reason than that was where Anton had kept them. Nathan was able to verify online that the red brick building he saw in the background was the Chorin Cloister. He was also able to access a satellite image of the area, but could not tell which face of the monastery building was shown, and therefore could not tell from which direction, and which house, the picture had been taken.

Nathan is familiar with the Cloister. He, Anton and Johanna had made a day trip from Berlin in 1990 while studying abroad, in that gray time after the fall of the Wall but before Reunification. Anton suggested the trip, and then disappeared while Nathan and Johanna wandered around the small Eastern village of Chorin. Nathan had been unsure about the journey; there was so much to see in Berlin and so little time, and he would rather have gone to Potsdam on a day trip. However, the ruins of the old cloister were remarkable, and he ended up intensely studying and sketching them. Seeing the village, frozen in time, with its rough narrow streets leading past a small church and low wall, Trabant cars parked in front of the brick and stucco houses and almost no one around, was a memorable experience in itself.

Preferring all information on a drawing, Nathan spends some time in the car transferring Anton's notes onto the copy of his sketches. Still a matter of interpretation, it is easier being here and seeing the real things to which Anton is referring. After some time he gets out, scampering up to where he can get a better view. Turning Anton's sketch around, Nathan stands on the new concrete wall where the men had been sitting yesterday and assesses the site.

The morning had begun mostly sunny, with big fat clouds rolling lazily in off the ocean. Now, the clouds had banded together creating an eerie arctic light and dropping a fine mist spraying sideways with the strengthening wind. Identifying the four huts Anton had searched most carefully, Nathan steps inside the largest one of the five remaining and begins to slowly and systematically survey from the center of the roof down to the base of the walls, beginning just left of the doorway. He studies the stones carefully–their subtleties of color, shape and size–marking possible abnormalities with a piece of chalk he borrowed from Padraigh.

Working intently through lunch, he finally stops in the late afternoon. Nathan guesses he must have marked forty or fifty possibilities in the huts, and those just in the five noted as unchecked by Anton. Eischen may have just as easily missed it, and that would mean another forty. Some were quite low in the wall, and the way these structures were put together would require an almost complete removal of an entire side just to check it out. All of this assuming the damn stone was built into the wall at all, as Moyne believes, and any part of it would be showing. Some of these walls are thick enough to fully encapsulate a piece its size. Or it could be buried underneath, or simply not be here at all. Still invigorated by the design work he had come up with the previous night, or at least hyper from lack of sleep, Nathan fights his natural pessimism.

He has time, he knows, since he has to wait for approvals before going any further with construction. He would call his client and suggest a trip to Chorin. It would be fairly easy to find the house in the picture once he is there, and any insight or clue regarding these things might help him narrow down its location. The big question would be if his client would approve of talking to this other collector, given his earlier statements. Convincing Mr. Moyne that he could gain access under some other guise, such as an architect writing for a magazine or some such excuse, would probably do the trick. Nathan smiles at the thought of spending a couple nights in the beautiful chaos of Berlin, after being stuck in this idyllic countryside.

He takes the long route back to Dingle, around Dunquin and through Ballyferriter, pausing to enjoy the feeling of the land, sky and ocean all around. Knowing he may not be back for a few days, there was a new immediacy to experiencing the place which he had not felt before.

Once back at his hotel, the phone call goes better than anticipated. Moyne is curious about the photo and fellow collector in Chorin, asking for specifics Nathan could not give. With the impending delay and lack of other leads, Moyne agrees to a couple days to follow this lead. He makes it very clear, however, to not allow this other collector any information about the site in Dingle, his name, or even express much interest in the other stone remnant. Excited by the cloak and dagger drama, Nathan agrees and convinces Moyne that, for whatever reason, people let architects into their homes to snoop around; he has a cover that does not even require lies.

A few minutes later, the hotel room phone rings. The first call he has received on this phone catches him by surprise. Padraigh checks in that not everyone is happy about changes, but as long as the owner knows it will delay the project and cost more, they have agreed to talk to Building Control and the Heritage Council. The sketches are sufficient, he says, until they get a sense of how the changes will be viewed. After that, they can reset the timetable and discuss working drawings to build from. In the meantime, his company has identified a couple sections that are not expected to change, and can continue on those to keep their men working.

Suddenly free for the evening, Nathan washes up and changes clothes. He would never eat dinner at this time in Chicago, but remembering that closing time for pubs is about the same hour he would normally go out, he decides an early start may be in order.

12

July 2, Dingle, Dingle Peninsula

AFTER A BEER APPETIZER and pub grub dinner, Nathan walks up the street, his mood the kind usually reserved for vacations or long weekends. A fleeting guilt makes him take a mental note to call Johanna. Tomorrow.

At the bottom corner of Main Street, he steps into a large pub. Nathan does not care if it is for tourists; meeting fellow travelers can make as good an evening as locals, and he feels he already has some good local time put in. The place is dark inside, moody but warm. Two musicians are either playing or warming up–he cannot tell the difference sometimes–at a large table against the wall by the door. He has seen this before; by end of the evening the table will be surrounded by musicians and full of beer glasses. Nathan is not a fan of traditional music, which is a sacrilege to admit in his Irish enclave of Chicago, but it creates a lively atmosphere. He is looking forward to some life after being alone in the middle of a field at the edge of the old world all afternoon. Nathan chooses a seat near the far edge of the bar, leaving enough chairs to make sure people will be sitting both sides.

The pub proves a good choice. Within the first hour he has an in-depth conversation with a gorgeous Australian woman and her boyfriend regarding politics and the advantages and disadvantages of each other's employee benefits and cultural attitude towards work, as well as a more boisterous exchange with three large golfers with red faces who bought Nathan a pint to toast the wives they left in Missouri. His guess was that somewhere in Missouri there were three larger red-faced women likewise accosting some poor bartender at a country club, proud they sent their husbands away.

No sooner had the red-faced golfers left to check out the half bar/half hardware store Nathan told them about ("What, you're shittin' me! We gotta see this."), when a woman he had noticed earlier leaning against the wall watching the musicians moves over quickly to grab a vacant chair.

"Hi, is anyone sitting here?" she asks politely, having seen the previous occupants exit. Her hair is dark and straight, down on one side somewhat consciously covering a burn mark or scar on the side of her jaw, which Nathan found attractive itself. She is in her middle to late thirties, Nathan guesses. Beautiful. Not the unavoidable beauty of youth, but the kind that comes from taking care of oneself with some decent genetics thrown in. The kind of beauty men his own age cannot help but stare at, feeling guilty but at least not feeling like a pedophile or dirty old man.

"No, go ahead," he offers and she sits next to him. Leaning slightly, he introduces himself "Hi, I'm Nathan."

"Audrey." The accent is familiar but much more northern than his previous drinking companions.

He smiles to cover that tinge of guilt as he judges her like an object. However, it is his nature or training to objectify people, and alternately personify objects, until everything melts in a big meaningful whole. It may not be considered morally correct or psychologically healthy, but Nathan thinks it makes him better at what he does.

"Wisconsin or Minnesota?" he asks.

"Canadian, actually. You from the States?"

"Chicago."

"Well, excellent. We're practically neighbors then." She smiles easily and extends a hand. Nathan instinctually checks the other hand for a ring before meeting her eyes.

"Which province?"

"Well done," she smiles. "Most Yanks think we're just one giant state that just hasn't found a star on your flag yet. You know much about us?"

"I know it's where the cold fronts come from that make me curse generally northward. Perhaps you've heard me?" Nathan jests.

"That's alright; I'm from the Halifax area. Atlantic coast. We curse in the same direction you do." She turns her attention to the bartender. She sets down an empty pint glass, ordering another Guinness.

"What brings you here?" Nathan asks, not wanting to lose momentum.

"Just traveling. The guidebook says it's less touristy here, and gorgeous scenery. Plus my ancestors are from Ireland and France, so I thought I would make a bit of a heritage trip." The term "heritage trip" sounds to Nathan like a recent life change. There is no ring, but that might not mean anything; some unmarried women wear a ring to avoid getting hassled, and some women who are married simply do not wear one. "Alone?" he asks, immediately regretful. Too soon, too prying.

"I like to travel a lot," she sidesteps, "I was even in the VSO, Volunteer Service Overseas: like a Canadian version of your Peace Corps, but not government. I spent a year in Kazakhstan, and after teaching and traveling in a place like that, especially as a woman, I figured I can take care of myself anywhere."

"I'm sure you could. What was it like there?" he asks, thinking he averted a potential conversation killer, and the best thing to do would be to keep her talking until she forgets about it. Plus, he usually finds it better to get others talking first; because once he starts talking he has a tendency to go on. It also gives him a chance to move his eyes around a bit, as discretely as he can, knowing full well she is aware he is checking her out. All part of the dance, he thinks. It never occurs to him she may be checking him out as well; she is just able to do it and talk at the same time.

Nathan is listening, but focus is lost a bit as he pictures himself slowly unbuttoning her shirt. She had given him a head start, the top two undone and one side hanging open revealing the perfect roundness as it curves toward her cleavage. He is trying to look her square in the eye, with limited success. Nathan feels out of practice, since the girls at the club prefer you not look them in the eye; it is too personal, too intimate. He has to at least pay enough attention in case she asked a question.

"So what do you do?" she asks the volley question, the easiest one to snap someone back to attention.

"I'm an architect, actually working on a project not too far from here," he smiles and ducks his head in a nod of affirmation and false humility. For some reason people are impressed with this, like many of the one-word careers such as "lawyer" or "doctor". Rarely do they know what architects actually do, or what they earn for spending all that time in school. However, as far as Nathan is concerned, the mystique is one of the benefits, so there is no way he would set her straight. He loves to talk about meaning and form, psychology of place, and the mystical aspects that are not just part of history but still find their way into the better projects today; the philosophical underpinnings and physical forms reflecting a mental condition. Not just talking, but trying to interpret these concepts into built form are an important aspect of Nathan's persona in his mind. He realizes, however, it is more important to know when to pull out this persona. Right now is not the time, he thinks, doubting it would impress her.

"Wow, that's great," she says, not fully impressed. "But don't they have local architects, or are you somebody famous in the field?"

She knows how to turn it back to his ego. *This woman is good*, he thinks. "A friend from school had been working on it, and I was tapped when he couldn't finish."

"What is 'it'?" she asks.

"A museum for those beehive huts you see around here," he keeps it brief. "Have you driven the coast road around the end of the peninsula?"

"Twice. It's fantastic. You'll have to let me know where you're building."

There is a pause as they both drink and turn in unison to order another. Nathan puts down enough money for both, as does she. He is imagining moving her collar back just far enough to see the nape of her neck, wanting to know what it would taste like. Salty, slightly sweet, his lips moving with the slight dip as he crosses to her bare shoulder. "You have a favorite architect?" she asks, her slight beer foam mustache breaking his fantasy.

"Favorite? It's always changing, depending on the project I'm working on. Right now I would have to say Bernard Maybeck."

"Never heard of him."

"He had a penchant for dramatizing the practical. Completely whacked, but still managed to get things built."

"Something you aspire to?" she jokingly inquires, rather close to the mark.

"And what about you?" Nathan feels it time to turn the conversation back. "What are you doing when you're not traveling? Did you continue with teaching?"

She smiles and looks down at her drink on the bar, folding her arms protectively around it. "Sort of. When I got back from Kazakhstan, I thought I had done something amazing and would be rewarded for my initiative and work helping others. Not so. You know how you feel time stands still when you're away? I came back and everything had changed. The guy I discovered I loved by being away from him had moved on, my coworkers had gotten promotions and pay raises, and I was basically starting over. Actually, it was worse than starting over. There's this new principal, Parker, at my school and he doesn't know me and I'm not used to his leadership style. He sees me with this scar," she points at her cheek, "and decides I'm damaged. He basically places me back as a teacher's aide."

"That sucks," says Nathan.

Audrey shakes her head in agreement. "But then it gets worse. I may have copped a bit of an attitude since I had actually put in more time at that school than this Parker did, I don't know. Anyway, none of the other teachers liked him. He's a bit of a dictator and rather incompetent, which is a bad combination as you Americans know," she winks, and Nathan thinks he knows but doesn't want to break the story to ask, "and my friends were afraid of the power he held over their jobs. I had the least amount to lose at this point, so I kind of took it on myself to make it a better place. That got me demoted to teacher's aide in the worst room in the school."

Nathan tries to think of something better to say than "*that sucks*", but in truth it was the most polite thing he could think of. *If*

I could meet this asshole, I would pound his tongue flat with a lead cheese grater and then nail it to the ground with a railroad spike, is his first thought. "I hope your friends stood up for you and there was a mutiny," he finally says.

"Hardly, they all had families now and I barely had a boyfriend. So then there was an incident with one of my students, totally outside of my class, where he ends up killing another guy over a girl. This was the worst thing to ever happen at the school, and because the kid killed this guy with a poison we had just read about in one of the stories I was teaching, Parker tries to accuse me of being an accomplice and telling him how to do it."

I would snap his neck so he was paralyzed but not dead and he would have to watch me put a meat hook through his sac between his balls and slowly lift him up to the ceiling until it ripped away and he fell to the floor. Nathan surprises himself with the protective violence he is feeling towards this woman he hardly knows. He is shocked he feels it at all.

"What's even worse, is this whole time he is trying to pressure me to sleep with him, saying it could all go away and I could get my old teaching job back. He even grabbed my ass a couple times," she shakes her head.

Nathan feels bad for his own thoughts regarding her ass. *If I was her boyfriend, I would have cut out his balls, and after slightly warming them in the microwave, wrapped them up in a tortilla made of his own shit and made him eat the whole thing.* He shakes his head, mirroring her gesture, wondering *Wow, where did that thought come from?* "That is awful," he says, "I hope you got him fired for that."

"Hardly. I wouldn't budge and the board loved the guy. I was waiting to be fired so I could get unemployment, but another teacher friend of mine got me a job at a private school in Halifax; uniforms and polite kids and the whole thing. I love it, so it kinda worked out for the best." She pauses and takes a big drink.

"I'm glad it worked out," Nathan concludes, curiously hungry for Mexican food. After this long unloading on her part, he now feels free to talk about anything he wants.

"So what are you doing tomorrow?" she asks, changing the subject.

Nathan reads it more as a question of interest rather than a lead-in. "I have a bit of work to do and then get ready for a short trip. I need to go to Berlin for a couple of days, but then I'm right back here." Nathan pauses, hopeful, "Would you like to get together tomorrow, dinner or something?"

"I can't tomorrow, sorry, a scheduled trip with some friends I'm meeting here," she gives a mock sad expression. "What's in Berlin?"

Nathan concocts a story about some materials for the project he is working on, German technology and so on. Instead of a possible wild goose chase to an abandoned abbey in Chorin, it is now a high-tech junket to a factory in . . . well, he was not thinking so fast so it is still Chorin. He chastises himself, thinking there are no factories within miles of the little village, and if he is going to succeed when he gets to that house he needs to become a better liar.

Audrey excuses herself to the bathroom. She leaves her jacket behind but takes her purse, a good sign she is coming back but not so good that she trusts him completely. He turns his attention to the group of four on his other side: two sitting and two standing. Engrossed in conversation, he did not even notice how long they had been there. The woman sitting directly adjacent has a pack of cigarettes laying just his side of her almost empty pint glass. All four are turned towards the table of musicians, their backs to the bar belting out the words to some song that involves a poor "Molly" and someone dying, but is incredibly upbeat about the whole thing. Without thinking, he secrets a white-colored cigarette out of the pack and into his jacket pocket in a single smooth move.

When she returns they talk for another hour steadily, even intimately at times. She brings up his trip to Chorin again, suggesting it is too bad and hinting that if he would be sticking around, maybe he could show her a few sights. Where exactly was he going again? What's there? Nathan regrets his formerly great idea, the possibility of something happening here far more intoxicating.

Even as drunk as he is now, he thinks this girl is good: like a stripper knowing the angles, picking up on hobbies and speaking at all the right times. *Always be suspicious of perfection*, he reminds himself. The lights come up, and as she stands to leave she steadies herself with one hand on the back of Nathan's chair and extends the other in a handshake. Not what he was hoping for, but he grabs it anyway.

"It was very nice meeting you Nathan. I really hope I'll see you around."

"Can I walk you back to your hotel? It's a small town, and with only three possible directions, chances are pretty good we're going the same way."

"No, please, I'm fine," she smiles and hurriedly turns into the crowd heading out. He tries to follow, but the number of people in the bar seems to have doubled and is now bottlenecking nears the door. Nathan is left behind seeing her long, straight dark hair pass outside with two dozen people between them. *Damn, she's fast*, he pouts as he takes the final warm creamy slug of beer.

Nathan leaves, one of the last stragglers. Even after so little sleep the previous night, he is disappointed at the preposterously early closing time. The street is busy for a brief moment as everyone heads to homes, cars, and hotels. No sign of Audrey, his last hope that she reconsidered and is waiting for him outside the door. He remembers the cigarette in his pocket, and removes it along with a book of matches he had snagged as a souvenir. It is a pleasant cool evening, and leaning against the side of a shop entry he puts the cigarette between his lips and lights it, turning and raising his arms to block the wind in a practiced move. He takes a deep drag, feeling a bit guilty at the pleasure, and raises his collar to walk down the dark and quickly emptying sidewalk. He coughs at the second inhalation. Thinking better of it, he drops the lovely glowing pilferage to the ground and stamps it out.

13

July 2, Dingle, Dingle Peninsula

NATHAN LIES DOWN with his world quite literally spinning. He tries to focus, his arm over his eyes, willing the room to stop. Too much drink, too little sleep, and an unfamiliar place all conspire and converge at this very moment. Not yet midnight, he sits up hoping the alcohol will wear off and fatigue will eventually win the balance.

Sitting in boxer shorts at his small table, Nathan concentrates on the sketches he had taken from Anton's room the day before. *How did he get this project? What has he been doing all these years that I haven't heard a single thing about him? What the fuck am I doing here?* Nathan smiles, certain Anton would be proud of dragging his old foil across the ocean, out of the funk he had been feeling, and into . . . what? *What am I feeling now?* Alone in a hotel in the middle of nowhere far from home, over his head in a project and process he is foreign to. Almost a dream job, now that he thinks about it. *Thanks Anton, but you're still an asshole for disappearing.*

He turns the sketch over and back, studying both sides, judging that Anton's line-work and printing has not improved since school.

Nathan would never forget their first meeting; the first day in studio at the University of Illinois and he was overcompensating by being aggressive and obnoxious. When a quiet Anton joined the group of girls he was trying to impress, he blurted out "Your mom keep your tongue at home?" Turned out his mother had been killed in an auto accident. Of course, Nathan thinks, if he had said "cat got your tongue" it would have turned out Anton's cat had just been run over: it was meant to be a no-win situation. They would eventually bond over the mutual loss of a parent, but at the time it was one of those mean things you say that stick in your memory, lingering far longer than any mean thing that was said to you.

One of their first assignments had been a town design, an exercise in form and context. Anton had named all the streets after deadly plants: Curare Boulevard, Hemlock Avenue, and Arsenic Lane all laid out on his drawing in beautiful poison greens. While the professor was considering whether to report the guy for psychological observation, Nathan was drawn to his dark sense of humor.

Anton tended to think and design very practically, yet had a very incisive intellect. When a juror during one of the ritualistic humiliations known as 'critiques' accused him of thinking way inside the box, Anton confronted him on what this 'box' is. *What if the 'box' is a good thing*, Anton argued, *and that if everyone is successively thinking outside of it, the box itself will keep growing and expanding until it just got too big and simply could not contain anything anymore? All thought would be rendered meaningless.* Nathan had a hard time understanding the fear that seemed to be underlying this view, but appreciated the quick thoughtful defense. At the time, in the safety of the university, Nathan thought much like his faculty that creative unfettered ideas–even the ones that fail horribly–are the only way new things are discovered. There would be time to learn the rest later, after all this was not a technical college but a University. The primary skill is how to think, not what to think.

The confrontation exposed the fundamental difference in nature between them; of Nathan being reckless and trusting, Anton as careful and suspicious. Now, looking back, it seemed to boil down to contrasting world views. Anton saw things more simplistically, homogenously and morally, with the rules and precedents of design as an actively good or bad feature of his ideals. Nathan remembers seeing things more complexly, contradictory and ethically with rules as neutral to referee and not govern his thoughts. They could both dabble in the opposite extreme and be devious in their own ways, and Nathan had admitted more than once that his way was worse in consistency, if not sometimes more effective and sexy. Their contrasting natures had led to many an architectural discussion, the best Nathan remembers. At the time it was all big words and recently discovered ideas. Since then, he believes, a balance has been struck thanks to Johanna and some early failures in his career.

Their semester abroad had also helped them both. The first year of graduate school, second semester, he and about fifteen of his fellow architecture class studied in Paris and Rome. Paris ended up not intriguing him as much as he expected, but having a home base to explore was invaluable. Rome was overwhelming. The professor leading this trip, Cornelius Moynihan, was unknown to Nathan before the trip. Anton and Professor Moynihan seemed to develop a close relationship; odd since Nathan was usually a favorite and Anton had never tried to impress any of his teachers. He was not jealous, but rather felt relieved Anton had found a mentor and Nathan no longer had to administer his pep talks.

Nathan remembers the professor mostly for odd little assignments he would give, much like the warm-ups he had seen from acting coaches. First there was a scavenger hunt for architectural details, most of which they had to look up in a dictionary first. Then, a quick sketch where Professor Moynihan would throw things off of a roof and the class had to sketch them before they smashed on the ground. The third exercise Nathan remembers vividly, because it was the one he did the best at; they had taken what seemed to be a routine historic tour, and then only afterward Moynihan required that they draw the plan of the building to scale, from memory.

There were typical studio projects in between–a small museum, a bus shelter, and a memorial–but every now and then would come the pop quizzes. In Rome they would have to find places that made them feel happy, sad, at home, or uncomfortable, and then analyze exactly why. In Paris they had to talk their way into someone's home without calling ahead, and document the architectural form and function; an assignment, he thinks, which might come in useful in the next couple days. This project would have been easier in friendly Rome, and Nathan wasn't sure what he learned although it had provided a boldness to walk into places on behalf of architectural curiosity. Later, the professor asked questions regarding personal aspects of the people they had just invaded.

It seemed stupid and pointless at the time, even tortuous, but they had all learned something about themselves. Nathan had a photographic memory for form and layout, even though he could not remember a name, yet his loose tongue had failed miserably at discretion; valuable when working so closely with a client. He had learned to pay attention, and that not everything was about the object. He has just forgotten that lesson since.

Moyne and Moynihan: a bit of a coincidence. I suppose as coincidental as French and Irish could be. Nathan gets up unsteadily and pours a glass of water.

In their early twenties, the whole aura of what they were doing seemed avant-garde, almost like architectural spying. It was, the professor would admit, a grooming to think a certain way. He always had an answer to their questions. Many times it was to just be aware of how to look, how to see the world, how people actually need the physical spaces around them and how environment affects their mood. Sometimes it was incredibly simple, like "don't forget to look up". Professor Moynihan viewed the world "as a parchment", he would say, "and unless you learn how to read it, anything you try to add will be little more than a scribble." Everyone accepted his reasoning, or simply did not care: they were young and in Europe.

Anton did naturally well: solid and trustworthy, people confided in him. Nathan also did well for opposing reasons: he talked freely and made intuitive connections, so pure in belief that people were drawn along and in the process spilled everything. Anton took it very seriously, encouraged for the first time in his academic career. Nathan thought it was fun. Johanna was average, which she was not used to, and focused instead on experiencing and sketching the places they traveled.

And there were so many places they had been able to see, to study: Prague, Paris, Amsterdam, Bruges, Florence, Rome, Venice, Berlin, etc. In between classes and before and after the official start of the semester they may not have been jetsetters, but certainly became second class trainsetters with more passion than money. They had much to see and limited time, so they settled on the 'perfect moment' method of deciding how long to stay: sometimes it would be a couple hours in a place they planned to spend a few days, sometimes it was a whole week in a place they had just planned on passing through. As a result, the three, and sometimes four or five, of them had spent only a tumultuous afternoon in the rich history of Avignon, but an entire beautiful week in relatively unnoted Bayeux. They left Prague in the middle of the night when after one incredible evening where everything–architecture, food, drink, dancing–all hit a pinnacle, and they knew it could not get any better.

The university, that semester in particular, had helped him learn to think. However, when it failed to temper his creativity with any discipline, it just created an ethos in him where intentions were more important than the final product. Nathan's early career was filled with meaningless creative drawings and multiple failed buildings with unhappy clients. There were a couple of bright spots, but it was too hit or miss, mostly misses. Soon after his first job, he went back to Berlin with the US government, trying to recapture the magic of his time overseas in school. But without his friends there, without Johanna and Anton, it was a very different experience, and he failed in spectacular fashion. Maybe not failed, so much as imploded. He needed a partner. He returned and sought out Johanna, who had been working at a large downtown Chicago firm. It was her convictions, and her philosophy, that saved him.

Nathan had always considered himself cutting edge. Despite sometimes being aggressive and loose-tongued when nervous, he could also be the introvert that people mistook for thoughtfulness. He did not, does still not, see a contradiction in this nature. All of his profession is a bit of that peculiar form of manic depression that architects create for themselves: of thoughtfulness to desperation, of procrastination to feverish work sessions before the deadline.

Nathan downs another large glass of water and moves over to the bed, propping himself up with pillows against the headboard. He thinks about tonight, about Audrey, and the days to come.

Tiredness has won, and Nathan attempts to lie down again. In those strange-thought moments, with head nodding before sleep fully comes, he swears he hears the door open and unable to move or speak Anton is in his room, covering his mouth with one hand while the Friendly Courier is covering him up with a sheet: first to his waist, then to his neck, then over his head as everything goes dark.

14

July 3, Dingle, Dingle Peninsula

HEAD POUNDING, STOMACH QUEASY. Waking up hung over, Nathan realizes he is too late for the hotel breakfast. He thinks it is for the better, the heavy eggs and sausage would not sit well. Then again, moving around at all is hell. He goes to the bathroom sink, fills the small plastic cup with cold water and tosses it back like a shot. Repeating the process a few more times, he knows from experience he did not drink enough to deserve this feeling. It must have been that damn cigarette.

Fresh air. A walk, and then food. He takes three more drinks of water before putting a hat on to cover his unwashed hair. Pulling on his jeans and shoes with yesterday's socks, he dons a jacket and grabs the key to Anton's apartment. Something he remembered before passing out last night made him curious.

The walk, unsteady at first, begins to take its desired therapeutic effect. Nathan makes his way to the western edge of town, a mostly uphill climb, before turning around and heading down to the intersection, then back up to O'Malley's at the opposite eastern edge. Once there, he takes advantage of his incognito look to check around outside, careful to stay out of Mrs. O'Malley's line of sight.

He lets himself in quickly and ascends the stairs. Nathan unlocks the door and surveys the room, much as he had done the first time. To his surprise, it appears some of Anton's things have been moved slightly. Not ransacked, but things were certainly moved and put back in almost the same place, but not quite. Anyone who is not as obsessive-compulsive as Nathan may not have noticed.

Professor Moynihan's words resonated clearly in his thoughts, as they did last night: "Don't forget to look up. People rarely study what's over their heads, and of those that do–designers and investigators mostly–one is looking for how it all fits together and the other for what is out of place. You have to do both."

Nathan looks up at the ceiling. Nothing. He has another idea, and steps over to the models sitting by the table. He rotates the model upside down for better light and peers through a tiny window. The pattern on the ceiling, from this angle, seems to be a series of beams sketched in pen on the surface. As he looks at it closer, the scribbling is too regular, and separated in tiny lines: writing.

"Sorry, Anton," Nathan says as he pries the roof off with a snap. The writing is tiny, and he looks around for a magnifying glass. Then he remembers the glass case in the bathroom medicine cabinet, hoping Anton left his glasses behind. No luck. The bottom of the whiskey glass on the shelf provides his only option. He takes it from its perch and lays the bass wood ceiling of the model flat on the table.

The individual lines of text, each spaced out to form equal length 'beams', read:

Nathan if you read this something has happened to me

Make a choice to leave now or follow this through

It is a specialty, reading the language of the built world

helping people find what has been hidden and hiding

things for people they do not want found Things I

know you would risk all to satisfy your curiosity

You know what to do and how to do it. We learned together

"What the hell?" he sits back in the chair and swears a bit more vividly in his mind before rereading it. *Some kind of mafia thing? No,* Nathan decides, *it seems like Anton is an independent contractor, and now he is getting me in on it. He probably even has a few government contracts. Secrets? The travel? That part might be intriguing. I'm a bit higher profile than Anton. This would have to be side work. What was he thinking? Is the pay that good?*

The arguments swirl in his head.

Maybe just for a few jobs, see how it goes. It's been pretty fun so far: I'm sitting in Ireland, heading for Berlin tomorrow morning. All I was doing in Chicago was maybe driving to Wisconsin every now and then.

What did he mean "We learned together?" They were only ever in school together. If Professor Moynihan was testing us, then he recruited Anton and then what–I came in second? Nathan sits in silence for moment, thinking nothing. Deciding. Deciding nothing. Has he chosen this, or is the momentum choosing him?

Make a decision, right now? Why not after this job, he wonders, *see how it goes.* Analyzing his life, as he had done the past few days, he suddenly feels committed to seeing this one through. Then, when and if "they" call he can decide.

Are these the kind of people you say "No thanks" to? he ponders for a second. *What if I don't want more? How do I get that word out. Seems the car is already rolling.* Nathan thinks about nothing for a while longer, sitting and staring at the broken model.

"I have to find what happened to Anton," he tells the room. Go to Berlin and find something new, a clue. If he can find the stone, and Mr. Moyne knows something about Anton, then he will have some leverage.

Now I'm thinking like a criminal, Nathan decides, satisfied.

He looks around one last time, peering at the other models to make sure he has not missed any other messages. Closing the door behind him, and descending the stairs he is barely out the bottom door when he sees Mrs. O'Malley crossing the street towards him. "Well a fine morning to you. Another look? You interested in the lease?" she asks.

"Sorry, I forgot," he says, stuffing the paper deeper into his pocket, "By the way, did you clean Anton's room in the last day or two?"

"No, haven't been in there."

"I'm going to be gone for a few days, I'll be sure to stop by as soon as I get back."

"Where you off to?" she asks.

"Berlin. Two days, tops. We'll see you then." He waves and turns to cut her off. Nathan suddenly feels self-conscious about his unshaven, very pale face. *What if I run into Audrey?* he considers the worst-case scenario.

The air is still doing its work cleaning out his head. At the corner, near the pub that did this to him the previous evening, he turns left and walks down the Mall towards the harbor. He begins to feel hungry, and the thought of leaving the next day, even though he is coming back, reminds him to pick up few souvenirs for Johanna and Sharon and something the office could share like a bottle of whiskey. Maybe not whiskey, he reconsiders, as his stomach moves in response.

Nathan looks in the shop windows along the waterfront. There is a light sprinkle, so he tries to stay under protective awnings. There are not as many people out on the street today, so he begins to notice a tall thin man wearing a fisherman's hat and carrying an umbrella. A guy like that, he thinks, would not be caught dead using an umbrella.

The light sprinkle builds into a quick downpour, forcing Nathan into a shop. The fisherman with an umbrella stops across the street and stands there, looking out at boats in the harbor. Nathan peers out a display window as the downpour reaches its climax; he is still standing there, umbrella unopened.

Rain stops and sunlight streams through big billowing clouds. Nathan steps out of the store with a painted plate for Johanna. He is certain she will hate it. As he continues his search for a more appropriate nick-knack, if there is such a thing, he glances over his shoulder to see umbrella man moving again. Is he being followed, or is this just a small town? Anton's paranoia may be contagious. Perhaps Anton had reason to be paranoid, Nathan thinks, he is missing after all.

Nathan decides to force the fisherman's hand. He ducks into an alley and heads back between two narrow sheds to a courtyard in the back. Looking back down the way he came Nathan sees no one. The courtyard has some beautiful old buildings, probably shops to repair small boats and fishing gear, given its proximity to the harbor. They do not look used, and Nathan cannot resist nosing around.

The back edge of one building is a series of brick vaults covered in plaster, but exposed where the finish is cracking. The wooden doors are side hinged, beautifully detailed and efficient. He calls out a "hello?" to cover his intrusion. Hearing nothing, he peaks his head into a dark shed, stopping when he feels a knife-edge at his throat. Without moving, the weapon's owner smoothly moves his head over into the light. The face is weathered: a fisherman's face. His head is shaved, a close-cut beard barely covering deep creases, especially deep around the eyes from staring out into sea sun and reflection below. One eye is missing or damaged, but he does not bother putting a patch over it; perhaps he thinks it would be too stereotypical.

"You think you can walk in wherever you want?" the man asks.

"Would it help if I told you I was . . ." Nathan does not have a chance to finish his sentence.

"I know what you are. I know who you are. That may work in that world," he nods towards the street from where Nathan had come, "but not in this one." The knife seems unnecessary, as the man's breath on Nathan's hangover is enough to subdue him.

"How do you know who I am?" Nathan asks.

"You're not just some tourist here, word spreads fast in a small town. And I looked you up online." He studies Nathan's eyes with his own good eye for an intense moment. "You think that's funny? Me sitting at a computer and typing?"

"No, no . . . I, I . . ." Nathan composes himself after a second. "I thought I was being followed."

"Ye might be. We all are. But it's not the police, and it's not my people."

"You . . ."

"I'm holding the knife. That's all. You stay out of our business, we stay out of yours."

"Okay."

"Brilliant. You should sign that lease."

"What?" asks Nathan, confounded.

"The lease, sticking out of your pocket," the fisherman gestures down with his good eye.

Nathan pulls it out, and stares at the man dumbly as he is offered a pen. Holding it flat on the palm of his hand for support, he signs the bottom. The man takes the pen and the piece of paper back.

"Thanks. Mum will be pleased."

Nathan snorts, unable to hide his amusement. "Your mother. Is that what this is about?"

"No. This," he gestures around, "is just happenstance. You came here, remember. I wasn't looking for you. You saw nothing." The man hands Nathan the knife, snarls again in what must be his version of a smile. "A housewarming gift."

The figure recedes back into darkness. Nathan turns to retreat down the alley, preferring to take his chances with the other fisherman holding an umbrella. Halfway down he hears from somewhere beyond the courtyard, "welcome to our neighborhood." It sounds more menacing than welcoming.

Nathan walks into the street, dazed. A young couple wearing matching rain jackets, jeans and tennis shoes suddenly stop, looking at him wide-eyed. They turn and, still watching him from the corners of their eyes, cross to the other side of the street. Nathan realizes he is still holding the knife, and reaching up touches his neck where the knife had been. He is surprised to see blood on his hand, a few spots dripping down on his shirt.

He sticks the knife quickly in his pocket where the lease had been, and considers himself fortunate to be leaving for a few days. Running into the O'Malley boy may have been an accident, or a conspiracy that the fisherman with the umbrella had led him into.

Returning to his hotel to dry off and pack, Nathan decides it may be time to lie down for a little while. This evening back home, he remembers, will be holiday fireworks. Here it is simply Tuesday, and he feels very far from home indeed, especially for someone who just signed a lease.

15

E R RENNT! Ciaran does not understand the words yelled from behind but he knows their meaning, feels the action of it in his running. It is dark in his dream, being chased through the woods, the men in pursuit intent on killing him. He is dressed in monk's clothes, much like he wears in his waking life. Ciaran realizes, however, this is not a vision of his own future, but one of his brothers many years from now. So far in the future, yet so little has changed.

In his vision he had been traveling with two older monks, delivering holy artifacts to a new monastery being built far away on the mainland. Those that had been promised these objects, the benefactors who desire some degree of legitimacy and status for the monastery they were helping construct, were unhappy with what they had received. The novice monk he is in this dream was not at the meeting where these artifacts were presented, but had heard his two elder monks discuss in hushed and worried tones afterwards what to do next. They decided to make camp for the night and try to send advanced word to monks of their monastery before making the long trip back home. There had been one monk from the new monastery at the meeting who, though he remained silent then, had afterwards, privately, extended an invitation.

Ciaran's dream-self had been returning to their camp with firewood, the novice sent out into the dark woods while his two brother monks had stayed behind to tend the fire and clean up from their evening meal. As he trekked closer to the campsite, he saw another group of men. Men from the meeting, something told him. They are yelling in their strange language and holding the oldest monk down on his knees. The other monk is lying on his side, motionless and facing the fire with unblinking eyes. A man standing behind his elder raises a heavy club over his head then brings it down flatly on the top of the old monk's skull. Ciaran's vision-self had flinched at the brutal action, and he shuddered again when the thudding, cracking sound reaches him a few seconds later over the distance.

After a frozen moment, he dropped the wood from his arms and turned to run, it did not matter where. The sound of falling wood and clumsy movement through the strange woods quickly gave him away. Had he stood still, they may have not realized there was a third traveling companion. Now he is running for his life. He is not sure, if caught, if he would simply be beaten to death as a witness or if he would be questioned as to where they had hidden the artifacts. He hoped to not find out.

The artifacts. They had traveled many weeks only to be met with greed and violence. He had to admit the stone piece looked rather ordinary, having expected a more traditional relic, such as bones of a saint, when he was told of their errand.

During the long journey his elders had filled him in on the history of the tablet. This was the third of three pieces brought back from an epic journey whose history had reached mythical proportions; the Irish love of storytelling exaggerated and skewed it even further. The writing on them, his elders informed, hold secrets of a far away people. This one had been kept at *Sceilig Mhichil*, the Skellig Michael rock, within sight of mainland but surrounded by treacherous waters where many of Ciaran's brothers would one day find splendid and safe isolation. There it would stay for hundreds of years until the place was abandoned, and it would then find its way to the monastery in Ballinskelligs and then to Clonfert, home to the monk in his vision. In all this time, not one of their scholars had been able to decipher the writing. It had become holy by age and mystery, yet the new Bishop of Clonfert saw it as of little use amongst the more apparent treasures. Amongst the three items they were carrying–a golden chalice, a small stone and a large stone–the Bishop considered the large stone tablet the least valuable. Among the monks who had guarded these items, however, the stone held a powerful fascination, both for its link to the great abbot Brendan but also for rumors of healing power.

The other pieces were scattered, they said, because of a power they held when brought together. They were both said to be in Ireland, under the protection of monks. Ciaran, however, knows there would be more pieces, not all in Ireland. He had seen where they came from, and what they looked like together. It was a part of the vision that had brought him to the monastery in the first place: the beginning of his faith, the bridge of his destiny, and a source of his current crisis.

In Ciaran's vision he is still running, jumping over fallen logs and brushing aside slashing branches as he moves quickly through the woods. He feels as if he had run for an hour when he sees a fire in the darkness and heads toward it, hoping for a friendly group who would protect a young monk. Entering the clearing, he looks in horror upon the bodies of his fallen brothers and realizes he had been chased in a circle back to where it started. He stops in disbelief, hearing the laughter of his pursuers who had now caught up with him.

Both of his fears come true. He cannot answer their questions since he does not understand their language–only the oldest of his companion monks spoke it–and so they beat him without mercy. As he lay battered and dying he is certain the relics are safely hidden, and that his fellow monks would find and protect them. He gasps, a heavy sigh that brings blood from deep within to his lips. Ciaran is now outside this body, staring at the young man's empty eyes as the dream world morphs, colors brightening as great red arches with delicate stone tracery arise from the dead monk. He stares in wonder, thinking it like an illuminated manuscript made into a building: a gift to God from the evil that took place here.

Ciaran awakes, alone in a broad field. He had been stuck in the middle of this dream before, running through the woods not knowing from what or why. Now that he has worked his way through, saw the beginning and its ending, he feels his forced retreat has served its purpose. The problem, however, is that it is only his first night away. If he were to climb a large hill he is probably still within sight of the monastery he had been sent from and told not to return to for a fortnight. Lying there in the early morning hours, he feels both happiness and despair: happy that he had faced the rut he had been in and moved past it, both in his faith and his dreams, and despair that he still has a long trip ahead.

Ciaran had been sent away by the abbot, a forced retreat to face a crisis of faith. On his first day journey, heading southwest to the peninsula and over its mountains to the coast, he had traveled with a fellow monk. They talked about their similar background, growing up with the gods of their ancestors and then trying to change belief to a single all-powerful God. They agreed it could be frightening and alluring at the same time. Families feared the wrath of the gods for their son's abandonment, and any tragedy that befell their families since they left has probably been blamed upon this heresy. However, the world had not come to an end, and Ciaran had found a freedom and use for his talents he had no chance of finding at home. He has seen many wonderful things, and knows it is nothing compared to what still lies ahead. Whether he fully believes or not, he knows in his heart that this is the right place, and life, for him. He simply needed the right person to talk it through.

For a time he had a traveling companion, who turned back halfway through the first day, returning to the monastery before nightfall. Now alone, and with a serenity of acceptance back in place, his vision that night would also finally be free to run its course.

Ciaran's problem is that his gift provides too much information. He knows that he will barely arrive at his destination before being summoned to return. He also knows what the summons will be for, as he has seen it in his dreams: the Voyage. The Crossing. The dream from which he has just awoke is but a part of it, seeing the death and greed that will follow items they would bring back, and the myth that will emerge. He will warn the Abbot, whatever good that would do. He had never known his actions to change the future he had seen. If anything, Ciaran believes he causes them to happen, fulfilling his forethought.

He rolls up his sleeping mat and takes down the small animal hide shelter, wet from the previous night's rain. He stores the few precious utensils given to him by the Abbot–a sharp-pointed iron knife with wood handle, a spoon carved from wood–in the middle of the roll. He slings the bundle over his shoulder, steadying it across with his opposite hand, and begins the next leg of his journey.

Having faced his crisis and gained closure on his visions in a single day and evening, he is now left with a long journey through the wilderness that seems pointless. He thinks about turning back, but who knows; maybe he would find something out there.

Ciaran feels the awakening, the reconciliation as the Abbot had promised. However, for him it is different: he knows parts of his future, he just needs the patience, the serenity and the acceptance for his part to unfold. For his fellow monks, the crisis of faith is in the unknown. For Ciaran, it would always be the known futures that trouble him most deeply. He has often prayed to his new God to be like his brothers, for the gift of the unknown. This vision had taken him past his own future, to the impact of items they would bring back from a trip he is has yet to be told he will be taking. It makes as much sense to him as anything about his Gift. The main difference, he thinks as he begins walking again, the sun low over his left shoulder, is that he now accepts it is a trip he will take.

Like the monk in his vision, Ciaran thought for a moment that he could outrun the future that is chasing him. He thought he could avoid running in the circle that would leave him stranded far from home. He would be wrong. Errant.

16

July 4, Berlin

NOSTALGIA, NATHAN THINKS, is a tan-colored feeling, in the same color family as déjà vu or a remembered love long past. Trying to pinpoint the correct tone he settles on a somewhat warmer color than those other feelings, perhaps caramel. When the nostalgia is for an environment that had truly changed you, it would be as deep a hue as one could imagine: having dreamt about it, brooded over it, modified the place in your memories to be something that is too fantastic and meaningful to really exist. Berlin had that effect on Nathan. Its nostalgia so powerful he had been afraid to come back here, as it could never measure up.

He had been to more beautiful places, more historic towns, more wondrous landscapes, even more cutting edge cities, yet none had fit him better than Berlin. It was as much the time in his life as anything the city had to offer. Sprawling, historic, political, cutting edge, dark, depraved, vibrant, cultural: Berlin is a huge park teeming with a restless population always willing to try the unexpected and sometimes questionable. Like his own life, the results have been mixed.

The mid-morning air is crisp and cool as Nathan steps out of the airport terminal. The sky in Berlin has always felt lower and more intimate than the huge skies of his American Midwest. This is his first flight to Schönefeld Airport, the former airport for all points East and far from the Berlin he knows, but now the destination for flights from Dublin. As he passes by the drop-off lane there is a crowd gathering around a new Porsche 911. Two security guards standing across from him, weapons slung menacingly across their chests, are eyeing it with a suspicion in perfect contrast to the look of lust on the faces of the crowd. Beauty and power are strong diversionary tactics, and in Germany a car can be more alluring than a Hollywood actress.

He passes the scene with a glance, also drawn briefly to the gravity of the car's beauty, and then crosses under the Am Chaussee Mittel Street to the train station. Before climbing the steps to get on the familiar maroon and caramel train he orders a doner kebab from a Turkish vendor near the station entrance. It had been years since he tasted one of these bread, meat, veggie, and sauce sandwiches. With his first bite he realizes not all nostalgia is beyond reality.

"Sweet mother of . . ." he looks up from his bite and realizes people are staring at him as if a public orgasm is unacceptable. He smiles. "Sorry, we can't get these in the States," he offers in defense. It was probably better that way, Nathan thinks, or he would eat nothing else.

His first trip to this city was as a foreign exchange student, sixteen years old and had never been outside his own State. Berlin in the early Eighties was a shock, an epicenter of politics and culture. Parts were still wasteland from World War II, other parts the latest in architectural design. It had opened his eyes in so many ways, changed him at such a crucial point in his life. His family did not have money where college would be an option, but they found a way. Indeed, when they realized he was smart rather than on drugs as first suspected, they panicked, knowing it would end up costing them more in the long run.

The duo-colored train, the S9, sits doors open and waiting for passengers. This stop is the beginning of the line, and Nathan has the luxury of walking down a few cars to the middle before stepping aboard and leisurely picking a seat. He checks the map, following the multi-colored lines in the hope this train would eventually get him to Zoo Station. Nathan knows the Zoo is no longer the center of life and movement that it once was, but to him it remains his central compass, his point of reference for everywhere in Berlin.

Doors close and the train quietly picks up speed as the outskirts of the city begin to fly past. Staring blankly through the glass, his overnight bag set on the floor between his feet, Nathan's mind wanders first to the events of the past few days that had led him here. Not sure if he is ready to process all that yet, he shakes it off and focuses on this respite, this city he has returned to after so many years. When you leave somewhere truly strange, as Dingle had certainly become to Nathan, it is not often you come to a place that has potential to be even more surreal.

His mind does not comply, and his thoughts quickly flit to the past few days. Nathan does not remember being scared when the knife was held on him; surprised, yes, but he had not thankfully shit his pants. It had actually not been the first time, but it has been a long while, another lifetime. He has grown soft and complacent. Hell, he thinks, maybe he even made a new connection; there are stranger ways to meet people.

Looking back at his first stay in Berlin, Nathan had matured and adapted far better than he, or his parents, thought he would. It was here he developed a love for the urban fabric and all things architectural. Still in high school but already planning some type of design career, this influence would later surprise many of his classmates and professors who drew inspiration from Rome or Florence or Paris. Berlin, they would say rather correctly, was a "mess". For Nathan it was *his* mess, and he reveled in the avant-garde culture of Kreuzberg, the unexpected public art, the homey neighborhoods, the wounded diplomatic quarter, the shiny display of the Ku'Damm, the villas of Wannsee, the gothic piles and modernist cubes: it all seemed to fit here, like a halfway house for the world's imagination.

He had also become more aware, through his wonderful host family, about the culture of the place. He saw the direct relationship between what is built and how we live. A chicken and egg type of thing, Nathan realized what is built is drawn from a community's priorities, but thereafter the space created would shape the next community that forms. It was a lot of responsibility, a lot of opportunity, but not nearly the Creator-of-Things aura his professors would have him believe. There were spaces here he had fallen in love with, and knew he could never recreate them as hard as he tried because that is just not how Americans live. And then there was East Berlin, East Germany, where everything tried to be opposite.

When he first came here, Nathan saw an opportunity to just start being someone else, someone other than who he was. After some time, some adjustments, he actually became that person: like telling a lie so many times that it eventually becomes a truth. The question was, in the end, did he become anyone better than who he was before?

They slow down again and come to a stop. *Adlershof.* The previous two stops were rather quiet and empty, but this one had a busier feel with more people mingling on the platform. He felt the city getting closer, his excitement building.

It was not until he came back in college that he had the capacity to explore the darker corners of the city. He was twenty-one, indestructible, with equally adventurous friends, and on a tight timeframe: the ingredients for an out-of-control approach to sightseeing. He wanted to experience everything he could, everything he would be afraid to be caught doing if this city was really his home. Not just drinking, dancing, and seeing the sights but staying out all night, going to underground clubs where anything could happen, seeing drug deals made and prostitutes picked up and robberies take place. He could be homeless, if just for a short while. One major obstacle was that he did not generally know where these things occurred, and even the really out-there clubs did not have a sign. He needed a guide.

Anton and Nathan planned on staying for two weeks. They had a cheap, not-so-clean hotel room on a side street near Nollendorfplatz. Johanna had also come with them, but after two days returned to Paris. Soon after that Anton disappeared for a few days, receiving permission to visit relatives in the East.

That night Nathan walked out the door with only his passport and about twenty Marks in his pocket, and ventured across the street to the small store where Yavuz worked. Yavuz was a Turk, about the same age as Nathan, who he had met and struck up an acquaintance over several visits to the shop. Nathan had first contacted Yavuz through Ian, a British doorman at the nightclub around the corner, as someone who was "in the know" and friendly enough to take him around–for a small price. Ian would later help Nathan discover the underground clubs, which required a different kind of access.

Nathan thinks he could not have been the first, that there was probably a good market for this type of adventure tourism. There were rules, and he understood he was just getting a small taste. Nathan knew even then he did not have it in him to truly cross the line.

Nathan smiles at how reckless he had been, and how wonderful and frightening the things he had seen and done. Glimpsing that world was addictive, and if it was a path he would get caught up in he knew it was not for the better. When Anton returned he sensed a change, even questioned Nathan about it. Nathan was too embarrassed, defensive, or just cautious to talk about what he had done. Certainly not that he was secretive, but he felt exploring your dark side is something not easily talked about, except with others who may have done the same thing to the same extent. Nathan doubted that Anton had even considered it. For those final three days, Nathan avoided the shop across the street and the nightclub where his "guides" worked.

Treptower Park

Nathan focuses through the window and beyond the station for a glimpse of the huge Soviet Memorial, but could not see any sign. He had stopped at this station once before with his girlfriend, Natalia, on a romantic day of visiting five thousand dead soldiers of the Red Army.

He met Natalia on his third stay in Berlin, a side trip that seemed sort of a different life to Nathan. *No, not sort of*, he reassesses. *It was.*

Natalia. Where was she now? Dead, Nathan hoped, as it would be much easier than the thought of running into her again. Maybe not completely and really dead, but at least miserable in a broken life, or incarcerated. He thinks fleetingly that his current situation as forty and unmarried leads back somehow to her, but decides not to give her so much credit.

He rarely mentions, even if he thinks constantly, about that time between school, his first few jobs, and his current work. Berlin figured centrally, again, to that middle time. With graduation

Nathan faced a crisis. It was not that he thought he chose the wrong career, as many do. He had worked a few beginning jobs while in school, getting his foot in the door. Instead, he wanted some adventure before settling in, rather than finding a job and staying there forever. He could not wait to get his hands on some major projects, but he just was not ready for a house and wife and family and then end up laying on his deathbed wondering what the hell happened. He did not think he was destined for a normal life. This makes Nathan smile, as if there is a thing such as a normal life in the world. Part of him is still reckless and indestructible, but it was so much worse back in his twenties. His earlier adventures had not so much quenched a thirst as stoked a fire. And back then he was completely broke, so when he got an offer through Professor Moynihan to train for analysis work he took it. He needed a foot in the door, and this door looked perfect and exciting.

A few weeks after graduation, he quit his job and left for a small school just outside Williamsburg, Virginia. Nathan was in a group with a variety of disciplines, some were even military and CIA in the Professional Trainee to CST program. Everyone else seemed to know what they were doing, what they wanted to be. Nathan said all the right things, but had no idea where he would fit in. He had simply taken a bunch of placement tests and hoped they would sort the rest out later.

They trained. He was physically and mentally sharp, and his architectural education was not entirely useless. Everyone else seemed to have an edge or a particular focus that set them apart; for some it was military strategy, others were accountants and knew that most crimes could be solved by following the money. If there was one thing that gave Nathan an edge, it was his photographic memory for space and form, and his ability to extrapolate layouts and functions and even events occurring within from very little data. It was, in the words of some of his teachers, as if he could see through walls. Nathan assumed he was not unique, and since some of it was strictly instinctual he also assumed he would be wrong as often as he was right. Most often, he would find out to his surprise, he was right. He may not have been a model recruit, but could certainly be useful as an analyst in the days before technology actually let people see through walls.

Nathan became the guy who could remember floor plans, anticipate and extrapolate physical environments. He was a top-notch environmental behaviorist; he knew how a place would effect the way people acted in it, and alternately where to find people who wanted to act a certain way. For whatever reason, probably because he had learned it in bars, he spoke German with a Dutch accent. At least it was not as blatantly American as most of the other students in his class, even if his grammar and vocabulary were not as polished.

After a year he was sent back here. Berlin. A perfect fit, with so many connections he had built up and maintained. They placed him with an architectural firm. Come to think of it, Nathan is still not sure who "they" were: he assumed he was with the Department of State in support of the CIA. Reading the news today, he doubts however that they had ever worked that closely. He never actually saw his paychecks, which were deposited directly into an account in the United States. He made enough at the architectural firm to support himself, and the savings account back home would later help him found his practice with Johanna.

During the morning and afternoon he would put in a full day's work, drafting plans, sections and elevation by hand with ink on vellum paper. Nathan doubts his draftspersons now could work on anything other than a computer. In the evening there would often be a package: plans and specs for him to comb through, analyze, and write up a report. Every now and then he would get a call to come to some location for on-site analysis, backing up field agents and giving them the best information he could to navigate through or find something. This would often involve reconnaissance beforehand, which his day job as an architect gave him a certain amount of access and professional courtesy for. Of course, anything secure was just as off limits, but sometimes he could get closer, and that was all he needed.

He had originally come to this divided city to understand the mentality of a time, his time, which could produce such a thing. While there he thought it incredibly meaningful that he took an interest in Native American culture, the idea of a Vision Quest consuming him. The usual means of such a quest was through a deprivation of food and drink, but Nathan was trying to do the same thing through overindulgence. The irony was not lost, and when he returned from thought he had visions of having all the answers, of providing some insight, but all he really had to offer was more confusion. And he missed his friends.

So on the evenings with no work, he went out. In his twenties he had the energy; Nathan excelled at both lives he was living, and for a while it worked. He was too impatient, too cocky, he recalls. He wanted to be in the field, an operations officer and not just a consultant for a Collections Management Officer. Too soon he would get his chance, and it would all fall apart.

Alexanderplatz

The last two stops had been just as congested, the pathetic milling about of so many people struggling to get an idea of what it is like to have an idea. He is now scrunched to the inside of the seat, feeling a bit guilty that he has a seat at all. Nathan looks around to see if there is a little old lady, or a pretty young one, that he could give it up to. He spots several, but thinks "screw it". He turns his head back towards the window, briefly wiping the right side of his chin on his shoulder now pressed firmly against the glass, and returns to his musings.

East Berlin, Friedrichstrasse

My God, this was one of his old crossing points. West Berlin papers allowed him to enter East Berlin here rather than Checkpoint Charlie. If you entered at Charlie, unless you were sticking to typical tourist sites, you might as well have worn a bright orange jacket so you could be followed more easily.

This platform was where he had first met Natalia. They were both here on a subway stop buying cigarettes and vodka on the cheap, no intention of leaving the station to go into East Berlin. Just a quick hop off, make your purchase at the kiosk, and catch the next train back a few hundred yards to West Berlin. They talked in line. They talked while waiting for the next train. They talked on the train and made plans to meet later that evening. Nathan could pinpoint that moment as the beginning of the end. So often, love is an ache barely whispered, never known to the other. With Natalia it was loud and frantic. His free nights were now filled completely, a non-stop life of work, drink, work, dance, sex, clubs, and walks in the middle of the night. Sleep was giving up, a defeat that he could not fit any more into that day.

Nathan calculated he was actively useful for less than two months before exhaustion turned to recklessness and brought the full attention of the Stasi, who had monitored him every time he crossed the border. He had to be more careful, make sure none of his contacts were jeopardized by the increased scrutiny of his movements. Soon, none of it would matter.

In truth, he was only peripherally involved in what he deemed "the Accident". He did learn one thing from it, the hard kind of lesson you never forget: how to spot a fake. It would eventually help him in his business life, also. The other thing he became good at was playing the clueless innocent which, in retrospect, he actually had been. He had no business being in the field, but it was a strange time when the Wall had fallen, and exceptions were made.

Nathan had been following a possible recruit, an engineer named Carsten Strackapfel. The man was in his early forties, and worked for the state agency that controlled the city's sewer and water infrastructure. In addition, he had knowledge of all things under the city: subways, bunkers, even the very old network of pneumatic pipes that blew post cards, letters and telegrams around the city in the late 1800's. Nathan's initial assessment was that Herr Strackapfel was exactly who he said he was, and could provide valuable information on how the Stasi monitors any movement or communication under the city. More importantly he would know what gaps may exist.

During Nathan's third evening following Herr Strackapfel, he had set up a route covering a few blocks around his apartment. It was usually more difficult to monitor someone in East Berlin in the evening, as the streets emptied at an alarming rate leaving you exposed. Nathan had tried to keep moving, out for a walk with a steady stream of cigarettes to help him fit in. He had come to like Strackapfel, mostly through his walk. He did not walk like other easterners; more of a glide, straight with his head barely bobbing up and down, his left hand usually in his pocket while the other swung easily with his gait. It was the walk of an open man, of confidence and optimism so very different from the walks of defeated, bitter, secretive men Nathan had previously followed. He had a wife, quite beautiful other than the typical bad hair dye, typical of the neighborhood, and an energetic if rail-thin daughter about eight years old. Although Strackapfel's routes during the day were inconsistent, meandering all over this half of the city–an advantage for anyone who might have to slip away for a few hours–in the evening he always returned home at the same exact time. This evening was no different, and once his mark was inside the door Nathan continued around the block, prepared for a boring few hours of routine surveillance.

Nathan was barely two buildings down when three cars came around the corner ahead of him and sped past, abruptly stopping in front of Strackapfel's apartment. His heart sped and throat clenched as five Stasi exited from the vehicles in their typical leather jackets, a driver staying in each car. One from the lead car briefly glanced at Nathan, eyes meeting in an emotionless glance, before he continued up the front stair. In retrospect, Nathan thought it may have been a professional courtesy on his part, warning him to stay out of this.

A few moments later, Strackapfel is brought out, a guard holding each arm. He is protesting, his feet out in front and weight shifted backwards towards the steps they are bringing him down. Nathan is still frozen, watching, feeling it is his fault. They must have discovered his surveillance, did their own investigation. The poor soul being taken away would never know who Nathan was, had no idea he sealed his fate.

Suddenly there is a change in the prisoner's demeanor. He stops his protests and the look in his eyes change from incomprehension and fear to decision and resolve. He calms, lulling his captors, then jerks violently back and forth, first freeing one arm then the other, lurching forward onto the sidewalk and then running directly towards Nathan.

There was only a brief glance before Strackapfel swerved towards the street and in front of a truck moving at high speed. Nathan instinctively moved, which distracted one of the five agents who were close behind, and as the sound of squealing tires and a sickening thud of Carsten Strackapfel crushed against its front grill, a quicker second thud hung in the air. One of the Stasi agents had grabbed Strackapfel by his waist, so that only his head came in direct contact with the truck, almost decapitating him.

Nathan stood dumbfounded, staring at the blood on the street and the two bodies lying in front of him. A few seconds of silence and then Strackapfel's wife appeared in the doorway and screamed, breaking the thickness of the air. At that moment Nathan was wrestled onto the ground in a quick move by two of the Stasi.

Lying prone, belly down on the pavement, the Stasi agent from the lead car held his knee in the middle of Nathan's back and pulled his head up by the back of his hair, an awkward lift just high enough to get the very large knife under Nathan's neck. Tears welled in his eyes and snot ran from his nose in fear and helplessness.

"I suggest you never come back here," the Stasi agent said calmly in accented but perfect English. It was more than a warning; it was confirmation that this was indeed Nathan's fault. The knife slid away quietly and his head was pushed down, hitting the pavement. He just lay there quietly for a few moments, and then slowly got up to his knees composing himself along the way. Nathan knew it would be wise to get across the border as quickly as possible, but even then he might have some trouble at the crossing point. Word travels fast.

As soon as he returned that night he contacted his Collections Management officer. The officer was suitably disturbed by his report, but spent most of his time trying to calm Nathan down and convince him it would fine. Then a further accusation was leveled, saying they fully suspected Nathan's new girlfriend, Natalia, of providing information to the Stasi. She had been monitored, unbeknown to Nathan, since they first met. They did not offer any proof, but in Nathan's paranoid mind it all made sense. Events, coincidences, everything just slipped into place until her betrayal was the only answer.

So Nathan avoided her, not answering her calls or even his door. He was not even sure if she had anything to do with it, but his need for self immolation convinced him. During the day he kept going to his job at the architectural firm, but at night he drank, brooded, and spent nights writing impossibly meaningful observations down by candlelight that in the morning proved to be mostly incoherent dribble. He was not eating, not seeing any of his friends. The drink made him feel in control, but daytime he was a fragile, broken, borderline psychotic shadow of himself.

And he blamed her for that, whether she was guilty or not.

Nathan simply never received another call or another package after the Accident. Not even a review or formal reprimand, which would have been better than complete silence. In a few months his Aufenthaltserlaubnis, his Work Permit, ran out. He received notice that his position was phased out, the Cold War was ending and resources were being directed elsewhere. He loved Berlin, and the thought of going anywhere else seemed ridiculous, not that any offer was made. He was already compromised everywhere East, and he was far too white American Midwestern to be useful in the real trouble spots of the Middle East. It was time, he knew, to go back and face the real world. He had to assume others faced the same experience; thrown in like a bunch of hand grenades to see if they hit anything.

Nathan was disillusioned more quickly than most. In a world he thought would be so carefully choreographed–events unfolding with everyone playing their parts, outcomes carefully planned–he was shocked by its random, brutal, haphazard nature. He may have only been a bug on the skin of the Beast, but that was enough for him.

Did Anton know? He didn't think so. He had never talked about it. Not necessarily because of any confidentiality agreement, but because he thought people would think him laughable, making up stories or another pick-up line for the girls. He wanted to build a reputation, and he did not want to be seen as someone making up fantastic stories to get attention.

Nathan rethinks Anton's message on the ceiling of his model. When he had written, "You know what to do and how to do it. We learned together" what did he mean? Was it merely those little exercises in school, or did Anton actually know about Nathan's time here? Did Anton do something similar, and have the same training? It was possible: they had the same professor who helped them both.

Hauptbahnhof

This was the largest and most modern station he had seen so far, a huge shelter of glass and steel. The first thing that came to Nathan's mind was the lawsuit he had read about in an architecture magazine a few years back. The architects of the building actually filed a suit against the government for not following their design. The boldness of that! He would love to do that to some of his clients, but he is certain he would be out of business rather quickly.

The train stops, and Nathan finds himself staring directly at a wall. A sign in English announcing "Most Exciting Juice for You Life" made him look at the picture and read it again. It reads like an English sentence that was translated into Japanese and then German before being translated back into English again. However, he did read it twice, so Nathan admits that it may be the kind of wording a marketing agency pays good money for: a slogan memorable for its awkwardness and originality.

The train picks up speed again, and though the landscape looks familiar something is missing. There is a line on the ground extending off into the distance and then it occurs to him that he is passing through what had been the Wall.

The Wall. It would probably remain the most famous structure to ever stand in this city. A decommissioned monument that once had the power to kill; it was now dismantled and crushed or sold in little pieces and displayed on mantels around the world. He thinks it a curious way to divest something of a brutal and murderous aura, by making it into a nick-knack. Even while it stood in the months after its symbolic fall, the Wall was referred to in the past tense, even as people stood next to it. Nathan knew well the power of attaching meaning to an object; it was part of his job. However, the Wall was never meant to be a monument in the sense of a Lincoln Memorial or Washington Monument, and therefore its demise–though now somewhat nostalgic even in the minds of former East Berliners–is a quiet footnote to its existence.

Berlin Zoologischer Garten

The train slows and the blur of people on the platform coalesces into individuals all looking in his same direction; an eerie focus of businesspeople, homeless, backpackers, and parents with their children all waiting for the doors to open and Nathan to step out. Zoo Station. The tiny stop, now eclipsed by the larger central station in the former East that he had just been through, was once a center of Berlin life and travel. Arriving here for the first time in the 1980's as a young man, Nathan envisioned it as the meeting place of spies, with conspiracy and double-dealing around every corner. There were in fact, a lot of shady characters around back then–the place had been notorious for prostitution, teen runaways and drug addicts–and if one squinted just right you could imagine them passing information to well-dressed men in trench coats or Stasi in their leather jackets. That Berlin has moved on like a huge silent beast; the allure of the Jascon slipping silently into the ocean, leaving a mess of discarded plans, people, and relationships in its wake.

Though it destroyed lives, the Cold War seems quaint and old-fashioned to Nathan. There were rules here, a balance and code of ethics. Its underbelly, still here, seems darker and far more chaotic and vicious. Nathan could feel it in the cut in his neck, like a knee injury might act up when it was about to storm. This underworld was woven into our fabric of humanity, and its allure of espionage as a gentleman's game has been replaced with a far more sinister and brutal darkness, the façade of rules stripped away.

Rolling his luggage up to the display board middle of the platform, Nathan checks the train schedule and return times, then walks over to the booth to buy a ticket for early afternoon. His plan is to go to Chorin and return yet this evening, just to scope out the area. He would find the house, get the name of the owner and make contact if possible, before coming back to go out in a real city. If there is time, he might find an internet café computer to learn more about the home's owner, but right now his primary desire is to spend an evening in Berlin.

The dichotomy between the modernist Europa Center tower with its large rotating Mercedes Benz symbol up top, and the bombed out ruin of the Kaiser Wilhelm Memorial Church, form a dueling focal point for everything around. Later, he would sit in the plaza between the two and have a beer, as he had done on his first night each previous time he had arrived in this city. It has been his ritual, the Berlin equivalent of throwing a coin in Rome's Trevi Fountain: a superstitious ploy that he would someday return.

Nathan lingers a moment and then steps under the big blue "U" sign, descending the stairs to the subway platform. Time for the new, and see what the future has brought to this city. The yellow form of the U2 train, direction Pankow, and its single headlight emerges out of the darkness of the subway tunnel and comes to a stop. He would take it as far as Potsdamer Platz, and then walk for a bit to stretch his legs.

He thinks himself quite different then the former boy playing dangerous games. Of course, we always view our younger selves as naïve and unprepared, no matter what our age. Nathan thinks, however, that he had truly changed his way of thinking. He used to view things, the entire world, through an analytical and scientific view. It helped him understand, and learn, being able to dissect its components and try to understand the bigger picture by understanding as many of its parts as possible. He truly believes he has reversed that, that he now accepts a big holistic world view and tries to understand the parts as they relate to it. In this way, his feelings and instincts are just as important and just as valid as any other facts.

Potsdamer Platz

Nathan ascends concrete steps, emerging once again into sunlight. He looks around, amazed at the new construction, like crystals rising up to the sky. It was not particularly inspiring, a bit contrived if not generally pleasant, but the remembrances of what it was like before make it far more fascinating. Before the War it had been a fashionable boulevard where Berlin's glamorous couples, dressed in their finest, promenaded along a street lined with café's and waltzed under the crystal chandeliers of ballrooms. Perhaps the inspiration for the center plaza, Nathan thinks. Destroyed during the War or at least soon after, Potsdamer Platz remained on the edge of No-Man's Land, and in the decades before the fall of the Wall was a litter-strewn red light district with peep shows, squats and dive bars haphazardly lining the street north towards the border, culminating in the wood viewing platforms overlooking the Wall. Nathan remembers it well.

What now stands before Nathan is a complete reinterpretation by a roster of the world's best known architects. Helmut Jahn's Sony Center, with a dramatic tented plaza and svelte glass skin, a showpiece of intent if not execution. Steel beams radiate from the center and at night, Nathan hears, a light show of changing colors bring it alive. The plaza and its fountain look ideal for people watching. The one original structure, the Weinhaus Huth, a six-story 1912 art deco limestone pile, stands gracefully as a lesson in proper proportions.

Potsdamer Platz had been a place of decadence. Well, at first decadence, and then a more corrupted version. They seem to have missed the mark, he judges, even with its Las Vegas-style light show it is now just a corporate center; suits and ties, no matter the country.

He tries to find the right word that describes his simultaneous amazement and disappointment, but cannot find one. He is sure there is one in German. Words guess at meanings like Nathan assigns colors to feelings. Even seeking solace in a dictionary, all you would be met with were more words and the odd diagram. When not in argument mode, he is a visual person. Nathan finds words lacking at those times. Especially when his first instinct is to find that one perfect word which wraps it all up, it is most elusive.

He looks around the crowd. If you were ever being followed in a place like this, you would never know until you test it. The best test is by going somewhere you should not be, anywhere marked "Eintritt Verboten" would work. It is a tempting thought, a bit of his old self egging him on. *Do it*, the voice says. *Not right now*, he answers, hoping his other self would accept the answer, even if just a stalling tactic.

The Reichstag is almost unrecognizable with Fosters' Dome sitting like a jewel atop, as fantastic as Nathan thought it would be. Any hope of getting up to see it is quickly dashed when he realizes the wall of people extending towards him is the line to get in. The previously empty area beyond the big plaza area in front is now filled with all manner of government-looking buildings: the new

Capital City. Returning to his nostalgic feeling, he searches for that same word of disappointment and amazement until giving up and deciding he just liked it better before. He would take irrationality over progress any day. If he has an advantage now that he did not have before, he thinks as he looks around, it is that now he knows people in power. His position puts him in direct contact with those who run things, make decisions, and build towers like the ones at Potsdamer Platz.

Nathan feels his love for the city is like a damaged mistress he could never marry; all energy, fun, tragedy, and sadness. Some of what is left of the Old Berlin was preserved to remind of crimes past. So much of what was new, Nathan thinks, point out crimes present. Yet despite its aura on the edge and the "party all night for tomorrow the tanks may roll in" life, Berlin was probably the safest place to be in the Cold War. What could be safer than a city occupied by both sides? Which country would attack its own people? Berlin had seen glory, was the center of an empire, devastated by two world wars, had been nearly completely destroyed, then divided during the Cold War, liberated once again. It has survived extraordinary circumstances over its history and emerged as a center of power and culture once again, with a certain amount of cheekiness and sense of humor. She is a survivor changing with the times, but never letting go.

Nathan also had problems letting go. He held on to his anger; at the Stasi agent who threatened him, and at Natalia. He spent months at the end of his stay finding out who the agent was, where he lived. On the night before he was to leave Berlin, he first went to this agent's apartment and letting himself in, slit the throat of the man's cat. He was glad it was a cat and not a dog, since he liked dogs. Then he went to the house where Natalia was living, lit a crudely made Molotov Cocktail, and tossed it through her window. Nathan paused to watch the flames rise before going back to his apartment, collecting his things, and leaving for the airport.

These acts were horrible, and Nathan has no excuses. Yet he feels if had not done them, he would not have been able to move on with his life. There was some childish satisfaction in their closure.

After checking into his hotel, Nathan steps back outside, ready to begin his next adventure, to have a new history to look back on. He is hopeful, and has a hard time composing his stupid grin as he walks down the street back towards Zoo Station.

It is early afternoon in Berlin, when some of the city is just waking up. He still has an hour before his train leaves, and with all he wants to see, he stands at a crosswalk unsure of where to begin. He finally decides most of what he wants to see is at night, when he returns from Chorin.

The thought helps Nathan refocus: Chorin. If he is going to do this, what his instincts were telling him it might be, he needed to come here anyway and reawaken the man he had been. No matter how brief, no matter how long ago it was, he needs some of that back. He needs to become a part of the underworld he had once been a visitor to. Or is his mind making more out of recent events than really happened? Was he, like Josef K., condemning himself for an unknown charge that may not even exist?

A sign above the door of a nearby building reads "Erotik", flashing neon either side alternating "Tanz" and "Girls". Nathan moves helplessly towards the door, which is not a door at all but an opening to a black wall blocking out the sights beyond. A familiar music beckons, wafting out with smells of skin and stale cigarettes.

17

July 4, Chorin

NATHAN STEPS ONTO a small open train platform at the edge of town. Even after two decades, the village feels rural as remembered, but the gray pallor of coal dust and whine of the odd Trabant are gone. The old uncurbed street running past the small square-towered church, a car-less ghost of a path at his last visit, is now vibrant with activity. He walks past the low stone wall surrounding the church yard, brushing his hand across the top, and instinctually follows the curve of the road left and back out of the tiny village.

He glances at his watch, knowing it will not be a short walk. Almost four o'clock. The sun would stay up until after ten in summer here, and if he is quick he may even catch the house owner for dinner. An hour or two each way, Nathan approximates, and still back to Berlin just before dark.

Nathan's first visit to Chorin exists in a surreal haze. It was the first small village he had visited in the East, a recommendation from Anton, and had opened his eyes to the "Other Germany". It was not all doom and gloom as he first expected. People here actually seemed more open, more American in a way, than those he knew in the West. It was the first time in a while he had been invited to a cookout, neighbors gathering together and laughing heartily, welcoming him in. There was little of the reservation he had felt among the West Germans. He also knew it may be part of temporary euphoria on behalf of the "Ossi's", the easterners. There were deep concerns the "Wessi's" had on the impact of their system, trying to absorb the workforce and bring the infrastructure up-to-date. Either way, he left here having had a genuinely good time and fondness for the people he had met.

Following the signs, Nathan keeps to the trail as it winds through a more heavily wooded area. The afternoon is warm and sunny. Treetops filter the sunlight, leaving a patchwork of lights and darks on the path in front of him. No traffic sounds, only the chirps and whistles of woods and rustle of leaves as the wind blows gently from the west. He is alone, such a contrast to the throngs of people in Berlin. Every now and then there is a strange noise, a feeling of being followed or watched; the buzz of a pixie's wing behind him. Nathan stops and looks around, comforted that his paranoia is increasing, convinced it is a useful and necessary quality he will need.

Rounding the bend, familiar high red brick gothic arches fill the framework of trees at the end of the path. Nathan stops again, this time focusing intently on the artwork before him, instinctively reaching for his camera. The deep red is a perfect complement to the green canopy. He is enters a clearing, approaching from the northwest corner where the brick is pushed to soaring vertical forms, arches, corbelled details, crenellated stone coping forms poking playfully at the sky. A true gothic pile, almost perfect except for the distracting circular inlay and trefoil near the top, he thinks.

At one time this may have been the entrance to the complex. Now closed off, he would need to turn right to see the courtyard and other buildings of the complex. Looking in that direction, Nathan sees a group of six tourists walking around the edge, slowly coming towards him. He has to remind himself that he is not on vacation, and there is no time to enjoy the beauty of the place, its summer gardens, or tranquil setting. He veers left around the northern edge of the façade he had just been admiring, stepping off the path and onto the grass between building and edge of lake.

He removes the picture from his backpack, studies it before slinging the pack over his shoulder. He analyzes the building form from the angle, the view, the character of the façade shown, continuing west past where the transept of the church breaks the plane of northern wall. There are some trees between this corner of the building and the lake. Standing where he gauges the angle in photo to be, Nathan gazes across the lake to a single house. The photo could only have been taken from there.

From where he is standing, he assumes another twenty-minute walk. The character of the home's windows would verify it as the site of the photo. However, given its distance, if he spends any amount of time he would be cutting it close to make the last train back to Bernau and Berlin. At least, from what he can tell, he will be heading back north and closer to the village of Chorin rather than further away.

The lake proves bigger than first thought, and there is a channel at the far west end that swings him further out of the way. Following a country road back north, he finally arrives in front of the house about thirty-five minutes later. Only once did he glance back, the architect in him feeling guilty for traveling this far and not exploring the cloister.

The windows match: color, muntins, and proportions of the panes of glass. He walks past the house at first, seeing if the view back towards the cloister matches the angle in the photo. He stands at the gate and readies himself. The key to entering someone else's home without them questioning you too deeply, he reminds himself, is to appeal to their sense of pride or vanity. It rarely turns out well for those who make the mistake of trying to sneak in, unless you truly have nothing to lose. Nathan visualizes the welcome, the tour, the description of recently remodeled areas and apologies for rooms they are still working on. Like a salesman psyching himself up, he puts on his confident smile and opens the gate.

Nathan walks up the straight pathway and up the three low steps to a large door, rather bare but impressively heavy-looking. He reaches to his right and presses the small black button surrounded by ornate metal filigree, as if surrounding a simple doorbell with such finery would somehow make it look less utilitarian. He hears it ring inside, and continues to study the strange contrast, the proverbial lipstick on a pig, before pressing the stupid black button again. He thinks a wrought iron doorknocker would look so much better. Instinctively he raps the big wood door with his knuckles. There remains no sound, no movement. He tries the door handle.

"Have you ever known a German door to be unlocked?" someone from his right asks, a hint of humor in her voice. Nathan pulls his hand away from the handle, startled, and turns his whole body to the source of the question. A woman is standing at the corner of the house, leaning one shoulder against it and her right arm obscured behind gray plaster. He may have been drunk and it may have been a dark pub, but he recognizes her instantly.

"Audrey?" Was he followed, set up? A hundred possibilities race through his mind. Certainly not coincidence, though it is the most hopeful of all possibilities. She looks beautiful, exactly as he remembers. Sometimes the low lighting and high alcohol skew the results, and people do not translate well to the daytime. This is not the case, yet Nathan is still less than enthused. He glances around and then steps off the stoop and onto the grass towards her. "What the fuck is this?" he asks, his intonation somehow sounding curiously polite.

"I'd like to say that it's fate," she motions for him to follow her away from the house and back towards the edge of trees about fifty feet away, "but the truth is we're working for the same guy, and probably looking for the same thing."

"I'm just . . .," Nathan begins to counter, his pride falling, "So if you're looking for the same thing, then the whole meeting in Dingle was about finding out what I know. Why not just ask, or is this some kind of competition?"

"Look, I'm here to help you. I might have slightly different instructions, though, so it's not like we're working at odds. I didn't say anything before because I didn't know how involved you would get, or if I could trust you."

"So, you're supposed to help me get inside and take a look at whatever this guy has, and find out where he got it from, and then what?"

They were inside the first row of trees now, and she pauses to look at him. "And then steal it," she says matter-of-factly. Audrey turns to walk in a bit deeper into the woods.

"That is different from what I had in mind," Nathan follows her, thoughts and feelings a jumble. They both sit down on some rocks that look to be part of an old foundation, the gray house still in sight through the trees. He realizes that he will probably have to reconsider his evening. "So what's the plan?" he asks.

"How do you propose we go in?" The question from her seems half-hearted, simply asking to if he had any better ideas then the course of action she has already decided on.

"Wait till someone comes home. Knock on the door."

"Believe it or not I tried that. No answer, and no sign of

movement. No one left this morning, so it's not like they just went to work and will be home soon." She glances at her watch, it is almost six o'clock. "I did notice the security system. A quick scope around the house, and there is a back window open, what looks to be a patio door."

"Did you try it?"

"We need a plan first, just in case security is on and we don't have much time. If we set it off, we'll never find it unless we're extremely lucky. I'll have to reconsider my plan, but two can get around faster than one," she looks at him discouragingly, "you might be useful."

Nathan pulls the picture of the stone on the table out of his pocket, the same picture that led him here. "This might be useful, too. The room has to be on the lake side of the house."

Audrey studies it for a moment. "I glanced in there, that's the room next to where the window is open. The table was empty."

She grabs a stick and draws a rectangle on the ground. "This is the house." She draws a curve to one side. "The edge of the lake." She points to the edge of the rectangle closest to the curve, "if no one comes home, we have it easy. I need to make a call or two regarding the security system. I find out how to dismantle it. If there were any guard dogs they would have gone nuts when we rang the bell. We wait till the early morning hours, dismantle the alarm and then enter here. It would help to have a layout of the place."

"I can do that," Nathan offers.

"You haven't been inside yet."

"It's a house, I can tell from the outside. It's not too hard to figure out," he considers for a moment. "If we wait until dark, we'll have to go buy some flashlights. Maybe a crow bar to open anything under lock and key."

She reaches behind the rock and shows him the strap to a bag.

"All the stuff we need, plus a sleeping bag."

"I do like the idea of that," he quips, adding, "Nathan Bang, Architectural Detective."

Audrey looks at him sternly. "We'll take turns until its time to go in, and if you refer to yourself in the third person again I will hurt you."

"Okay," he feels sufficiently chided, "now what do we do until then."

"Surveillance, and figure out the security. You can draw up that plan."

Surveillance on a stationary object like a building is easy; you just sit there and watch it. If the building is simple in form you can do it with two people at opposite corners. Audrey felt comfortable staying where they were and just watching the driveway. Nathan, unwilling to bring up any training he may have had, simply does as he is told. Every now and then, he realizes how much you know just from watching the rhythms of the world; like the sudden absence of the woman working across the street for longer than usual lets you know that it is not just a vacation but also a honeymoon. Watching a building, like watching people, gives you insight into its character, its patterns, mood, and inner workings. Nathan sits and just stares for a half hour before pulling out the notepad and pen from his pack sketch the house plan. Finishing it up, he hands it over to Audrey who had been talking quietly on her phone.

"Nice. How certain of it are you?" she looks genuinely impressed, which Nathan finds sadly thrilling.

"Best that I can do. I'm usually pretty good at this. How's security?" he asks.

"Not getting too far yet."

"What kind of security system is it?"

"It's an ADT sign in the window, which is good and bad. Good that it's known and probably standard, bad that it's a good system. Size of house, status of owner, I would say something like the Power Series 632 Intruder Alarm, or whatever the German equivalent is. Inertia sensors and probably trap detection, your usual common passive infra red detectors dueled with microwave."

"All right, I understood the 'ADT' part. I don't know these things myself, but I do know people who know these things. If I can use your phone, I can call a guy who installs these in the States. He might know a gap or workaround of some kind."

"Just don't give us away," she hands him the phone.

"Nice," he says, looking at the satellite phone. He reaches in his pack and pulls out a black leather folder he keeps his contact numbers in. He dials the number, and is relieved when it is picked up rather than sending him to voicemail. "Hi Bill, not sure you would be answering your cell today with the holiday and all, but I have a bit of an emergency." Nathan listens for a minute to the *no problems* and quick story of what Bill and his family are up to today. "I'm actually in Germany, and the lady I'm with is locked out of her friend's house with the alarm on, but her baby is inside and we want to know if there is a way to get in without all hell breaking loose." *I assume you can't get a hold of the friend. Can you call the local technician?* Bill asks. "It's a bit complicated. She's going through a nasty divorce right now, which is why she's staying with this friend, and doesn't want to have something on record that she's an unfit mother or anything."

Audrey throws him a dirty look, warning him to keep it simple.

Nathan listens for a few moments. "Uh huh. Uh huh." A longer pause. "Nothing simple like a master installer code or anything?" He listens for another minute. "Why don't I have you talk to her, she can tell you what kind of tools she has."

He hands the phone back to Audrey, his hand over the receiver whispering the direction "sound distraught," and then adding, "don't sound like you know what you're doing."

She takes the phone from him and begins with an exasperated "I appreciate this so, so much." An impatient snapping of fingers at Nathan for his pen and paper contrasts the sweet tone of voice.

"Sure, I can get a drill." A pause as she listens. "No, I'll pay for whatever damage is done, don't worry, I just have to get in. My baby's still sleeping but will wake up soon," she answers and begins jotting down notes. After a few minutes of questions and answers, she hangs up with an equally urgent 'thank you'.

"All set?" Nathan asks. "Do you have what we need?"

"How thick do you think that wall is?" she asks in return.

Nathan had seen the construction before. "Probably stucco over a clay block. Furring and interior finish. At least twelve to fourteen inches."

"I think we're all set then."

"You just happen to have a drill with a bit that long?"

"Actually yes. I assumed I would have to break into a safe or something. We may still have to, once inside."

"Damn. So now what?"

"Now we wait," Audrey says and slides down until she is sitting on the ground, reclining comfortably with her back against the rock.

Time passes quickly, if not more silently than Nathan had hoped. It begins to get dark, and still no movement around, or in, the house. Audrey offers to take first watch while Nathan gets some rest. He unrolls the sleeping bag on the ground behind the rock where she is sitting and climbs in, convinced there is no chance in hell he will fall asleep.

18

A QUIET CORNER *of the park, the breeze picking up and branches swaying. A lone plastic cup chattering across a gravel path until it knocks into a limestone base with ding. A forgotten sculpture in a forgotten clearing. Nathan, however, knows this park, and, knows this piece of art. He walks around the sculpture, looking up at the two life-sized bronze figures in a lover's embrace, intertwined bodies with lips barely touching. The overcast sky grows darker and the wind dies completely to an unnatural stillness. He is inside the sculpture now, inside her. Cold. Hard. He is her. Anna.*

An awkward scrape as bronze eyelids force themselves open, a repulsive sound sending shivers through the rest of her body as she rides the wave of consciousness up. Unable to move, she blinks a few more times until her lids lose their sluggishness and open smoothly. Warmth spreads, the hard metal softening. Anna wants to look around, but is only able to see the face an inch in front of her. Seth.

Consciousness returns, memory telling her they have awoken from their embrace only a few times since they had been placed in

140

this secluded corner. Her overriding feeling is that she could not endure one more evening together. She is sure he feels the same, all pursed lips and chiseled jaw. God, she is so tired of staring at that face!

Trying to look around, Anna strains and focuses all energy to her neck. It gives way, the movement accompanied by a sound like so many bones shattering in the dark. Unable to scream, tears well up in her now human eyes and run down a still frozen cheek. She decides to wait it out, hoping her transformation would be complete before Seth's even begins.

The sensation is intoxicating, much like the painful warmth of liquor as it travels down the throat and beyond until no feeling, neither pain nor pleasure, is left. It could have lasted minutes, or hours, this melting of metal to flesh. From unyielding to elastic, she stretches her newly free arms and arches her back both in pleasure of being released, and in reaction to Seth's cold bronze embrace. Once she can finally flex her toes, Anna slithers naked down through his arms and steps lightly off the stone pedestal. She turns back, oblivious to the now increasing wind and vulnerable state of her newly soft body, and ponders her partner. She thinks that perhaps she should just leave now, before he wakes up. No, too dramatic. Besides, why let him off that easy?

Feeling the chill, but in a way very unlike the cold she had felt for so long, Anna looks around for something to cover her body. Modesty is not an issue–she has been nude and stared at for so long, perhaps a hundred years–that she could walk with no hesitance into a crowded cathedral just as she is. Leaving her clearing she walks confidently down the path to a small open field where kids often play. She could hear their laughter day after day, feel their movement. At night, real lovers would sneak in here to make love under the stars. She could hear them, too.

A few jackets are left behind in the trees, a dirty towel draped over the back of a bench. Anna finds a hooded sweater that says "Pink Power" in English and is only slightly too small, the sleeves stopping short of her wrists. She wraps the towel around her waist, and then spots a piece of canvas left by one of the groundskeepers that is a bit longer, and a better windbreak. If not quite fashionable, Anna is comfortable as she walks back to check on Seth's progress.

When she passes the edge of the manicured hedgerow, she stops at the entry to her home. Their home, she corrects herself. He is not only awake, but fully human, sitting naked and smirking on the bench opposite their base. "I knew you would return. I knew you would be back," he repeats, reassuring himself.

"Running away won't work. We've tried it before, and when it's time, we end up in our original form. Like gravity." Her voice is cold, resigned. She takes a few steps in his direction, thinks better of it, and stops.

Seth looks up at her curiously as her motion towards him halts. He thinks for a minute, coming up with the words she wants to hear. "So how do we end this?"

"I think you know. We've tried everything else."

"Yes. But how do you kill a statue?"

She furrows her brow at the insult. "We are not 'statue'. A statue is a dead politician, like Kaiser Wilhelm over there." She gestures down the path in front of her, opposite the way she had just returned. "We are a sculpture. We are art. And I'm not sure how to kill us—maybe when no one looks at us anymore?"

"That is probably why we feel as we do isolated back here."

She moves quickly towards him. Seth is frozen by her suddenness of motion, and simply stares in disbelief as her foot lands squarely in the middle of his chest, sending him backwards off the bench and into the hedge. The sound of breaking branches and sight of his awkward form, all naked legs and ass, draw an involuntary laugh from deep inside her.

Seth slides his legs off and stands up between the bench and the foliage behind him, a furious look on his face. "What in God's name are you thinking!?" he asks incredulously. She crouches a bit in response, and he raises his hands in defense. "Are we going to fight this out? Then fine," he says as he jumps over the bench and with both hands pushes her hard down to the ground. Landing on one side, Anna swings her free leg, sweeping both of his out from under him. As he lands hard, she springs back up and runs toward the pathway.

Seth is up quickly and Anna feels his hand grab her shoulder. She spins and slaps him on the face, the momentum of her body providing additional force. He takes a step back and rubs his cheek, tears welling in his eyes. He turns his back to her so Anna cannot see.

No remorse, Anna quickly thinks how to end this. A branch? A rock? Ram his head against the paving stones? As she is weighing her options, Seth simply walks away.

"Where are you going?" she snarls, adding "you coward."

He simply keeps walking. As he gets to the edge of the clearing opposite the hedgerow, he climbs the wrought iron fence and then begins to scale a tree on the other side. He moves quickly, deliberately, branch to branch until he is standing easily on a large trunk facing her.

"You really want this?" his voice is sad, but not plaintive.

"Yes." The words are quiet, resigned and less sure than she thought they would be.

He falls forward, his arms out and body forward so that he is perfectly horizontal when the top spikes of the wrought iron fence pierce. He was high enough so that they went all the way through, appearing out his back, a screech of breaking bone and tearing flesh. Anna stands shocked by his sacrifice. Could he have actually loved her? She wonders.

Is she free, or simply a solo sculpture—just a statue really—never to wake again? Anna feels the change come, foreseeing the morning when police would find a human body near a statue of a lone woman on a pedestal. Breathing becomes more difficult, and in the half-waking effort Nathan can feel himself separating from her and his own lungs gasping.

Nathan is awakened by a shake of his shoulder and Audrey quietly repeating his name. He feels dew on his face and, collecting his reality, breathes in the cool night air. Perhaps the nature of dreams, unlike epiphanies he thinks, are that their insights never occur when you need them; you just have to file it away and hope to remember when the right time comes. He knew there were a lot of things he should be feeling, that there was a message there: his own inability to make a lasting connection, the issue of only seeing the surface beauty and not realizing the damage beneath, or perhaps having space to become who you are, even if it is not human.

"You were having trouble breathing," she informs him, her look more annoyance than concern, "but it's time to get up anyway."

The dream echo of pain is slippery, its loneliness and lies barely a forgotten taste. The feeling of poison greens fades to earth tones, and as he awakens more fully all he can remember is how beautiful the garden was, how enticing the form of the sculpture was when together, and a feeling of wonder why anyone would leave such a beautiful place. Therein somewhere, he knows, is his problem.

19

"YOU READY TO DO THIS?" Audrey asks.

Nathan is nervous, unsure. He can hardly see her in the darkness. "Don't you think we should give it another day, try the front door approach?" he suggests, "I'm just worried if we mess up the breaking and entering, that we lose our chance altogether."

"I don't think so," she continues a bit impatiently, "You might think you've figured everything out, but you have only focused on physical aspects: the house, the security, which room the stone might be located in." He can hear more than see her moving around efficiently, packing things up and organizing her tools. "You didn't even ask the most important question."

"And what's that?" Nathan asks.

"Who lives here," she answers. Nathan admits she is correct; it was his whole point in coming here. He chides himself for becoming so distracted by the girl, the setting, and the thrill of it all. *Time to focus, or this will be a monumental disaster*, he thinks, *and I'll be calling Johanna for bail.*

A few moments of silence pass, Audrey checking the operation of a few tools in the duffel bag lying next to her. The soft whir of a drill is almost imperceptible before she sets it down opposite the open bag.

"Okay, who is it?" Nathan finally queries.

Without being able to see her in the black morning, Nathan can feel her stop and stare at him. "His name is Ruppin. German mob, but antiquities rather than protection or contraband or drugs. He's got people. Even if you had made it through that door, and he was flattered you noticed his nice home and yard, he certainly does not want any exposure and certainly wouldn't let you look at the merchandise unless you were ready to buy," she pauses for effect, "and even then he might kill you." She picks up a wand-like object from the duffel, telescoping it out and back before setting it next to the drill. "The good news is he should still have the object, and doesn't know anyone else is interested in it. The bad news is he may have taken a personal interest in it," she explains, "and that may complicate the security he puts around it."

"You said 'we'. So who are you?" Nathan wonders.

"I'm your Owner's Representative. You know the 'we'. You're part of the 'we' now, ever since you signed on with Moyne. Anything else, we can talk about later."

"Fine. That's fine," he is calm but a bit exasperated. "Can you at least say why me? Why an architect, rather than an archeologist or historian?"

"Our boss tried that," she chooses the word 'our' carefully, trying reel Nathan back in line. She needs him on board, or completely out of the picture. "He's been chasing some of these clues for a long time, but they all seem to be in different forms. Architects, according to Moyne, think more creatively about rather mundane things, know history, are decently cross-trained, know people, and can imagine in three dimensions. Most of all, they can alternately see the world exactly as it is and then look at it completely cock-eyed, making jumps of logic that others might not."

"I'm flattered," Nathan says unsurely.

"Don't be. It's what you get used for, and not particularly well paid for, which is fine with me. I find it all too hit-or-miss." She zips up the bag and rests her arm on it. "Anton was a right Prima Donna asshole, thinking he was all that," she considers him carefully, "You have, however, already made more progress on this in a couple days than he had in a couple months."

"Well thanks, but I think he knew this lead, he just didn't follow it for whatever reason. Anyway, I think you're wrong about us. We usually have to be disciplined in our reasoning, even in the creative part of it." He thinks about the lines he has used to impress women over the years, adding in his most scholarly voice, "Even above Plato's Academy the inscription read 'Only he who is familiar with geometry shall be admitted here.'"

Silence. Just a bit of wind and some rustling sounds from the woods, a small animal losing its place on the food chain. "Updated rules," she admonishes in icy undertones, "if you bring up Plato again, or refer to yourself in the third person, I will kill you. Do you understand?"

"Yes," he says without protest.

"Now are you ready to do this?" Audrey asks again, annoyed that fifteen minutes have passed since the first time she asked. "And for God's sake, take those damn white socks off."

He complies, removing his shoes and socks and then putting the shoes back on. He nods his head, thinking twice about speaking but then realizing she probably cannot see him. "Yes."

"Alright. Stay close. I was expecting to be alone, so I only brought one flashlight. We're not turning on lights. If I hand you the flashlight keep it pointed down on surfaces below window level, and not towards any windows. Don't flash it up on walls unless you really need to, and then always check if there is a window behind you before you do."

"Got it boss," Nathan tries to lighten the mood.

"Grab the bag. Check the site, leave nothing behind," she directs, "Will the floors be stone, tile, carpet, wood or what?" Audrey already knows the answer since she had peaked inside. She just needs to make the point.

"Probably wood in most rooms, at least from what I saw. Entry, kitchen, bathrooms will be stone or tile. Not too different than an American house from the same time."

"If it is wood, stay close to the walls where it's less likely to creak."

"I'm not stupid. I've snuck out of homes before," Nathan protests, feeling patronized.

"Well sneaking out of mom and dad's house or some one-night stand's apartment is a little different than sneaking into a mob boss' mansion. Just focus, and don't do anything . . . rash." She almost said 'stupid', and they both silently acknowledge the possibility.

She crouches, holding the drill and telescoping rod. "Behind me," she looks back to see if he is ready.

"Gladly," he remarks, and with his backpack on one arm and the duffel over his shoulder he prepares to move, feeling a bit like a pack mule. They traverse open lawn to the house, retracing quickly the same path they had so casually walked the day before. Nathan questions why the front door, rather than a hidden side or back entrance, but chides himself for thinking at all. That is not his job; she would get them in, he would take it from there. Crouched behind her on the stoop, he cannot help looking at her ass before being distracted by how cold his ankles are.

She stands low, gauging a specific distance and height from the edge of the door. Nathan sees a quick flash of blackened steel from a long drill bit as she sets it against the wall. Used to the louder whir of construction equipment, he is surprised when a few small curls and dust begin to form a pile on the stoop near him in near silence.

Nathan waits. Nerves return, he feels his heart pounding, his palms sweating. With one hand still holding the strap of the duffel bag he wipes his free hand on his shirt, shifts the weight over his shoulder, then wipes the other.

He looks up to check progress, just as she is easing the drill and bit back out of the hole she had formed in the wall. Audrey hands him the drill, and he slips it in the open corner of the bag she had left partially unzipped. She takes the telescoping rod, which he sees now has a small mirror at the narrow end and a small scope on the end she is holding. Audrey feeds it through the small round hole and then follows it around with her entire head as she turns it into position.

Without looking down she grabs a second rod slipped through her belt and feeds it through, keeping her eye on the scope. Once she is satisfied, Audrey takes a heavy glove tucked into the waist of her left side and puts it on, pulling it down with her teeth. The two rod-ends left dangling out of the wall, she does the same with her right hand, and then removes a canister from a side pocket of the duffel bag. She attaches it to the end of the second rod and presses a button on top. A low hiss and Nathan sees frost develop on the outside of the exposed rod.

Audrey peers through the scope again, and then begins dismantling canisters and rods in reverse order. She takes one last look through the scope; turning it all the way around before pulling that last piece out and collapsing it back into its shorter form. Putting her tools into the duffel back and taking off the outer gloves, she bends back down and whispers to Nathan, "Should be clear."

She then takes a small plug out of the bag and fills in the hole she had made. Nathan helps by brushing shavings off the stoop.

"Should be?" Thinking of a real question yet knowing better, he asks, "Bill told you to do that?"

"Not exactly, but I didn't want him contacting the local rep," she replies. She takes another look around before pulling out a small black pouch from her back pocket and focuses her attention on the door handle. It takes a few moments for Audrey to pick the lock, with a quiet mutter of "damn German hardware" in the process.

She looks at him. Turning the handle she reminds Nathan, "If the alarm goes off just run back to where we were. Don't try to do anything." The handle clicks and the door opens. Silence. He follows her in.

Sensors near the door look to be working, but Audrey's disabling of the main control panel have stopped them from relaying their alarm. They move through the foyer and stop in a wide hallway. Ahead of them is the stair to the upper level, to their left a dining room and to their right a living room. Both of these rooms look like furniture showrooms, too formal to ever really be used.

According to the plan Nathan had drawn, straight ahead through the door should be a family room, more of a conservatory in its previous life but converted to the main living room due to its views to the lake. Just to the right of it, also adjacent to the living room, would be a library containing the table in Nathan's picture. To the left and adjacent to the dining room would be the kitchen with a pantry and pass-through to the garage.

The door ahead of them is closed, so they peak their heads around the corner in the living room to see if there is a more direct access. There is a door in the middle of the wall that should lead to the library, but it is also closed. Audrey steps back into the hall and motions toward the closed door at its end.

It is even darker inside. Nathan puts his hand on Audrey's belt and uses it as a guide. He feels more vulnerable carrying the weight on his back, aware of its length, and as they stay close to the wall on their right he is careful to not let the bag brush its surface. She opens the door slowly, stopping when it begins to creak and then continuing when it submits to her will. They look around. So far, so good: no people and all rooms where they should be. She leads the way right, still hugging the wall, moving around a small table with a vase on it before reaching the door at the end. According to the plan, this should lead to another small interim space, Nathan thought, containing a powder room or wet bar, and then another door to the library. As he glances around this family room, a little lighter due to tall windows, he sees the table upon which the stone had laid. It is empty.

Audrey takes the door handle, cursing the German propensity for closing every door. There is a slight click as she rotates it down. Nathan has to back up slightly with her as it swings open towards them. They pass through the small anteroom and get to the door of the office. The same delicate turn of the handle, but this time the door swings in towards the library.

It is the kind of library office traditional to an old home. Lots of wood, which make it appear darker than the last room despite similar windows. One of the windows is open slightly, angled inward like a hopper, enough for air but keeping rain and any intruders out. There is a desk facing them, fairly well organized from what they could make out, with a large empty bottle sitting in the middle reflecting what little light there is. Bookshelves along the wall they just passed are filled, and deeper than usual for books. It may take some time to look through, Nathan judges.

Audrey motions for him to begin at the far end of the shelves.

He sets the bag down between two guest chairs angled towards the front of the desk. His eyes have adjusted rather well, enough to tell book from stone anyway. He begins a quick methodical scan, shelf by shelf, up then down, down then up and over, until after a few minutes they meet in the middle. Audrey shakes her head; nothing.

Nathan moves back to the side wall, behind the door they had entered through. The wall is almost covered, rather haphazardly, in a series of frames. Some have glass, some open; Ruppin's collection of photos and paintings of beautiful women, beautiful things, like his own modern version of Ludwig's Gallery of Beauty at Nymphenburg. As diverting as it may be, Nathan is focused on finding the stone. He looks back out at the small anteroom through which they came. There should be another door, but instead there are more of these same framed photos and paintings.

Stepping over to Audrey he whispers "the plan is wrong. There's a space between these two rooms." She nods and focuses on the series of shelves, looking for double supports or anything that might support a hinge. After a few moments she stops just right of the middle. Nathan studies it with her.

Not enough room to swing, he thinks. The other shelf sections have books and other knick-knacks, but this one only has books. He reaches forward and pulls one out. *Not false books,* he concludes. Comparing it to other sections, he notices that most of the bindings align on the others, but this one has some pushed back. Nathan reaches down and pulls the bottom towards him, and there is a slight give before a lock stops its movement.

He searches the bottom row for the most worn book. A leather-bound volume with the simple name 'Die Odyssee' is slightly raised from its neighbors, its dark cover almost light near the top. Nathan lifts it out. There is no click or other signal, but when he attempts to pull the case towards him it swings free, rotating easily and smoothly up and over his head. It is hinged about six feet high, which requires both Nathan and Audrey to crouch a bit to enter.

Nathan is temporarily blinded when Audrey turns the flashlight on, shielding his eyes with his forearm until they adjust. When he is able to see again, he is amazed at the scene: like walking into a pirate's treasure trove, he thinks. The shininess of gold and silver objects reflecting the light distracts him again from his purpose.

Audrey spots the tablet first. It is uncovered and on a middle shelf, the area around it relatively uncluttered compared to the rest of the small room. The stone is clean and laying flat, obviously accessed recently. She lifts it straight up carefully, holding it on each side, until it is clear and can pull it into her chest. Crouching again, they step back under the flipped-up casework and out into the room.

Focusing on the stone, he snatches the flashlight from her hand and begins to study it. The top flat part is like the picture–both pictures, from Anton and Moyne–lines of inscription in an unknown alphabet. It has a dull smoothness, like it had been highly polished at one time but the years and handling have worn its finish. The sides are irregular, and in two areas actually extended out a few inches. Writing extends all the way to the edge, giving the impression that it had been broken off from a larger tablet. If so, Nathan thinks some of these edges had been retooled, or at least worn down, to a more regular shape. It may have been broken with tools, or along a natural vein. Whatever it is, this piece does not have the sharp edges or pits of a shattered stone.

There is something about the stone itself, its color and veining, he also notices. It certainly does not look like any stones he had seen around the site in Ireland.

"Help me turn this over," he asks. The piece is not too big or heavy, he just wants to handle it as carefully as possible. Its age is palpable, a strange vibration of meaning and history. Nathan knows his imagination, but he swears it gives off a glow, a pale aura of whitish gold. Had it really done so, Audrey would have noticed. In contrast, after helping him turn it, she resumes looking around at other objects in the alcove, seemingly disinterested in the object they had traveled so far to find.

Nathan bends over it again, shining the flashlight on its surface. The back is finished same as the front, a dull smoothness. There is some more etching, not quite as deep. He thinks it looks different than any of the letters on the front, more like a diagram of eight rough circles, with lines emanating at different angles. Underneath is a very shallow impression, almost written on top, of two words *'diatoni'* and below that *'araeostyle'*. *A translation*, he wonders? The letters are crude but plain, like initials carved hurriedly in a tree by lovesick teenagers.

He knows that word, Nathan ponders. *'Araeostyle', something to do with columns, or distance between columns.* Something he studied. *Systyle, Diastyle, something, something, proportion. Screw it*, he thinks, *I'll look it up online later*. He regrets not bringing a camera, although his partner would certainly have a rule regarding flashes.

"Just wrap it up," Audrey commands, "we're getting out." She pulls a cloth out of her duffel bag and hands it to him.

Nervous that they have stayed too long, she nonetheless goes back into the hidden chamber, curious about the other treasures within. Nathan, having placed the cloth over the stone and then lifted it slightly to cover its bottom surface, also begins to looks around out of curiosity, waiting for Audrey's return so they can get the hell out. The wall with all the photos is opposite the window, and he remembers her warning. Thinking of a loophole, he shines the light on the wall behind the desk to see if the Gallery continues.

There is a dark splatter on the wall. He moves around the desk, still studying the wall and hoping to get a closer look when his foot hits something hard. Nathan glances down and, to his horror, sees the body of an elderly man lying on its side with the back of his head missing.

"Holy . . .!" he stops his voice but cannot help his body's quick jerk of repulsion. His hand swings out and knocks over the empty bottle on the desk, which rolls for a moment before falling and shattering with a piercing crash on the floor.

Audrey comes rushing out, grabs his arm. "Jesus, what the fuck are you trying to do, make as much noise as poss-" she sees the body on the floor, "shit, what did you do!?"

"Me?" he steps back, "no way, I found him like this!" He feels the need to explain, "You know how you said keep the flashlight pointed down? Well, I didn't," Nathan admits. When he sees she is looking at him instead of the body on the floor, he points the beam of light back up on the wall. "And I saw that." The smear and splatter extending up the surface of the wall and over the painting hanging is almost black against the light wood surface.

"That looks like blood and probably some brain," she confirms.

"Christ, he's almost petrified," she whispers. "Hole in his head," she points out, rather obviously. "I guess we know why there was no answer when you knocked."

As she bends down to look closer, Nathan peers over her right shoulder.

"Full rigor; he's been dead at least ten hours," she proclaims. Suddenly she bolts straight back into him.

"What!" Nathan asks startled.

"He's alive. His eye moved."

"Impossible. The back of his head is missing," he points. Then Nathan sees it too; the eyes move up, first at them and then over

155

their shoulders. They turn around and see the wrapped stone still lying on the table. Ruppin's eyes come to rest directly at it, then remain dead still.

Audrey recovers, and bends down to study the elderly man's body. She has trouble moving his hand, clenched in a half-pointing position. There is a gun lying under the knee space of the desk, but she is careful not to touch it.

Nathan stands over her, trying to see what she is doing. Glancing around, he sees a faintness of light flicker under the bottom gap of the closed door. He strains to listen, swearing he can hear a heavy panting and someone in a low whisper command "Ruhe!" Nathan's eyes widen. He looks back down at Audrey who, focusing on the body seems to have not noticed. Nathan continues to stand dead still for a moment, his mind weighing the options, searching for the perfect words to alert Audrey and suggest a plan of escape, conveying the gravity of the situation–that they have broken into a mob boss' house and were now standing over his dead body, ready to steal one of his prized possessions–when at last and in the interest of time Nathan finds the perfect phrase.

"Oh. Shit."

20

July 5, Chorin

AUDREY LOOKS UP, and Nathan swears the eyes of the corpse move in unison. Both of them stare intently at him. "What?" she hisses.

"Someone's here, in the kitchen," Nathan whispers, unsettled by the dead man's troubling awareness.

"I knew this was too easy."

"You call this 'too easy'?" he contests, pointing at the body.

"Better get out," she states quite obviously, "if it's police they'll figure it out, but not until after a lot of questions. If it's his men, they'll just shoot us." Audrey gestures towards the wrapped stone sitting on the table, commanding, "Grab it and follow me."

Nathan complies, with only the briefest thought that this action makes him the primary thief. The back of the stone still lay upward, slightly uncovered. He has a moment of recognition for the etched pattern he had been studying. Before he can place it, he quickly flips up the flap either side so it is completely enveloped. It slides easily across the table as he loops one arm underneath and lifts it up into his chest. It is heavy, but not as heavy as he thought it would be. He thinks that with the adrenaline of the moment he could probably lift a small bus.

Audrey is at the door leading to the living room, on a wall adjacent to the way they had come in. She opens it slightly and motions for Nathan. At the same moment, he glances back at the bookcase to his right and stops even before he takes his first step. There is a picture there that catches his eye. Even in the dimness of the room he recognizes his old friend. He shifts the weight of the stone to one arm and takes the flashlight out of his back pocket, flicking it on the photo. It is Anton, standing next to a younger and more active version of the corpse on the floor.

"Come on," she urges, breaking his reverie.

They move quietly, deliberately, along the living room's perimeter. Audrey stops a few times to navigate around furniture, but follows a rather direct path to the small hallway and front door where they had entered.

As they approach the entryway, they can hear and see movement beyond a closed door at the end of the hall. Light shines from below the door, a shadow of footsteps moving into the slot of light. Audrey moves close to his ear. "Remember how your eyes work: motion, then form, then color, then detail. You see anything, freeze and remember we have the element of surprise. Assume he doesn't know we're here, or he doesn't know there are two of us."

Nathan nods in understanding. Audrey moves to the door and with both hands opens it a crack. She sees two cars, one near the garage to their right and one at the end of the driveway. Someone is waiting in the car closest to them, and there are two men standing outside either door of the car further away.

She motions to go through the dining room, hopefully circumnavigating their visitor. Just then the door at the end of the hall opens, startling them with light. A short black form, unbelievably fast, is heading straight for Nathan. The German

Shepherd's nails make sharp clicking sounds on the hard wood until it is within a few feet of Nathan, and then lunges toward him. In that instant, Nathan crouches and sets the stone down with a bit of a thud, afraid he is unable to defend himself, or run, while holding the additional weight. The door swings shut behind the dog and he loses site of the snarling animal, now in mid-flight somewhere in the darkness in front of him.

Still in a crouched position, Nathan raises his right arm and as soon as the dog sinks his teeth in, he uses his free hand to grab it under its jaw, wrapping his fingers around the fleshy skin aside its back teeth and folding it over, pressing down hard against the dog's back teeth. The fierce dog instinctively opens its mouth with a whine. He quickly moves his injured arm through its gaping mouth and cups his hand on top of the dog's head to spin it counterclockwise, snapping its neck.

Audrey stares at him, stunned not so much by the violence but by his efficiency. She moves sideways from the door and hides on the edge of the stairs as Nathan takes a step back into the doorway, holding his arm and wishing he had just held on to the stone, using it to brain the damn thing.

The door opens again and a man enters, holding a flashlight in his left hand, his right hand supported over the left wrist and pointing a handgun in the same direction. Nathan is hidden from direct view by the thickness of the opening to the living room, but he can see a reflection of form bounced by a mirror somewhere in the hall. Light dances around walls and floor until it comes to rest on the dog's body, just a few feet from Nathan.

"Halt," the voice commands, "Ich weiss, dass du hier bist." The guard used the singular 'you', confirming Audrey's thought they may only expect one person. Nathan stands still as the figure approaches and the angle of the light shows he is ready to look around his corner. He tries to see if Audrey is still on the staircase, but the contrast from the light shields her from view. Nathan sees a black boot, very stylish, step over the dog.

Just as the light shines in his eyes, there is a grunt and a crash and the same light goes spinning off back down the hallway. Audrey had swung around the newel post at the bottom of the stair feet first, catching the guard with a high kick directly to his throat. The guard falls over the dog's body, twisting to land on his back. As he hits the floor she is on top of him, knee in the groin and a flurry of right fists into his throat. Within a few seconds he is lying as motionless as the dog.

"Hier!" another voice exclaims from further beyond the door. The guard is also not alone in the house. There is some more commotion, a third set of boots on the floor, yelling in German. Someone must have found the old man's body. Audrey grabs his hand in a forceful motion, leading him past the front door and through the dining room. There is another door in the center, similar to the one from the living room leading into the library, and she opens it slightly to peer through before opening it the rest of the way and pulling on his arm again.

Nathan is beginning to feel the stone's weight as they pass through kitchen and into the small pantry that separates it from the garage. There is another door that leads to the backyard. Between the two doors are a series of keys hanging in a neat row. She grabs them all, and chooses the door leading to the garage.

Three cars sit in a row, not much of a collection if it was meant to be one. A BMW or Mercedes-looking sedan closest to them is, or was, Nathan judges, Ruppin's main car. Beyond is a Lada Riva, a dark-colored sport utility vehicle, rising above the sedan. Built for Russian roads, Nathan had seen quite a few in East Berlin, and this one seemed in excellent shape with little dirt or damage. From its style, Ruppin owned it before the Wall came down.

What catches Nathan's eye, however, is next to it. Just the front end is visible beyond the Lada, but he recognizes it immediately: a Porsche 959, gleaming silver even in the barely moonlit blackness. He had seen only one before, but it made him understand what the crowd at the airport the day before was feeling. All-wheel drive, computer-controlled, incredible top speed and only a few hundred have been made road legal. This car is probably more valuable than most of the treasures in Ruppin's secret room.

"Brawn or speed?" she asks, surprising Nathan for his opinion.

"I don't know what that is," he says pointing at the Lada, "but driving that Porsche would make the jail time worth it."

She assesses their options. "We use both. Get in the Porsche."

Yes, Nathan thinks. He holds out his hand for the key as Audrey tries to distinguish them in the low light. She finds the car key and hands it to him.

"I drive. Just get it open and turn out the dome light. Hold on to the key. DO NOT put it in the ignition." Her emphasis makes him feel like a child. Chided, he does once more as he is told. He opens the passenger door first and hopping in the seat quickly turns out the light that comes on. Nathan sets the stone in the small back area behind the seats. His arm hurting from the dog and carrying the stone, he settles in and looks around the interior, trying to enjoy the moment despite his fear before turning his attention back to whatever Audrey is doing to the Lada.

Nathan sees she has taken a garden tool–some kind of shovel or hoe with a long handle–and after breaking it to the right length, wedges one end into the head rest of the driver's seat with its other end holding the clutch down. She takes a brick and sets it on the accelerator. Reaching over the wood handle spanning the seat, she puts the truck in first gear and then steps back out, closing the door.

"You ready," she mouths the words at Nathan through three car windows, just catching his eye to make sure he knows it's going to happen.

Audrey starts the truck and grabs the wood handle. As it crashes through the door, she runs straight through the void it leaves, a direct path to the driver's seat. Nathan opens the door for her and has the key ready. She jumps in and has it started before the back end of the Lada is fully through the former garage door. They hear gunfire as Ruppin's men outside open up on the innocent truck.

Nathan winces and shields his face as the Porsche leaps through the wood garage door. Shielding his face was natural fear, but the wince was for the damage to the beautiful machine's front end, feeling it his fault for choosing her.

They both crouch low in their seats, following their blocker like a good running back. The Lada, revving high in first gear, is still moving slow and taking fire. Audrey keeps the car slow, so the truck remains between them and the men with guns. As they approach the end of the driveway and the second car of Ruppin's men, a tire is blown on the truck and it begins to veer left into the yard. Audrey pushes down hard on the accelerator, and both she and Nathan are shocked by how fast the car takes off.

"Holy shit," she gasps as they blow past the parked car and onto the country road, squealing tires as they turn left. Ruppin's men seem equally surprised by the second car, providing a pause before they jump in and back out onto the road to give chase.

The car easily picks up speed as they lead the way up the road. They only travel a few miles when Audrey skids the car left again onto a much narrower road and guns it again. Nathan feels a bit nauseous as he sees the lights of Chorin appearing in front of them.

"Were you planning to slow down?" he asks, involuntarily placing one hand on the dashboard. No answer as they bear down on the edge of the town. "I've just never entered a small village at 120 miles per hour before."

Audrey is still silent as they approach narrow streets at ungodly speed, headlights off. The sleeping rows of houses begin to blow past at a dizzying pace. Focusing on the road, she finally speaks up and encourages him to hold on before taking yet another left at high speed, exiting town as quickly as they had entered. Another few miles and another left, Nathan thinks they must have made a circle back to the house.

They were, however, entering another small town. Nathan barely has time to read "Golzow" on the sign before they are again passing through narrow streets at the speed of a low-flying aircraft. Finally she takes a right and Nathan sees her destination, an autobahn straight ahead of them. She slides left to the on-ramp. Nathan gasps again as she steps down hard on the accelerator and the car picks up even more speed.

Traffic is light, and they feel comfortable that they have lost their pursuers. Audrey sits back into the seat, relaxing her posture a little.

"You did well," she offers.

"I froze in the library. There was something wrong there." *Besides the corpse*, he thinks back. "There was a picture I saw on the way out. It was of Anton, with the mostly dead guy."

"Anton? Are you sure?"

"That's why he didn't follow up on this lead. He didn't have to. He was already here," Nathan concludes.

There is an inverse proportion of the length of a chase to how successful you are in getting away. The longer it goes on, usually the more time police or whoever is chasing can muster their resources and organize around you. Just as Nathan is thinking this, a car enters from the ramp in front of them and picks up speed, cutting across lanes on a collision course. Nathan braces again, for impact this time. Their speed carries them just past, missing by a couple feet.

"That was no accident," she decides and tenses back up to her earlier position at the wheel. "We should have the speed."

"The 11 takes us towards Berlin."

"It will take us to Bernau bei Berlin," she corrects him, "where you caught the train. We'll catch the 10 from there and then the 114 into Berlin."

The black BMW that almost rammed them is turned around and doing a good job keeping up, which leads them to believe it has a better engine than standard. As he looks behind, he sees it gaining, headlights right on their tail. He feels the back end of the Porsche slip as the air is taken away, not making total contact but close enough to cause a spin. Audrey struggles with the wheel for a second before computer control take over.

"Damn. Nice car," she remarks.

"How did you know where I got on the train?" Nathan asks.

Now there are two sets of headlights closing in.

"This car must have a tracker on it. Shit," she adds and swings far right almost to the shoulder opposite of where they were. The car slows and skids slightly and Nathan lets out a guttural "whoa" as they head directly for the dividing strip between the two directions of the autobahn. They pass through a police crossover and swing far over into opposing lanes before leveling out on the right hand side. Nathan stares wide-eyed as they speed the wrong way, headlights out again, down the fast lane of the oncoming autobahn.

The chase car makes the same maneuver and is directly behind them. A second has now caught up, and is continuing down a parallel path in the left lane opposite the divider.

The highway is fairly empty at this hour, but in the distance

Nathan can see headlights. It is impossible to tell what lane those approaching lights are in, and at this speed he is not sure if it matters. Someone, he is sure, is going to die.

"We can't stay here," she swings wide left, headlights coming right at them before braking hard and swinging again hard right through the cross-over between highways back to the proper side. The maneuver cost them some distance, one chase car right behind them while the other that had stayed in the correct direction is now in front. They pick up speed and try to take air away from the front car, hoping it does not stop suddenly to trap them. The gambit does not work, but neither can the car slow down to sandwich them without creating an opening.

Suddenly, the back end of the car in front goes up straight up into the air. Audrey maneuvers around in a blinding fast motion as Nathan looks to see what happened. While concentrating on what was behind they must have hit a slower car in front, which is now sliding sideways on its roof sending sparks into the dark. The chase car rolls end over end twice before also landing on its roof next to the car it had hit.

Such an exhilarating blast can only be heightened by the mortal danger lurking behind it, Nathan thinks, spying the other black BMW closing in after them, his heart racing. They are now at a relative balance; unable to lose them yet the other car unable to gain. Passing Bernau bei Berlin the high-speed parade makes a right bend onto the 10. The ten kilometers takes only a few minutes before they have to make a hard turn onto the 114 that leads right into the city, dropping them off at Hennersdorf/Pankow and into Prenzlauer Berg. They slow considerably as they enter city streets, but the roads are still wide and clear enough at the early morning hour to allow some speed.

The sign on the right hand side says simply "Berlin". Nathan grips the dashboard more tightly, shocked by how differently he is returning to the city he had left so innocently just the day before.

21

July 5, Berlin

ANOTHER CAR APPEARS behind them. "They must have a tracker and radios. We're not going to lose them with speed; time to get lost in the crowd." Audrey begins to weave into the city's thickening traffic. "Police are a factor now, though that might not be bad." She looks over at Nathan, "Put your visor down; it'll help keep street cameras off our faces."

"We're in a stolen car, and the car's owner is dead."

"That part might be bad," she concurs.

"Tegel Airport is direct west." Nathan suggests.

"Not going to Tegel. I have a plane at Templehof." They are heading south after making a few turns, right then left, cruising just a bit faster than traffic down a wide street, four lanes each way. So far, traffic lights have been with them. Approaching the darkness of woods, he recognizes the Siegessäule in the middle of central Tiergarten park. She follows the curve around the tall victory column's encircling road and is now heading back east, directly towards Brandenburg Gate.

"Nothing like staying low profile," he quips.

Audrey does not seem amused. Just before the Gate she takes

another hard right and follows the wide street heading towards the airport. She glances in the mirror and looks alarmingly at Nathan. "Hold on, they're making their move," she warns.

Nathan glances in the mirror and sees not only the two familiar chase cars, but also a large truck moving up alongside; the three of them together are sufficient to trap any vehicle. Further back, he can see the blue flashing lights of two white and green Berlin Polizei cars joining the parade.

One of the black BMWs pulls along their right side and accelerates. Audrey speeds up to shift into the lane directly in front of it, cutting the BMW off hard. It brakes and turns, setting it up on its two left wheels and almost rolling over. A chain reaction starts and Audrey–preoccupied with the action in her mirror–misses the fact that traffic has come to a complete stop in front of her.

She takes a hard turn to the right, sending their car over the curb and onto the sidewalk. There are no people walking at this hour, just a few stragglers moving through the wide plaza area beyond the steel street edge bollards. He looks behind for the other BMW and the truck, which he now discerns is hauling a large tanker trailer. Nathan guesses it was hijacked from its early morning fuel deliveries. Probably not the wisest choice, depending how full it is.

"A tanker?" he questions.

"Big horrible accident, all the evidence burned up," she surmises, "It's a good choice; what I would do." Nathan looks at her as she casually speeds down the wide sidewalk, stopped traffic buzzing beyond her driver side window. "I have an idea," she adds ominously. "It might be a bit dangerous, but who wants to live forever?" she asks rhetorically.

"Me," he answers anyway.

"How fast can you figure out where a car can fit through that building?" she points at a glassy high-rise Nathan had noticed on his previous tour of Potsdamer Platz.

"Fast, but anyone including those guys behind us know the big parts of a building, at least the parts you can drive a car through. We're not going to lose them."

"Right, but how many can figure out the way to the service entrance from the lobby?"

"Anyone who's ever been in there."

"Who can do it at sixty miles an hour?"

"Say what?!"

"And remind me, we need to make a stop." She turns the car hard, sending it up on two wheels and curving off the sidewalk between narrowly spaced bollards–designed to prevent exactly what they are doing–and onto the large open expanse of open plaza. Audrey aims the car directly for the double glass front doors and picks up speed again.

"No, no, no, no," Nathan mourns for the car, covering his face and ducking low behind the glove compartment. There is a thud of metal on metal and then the shattering of safety glass.

"Left or right!?" she yells over the noise.

"Left," he answers before he is fully upright again. He had prepared for that decision before the car made its very rude entry into the building.

They are screaming through an open lobby and heading past a reception desk towards a long, wide hallway running the length of the building. The driver side of the corridor is all glass facing a courtyard and a similar glass-enclosed lobby in a neighboring building beyond. A row of circular steel-wrapped columns standing outside the glass wall accentuates their velocity, marking their distance in rapid succession one after the other. *Nice desk*, Nathan thinks as a blur of wood and brushed aluminum passes his right shoulder.

One car has followed them through, the other still caught in traffic. Nathan glances behind and sees the tanker in mid-roll as the bollards do their work, causing the rig to jackknife with the cab upright and pointing towards them and the trailer now perpendicular, exposing the tank's full length.

"Right," he yells, returning his attention front and seeing the upcoming elevator lobby.

"Not a dead end?" she asks even while turning the wheel.

"Left at the other end," he says, spotting the double doors he had hoped would be there just past the bank of elevator openings. As they make their turn Nathan sees the black chase car slide on the slick floor and hit the elevator wall hard on the passenger side.

The double doors fly off their hinges and travel with them a bit down the service hall. This hall is plain, with a number of single doors. At the end there is a set of double doors on the left, a set on the right, and a set at directly in front of them.

"Which way?" she asks hurriedly.

"Right."

"Not straight? I think its straight!"

"Right!" Nathan repeats.

She goes straight anyway and as soon as the car enters the room she has to break and turn hard. The Porsche skids through a number of tables and HVAC ducts before hitting a large vertical pipe with the back quarter panel. The impact on the pipe pivots the front end around and they hit a second time with a thud, coming to rest slightly angled to the wall.

A gush of water begins flowing out the broken sprinkler main and over the car and floor. Their vision obscured, Audrey throws the gearshift in reverse. The wheels spin and with another dull impact the back end goes through the partition wall behind them. A web of bent and scattered conduit and shower of sparks announce that they have entered the electrical room.

In front of them the chase car has entered the room at full speed, the location of the wall screened by a waterfall. Unable to stop in time they hit hard, the front end lifting up out of the water now pooling on the floor and then bouncing backwards a few feet. Audrey moves forward around them and back out the door, flames starting to form near the front end of the black BMW.

She drives more slowly, sheepishly even, through the doors Nathan had originally recommended. At this speed the double doors open and close easily behind them, like a janitor's cart being pushed through. Straight ahead is an overhead garage door, towards which Audrey aims the car.

"Left." Nathan says, and this time Audrey listens without question. They have to pick up some speed to break through the set of exterior doors, but within moments they are outside in a service drive behind the building. Audrey sees a guardrail and ramp at the corner leading to the overhead door, the door she first chose, which would have taken them over a four-foot drop-off at the loading dock.

Audrey follows the service drive as it leads to an opening near the plaza. She stops the battered car, sitting for a minute to reassess the situation. There are fires and people running near the street they had come from. A few charred objects fall out of the sky and land on the car. Audrey steps out to see what they are and then quickly gets back in. The brief moment the door was open Nathan could smell it: the truck was not a fuel tanker, but carrying ammonia. Within seconds they are bombarded with more flaming, foul-smelling objects of different size from where the tanker truck and several other cars had ended in a fiery pile-up.

Audrey closes the vents of the car and turns back onto the plaza towards the fire. People are scattering from their cars, holding shirts or arms over their faces. Audrey points at the stone in the back, directing Nathan to take it.

"Shouldn't we go away from the danger?" he asks, picking up the stone and setting it on his lap.

"There is a subway just over there. I'll get us close and then we're on foot. Be ready to go, and get something over your face."

Nathan sees a large canopy announcing "Potsdamer Platz", their new destination. He lifts the neck of his shirt over his nose. People with a similar idea are holding their hands up to keep the shirt in place and are not watching where they run. Many appear blinded by deadly fumes. Audrey stops in frustration, afraid of running over someone trying to flee.

They exit the car at the same time, and with heads down make a direct run for the steps leading downward. Nathan could not remember if the fumes would be worse down here, or if the ammonia vapor would rise. His guess was that they were screwed and that the whole station would soon be evacuated anyway.

The stone is feeling heavy again, and Nathan cannot keep the shirt over his face while running with the stone cradled in both arms against his chest. He gets in front of Audrey as they skip down steps amidst a throng of people. A bigger crowd is coming up towards them and then stopping. It is clear from their expressions they just got off a train and have no idea of the mayhem unfolding above.

Nathan spots the train. At this point it does not seem to matter which direction it is heading, just get out. He sprints across the platform and through the open doors of the yellow car as warning lights above the door flash that they are about to close. Turning as the final warning bell sounds, he sees the doors close just behind Audrey. He sets the stone down on the open seat near the door, and studies the multi-colored line map with Audrey.

"You know this?"

"Yeah, we're here," Nathan points towards the middle where three colored lines cross at Potsdamer Platz. He looks around the car. A small rectangular screen above the door at the front is scrolling "Mohrenstrasse". He follows the lines with his finger for a moment.

"Second stop from now we get off. We're on the U2 direction Pankow. If you want to go to Templehof, we switch at Stadtmitte to the U6 direction Alt-Mariendorf. Four stops and we're there."

"Good," she says simply.

They sit in silence among the early morning commuters, their prize occupying its own seat next to Nathan. The quiet continues as they switch trains, arriving ten minutes later at Templehof Airport. As they crest the top of the steps and enter into the glass atrium, Nathan sees the sun beginning to rise beyond. Just to the left of the bright orange sphere is a small second sunrise, in the direction they had just come.

"Holy shit, did we do that?" he gasps. Audrey stares out the window. The glow is from a burning high rise near downtown. Others have joined them at the glass.

"I didn't think that was supposed to happen," she whispers to Nathan.

"I suppose if we disabled the sprinkler system and electrical, and then started a fire with fuel near vertical ducts in an office building with a lot of paper, something bad might have happened."

"Holy shit, we really need to get out of here."

"Am I coming with? Won't tickets on credit card leave a trail, or give us away if they are already looking for us?" His mind fills with questions, not the least of which is *what the hell did we just do?*

"You may be useful–you know how to think. The rest I can teach you." She leads him away from the growing throng at the window, heading towards a quieter portion of the large complex.

"My stuff is at the hotel," Nathan remembers.

"Go back and get it, then. I'll put bets on who gets you first, Ruppin's men or the Polizei. Too bad the Stasi aren't still around, I would have given them the best odds. Of course," she adds thoughtfully, "we wouldn't have made it over the border."

"So you'd just leave me here, head back to Canada with that thing as a carry-on?"

"I don't know, I may check it. It's a bit bulky."

"Isn't there a law about removing archeological artifacts?"

"Then it's lucky I have the credentials and paperwork I need." She smiles wanly. "You at least have your passport, don't you?"

He pulls it from his backpack. They enter an area for charter flights. Audrey is calm and smiling as security checks her over and examines the stone. The officer studies her paperwork and then calls another guard over to confer. She chats easily with them, but Nathan feels like the sweat on his forehead and clammy hands will set off an alarm. The new guard picks up a telephone and confers yet again with an unseen superior before coming back. The three of them chat some more, and with a few well wishes Audrey passes through a metal detector. Now it is Nathan's turn.

His backpack is innocent enough. In that moment, as he passes through the detectors, Nathan remembers the duffel bag left at the dead man's house. He feels rather certain Audrey is professional enough to not leave anything behind that might lead back to her, but he suddenly panics about his involvement. Had she wiped everything down, or are his prints on something, set up to take the fall. He does not think so. If he was meant to be a patsy, he would not be standing so close to her right now; she would have left him somewhere to be picked up alone.

Through security and calm once more, Nathan contemplates how to get a better look at the stone, and back to his original job. He thinks he may have seen what he needs, but is certain there might be additional clues. They pass through a door and onto an outside walkway connecting to a smaller hangar.

"I have the location of the other stone," he blurts out suddenly, "back on Dingle."

"How?" she looks suspicious but curious.

"This piece," he gestures awkwardly, wishing he had an airport cart to push it in.

"You're sure?"

"Yes."

Audrey steps away, taking out her phone. She is talking loud out in the wind and sounds of airplanes landing and taking off, but Nathan cannot make out what she is saying, or to whom. She puts the phone away and points across the tarmac at a small jet near the hangar. "This way," she commands.

It is fitting, Nathan thinks as he follows her, that he is once again leaving Berlin with flames in the distance, unsure if he can ever come back.

22

NATHAN SITS ALONE in the cabin of the corporate jet. A few moments after takeoff he breathed a sigh of relief, before the ensuing quiet and solitude began to unnerve him. Audrey is up front with the pilot, forcing Nathan time to relax and just stare out the window. His mind is too exhausted to think, the steady whine of the engines lulling him, yet his body is too wired to sleep. He is not enjoying this kind of thoughtlessness right now, and hopes Audrey will come back to distract him.

Never having been in a private jet before, his imagination has proven remarkably accurate. Two sets of wide leather seats–recliners, really–one set facing each other with a wood fold-down table in between, either side of a central aisle. There is an open space behind where he is sitting, presumably for another bank of seats when needed, which does not have the same beige carpet but rather a more resilient floor. Perhaps they often haul cargo, he surmises, or pieces for his client's collection. There is a faint smell of antiseptic. Nathan is facing forward, the closed door to the cockpit about fifteen feet in front. In his imagination there would be a simple curtain, but the wood panel door that covers the entire front gives a much cleaner look, and a nice contrast with the beige of the rest of the interior. This is luxury, even for a private jet. His client should certainly be able to pay his bills, Nathan decides.

The cockpit door opens and Audrey appears. Nathan looks at her as if for the first time. It may actually be the first time in decent lighting, or without being in imminent danger. Her dark hair is pulled back in a pony tail, accenting the scar he had seen that night in Dingle. She is still wearing the same clothes from the past two days; the dark blue and somewhat muddy jeans and a black top. He finds the color and shirt, which is not really a blouse but a collarless cotton pullover with long sleeves, is a nice contrast to her lightly tanned skin. Its five buttons at top are all undone, exposing an amazing collarbone. She is dressed dark for breaking and entering, he judges, yet nondescript enough to get lost in a crowd. Throw in a black leather jacket and the outfit would meet standard uniform for living in Chicago.

He watches as she places a tray high up in a compartment near the doorway. Her hands belie her age, and seem disproportionately large for the rest of her body. Nathan wonders why he had not noticed them before. A shield mounted on the wall near her reads "JASCON". Nathan wonders if it is the name of his client's company, or simply of the jet.

Reaching up to another overhead compartment, the bottom part of her shirt gaps from the waistline of her jeans, exposing a flat belly with toned lines either side where it joins her hips. As she lowers her arms a bit of paunch appears, the two lines disappearing. She does not have a particularly feminine figure, Nathan observes. He finds the word 'sturdy' to be more accurate. He likes 'sturdy'; there is something very sexy about a woman built to do real work, something so much more beautifully human over dainty wallflower types. Of course he would never say 'no' to either, Nathan thinks, or any shade in between for that matter.

Audrey finishes her work at the bulkhead and sits down opposite Nathan, not bothering to buckle her belt. "I don't think you should go back to Berlin for a while," she recommends.

"No shit?"

"So you've been to Berlin before?" She tilts her head slightly and rotates in her seat, bringing a leg up underneath her.

"Yeah, I was a student there and worked for a while too. Actually, my first real job in architecture was for a firm there. Screwed me up a bit, since I learned a whole bunch of technical terms in German and measurements in metric, and when I got back to the States had to learn it all over again."

"You handled that dog well. Military?"

"Do I look like the military type?" he smiles, "No, I've never been good with authority."

"I figured you did some time; that kind of move doesn't usually happen through luck." She waits for a second, gauging if he will respond. Nathan finds it rhetorical, and after a brief moment of silence she fills the gap, "So how did you decipher that plan?"

"You know," he shrugs, "it's kind of my job. I just have a really good spatial memory and intuition for that kind of stuff. I can't remember people's names, though."

There is a short beep from a timer at the bulkhead. Audrey gets up and walks back, reaching for the tray she had previously stowed. Nathan's eyes are again drawn to her exposed midriff. He begins to salivate from the smell of food, finally realizing how hungry he is from having not eaten for the past day. She returns to place the tray on the table between them and sits down. Some type of chicken and vegetables, a bit odd for breakfast, but they both dig in ravenously.

"What do you know about our employer?" she asks between bites, raising her hand to cover her mouth in a loose gesture of manners.

"He's some kind of collector, that's about all. I've never met him, only talked on the phone."

"Why do you think he picked you?"

"Apparently he likes architects. I had a friend who was working for him, an old schoolmate who referred me. I seem to be filling in for him."

"Nobody's missing you back home?" she asks.

"Well I hope someone is. But I'm not married or living with anyone, and then a major project went on hold. Seemed like a perfect fit: a short-term job filling in for an old friend, plus a trip to Europe. Who wouldn't have jumped at the chance? I thought it would be like a working vacation."

"So you think you found what you need? You know where you're looking in Dingle?"

Nathan notices she did not query 'what' he is looking for in Dingle. "I really won't know until I get there, but I'm obviously looking for a piece like the one we stole," he gestures at the mass, still wrapped, sitting on one of the seats across the aisle. "What is all this about, anyway? And what about you; who are you, really? How much of your story in Dingle was bullshit?"

"I think we're about even in bullshit levels here," she studies him. "You know, you've been rather flippant and kind of evasive. I don't think you're the modest type, so you're purposely hiding something. You should just tell me," she smiles and leans in, inches above the food on the table, "because I'm going to find out."

Nathan struggles to meet her eyes and not look down her shirt. "What is that? A threat?" he half jokes.

"Well, if we're going to be partnering up here," she rubs her hand down his forearm, "I need to know I can trust you."

He tingles at her touch. "I'm sure our mutual boss checked my references."

"I've got my own criteria." She walks away with the tray, putting it in another compartment. "And our employer may have more questions if he's going to invest additional time in you." She pulls out a small white box. "Take your shirt off."

"Not exactly romantic, but I'm game."

"Get real. I need to look at that dog bite, unless you're immune to tetanus and everything else."

He takes off his shirt, and it sticks a bit where blood has dried around his wound. The bite did not appear deep, barely a puncture of the skin.

Audrey sits opposite, folding the empty table against the wall. She takes his right hand and leans in even closer to get a good look. Her hair just under his nose, he can smell her now. He clears his throat and nervously looks out the window. The smell of her is replaced by disinfectant as she opens a bottle and sets it on the floor near her foot. There is a sharp sting followed by a dull throb as she wipes the wound clean and then wraps it in a white bandage. She pulls out a syringe and removes it from a sterile package.

"Just to be safe," she says, jabbing him in the arm.

"Nice plane," he winces as she slowly presses the plunger. On queue, the door to the cockpit opens, and a large man in a white short-sleeved pilot's uniform steps through. Nathan has no doubt that despite the lack of traditional hat that he takes his job–and from the size of his forearms, his workouts–quite seriously.

The pilot hands a file to Audrey. She says a quick "thank you" before he turns, and without acknowledging Nathan, walks back into the cockpit and closes the door. Audrey opens the leather bound folder and pages through before looking up, a serious expression on her face.

"We seem to have some questions for you." Audrey looks

around. "You're right, it is a nice plane. One benefit is we are completely private here, so you can tell me anything. No one else will hear." Her tone lowers. "If you decide not to talk, or you lie to me, we are very far from anyone who can help you."

"Excuse me? I thought I was here to help you."

"Strip," she commands, slapping the folder down on the seat.

"What?" Nathan becomes worried. "No, I am not stripping."

She moves quickly, one hand to his neck and the other knife that appeared from nowhere to his crotch.

"If you answer me, and no playing around, we'll get along fine." She looks him deep in his eyes. "If you do not answer me, or you lie, I will have an unfortunate mess to clean up." She loosens her grip on his neck, her palm and forearm still resting on his bare chest. The knife does not move. "Do you understand?"

"Yes," he submits.

"I need to know I can trust you. That you're not just stringing me along because you lust after me."

"Whoever said I . . . ," Nathan stops, realizing it would be a lie.

"Why do you think I was sent out here to follow you, rather than anyone else?"

"Because you're my type, and I would not only cooperate but spill everything trying to impress you?" he guesses.

"So impress me. Strip," she repeats.

Audrey backs off. Nathan stands up from the comfort of the chair, unbuttoning the top button of his trousers and lowering the zipper. He loses his balance and steadies himself on the wall, adjusting to the plane's movement.

"Don't you think I could be both telling you the truth and lusting after you?" his defiance returns and he stops, "and I am not stripping for you."

"Your call," she shrugs her shoulders, raising her eyebrows in a gesture of mock defeat, "I was just hoping you would undress yourself before you passed out."

Nathan comes to, being yanked up and slapped, standing legs crossed right over left at the knees and bound tight at the ankles, his arms tied at the wrists behind his back. A rope is attached to his wrists and up through a pulley attached to the ceiling of the cabin. Audrey is holding the other end and staring right at him as she gives it a pull. He is in a reverse hanging position, *strappado*, as he had seen in photos from Abu Ghraib. If left like this, it was as good as crucifixion. He would suffocate. Not to mention the pain as the sedative he thought was a tetanus shot wears off. Naked and bound, he is completely exposed, and she has all the power.

She ties off the end of the rope to a hook on the side wall of the plane. The pulley and flooring here is, as Nathan first thought, probably for cargo, or it can double for interrogation.

Nathan is marginally relieved that Audrey's hands are empty as she approaches him. She comes up very close, her breath on his face, and walks all the way around him, accenting her own power and his helplessness. She comes back to the side of his face, her breath on one cheek and her gaze fixed on his eyes. He feels her hand cup his balls and begin to tighten.

"If I squeeze too hard you'll throw up," she lets go, "but I like these shoes." She orbits him once more. "There's an easier way, but I may not have time before the plane lands, and I really would rather not do any permanent damage." She shows him a syringe, perhaps the one she had used before. "Do you know what haloperidol does?" She waves it in front of him, not waiting for an answer, "It's a neuroleptic antipsychotic, which in high doses has a nasty side effect called akathasia. We're talking an anxiety and torment like you're being burned from the inside out. You also will have tremors and uncontrollable motion, which in your present condition is not good; you might even tear your arms off your shoulders. It would also be inadvisable to drive for a while. In this hand I have some biperidem, which will counteract it as soon as you tell me what I want to know."

He stares back in defiance, not saying a word. At first he was just playing coy; he did not really think he was keeping any secrets. Now that it has come this far, he entrenches his position. Even if he holds some earth-shattering truth, he would not give her the satisfaction. Besides, he figures, they cannot fly for much longer: a few hours maximum. Drugs would barely take effect, and would have to be explained wherever they land. He supposes they could say he is drunk or sick. Or they could simply throw him out. *That would suck*, he fears. Realization sets in. This is no longer a game, or if it is, he has no idea what the rules are.

Audrey reads the defiance on his face, even though he is unable to respond through the fog of the sedative. "On second thought, let's try something quicker," she must have read his mind. She moves around behind him and opens another door. Audrey returns holding a small crank generator marked 'US Aid'.

"A little surplus left over from Central America," she explains, setting the box on the floor in front of him and unrolling wires. "Electricity," she continues, "one wire fine enough to fit between your teeth," he clenches his jaw but she is able to use a similar pressure to force it open as Nathan had used on the dog. She slides the wire between two teeth on his lower right. He tries to remove it with his tongue, but it is wedged so tight he cannot budge it. "And the other," she picks up the second wire, "well you can imagine all the different places I could put that." He bites his lip, tearing in pain as she grabs his penis and inserts the wire.

"Trust me when I say the pain is unbelievable, I know." She

183

moves back to the generator, one hand on the crank.

Nathan's chest is heaving in spasms: fear, confusion, and anticipation of pain. The heaves are horribly constricted in his current position, unable to take any deep breaths.

"What is this about? You want locations? You want to steal this from me and our client? I don't know enough to tell you anything," he pleads."

"It's a start. However, I don't care what you know. I just care who you say you are," she states.

Audrey gives the generator a quick crank, sending Nathan into convulsions. He screams in agony and venom, attempting to deflect the pain outward into laughter. As the shock subsides he is clenching his jaw in a half maniacal grin.

"You think you could stick that in a bit further, might take a few shakes," he spits out, his defiance returning.

"I'm going to ask a few questions, to see if our relationship can go any further, or if I will need to crank this up higher. I will know if you lie. We'll start with some easy ones that I may already know the answers to. Do you understand?"

Nathan nods his head, the motion hurting his already sore shoulders.

"OK, Nathan Bang, were you ever in the employ of the NSA?" She keeps her eyes focused on the file in her hands.

"No."

"US Military?"

"No."

"CIA?"

Nathan hesitates a second too long. She looks up at him, a mock sense of pity in her eyes.

"Oh, and you were doing so well." The crank on the generator is longer this time, and there is no way to redirect the agony. He thinks his eyes are going to burst. "CIA?" she repeats.

"Would you be upset if I said 'I think so'," he answers.

"Why didn't you just say?" she asks, playful concern on her face.

"Because I've been a fucking architect for fifteen years: you know the profession where bow ties are acceptable casual wear? I'm hardly some kind of badass."

"I don't know, badasses are rarely the large intimidating tattooed type. The guys who are really scary are the psychopaths who look normal," she leans in, "you know, just like you might be." She moves back out and takes a deep breath.

"Thanks," he responds, "and fuck you. Who's the normal-looking psychopath here?"

"What did you do?" she ignores the accusation and continues.

"I was a plebe: a young student, an analyst, with barely some training."

"You were in the field. Student analysts, even ones in the CST Program, aren't alone in the field. Operations Officers are in the field."

"It was a weird time; there were a lot of East Germans, Russians, and Polish coming in, offering information. Recruitment wasn't the issue, it was knowing who to trust. At first I offered support, looking at floor plans, photos of buildings and providing layouts and other information. Then it got really busy, and I was asked to follow people after they came in to see if they were who they said they were."

"Interesting," Audrey nods, "and how many other hidden talents do you have?"

"Why don't you strip and find out?" he taunts. This is obviously a transgression, but not serious enough to warrant a crank on the generator. She grabs his bandaged arm and presses the bite wound hard, eliciting a loud objection from Nathan.

"Who is Natalia?" she continues. "She was more than a contact, wasn't she?"

It is embarrassing to talk about a former love to someone you had hoped, however misguided, would be your next. Nathan is surprised he still feels some of this embarrassment in light of his current circumstances. "She was my honeytrap; she set me up, I was naïve," he admits, possibly for the first time to himself.

"Oh please, come on, with a name like Natalia? How stupid were you? If you're still that big of an idiot, is there any way I can trust you?"

"First of all, she was Lithuanian not Russian. And she was supposed to be working for us."

"You trusted her?"

"I loved her," he sneers.

"You know, there are a lot of things one can cut off, but you," she straddles him, "the thing most precious to you is your eyes. One good cut across the top here," she brushes the knife along his left eyelid, "and all the muscles that let you blink are severed. Your poor eye would dry right up. Make it very hard to sleep, too."

"What else do you want?" he is gasping short breaths again. The pain he had endured so far is temporary, but blindness is one of his great fears. She had found his weak spot, the one thing that would affect the core of who he is.

"All of this may seem a bit extreme," Audrey admits, gesturing around at the bondage and wires, "but when I read you burned her, that just sent a red flare up. You never even found out for sure she was the one who betrayed you. You don't know for sure anyone betrayed you; you might have done it to yourself and just needed someone to blame." She pulls him toward her from the back of his neck, extending his arms to their limit, "you need to admit what you did. You need to convince me you are not a psychopath. You need to prove to me you are not working for someone else, and that you didn't kill Anton knowing you would be called up next."

The disbelief in that someone knows about the firebomb numbed him from any other pain or emotion. *How could they know? Did I kill someone, someone I loved?* His thoughts morph from the relief he had felt for years in taking action, to actually thinking about the consequences. *Oh my God, did I kill her?*

"I'm not, I swear. I didn't. I didn't know," he stutters. Nathan looks her in the eye trying to convince her.

Audrey sits down in the chair near the stone, studying him. After a moment, she sighs and gets back up. She unties the rope from its cleat and lets it go, allowing Nathan to drop to his knees in the middle of the floor. She removes the wires as he kneels there motionless, hunched forward, eyes to the floor. Naked and hands still tied behind his back, she leads him over to the chair she had just vacated. His shoulders ache, but at least he can breathe again.

"Is she dead?" Nathan wants, needs, to know what is in that file, what had happened to her. Then he remembers the last thing she had said, and he asks, "Is Anton dead?"

"We don't know," she admits, "we don't know either one. Natalia disappeared after the fire, and so has Anton. It seems a bit too coincidental, but I think I believe you, at least about Anton." She picks up the stone, and before sitting down across from him sets it on his lap, "What do you know about this?"

"Holy shit that's cold." The weight of it presses his thighs, and with his hands behind his back he is unable to do anything about it. If he stands up to let it slide off it would land squarely on his bare feet. At least his private parts are covered, he thinks, looking for a positive. She leans down low, shows some cleavage through the open top of her shirt. Nathan is in disbelief that he is still compelled to look. *Perhaps I really am a psychopath*, he considers. "It's some kind of artifact. The client, Moyne, is looking for different parts to complete his collection." He looks at its inscription, "maybe some kind of Rosetta Stone, and when all the parts are put together it might be some big discovery, or it might be a really good recipe for bread."

Audrey considers this, then picks it up off his lap and sets it on the chair opposite the aisle. "You really don't know? It doesn't seem like you even care. If I'm satisfied, I've been authorized to tell you more, if you want to know."

"Seems the least you could do," he replies, a bit self-conscious at being exposed again.

"I wasn't really going to hurt you unless you work for someone else or had something to do with Anton disappearing. The key is to induce dread, or humiliation, or fear of your mortality: the precise pain, in the precise amount, for the precise length of time. It's really an art." She looks a bit remorseful for the first time. She bends him forward to untie his hands. "You made me do it, you know."

"Oh? I made you? Is this some sort of dysfunctional relationship and you just got done 'putting me in my place'?"

"You weren't being honest. I had your file, and the possible connections were too serious to ignore. Like I said before, you don't seem like the modest type, and so I had to wonder what you're really hiding." She throws his clothes back at him, "I barely turned it on compared to what I survived."

"And because you survived so much worse it makes it okay? This was some sort of a hazing to you? I could never do what you just did," Nathan contends, awkwardly putting his underwear back on, unable to fully extend his arms from the pain in his shoulders.

"Yeah right, history is full of people who could never do this, yet became very good at it, even seemed to enjoy it."

"So who the hell are you? How rude of me–I feel like I've been doing all the talking," he says sarcastically, "where did they stick the wire for you?"

She grabs him by the throat again in a burst of anger, then relaxes her grip and sets him down. "Audrey Mays," she extends her hand. He waits a second before taking it.

She had called Anton Eischen by his first name him, Nathan recalls. She knows him, personally. He remembers back to his search of Anton's room. No indicators that they were close. Maybe the "am" Nathan had seen in the matchbook? Audrey Mays?

"So, back to the bullshit," he asks, forgetting about the information she was about to offer him. He is much more interested in her. "VSO? Kazakhstan?"

"JTF2: Joint Task Force, sort of a Canadian Special Forces. Afghanistan." She watches him dispassionately as he finishes dressing.

"Not any women in our Special Forces that I know of."

"None officially in ours, either. That just makes it more special, and a bigger surprise, when they show up."

"I take it you were dismissed?" he asks.

"I was captured. After that some of my superiors couldn't tell the difference between bravery and having a death wish endangering others." As she continues unprompted, Nathan thinks he may have hit the button on his first try. "It's not a death wish, surviving something that intense; I actually never felt more alive. I mean, imagine the guys who walked on the moon. What do you do after that? The rest of your life something like that will never happen again, and all the time the moon is still there to remind you."

He finishes buttoning his shirt, and she hands him a pill. "For the pain," she almost apologizes.

"Fuck you."

"Oh, don't be like that Natey," she smiles. "You want to know what this is about."

"You don't get to call me Natey," he replies, not answering the question.

"Let me guess," she puts on a pouty face and tilts her head, "just your grandma and the love of your life, the one you never got over since heroically letting her go and is the reason you've never married."

No answer. It was probably in that damn file.

"Like I said, I know you, but I also know your grandma is dead and the 'love of your life' left you because you were a lecherous ass who was never going to commit." She sits back down, obviously eager to share. "Last chance, you want to know what you are really doing here?"

"Yes," he concedes finally, "Yes, I want to know."

"What do you know about the story of St. Brendan?"

"He was Irish. Like Patrick, but without a holiday."

"He was an explorer. The Voyage of St. Brendan is the story of monks setting out on a two-year adventure that describes some very familiar-sounding places, which were not officially discovered for another thousand years."

"And this tablet is proof that he made this journey? If it is," he points at the stone, "I'm afraid it might be a hoax. That stone doesn't look like any type native to Ireland. Nothing I saw anyway."

"And it doesn't need to be. Mr. Moyne thinks it's something Brendan brought back. From America."

"Well, that's cool and all; it might even rewrite a few history books and certainly be a collector's item." Nathan points at the pulley, "but is it worth all this?"

"Mr. Moyne thinks it has to do with the key to immortality: the

Fountain of Youth. He may be off his rocker, and I don't know what led him to believe this, but Moyne is certain Ponce de Leon could not find the Fountain of Youth partly because it had nothing to do with being an actual fountain, and mostly because an Irish monk beat him to it by a thousand years."

"So I'm supposed to believe this stone has some healing power, or tells some secret? I guess even as a myth that might drive some people to kill for it," Nathan admits, "but it sounds more like a tremendous pile of unbelievable shit."

"There might be some truth. You saw the guy in that house. That wasn't right." Audrey shivers a bit at the recollection.

"You think that stone, his exposure to it or something he read on it, was keeping him alive after he blew half his brains onto the wall?"

"It means he didn't know what he had, or he wouldn't have done that. Talk about a living hell . . ." she trails off.

"No, no way. That is too crazy." It is Nathan's turn to shiver as he considers the possibility. "Man, if it is true, he is not going to enjoy his autopsy."

"What about the afterlife? You believe in that?" she asks.

"Like ghosts and such?"

"Yeah."

"I don't believe in ghosts. They always seem to occur in buildings where good or bad energy happens. I think it's the building itself coming to life; achieving consciousness and confused about it."

"So for you it all goes back to buildings?"

"Science, engineering, fabrication and poetics all melding -it wraps it all up for me. I can search for beauty, and try to convert it to something that will outlast us all."

"So you look for your own immortality, for the big project, like a thief looking for the big score? I just assumed it was an older person's profession, or that it attracts slow people," Audrey quips.

She is good at lightening the mood. Nathan actually feels closer to her. Is this Stockholm Syndrome? He hates the thought of being so typical. "There's a lot to learn, and it takes a while; sort of like learning to write novels in another language. You need to learn the words and grammar, and then be able to communicate. Yet, on top of it all, you need a story to tell." He thinks about his own recent downswing, how he knows he is letting his partner Johanna down, and not achieving any of the things he had set out to do. "Architecture," he concludes, "is not so much a manic depressive exercise as it is a peculiar form of alternating thoughtfulness followed by desperation."

"Anton," she queries, "is he a lot like you?" Audrey asks the question convincingly, almost sadly, but Nathan thinks she is the one lying now. He thinks she was sent for Anton much like she was sent to watch over him. And like him, Anton probably fell for her. The two of them may have even worked together over years, and he was deeply in love with her. Nathan knows there is nothing sadder than having someone deeply in love with you, and you being unable to feel anything for them even if they are likable. It negates everything: spending time, a comfortable drink, any chance of even developing a real friendship. There is nothing sadder, he clarifies, unless you are the other person. Maybe she is the reason Anton disappeared. The 'am' written in a matchbook was perhaps a last attempt to meet and tell her how he felt, and it did not go so well.

Nathan is about to confront her on this, but thinks better of it since he has no basis. Glancing out the window he recognizes the Irish countryside. The plane bumps gently, descending through low clouds as it prepares for landing.

23

July 6, Dingle, Dingle Peninsula

NATHAN LOOKS OUT THE CAR WINDOW at Connor's Hotel. They sit in silence, he and Audrey, the engine idling the moments away with a guttural rhythm. The route from Shannon to Dingle, especially the last miles over the mountain, was still thrilling to him yet seemed lost on his visibly pale driver. Trying to point out the fantastic to someone who does not care drains the entire experience.

Of course, he considers, Audrey may truly be ill. After arriving on what he has now labeled in his mind as the "Fucked-Up Flight" in Shannon yesterday, she decided to stay the night near the airport even though the drive back to Dingle could easily be made before sunset. Nathan was feeling quite well, given his ordeal. Of course a pain pill or two each time he had to pee was necessary, but in general all his wounds were healing at an amazing rate, if not a little strangely. The cut on his neck had lost its scab and covered over in a bump of whitish flesh that feels rigid. Audrey however, though she would never admit it, is looking paler and weaker by the moment. Nathan considers it some kind of cosmic payback.

She still demanded to drive, despite his offer. He asked her more about the story she had told, as it begins to take root in his psyche. Brendan, Fountain of Youth, and Immortality? She was not in a talking mood, or did not know any more than she had already told. Nathan doubts that she has told him all, and her reticence makes him obsess about it even more. What could it be? What would it mean to live forever? To have the time to do whatever he wants, to acquire the means to create a monument unlike any on earth. Forget monuments, those are just substitutes for actually living forever. The things he could see one day! It could be like a Mayflower Pilgrim experiencing today's highways and computers. It is all fantasy, of course; fables to give value and meaning to objects that otherwise are merely old. Nathan has no doubt that the tablet they found—technically stolen—and the one he is searching for are valuable. Put together and translated they could potentially rewrite history books, and his role might give him a bit of immortality in name that he may never find designing monuments for others. *Immortality. Damn*, Nathan shakes his head, knowing logically it could not be true.

And so here they are, clues in hand but no plan since she 'didn't want to talk about it right now'. Nathan does not have unlimited time; he needs to be back at his office in a week. He would not be surprised if there are several messages waiting for him behind the heavy blue door of Connor's Hotel he is looking at.

"We should meet later, talk about what we're going to do," Audrey picks up on his thought.

"How about the pub where we first met? 8:00 o'clock would give us a couple hours to settle back in," he suggests.

"How about we start new. You know the hardware store place?"

"Yes, yes I do." He answers. "What about that thing?" Nathan glances at the wrapped form in the back seat.

"I will hold on to that," she says.

Grabbing his backpack from the back seat, the only part of his luggage to make it back from Berlin, Nathan opens the car door to exit the small rental. He slams the door shut and waves awkwardly as she speeds up Main Street heading east, realizing he has no idea where Audrey stays. Probably some B & B, he thinks, then dismisses the idea of her staying with some nosy hosts trying to serve her breakfast. More likely she is at a nice anonymous hotel, as basic as possible. They would never be good on vacation together, he concludes.

Nathan passes through the lobby, pausing to look at the portrait of a woman he swears could be his grandmother, when a voice calls from what he thought had been an empty reception desk.

"Ah, Mr. Bang, nice of you to come back and visit us so soon." Her voice is lilting, and he cannot help but be cheered by the accent.

"Just a few days away. I can't wait to get back and get a change of clothes," he apologizes for his appearance. He searches for his room key and pulls it out.

"Oh, thank you, we were wondering when you might be dropping that off."

"Dropping what off?" he asks.

"Your room key there," she smiles, gesturing at his hand.

"Won't I need it?"

"I would think you have one for your new room," she answers.

"I have a new room?" Nathan is truly confused now. Perhaps he was upgraded as a long-term guest, he hopes.

"No," it is the young woman's turn to look confused, "you are no longer a guest here."

Great, just what I need, he thinks "What?! I never checked out." He composes himself for a moment. "What happened to my stuff?"

"The O'Malley boy came with a few friends, said he was helping you move. He showed us a signed lease and we checked it against your signature." She offers a look of apology and apprehension, mixed with a tinge of defensiveness in having done her due diligence.

Nathan stands in disbelief for a moment. "They took everything?" he asks, following up more pointedly, "even the stuff in the safe?"

"Yes sir. Safes, as you can imagine, are no problem for the O'Malley boy. We were a bit surprised you hooked up with him," she smiles knowingly.

"Yeah, right. You and me both," Nathan accepts that he has a new home, and will need to walk a bit further to get there. He thanks his former host and steps back through the big blue door onto Main Street. Looking right he can see his destination, then turns into the gathering tourists for the familiar crowded trek down Main Street and then the more solitary climb up John Street to the house across from O'Malley's Bed & Breakfast. Nathan checks his pocket for the key, as he has no desire to talk to Mrs. O'Malley; he would probably end up leaving with an additional insurance policy or something.

He arrives to stand in front of a different heavy wood plank door, this time beat-up and grayish-black rather than the fresh blue of the hotel. He sets his key in the lock and turns. The small dark landing and narrow steps take on a more forbidding character than he remembers. At the top of the stairs, Nathan ponders Anton's door for a second before opening his own.

Nathan has to admit the boys have done a decent job; his clothes are hung up, toothpaste and brush in the bathroom cabinet, even the same pair of pants he had packed and then taken out and laid on the bed before leaving for Berlin is lying in a similar position on his new bed. The room does have a homier feel than his hotel room, he finally admits. He sets his pack down on the chair near the door and walks over to the bed. He lies down on his back, legs bent at the knees and feet still flat on the floor, mulling over what to do next.

He is anxious to return to the site, though Audrey may interfere with her 'plan'. *Should he trust her?* Not convinced of that yet, he thinks instead about how to kill time before they meet up. He is not in the mood for site seeing; it seems a bit trivial now. Nathan ponders a way to hone in on his task, come to his meeting with Audrey more prepared, or at least have information that he can keep to himself if worse comes to worse.

Where was the key to Anton's room? He tries to remember. Having left it in a nightstand drawer in the other room, Nathan hopes it will be in the same spot here. Finding it, thank you O'Malley boys, he steps back into the hallway and opens the neighboring door.

The room is exactly as he had last seen it, apparently no additional burglaries. He begins looking over everything anew, convinced he can refine his search now that he has a better idea of where the piece of tablet may be. The other models yield nothing, the photos a dead end. He focuses on all the architectural things, believing Anton would make his messages invisible to anyone without their shared vision. Still he finds nothing.

Nathan looks around again, studying the photos and notebooks more closely, even searching the pockets of Anton's clothes. His movements become more reckless as his frustration grows, and as he sits down a second time, he admits to himself that he was no longer seeking clues to the stone; he is looking for clues to Audrey.

Just then there is a knock at the bottom door. Feeling caught, although no one would notice or care, he steps out of Anton's room and locks it before descending the stair. At the bottom landing, his instinct is to open the door but he thinks better of it. "Who is it?" he asks through the heavy wood.

"Me," he recognizes Audrey's voice. He opens the door to find her leaning against the frame, her face ashen and car idling in the street behind.

"What's going on?" Nathan decides not to comment on how terrible she looks.

"I'm feeling sick, no meeting tonight," she says, "and you better take the stone." She gestures towards the car. "I'm in no condition to protect it."

"Okay. You'll call tomorrow then?"

"Yeah. I just need to rest." She looks at him seriously, "I'm trusting you here."

Nathan nods. "I know," he says quietly and walks over to open the car door. He looks up and down the street for anything unusual, and realizing how suspicious that makes him look, he simply picks up the heavy bundle from the back seat and carries it in a hug towards the door. "Have a good night," he wishes, feeling like a shmuck for wanting anything to do with her after that plane ride, much less wishing her well.

"Don't let it out of your sight," she responds, getting back in the car.

Nathan closes the door to the sound of her driving away, and then labors back up the steps carrying his charge. Once more in his room, he sits on the bed to unwrap the bundle. Running his fingers over the script, he stares at the pattern of the stone itself, its veining and crystals. He turns it over to check the image on the back, making sure it connects with the version he has stored in memory. Just to be careful, and in case Audrey changes her mind and comes back to retrieve it, he looks around for a piece of paper and a pencil. Finding none, he tries Anton's room and returns with a roll of tracing paper and a fat charcoal sketching pencil. Laying the trace over the stone, he makes a rubbing of the image. He turns the stone over and repeats it with the script on the front. The two charcoal covered sheets curl into a roll which he lays on the bed.

Realizing he has not checked for his safe, he looks around the room and, seeing nothing, checks the closet. There in the corner is the same metal box from his hotel; the boys had simply moved it without opening it. Nathan notes he should return it when done. He opens the safe and with a single folding is able to stash the rubbings inside.

Lying back down on the bed, staring at the ceiling, he feels restless; he needs to get out, see people, do something. He gets up and changes clothes, putting on a sweater to guard against the cool dampness outside. It was probably hot and humid back home in Chicago, but here one never knows; might as well prepare for the way it was an hour ago.

Nathan steps out the door, and is surprised the weather is amazingly similar. He walks back down the hill towards the intersection with Main Street and stands for a moment, deciding where to go. *Might as well start here*, he decides, stepping into the large pub on the corner where he first met Audrey.

It's early, but a good crowd has gathered; mostly tourists, which Nathan no longer considers himself. He avoids a group who may have been direct relatives to the 'Monstrous Men From Missouri' he had been happy to talk to on another occasion, and finds a seat at a more private corner of the bar. Here he could watch and think, and join in the scene later if the mood strikes.

Beer arrives as he muses over the story of Brendan that Audrey had told. He had heard of Viking explorers arriving in the New World well before Columbus officially discovered it, but not the Irish. It explains why so many waterfront places are called

Brendan's Docks or other such names. A man of God, an Explorer, fearlessly crosses the ocean in a small boat with his crew of monks. These guys were hard-core, he thinks, having seen some other outposts Irish monks had set up. A bit like the Polynesians on the other side of the world; explorers looking for the right kinds of clouds in the sky that signify land, completely unafraid of open ocean. Not for him, Nathan decides. He would have turned back as soon as he could no longer see people on the shore.

The whole basis for Irish monasticism seems unique: a withdrawal from the world and penitential exile. It was useful more than once to the Church—keeping knowledge and skills alive during the Dark Ages for one—and probably useful for bringing things back, and not necessarily plunder. How Christian would that be? Audrey's fantastic tale of an Irish monk visiting Florida a thousand years before the first Spanish arrived, and bringing back the mythical Fountain of Youth, is a compelling myth. Like the Grail or El Dorado, it is the kind of tale that inspires exploration simply for its own sake, with no real expectation of finding the truth.

Nathan takes another drink and thinks about when he and Anton were traveling as students across Europe, when they were most bonded. Nathan could guess that it may have been the only time Anton glimpsed true belonging, even though it was transient. Their 'perfect moments' often involved sunsets, or nightclubs, or other people they met that were truly characters. Most often it involved spaces that, as architects, truly spoke to their souls. We have forgotten, Nathan thinks, the extent to which our humanity, our ability to find ourselves, our bliss, our others, depends on the physical structure of the world. The things we make and the places we build.

Those ancient Irish monks purposely denied themselves this part of their humanity in order to find divinity. In the process, they probably could not help having an adventure or two, and probably found how much they needed each other. And what if they did bring back a treasure or two? They were still human.

Immortality. Damn.

Most people in the history of the world have come and gone with just their children as legacy, and belief in an afterlife. Some, he is sure, hoped for a complete end, an eternal nothingness. Some believe we keep coming back, without the benefit of a memory of life already experienced. So why is none of this good enough for him, Nathan is wondering? What drives him to keep searching for some other way to make his mark?

He thinks back to when he was a child, and his mother had died. For him, she had simply gone to the hospital one day and not come back. Nathan was only about six. At the funeral, he remembers standing holding his father's hand, and asking why he was the only one not crying. His father simply said "You will." It was a lot of years before he did. His life, as he figured it, was normal. It was only in his twenties, in hindsight and when he compared himself to his friends, that he began to think he was abnormal and maybe this loss was the reason why. He would alternately find solace in his loss, or feel it was just a lame excuse to blame things on. Anyway, he finally did cry, and for a long time. Not that he is unhappy with who he is. Nathan feels in his heart he is a lucky man who has taken advantage of most of the gifts he has been given. Getting older, however, he is starting to feel the press of time to accomplish those things he had not done yet: the famous project, the family, the happiness of being content.

At this very moment, he is only three years older than he wants to be, but that is not the problem. It is the bar he is in, and the music that is playing. The song, a slightly reggae-inspired Irish mix, reminds him of his last live-in love, Alex. Alexandra. He smiles as he thinks he would have broken up with her earlier, but was just waiting for the right song to come along. She would not have taken it as romantically has he meant it to be.

He watches the waitress, wondering if she notices him. She is one of those happy people; infectious smile and joy to be around. Easy and carefree it seems–so unlike Alex.

Once the tone of a relationship is established, it is tough to change. With her, Nathan was destined to be somber and serious, because that is the way she knew him to be and whenever he tried to change she threw a tantrum of her own to put the focus back on her. It was not worth it, and so he hid his emotions and became that person. If he had married her, he knew he would have to be either lonely and focused on his own little world, or unhappy with her, because that was his assigned role.

Alex had confronted him about it, but never in a way that seemed productive in his male mind. It was not about being a jerk or uncommunicative or even overly protective/obsessive. In general, he thinks, men just want to be left alone without being lonely.

Nathan looks at the other waitress, not nearly as attractive but ardently primping in the reflective stainless steel of a coffee machine. He looks around, judging ages. His first subject is twenty-two but a smoker, the 'primper' thirty-six, a new waitress coming out of the kitchen still has the look of baby fat and must be nineteen at most. Nathan wonders if he is so easily read. He flatters himself that he does not look his age, but realizes it is quite untrue. Everyone looks their age; it is only a matter if they look good or bad for their years.

A decent hobby, judging people. Some hobbies take a lot of time but little money, while others little time but lots of money. He had a number of clients with the latter kind of hobbies. The worst were hobbies that took a lot of time and money. This hobby does not take much of either. Unfortunately, Nathan feels he identifies more with the unattractive primping waitress; sure she looks better, but compared to what? What an asshole thing to think, he admits.

His attention follows the cute waitress as she takes an order and returns to the edge of the bar to deliver it. She smiles at something on the computer screen, her face reflecting its glow, and Nathan thinks she is either putting on a show for him or she is quite insane. Her smile accents big lips, deep dimples in her cheeks. Empirically she is attractive; all the parts are perfect, but somehow they do not come together. She returns to a table with two guys and lingers, joking with them and smiling at their lame attempts to impress her. She is flirting, and Nathan actually feels a pang of jealousy and betrayal, even though he has not even spoken to her. He realizes that perhaps he is that somber, serious person his last girlfriend stereotyped him to be. This girl probably has a boyfriend who does not care if she flirts at work; just part of the job, and it probably brings home more tips. Not for Nathan. If he had been involved with her, he would be hurt seeing this.

He has felt that same tinge of jealousy with girls at the club. Nathan always had to remind himself that the thrill, the titillation, was neither beauty nor meaning. Similar to his profession, where so many have confused the new and different with being beautiful, where they believe the intent of what they mean to do is more important than what actually gets built. If the beauty has to be explained than it probably is not beautiful, he decides. He is guilty too, he knows.

How did it start, this crisis with his work, even though he is getting more attention than ever? He could justify it is what clients have been demanding, what the market supports, all those excuses. All bullshit. Good design takes effort, and the demands of managing people rather than projects has been wearing him down. As for the clubs, for all the rationalizing he has done to himself and others it comes down to just being lonely, even though he had been with someone when it started. He was very lonely with Alex. It was good he did not marry her, he thinks, though it was not a choice he made on purpose, and it left him more alone and older.

Nathan shakes his head to change his thoughts, to something more positive. He certainly could not go to a club even if he wanted to. He certainly was not going to find one out here, and he missed his chance in Berlin.

Berlin. It has awoken something in him he had not felt for a long time. The kind of feelings all the clubs and projects in the world are just patches for. He needs some air.

Nathan stands up and steps outside for a moment, leaving his place at the bar obvious that he is coming back. There is a storm coming. He faces into the wind, wishing he was out at the site, bare to the ocean and the elements right now. He feels brave, liking the thought of tucking his chin in and facing the onslaught of wind and rain; walking straight in and daring it to knock him down. He opens his eyes and sees Audrey down the street.

"A miraculous recovery! You look much better," he smiles, actually pleased to see her.

"Just a nap, and I woke up feeling fine," she stops in front of him. "I thought you might be here, even though I told you not to let our little package out of your sight," she chides.

He holds the door open and she passes through. His drink is still half full on the bar. Audrey motions towards a small open table in the snug near the fireplace, claiming it with her jacket and then returning to the bar. She orders, and when a glass of green liquid arrives, Nathan pays and hands it to her.

They cross back over to the quieter table. Sitting across from him, she takes a sip and sets it down, cradling the glass between her hands. "What were you doing earlier? Drinking alone?" she asks.

"You know, just out, letching on some girls."

"I did not know that was a verb," she offers an amused quizzical look.

"I've created quite a few new verbs," he falls into operator mode, "I'm sure you have too."

"Whatever," she muses, confirming that she probably has, "so tomorrow I'll pick you up at 8:00 and go to the site."

"Sounds good," he replies.

"Anything else you need? Equipment? People?" she asks. "You think you've pinpointed this piece?"

"We should be good," Nathan decides, "the stones aren't that big and I have it narrowed down. The site superintendent seems to be there along with a few others, so if we need help we can get it. Anton trusted them." He tries to lighten the discussion, "you should see this guy–he looks like he's been through two wars but has this amazing smile."

"Wow that sounded gay."

"No. I mean . . . "

"I know," she confesses, "I've been out there."

"Really?" he should not have been surprised. He wonders if it was with Anton, and he feels the tinge of jealousy despite his best efforts. It is quiet between them again, and Nathan is feeling dizzy from the alcohol. He sits and thinks about all the things he just thought about. Then another voice comes, a much deeper and cautionary one from the back of his head very unlike the voice he usually thinks with, gently reminding him *Get out of your fucking head.* That would be impossible, of course. He is not wired that way.

Immortality, he muses. *Damn.*

24

July 7, Dingle, Dingle Peninsula

THE WHISPERS ARE vulgar and suggestive, the best kind of whispers. Taunting, compelling; hips moving in time with quiet need. Warmth of someone else's bare skin soaking into his own. Lids heavy, not wanting to open for fear it is just a dream.

Nathan cracks one eye to a familiar sight: the back of Audrey's head. This is not his room, and he has no recollection how he arrived here. He lifts his cheek off the pillow an inch before the weight of his head becomes too much for his neck, slumping back into the concave form where it had been. His skull splitting, mouth dry, he is more focused on the fact he is naked under this blanket. He lifts the down-filled comforter up, just to make sure. He then slides the top of his hand over, lifting up the blanket close to Audrey. Thankfully she is just as naked; how embarrassing if he had been the only one, he thinks.

He lingers a moment, studying the back of her legs as they meet the roundness of her bottom and then smoothly counter-arch to that perfect angle in the small of her back where they all meet. She begins to stir, and he quickly drops his hand.

"Hey!" she groggily exclaims, lifting herself to her elbows before also realizing she is naked and stops.

God, I hope we did something, Nathan pleads.

"What . . .," she stops mid-accusation and puts her hand to her head, obviously in as much pain as Nathan. She holds in this position for a second before turning her head towards the side table. With a sudden lurch she stretches her right hand from her head towards the drawer of the stand. Nathan, out of instinct and fear, echoes her movement and reaches over her. She gets to the drawer before him, but his longer arms and the advantage of being slightly more awake allows him to catch her hand. Looking over, he sees a large knife with serrated top; not a casual eating utensil. He is naked on top of her bare back, both facing down with right arms extended toward the weapon. She bucks him off, but he manages to reach in and grab it before landing on the floor, his right elbow stinging as it breaks his fall. He somehow maintains a grip on the knife. She is crouching, ready to tackle, but he springs up in time to stop her further movement and get the knife to her throat. She halts and slowly gets down on both knees, raising her open hands over her shoulders.

"What did you do to me?" she manages.

Raising her arms bring her breasts up to a perfectly-formed position, making it impossible for Nathan to keep his eyes above her neck. The question catches him off guard, not because she is so naked or even due to his own exposure. It is an honest question, or one meant to deflect blame. Nathan wants to give her the benefit of doubt, but after the trip from Berlin he is unsure. A metallic reflection in the corner of his eye draws him to a familiar-looking dark canvas roll-up, her torture tools organized on top.

"What I did? Nothing. This is all you," he answers.

"Not me," she considers shaking her head to emphasize her

denial, but the throbbing headache and knife stop her. She tries to meet his eyes.

Nathan sees nothing to immobilize her. He expects a length of rope, or handcuffs, or something she would need for her own use. Improvising, he shakes the pillow out of its case with his free left hand. "Back up," he commands, not sure how he would tie her hands if she resists.

Keeping the knife tight to her throat, she sidles back to the head board which is mostly solid but there are a few openings near the top, the top wood piece looking strong enough to hold her for a little while. He drapes the pillow case over top, careful not to straddle her yet feeling very open to attack.

"I'm going to tie your right hand, just so you don't try anything funny. Use your left hand, slowly, to hold the front of the pillow case," Nathan directs. Audrey crosses her arm as told and grabs the fabric. He reaches through with his left hand, still pressing the knife with his right, and grabs the loose end of the case to loop it around her wrist and then around the end she is holding. He pulls tight and repeats the loop a second time until he is confident some type of knot is formed. Lowering the knife, he sets it between his teeth to free both hands. Quickly emptying the other pillow, he is able to tie up her left wrist with far less anxiety. Audrey, resigning herself to her fate, or at least confident she is in no real danger, also relaxes, making the rest of his job far easier than it should be.

"What do you plan on doing with me?" she queries.

"This is another setup, isn't it?" Nathan moves off the bed to retrieve Audrey's tools. There is a clipper, about the right size to remove a finger or toe. He holds it open around her right little finger and stares her in the eyes. She sucks in a breath quickly at the feel of cold metal.

"I did not do this. I did not bring you here," her tone is

adamant.

"Why should I believe you?" he closes the clipper slightly, the first feel of pressure sending pangs of guilt and uncertainty.

"Would I have drugged myself, too? That's just stupid," she points out. Nathan cannot disagree with her assessment. She would choose to stay in control, and he believes there is nothing to be gained by questioning him again. If anything, she needs him to go out to the site and retrieve the other stone. Then, maybe after, she might feel the need to dispose of him. He would consider that when the time comes.

"What, no clever comeback?" she follows up, sensing his agreement and hesitation.

"Clever comebacks usually require something clever to be said first," he counters, trying to maintain some control until he can diffuse this. Nathan turns his thoughts to anything else he might want to know, since he is momentarily in control.

"If it wasn't you, and it certainly was not me, must have been someone else," she reasons, unaware he has already decided this and moved on.

"You think we . . ." he queries.

"What?" She does not understand until he looks her up and down one more time. "No. Absolutely not."

"You sure?" he barely masks his disappointment.

"I think I would know."

It is quiet; there is nothing else to say and Nathan realizes he is unable to treat her the same way she treated him. Despite the danger, he just cannot hurt her. Reluctantly, he sets the clippers on the night stand and hears Audrey takes a deep, audible breath.

"So unfair, so sexist—you could have electrocuted my balls and it would have been 'unpleasant, but for god and country'. If I even look at you bound and naked I'm a pervert."

"Then it's a good thing you are," she agrees. "I guess the only truth that comes from torture is what it reveals about the torturer."

"Yeah? What did I learn about you?" he asks, feeling he only revealed weakness.

"Do you mind if we put some clothes on before we have a heart-to-heart? Let's say we're even now," she bargains.

"Hardly," he scoffs. "You know, we could just stay undressed and . . ." Nathan offers, his innuendo trailing off.

"Oh please, believe me when I tell you I have a headache you would not believe."

"I believe it," he answers, feeling the weight of his own skull but unwilling to use it as an excuse. He unties her hands and steps away off the bed. She rubs her wrists, encouraging blood to circulate again before searching for clothes.

"You know what your problem is," she looks at him, buttoning up her top, "you personify objects even as you objectify people."

"Oh yeah, I objectify people. That's why I couldn't torture you."

"Exactly! If you saw me as human, you could have done it. Ultimately you just saw me as a woman you want."

Nathan thinks about his dream; the way Seth saw Anna was completely empathic, completely personal. The two of them actually were objects, but he felt her humanity so deeply he sacrificed himself to give her a chance at being a person. Has he ever truly cared for anyone that deeply, Nathan wonders? Did Natalia ruin him, his ability to trust? He had hardly given her a thought since leaving Berlin all those years ago, but since he found out, well, Nathan cannot think about it. More likely, he believes, his work has focused him on the permanence of things he builds rather than on the uncertainty of human nature. He is looking for immortality in a sense, but more as the designer of temples rather than patriarch of a clan. Nathan's crisis, or part of it, is that he is rapidly realizing he will never be Imhotep, Christopher Wren or Frank Lloyd Wright. He would not be surprised if Anton feels the same weight.

Audrey misinterprets his silent pondering, "Look, part of why I didn't think twice about my drastic approach to questioning you is what I read into your profile. I didn't have much time, and you may be far more dangerous than you let on."

"Bonding with your torturer, I know the drill. It's not me," he states, even while accepting it.

"You're still here, following my lead like a puppy, even after what I did to you. Or because of what I did to you," she proposes.

"And you will do the same for me?" he asks in return, knowing the answer. "So, again the question is if you didn't do this and neither did I, then who?"

"I'm not sure," she responds.

He senses it is not a complete lie, but Nathan remains unconvinced. The undertone is that she has an idea who it may be, but that she would take care of it. It might be worth checking out how exactly she might do that. If she makes some phone calls he has no chance, but that does not seem to be her style; Audrey confronts people in person, and that leaves a trail.

"Go home, get cleaned up and we'll go to the site as planned. Consider ourselves even, and start over." She is only wearing her blouse, highlighting the rest of her nudity, completely unselfconscious. Nathan is also struck by having this conversation without thinking about his own exposure, or that he has not even attempted to dress.

"Okay," he offers, and finally begins to look for his clothes. Once dressed and with a plan formed, Nathan leaves. He recognizes the area of her hotel as the west side of town, near the hilltop. It is quite lovely, actually, with wonderful views of downtown and the harbor to the south. Nathan plans to wait for a while, an hour at most, to see if Audrey leaves. Taking a position behind bushes in a field across from the hotel, he finds a piece of paper and pen in his jacket pocket and pretends to sketch a nearby house. It is difficult to actually do the drawing, given the pain in his head, so he just motions the pen over the paper.

He is rewarded a half hour later, as she appears in the doorway with her hair still damp from a shower. When you're following someone, and do not have the luxury of a team for zones, you have to create your own. Reversible shirts or jackets, hats, nothing too silly that might attract attention but still throws off initial image. As Audrey reminded him, the eye sees motion, then form, then color, then detail. Take care of any of the first ones, and you don't have to worry as much about the last. Of course, it never hurts to have a diversion in mind when you think they get suspicious. Most people who have been followed never know, even if they are expecting it. Nathan looks over what he is wearing, to see if he can change anything that Audrey would recognize. Seeing a lack of options, Nathan briefly considers that an inverse rule could also apply: the bigger deal, and more open the ploy, the less suspicion. It is too small a town and a bit late, he thinks, to work on Audrey. So he decides to do it the old-fashioned way, keeping his distance behind her.

Luckily she stays on foot. If she had taken a car he would have given up immediately. She walks downhill, into town, with a purposeful gait. Nathan gets up and begins his chase just as she turns right down the crossroad, heading instead towards the harbor.

The buildings are not very close to the street here, and as Nathan approaches the corner he has no problem seeing Audrey about a block ahead. He waits a minute before entering the same street, knowing if she looks over her shoulder he may not be recognizable from this distance but would still be in her line of sight. Nathan finds it becomes far more difficult to walk naturally when you are thinking about it.

Approaching an intersection, Audrey crosses the street on an angle. She quickly glances back in Nathan's direction, looking for cars. He involuntarily freezes for a second, but she just as quickly swings her head back the other way. Three houses from the next crossing she stops, reaches over the low metal gate at the edge of the street, and lets herself in.

Nathan knows she will probably check around at this point, just out of habit. He hurries his pace and ducks back around the corner where she had crossed the street, finding a decent view of the brightly painted red slab door that contrasts vividly with the whitewashed Irish cottage. Right on cue, she looks both ways and behind before ringing the bell. A few moments pass before the door opens and a gaunt man appears in the dark opening, smiling at Audrey. She raises both arms and pushes him hard at the chest and shoulders, both of them disappearing rapidly into the house. The door closes behind.

Nathan is left in disbelief on the corner. He only saw the man for a second, but that was enough: he never forgets a face.

Lost in thought, Nathan returns up the hill and walks down through the dip of Main Street to his apartment, showers, and changes. He only has to wait five minutes before his bell rings. Grabbing his jacket from the chair and a few of his notes, he runs down the steps to the bottom landing and opens the door.

"You just get done? You're worse than my girlfriends," Audrey seems cheerful.

"Like you have girlfriends," he quips.

"Where is the tablet?" she asks.

"It's safe," he nods his head up towards the apartment.

"Bring it along. If we find the other I can leave directly, take them back to our boss." Using the 'our' was a nice touch, Nathan thinks; she is trying to gain trust, rebuild the team. He returns to his apartment and reappears in the doorway carrying the bundled piece. She opens the car door for him and he sets it in the back seat before taking his place in the passenger seat.

The drive is beautiful, which Nathan decides it must always be as long as it is not storming or complete fog. Every now and then, however, Audrey makes an audible gasp or deep sigh.

"What's wrong?" he asks, less out of concern than breaking the silence.

"Nothing–just lingering effects of, you know . . ." she puts her hand to her head.

"Should I drive?" he asks out of concern, remembering the sheer cliffs coming up.

"No, I got it," Audrey replies, and they continue in uneasy silence as she tries to control her outward pain. Ten interminably quiet minutes and they arrive at the site's metal fencing. They pull in and park next to a red pickup truck. Padraigh is there, near the foundations, holding a middle-aged man by the arm and walking towards them.

"his *feirmeoir* from up the road just stopped in," Padraigh nods his head at the man, and although he used the Irish term for 'farmer' it sounded close enough that Nathan understood; besides, there is not much else up the road that he could be. "I guess he's gone to the Garda, but they just don't believe him."

"Don't believe him about what?" Audrey asks from behind, sounding concerned.

"He says he killed our Mr. Eischen," the foreman announces, pronouncing Anton's name correctly for the first time.

25

July 7, Dingle, Dingle Peninsula

"**I** SWEAR, I just wanted to scare him a bit. I broke in, then me sheep came through and right out into the road. I looked around, and a back part of the fence was also down which is how they must have come in," he points to the side of the site furthest from the road, "so I wasn't the only one breaking in that night. A bit later a car stops and I hide. The man came in, was picking around and then leaving with one of them rocks," he gestures again at the stones all around, "and I don't know, that just really made me mad. This is our heritage, and people always coming in and stealing bits of it. The British destroyed enough, I'll be damned if their Yankee cousins take the rest little by little." He stops, taking a deep breath knowing he was heading off on a tangent. "So I pick up a stone and hit him in the head. I move the rock he was carrying so he can't just get up and grab it again. Then I get the hell out."

"You 'scared' him with a rock to the head?" Nathan asks incredulously.

"I know, I know," stammers the old farmer, "but I was just so mad. I felt awful, and turned myself in the next day to the Gardaí.

But they didn't want to arrest me until they found something. There was no evidence except for a spot of blood, which could have been a sheep. Even his car was gone."

"That sounds like enough of a confession to me," Padraigh tightens his grip.

"I waited, checked back in. I heard they still hadn't found a body. It kept eating at me as time went on. I've been drinking myself to death, and the next morning feeling even worse. So I come to you," the old man pleads, "take me in."

"We're not the police." Nathan says.

"You're sure he was dead?" asks Audrey.

"Not really," the farmer thinks, "He was bloody but breathing when I left. I hit him pretty hard." He looks at each of them in turn. "I thought you'd all be more shocked, angry."

"Well, to be honest, I don't think anyone here ever liked him very much," Nathan states, "but if you felt so bad, why didn't you call for help that night."

"I must admit I had been drinking a bit. I don't usually–I'm not some Irish drunkard you know–so when I do I don't handle it so well," he looks down at his feet, and then back up at their faces again, "So no one will arrest me?"

"Go home. I don't believe Anton is dead," Nathan says.

All three stare at him.

"How do you know," the farmer asks.

"I just have a feeling," Nathan says.

"Do you know where he is? His car, his blood was here," Audrey asks.

"This isn't some psychic bullshit feeling, is it?" Padraigh follows up.

"No body, no trail to the cliff or the police would have found something. My guess is someone, maybe the other person who broke in, was still here and took him. With a blow to the head he might not remember who he is or at least what he was doing here," Nathan offers.

Padraigh reluctantly lets go of the man's arm. The farmer looks around and, defeated once again in his attempt to pay for his crimes, begins to walk up the road. He throws a few glances back, perhaps hoping the three of them would change their minds.

"So now what?" the foreman asks, "It is Saturday. I wasn't here to work if that's what you had in mind. Just checking security."

"I take it you know Audrey Mays here?" Nathan asks.

"Of course, ma'am. You've been to the site a few times, but I haven't formally introduced myself. Padraigh O'Malley," he flashes a grin and offers a craggy hand.

"A lot of O'Malley's around here," Nathan observes.

"We're a plague," he says with a wink.

Audrey and Nathan look at each other. "Excuse us a moment," Nathan begins to walk up towards the new foundations, Audrey a few steps behind. "I don't want a lot of questions," she says, "I think today we need to be alone. If we need help or any equipment we can call." They walk back and tell the foreman the job site will be shut down another day. He leaves with a wave and a promise to return early on Monday. They are alone again, buffeted by the sound of wind and waves. The sky looks ominous, threatening to break loose. "I wish we had a way to narrow it down," Audrey looks around the inestimable piles.

"Like a rock detector?" Nathan asks, mockingly.

"What if it's already gone? Either that night the farmer was here, or five hundred years ago."

"You're not a positive thinker are you?" he frowns at her, "Just give me a minute, I need to put it all together." He ponders all the pieces in his mind, feeling there is something he is missing.

Whenever he cannot remember something, Nathan tends to explore a different direction hoping it will come to him on some lateral path. "How well did you know Anton?" he asks, preoccupied. He is scanning the foundations of the structure Eischen had started. Some of Nathan's changes have already begun, but the remnants of Anton's previous structure are still there. Nathan studies their shape.

"Not too well. Professional; nothing like you," she quips, breaking Nathan's concentration enough for him to look up. "Great focus, well organized," she observes, watching Nathan move around the site.

"You respect him?"

Audrey takes the cue. "He's the kind of guy who feels he has built up so much strength that he feels useless when not using it," she expands, "but instead of waiting around, hoping for things to go bad so he can spring into action, he actually makes things go wrong." Her analysis complete, she turns her own question, "How do you know he's not dead?"

"Because I just saw you with him," he stops what he is doing to turn towards her, an awkward attempt at dramatizing his revelation.

Her eyes tighten in a look of dismay and anger at having been followed. "You shithead" she shakes her head in dismay, concern masked in her expletive.

Nathan walks over scattered stones to one of the ancient beehive huts. It is difficult to tell which stones were once part of the structures, and which are simply part of the earth. "I assume I get paid as long as I do the work. As to why he chose to disappear and bring me in, I can only assume he was failing. What I would like to know is why he drugged us. Did you find that out during your little visit?" he pointedly asks.

"He swears it wasn't him," she responds.

"Then who?" If it was not Anton, Nathan considers the more disturbing thought that someone completely unknown is toying with them. First angry, and then confused, at the sight of his old friend, he had found some comfort in knowing the danger.

"I don't know. I thought he was the only possibility," she admits.

"And here I thought he might be jealous," Nathan teases.

"Jealous of what?" she asks.

"This must be where Anton was searching," he changes the subject, pointing at an area of stacked stones, "the pile is different here, organized in that anal way I would expect from him."

Nathan spots a strange discoloration and moves closer. The rain has made something run like a rust streak down the stones below. It was especially odd that all the other stones were pitched to shed water out, typical in this mortarless masonry wall, except something is causing water to enter here. He pulls with some effort on a stone next to the stain's source. Working it back and forth, the stone finally comes loose. With a last pull he repositions his hands to catch its weight. The movement of the stone also dislodges something else–something almost as large as the stone itself–and Nathan jumps back to get out of its way as it falls to the ground near his feet.

26

YOUNG NOVICE CIARAN sits alone in blackness, waiting for his eyes to adjust, dizzy from the ghastly scenes which had awoken him. It is a small chamber, dark and cold and prone to receiving cooking smells from neighboring ovens; but it is his and his alone. He had never known such luxury, having always shared a small shelter with parents and older brothers and sisters, seven in a space maybe twice this. They spent most of their time outdoors, of course, in fields and boats. If his father knew how much time he spends inside now, in prayer and in his studies, he would no doubt declare it downright unhealthy, and certainly no way for a man to live.

His current home, much like his previous, is built of posts with wattle and daub. Unlike his family's little village, the monastery is rigidly organized, no doubt an influence of the Roman part of the Roman Church. Even here, at the edge of this spreading Faith, the physical structure, trappings, and sometimes arcane rituals become synonymous with core beliefs. Whatever its inspiration, for Ciaran this monastery is the largest settlement he had ever seen, at least until seeing the Vision still swirling in his mind. The greater dormitory structure, where he now sits, is clustered around an open courtyard marking the western edge transition between the most sacred space of the church and the rest of the enclosure. Ciaran's cell is part of a larger structure, though some monks inhabit small circular stone huts. The church itself is a small stone building devoid of windows, slightly rectangular in plan, with a thatched roof. The only light comes in through a door on the west side.

The entire monastery is surrounded by a slightly oval enclosure of stone and ditch, both of which he has helped build and repair. Everything they need is here: water, mills, gardens and workshops. Everyone awakes shortly after middle night, pray and then nap again until prayers at sunrise. After that they pray every three hours, they study Latin, read and labor between. Sometimes the labor is in gardens or shops, sometimes it is writing script. Ciaran enjoys the writing most, having done enough labor as a boy on fishing boats and in fields.

He moves over to a small chair and table, a journey of perhaps two steps. Ciaran guesses there is about half an hour before he and the other monks will be summoned to first prayers of the new day, after which he may return to sleep. This time of year the sun rises early and days are long, so every moment of sleep is precious. The fact he is wasting some of that time now is frustrating, but the Vision which woke him is vibrant, insistent. There would be no sleep anytime soon.

Ciaran leans hunched over, hands folded with his elbows on thighs, sorting through images and details. He keeps writing materials in his cell to purge himself of messages he receives, otherwise he would not return to sleep at all. He has become adept at writing in the dark, although sometimes the sight of his words in morning light is seldom as crafted as his memory. Even with the upcoming distraction of prayers, he doubts he could return to sleep this night without leaving these images elsewhere.

Picking up the cut reed he uses as a pen, he feels around for the rough parchment scrap he saved, and orients himself to the upper corner using his left hand as a guide. For private use he is allowed some ink made from egg whites, soot, and honey, mixed until a smooth paste. Unlike the expensive colored inks they use for manuscripts, this is simple and does not dry out easily when kept covered.

The greatest gift Ciaran received from his Church is the ability to read and write its language. What an incredible way to communicate, so transcendent from the word of mouth through which all other stories he knows had been passed. He could write something now, and even after he is gone others would read his words; not the interpretation of the next storyteller, but his very own words. There are many questions he has about this Faith, but such a gift is worthy of his time and dedication. As a boy, Ciaran had learned to read some of the Ogham script found on corners of large stone slabs near his home. It was crude and factual and mostly said things like someone was a son of someone else, and which tribe he belonged to. The Roman alphabet of the Church is a thing of wonder, able to capture stories and preserve them forever.

In septemptrione et meridiano duae urbes magnae nascuntur Ciaran writes, unable to see the words but feeling their release. Two large cities rise, one to the north and one to the south. They grow and press on the land, until the armies from the east come, *Ab oriente acies.*

Meridianus devictum, septemptio oppugnatum. The fortress of the south will fall, and a great city to the north is under siege. Ciaran continues, sometimes struggling for the words in his mind to write the most succinct translation. It is the description of a memory of a dream. The feeling is strong—horror, helplessness, hope—and his heart tells him he must somehow warn others, despite its inevitability. Telling the Abbot may help, but even as he describes it he knows these are events far in the future. The size of the cities!

He is still a very young man, just a few years from being a boy. It was just this kind of vision that brought him to the monastery in the first place, a warning Ciaran had felt compelled to deliver that intrigued the Abbot, who then talked him into staying. Ciaran had meant well enough; just deliver his message and go. On his way from his home, his mother had warned that he would not be believed, perhaps even mocked or seen as some kind of evil. He himself had thought it would be a long journey to deliver a message no one would believe. However, the dreams were insistent; if he did not make the journey they would continue to haunt him. Now it is two years later. He wondered even then if the Abbot had a similar gift, an ability to see as Ciaran sees, and perhaps even knows if this gift is truly divine or simply an anomaly of birth.

Like most dreams, many of his visions mean very little or fade into ether without notice. Every now and then something powerful, something ancient, disturbs his mind. Such was the recurring image that brought him here. Ciaran had an apparition of an object, in his dream vaguely stone-like but not like those around which his family tried to eke out an existence. This one looked different, felt different, and it actually possessed and radiated energy like the sun. Its power, however, was not the message; Ciaran had no interest in possessing such a force. The lesson was a warning of its effect on people, on society, even on what would become his Church.

He had seen his own arrival on a land familiar but unimaginably far away. Ciaran knows his fate is integral to these visions, accepting it much like his father accepted the struggle of the sea as his fate. Unlike the nondescript existence of his father, however, others would learn of Ciaran's voyage. He already senses these others in pursuit of him, of his crossing which has not yet occurred and a prize yet unseen.

This night's vision is related, he is certain, and will no doubt haunt him for evenings to come. The message is similar–the danger of these sacred stones falling in wrong hands–but the place of horror was set closer, here in the land that is his home.

Images in his mind fade. In the time before last, the pause between moments, it all seemed so clear. The feeling is still there, but the details soften to blurs. He stretches a finger from his writing hand, careful not to lose his place in the pitch black, and gauges how many lines he has written.

He will review this again in morning light, when he must also consider what to do with it. The parchment may not be ready to be shared, and Ciaran is certainly not ready to tell the Abbot. He hopes it is a message that will serve to warn, or at least prepare, his brothers for trials to come. The thought that he is crazy often crossed his mind, yet too many times these things came to be; they could not be ignored, no matter how far in the future these events may occur. It could also be that he is simply slipping a message into the ether for it to disintegrate, its only purpose to ease his own mind and let him sleep.

One of the older monks passes his cell, calling all to the first prayer of the day. Rushing to finish a final entry before leaving, Ciaran wonders if he is doing the right thing. This power he sees may too dangerous even for his Church. Yet these brothers, who he is about to join in worship of a god he is still unsure about, seem the only chance. They must know, they must be warned, the pieces must be scattered.

Fragmenta dilata et occulta sunt.

27

July 7, Dunquin, Dingle Peninsula

I T LIES THERE dried and cracked, yet still strong and flexible; like an old balloon skin, or a pig pounded flat. The bundle landed with a thud on the damp ground, and Nathan instinctively rushed to pick it up and protect it. Obviously an old package, it bears wear marks to show that it has been opened repeatedly, added to, and now seems stretched to capacity.

The outer wrapping is a strange material: burlap-like, but smoother. Probably some animal hide, Nathan thinks, certainly not chosen for its beauty but effective to keep moisture out. He unrolls it a few flaps, and inside is a heavy piece of paper with a number of phrases written carefully in black ink. The upper right corner of the top piece has a date on it: *1928*. It is wrapped around another, more yellowed piece. This second piece is blistered and warped from age and moisture, but Nathan can make out the same first few badly faded phrases. This is wrapped around several more pieces, some with a discernable mark here or there, but all either faded beyond recognition or completely blank. The two bottom pieces look like they had been written over in the same place so many times there are holes in the material.

"Do you understand what this says?" Audrey looks over his shoulder.

"No. Not the first four lines, but I think I know these last two," he points at the bottom of the page where there is a longer line of words. This script, however, looked to be in a different hand than the others. "This long one here is a Latin quote from one of the oldest books on architecture. If I remember, it goes something like 'Never let greed for glory impel you to embark rashly on anything that is unusual or without precedent.' Alberti, end of book 9 of the De Re Aedificatoria."

"Impressive," she says.

"Not really. I remember it because we studied this in school and Anton and I were on opposite sides of that argument. We had quite a few discussions, so it stuck. He was wrong, of course."

"So what about the last line?"

"Simple numbers. *Novem ex octo*, nine from eight. I've done a few cornerstones in Latin," Nathan explains. "*Antepagmentum superis* is the fancy architectural term for a lintel over a doorway."

"If it pertains to what we're looking for, that's the best clue yet," she says.

"The nine from eight confirms what I understood from the diagram on back of the Chorin tablet. I think eight of these huts were original, and a ninth one was built later with the stone in it. The lintel might be a location in the hut, but we have to narrow down which of the nine is the odd one out. I thought I recognized the layout when we were in Berlin, but now that I'm here–for lack of a better phrase–I don't know which way is up on the plan. But I think I know who might be able to tell us."

Nathan stands to yell at Padraigh, asking if the farmer is still around. Padraigh points at the old man, still within sight walking slowly up the road. The foreman gets in his truck, and within five minutes the two wizened men are standing in front of Nathan and Audrey, still crouching over their find. The farmer seems a bit nervous upon seeing the opened bundle of papers.

"Is this yours?" Nathan asks.

The farmer pauses a moment, considering his answer. Realizing he has already given it away, he decides on truth. "Yes."

"What is it?"

"Something my family has been charged with for generations. Ever since it happened, I imagine. Every two or three generations we recopy the script and put it back. For centuries, it's been. I suppose it doesn't matter now, it's all happened so long ago and I have no one to pass it along to."

"What does it say?" Audrey asks.

"My grandfather said it tells the story of the rise of Galway and Limerick, and then Cromwell coming, Limerick falling and Galway under siege, and how then our people are scattered. I'm not really sure, we just copy the words."

"So your family's been doing this since the 1600's?" Nathan is incredulous. His own family could barely keep anything for a single generation; he knew nothing of his grandfather, let alone his great grandfather.

"Possibly longer, my grandpa had a fantastic story that some of the paper were very ancient, and that the whole thing was foretold and not just a history. I don't know about that, but it has been a tradition, something that gave my family great pride, even if it is old news. I have felt a great burden that I have no children, no way to carry it on. After all this time, I am the one responsible for breaking the chain."

"Is this your writing, then?" Nathan asks, before considering the year written on top.

"No, me grandfather."

"But the fifth and sixth lines, they look newer," Nathan follows up.

"There're only four lines," the farmer replies, "I know them by heart, if not what they mean," he turns to Padraigh.

"Look, right here," Audrey points at the bottom of the sheet.

"Not me. There are only four lines," he insists. "It probably means shite," the farmer sighs heavily. "What are you going to do with it?"

Audrey answers, "I'm not sure it means as much to us as it does to you. We'll just put it back and you can do what you think best."

"Aye," he nods, "if only you would do that with all our history. I didn't trust that other fella," the farmer says, referring to Anton, "I think he would have taken anything he could carry."

"But is it important enough to brain him?" Nathan stands in confrontation. The farmer bows his head, avoiding Nathan's eyes, and turns back towards the road. He walks away, beginning his journey again without a word. Padraigh follows him out, offering the old man a ride but being waved off.

Nathan and Audrey are silent, and once more alone. "A hell of a tradition, who knows how far back," he observes. "Back in the day, farmers out here at the edge of the world learning to write enough to carry this on for hundreds of years; they must have felt part of something important, timeless."

"Maybe that's what he was doing here," Audrey gestures at the receding figure repeating his steps up the road, "seeing if we found anything."

"Why hasn't anyone found this before?" Nathan asks, "And are we really going to put it back?"

"It's probably been uncovered before, but put back out of respect. I suggest we do the same, or that farmer will come back for you," she warns.

"So let's get this straight, take the stone but leave the parchment?" he clarifies.

"Something passed down from generation to generation, cared for; that belongs here. The stone does not."

"Plus, if we leave it here they may not know the stone is gone," Nathan cuts to the underlying reason.

"I thought of that too," she admits.

"*Fragmenta*: fragments or pieces. This may tell us why it was broken up, but doesn't seem useful in finding it." He looks at the paper again. "The last two lines are by Anton or someone as close to finding it as we are."

Nathan studies the parchments a few more minutes, but getting nothing else, he repackages it and hands it back to Audrey. She puts the bundle back and replaces the stone that had exposed it, as closely as she could remember. Then they both find a low wall to sit for a minute.

"Precedent," Nathan mulls it over. "Something Anton studied to come up with his design. Maybe it's not as awful as I thought; just contorted because of some kind of meaning or message he put in it." He stands up quickly. "Help me measure this," he points at the new construction. Nathan hands her the end of a tape measure borrowed from Padraigh. As he directs her around the foundations, he jots down some measurements in the notepad from his jacket pocket; first lengthwise, then crosswise. Then they measure each hut, estimating the diameter and height as best they can. Once they have finished he sits down on the edge of the concrete wall, working through the numbers.

"So what is it we're doing here?" she finally queries.

"Phi, the Golden Section," he says, pointing over his shoulder at the foundations. Her quizzical look tells him she needs a bit more elaboration. "The ratio of 1 to 1.618. You'll find it prevalent through all architecture," he explains, "from the pyramids to classical Greek and Roman designs. You'll even find it in modern plans and elevations. Architects, craftsman almost everyone imposes some kind of numerology. They do it out of instinct or training, or out of a hope that by doing so–and after all you have to do *something* anyway–you are also imposing a meaning. Like the farmer was recopying an old manuscript."

"So it means something. Will it help narrow down the search?" she asks.

"Probably not; almost any architect would recognize it, and none of these huts fit the proportion. If it means anything other than Anton showing off his history, it would be a message to me that there are more numbers, more symbols, hidden here to look for." Nathan steps up on the edge of the foundation and points generally at the series of half-buried concrete walls below him. "Look at that! There's no need for all these foundation walls in this kind of soil and rock. It's a classic nine-square grid problem, pushed and pulled to not be too obvious, with only eight squares. The ninth square is that one over there," he points at a stray square of concrete, hollow in the middle, about the size of a garden shed.

"You know back in Berlin you said . . ."

"Well, I know *about* where it is," he admits, "I didn't want to be left behind." Nathan pulls the rubbing from the stone out of his inside jacket pocket. "The eight circles on the diagram are in exactly the same plan layout here, right down to that sort of offset hut over there. However, as you can plainly see, there are nine huts, nine circles total."

"So like you said, one was built later and we know it's not in there, which leaves us with eight, or the one not in the diagram is the one we are looking for," Audrey concludes.

"I think Anton is directing us here. If we orient the diagram with his foundation diagram, then the hut we're looking for is . . ." he searches for a second, "that one." He points at a medium-sized *clochán* in between a corner hut and the one that is a bit offset. "There was something else on the Chorin stone: the words 'diatoni' and 'araeostyle'. The first refers to a through stone, one that extends full depth of the wall. My guess is the one we are looking for is next to one, not a through stone itself. The other is a proportion, a space four times the diameter of a column. Since there are no columns, I'm going to go for a height four times the width of the wall. Now the question is," Nathan asks pointedly, "if Anton knew all this, why the ruse? Why leave us to find it, and take the wrong stone himself? More importantly, why doesn't he get his ass down here to help look for it?"

"He may have never seen the back of the Chorin stone. As for what he was doing here that night, I don't know."

"Why did you, why are you, keeping him secret?"

"You think I could have gotten the help? I don't feel like being out here forever, as lovely as it is I would rather be home," she explains. "Seriously, would you have taken this job otherwise? Come all the way out here?"

"Probably not. There was also a bit of a setback on one of my other jobs that made the timing fortuitous." Too fortuitous, he muses. "But why would Anton build in so many clues?"

"Anton says he always does that. He has a method for leaving his research so that someone he knows, namely you, could finish it if anything goes wrong. You would probably be surprised how many other jobs–other whole buildings–are out there with built-in messages to you, just in case."

"Sounds expensive," Nathan says, gauging the thickness of the wall near the doorway and then using his arm as a measuring device to find a height four times that. He then looks around that area above the door, ducking in and out, searching for a stone that appears to run all the way through. He marks two possibilities with chalk found near the new foundations.

"Meeting a budget is usually not a concern," she says, and as the sun comes out again she takes off her jacket, still protected from cool winds by a long sleeved shirt. "Should we get started?"

After removing just three stones off the top, Nathan realizes the complexity and subtlety of construction. He uses the chalk again, marking pieces so they can be put back later. They work in silence, paying attention to how each stone is placed. Although Audrey appears frustrated with the slow pace, Nathan suspects she may appreciate the opportunity to more thoroughly cover their tracks. He, of course, sees it more as a necessary historic preservation measure. After the first hour they step back and take a look at how far they had come, and how far they would still need to go to reach the lintel area over the door.

"This is going to take forever," she sighs. "And what if you're wrong? The ancient mind probably worked a lot differently than how we're guessing at this."

"I doubt it," Nathan replies. "The physical reality, the things we build, are an expression of the spiritual world. Though styles have changed, that simple fact has not. The underlying meaning or purpose of how they built, the way they would have gone about securing something of importance, is basically the same as today."

"So what's the purpose?" Her questions seem mostly aimed at passing time. It is difficult for Nathan to tell from her tone if she cares or not.

"Reminders, instruction on what it is to be human," he answers.

"Wouldn't the local cults have had different views on that, compared to the Christians who took over?" Maybe she does care, he thinks. Nathan begins to wonder what her religious views are, the way she had said *the Christians* was curious.

"If you walk into almost any civil building, especially neoclassical ones like we have in the States, you'll find the same alignments as Neolithic ceremonial centers; set to cardinal directions, every bench symmetrical. You can imagine future archeologists describing our worship of ancient leaders. If I learned anything in architecture school it's the perspective that we share an unbroken lineage across cultures and continents. We sometimes think to ourselves that it has never been better than it is now and we are superior to anything before us. They thought the same thing. We are just the next step of those ancient ages, and will soon be the next lost civilization," he hesitates a moment, examining his work more closely. "I guess I wanted to be part of that. Creating the monuments, hopefully creating those future clues."

As they fall back into silence, Nathan remembers Professor Moynihan's words. The first day of class the Professor had come in, full flourish, and after the effect of his entrance had settled in to the young students, he began in biblical tones "First there was the Line, and the Line became Form. But Form was already there, the line just captured it: the greatest capture since the naming of gravity. Think about that. Class dismissed." That was it, his first class lasting all of a minute and leaving young Nathan bewildered. Worse yet, he had woken up at seven in the morning with a hangover to get there. As much as he sometimes could be nostalgic for those days, there was no way Nathan would ever want to go back. *I've come too far*, he thinks before questioning, *or have I really*? There would be time to ponder this in the next hours, he decides.

The day goes quickly, despite painstaking work. A storm blows through, causing them to seek shelter in one of the huts. Nathan is amazed at how well the ancient structure still sheds water, even wind-driven rain. Twenty minutes later it is sunny again, but as they emerge they realize how much lower the sun is in the sky. In less than two hours, he figures, the sun would dip below the horizon and they would have to go home or find a new source of light, the latter choice certainly drawing unwanted attention. The rumbling of his belly marks a time all its own.

Still working together–Audrey clearing a piece, Nathan marking it and then laying it in order to the side on the ground–they reach the area he originally marked two feet above the lintel stone. If it is here, they should be close.

Removing the next stone they get a glimpse of something different. A portion below is lighter, even faintly veined unlike all the other ones they have seen. Although just a small corner is revealed, Nathan and Audrey look at each other and smile at their success. Success, and relief.

28

ONCE THE SIDES of the inscribed tablet are clear, Nathan and Audrey each take an edge, and with a concerted pull and gentle twist it comes free from its hiding place. There is at best an hour of sunlight remaining, but it is perhaps the first light this relic has seen in a thousand years. The stone had been placed sideways to completely conceal it, long edge vertical and slightly angled to accommodate the curve of hut wall. Once found, Nathan and Audrey had to resist the urge of prying it loose, and instead take the time to dismantle surrounding structure until it was clear and not in danger of scraping or chipping.

Each still holding a side, they maneuver their way down the side of the hut together and set it level on a nearby foundation wall. They stand side by side, transfixed with the piece. For Audrey this moment has been a long time in the making. This is what she needed to find; the second piece in Chorin just a bonus. To Nathan, this finding of an ancient artifact is an accomplishment, more of a thrill rather than the sense of relief and culmination Audrey feels.

"It look just like the other one, only the edges are different," she assesses. "Same markings on the front."

"Those markings weren't much use last time; let's see if there's anything on the other side," Nathan turns it over. Across the back are a series of arcs and circles. "Here we go," he proclaims. Nathan studies it for a few minutes under the flashlight. There is still some light left in the sky, but not enough to discern if the ancient markings are language or diagram. "The other was a map. I don't recognize this, but I wouldn't have recognized the other one either if I hadn't been here first."

"I might know this. If this small ellipse is Ireland, then these by proportion could be Iceland and Greenland. And this," she points at the deepest cut, a small point surrounded by an irregular line looking like a bird's beak and eye, located where the bird's cheek would be, "this is home." She shakes her head in amazement, tracing the line, "New Brunswick down here and Newfoundland up above, and if this arc is the north side of Nova Scotia, then this is my island." She looks up with an innocence of wonder and recognition in her eyes, "Trust me when I say there's nothing else out there."

"Well, maybe I was sent to watch over you, not vice versa." Nathan stands back up, "Let's get this structure put back together so we can study it further. Before we fly all the way to Canada, we want to make sure it's not just down the road here."

Audrey looks up again, this time seriously quiet. Nathan knows he is making a presumption; his job might be done. Excited and in the moment, he feels invested, wanting to see this through to the outcome. He would love to be there when they deliver the pieces, to meet his employer, and see when he behold not one but two artifacts.

Deciding not to push it right now, and have to *ask* if he can come along like some pesky younger sibling, he focuses his attention at rebuilding what they had torn apart. The first order of business is to find a piece about the same size as the one they had removed, to take its place. He scans the site, finally settling on two stones that together could fill the gap; there is a piece of concrete that could work, but that would be sacrilege to his sense of architectural morality.

The unknown behind them, having found what they were looking for, they are in a much better mood. At least Nathan is. Audrey is being very quiet, and stopping every so often to rest. His system for marking the stones seems to be working, and once she understood the order quickly falls into a rhythm of teamwork where she passes the stone up to Nathan, who stands partway up the hut to manage the brunt of heavy lifting and placing. Laying the dry stones without mortar goes very quickly when they have already been matched. They pause rather often to rest their arms, but otherwise progress quickly in silence.

As with most physical labor, Nathan's mind begins to wander while his body goes into automatic. If she does take him along for the next leg, would he actually be of any use? He thinks he has proven useful so far, surprising even himself. Maybe these years, learning and making connections, have not been wasted. Maybe his career choice was exactly what was needed in order to accomplish, what? What the hell is this anyway? Nathan realizes how little he actually knows, how little he has questioned. What fairy tale of immortality is he willing to swallow in order to get laid? That was probably his main motivation after all, he thinks, he may as well admit it.

Although as this puzzle, this latest diagram, redirects them from something he may understand to something only Audrey would have recognized, Nathan considers another possibility: perhaps he was hired to be the Watcher and not the Watched. If Anton and his client know his past, look beyond his innocent demeanor, they would understand his advantage. He is, he thinks, and always has been the walking epitome of "he seemed like such a normal guy"- the one neighbors are shocked by when they learn he did something horribly wrong. In high school he was the metal head with short hair and button down shirts, in college the alternative guy far more extreme than those wearing the right clothes and make-up. He had always just dipped his toes, though, only testing the waters of what lay beyond. Nathan still wonders what kind of Truth is out there; he has never crossed the Line, not fully. He marveled at, as much as reviled, those that made the leap he could not. The brilliance of those cannibals, those psychopaths, and the freedom they must feel after the first killing, the first transgression. Why the hell was he thinking this now, he wonders? Does he think if he continues with Audrey he might get that chance; that she has crossed the line and would show him the way? Nathan sees a dark knowing in her eyes, an acceptance of some experienced horror. She had no qualms stripping him raw on that plane, and that brief taste was probably just a fraction of what she may have endured. It is unlikely that kind of knowledge can be shared: to understand, to cross the line needs to be one's own experience. All epiphanies are solo, personal. Nathan knows himself, his patterns. He would only go so far and then flee when it starts to become real. *What am I saying?* he voices to himself, *I've been in more danger than I ever have been since I got here, and I want more.* Maybe this is his epiphany, and the Line is being crossed. He shakes his head clear, stretches his shoulders and back and then the muscles in his face around the eyes. He must be tired.

The low sun begins to lose color as strands of wispy fog spread. Soon the mass of fog flows in, heavy and swirling in winds off the Atlantic. Moving like a low cloud, its density not only conceals their vision but muffles all sound as well. As the outer edge envelops him, Nathan stops his work to experience the sensation. It could work in their favor, he thinks, keeping any curious passersby from stopping in, though surprisingly few people have passed by for a Saturday. The road past this site, though one of the most beautiful in Ireland, sometimes has a habit of washing out. Tourists were probably right now crowding the next peninsula south, and that was alright by Nathan, who felt for a moment he was alone on the edge of the world.

They continue to rebuild the hut, moving more swiftly as completion is in sight. Audrey passes the last two stones up to Nathan as he looks up and around, feeling watched. Standing atop the nearly rebuilt beehive hut there is no relief against increasing winds off the Atlantic, and the fog has brought a chilling dampness much worse than the earlier downpours. Dampness coats their whole bodies, covering even their eyelids with thick moisture and penetrating clothes, soaking them to the very bone.

The last piece is in place, and with satisfaction of a complete mission and relief to get out of miserable weather before complete darkness, he looks down toward Audrey with a smile. It quickly fades as he sees they are now half surrounded by nebulous forms in the gray mist. Twelve, maybe fifteen people materialize, about half women and half men in differently colored jackets. They stand quietly, motionless among the beehive huts, all focusing on Nathan. He stops in place, mirroring their frozen stance. Over a dozen people like statues in a small area, the only person moving about is Audrey just below him. *Audrey*, Nathan thinks.

"Get in the car," he commands in an urgent whisper.

"Why, what's up?" she asks, not looking up from the stone.

"Turn around," Nathan warns.

Audrey cranes her neck around, right then left. Looking back up at him she shrugs her shoulders and gives him a confused look.

"Don't you see them?" he asks, his voice hushed.

"See who?" she repeats the motion, pausing longer to look around, "is the farmer back?" She moves closer to the hut and Nathan, still scanning the area.

"Just get in the car," Nathan knows that out here, in this weather, all light may fade in moments and once gone it will be pitch black. The car would be the safest place, and chance for escape. Audrey looks at him quizzically, but complies. Picking up the stone with some effort, she clutches it against her chest and stomach, arms wrapped tightly around. With several steps she disappears into the fog, leaving Nathan to face the arc of watchers. As he scans the mist-concealed figures, he returns to a gaunt presence standing next to the neighboring hut.

"Anton?" Nathan calls out, "is that you?"

There is no answer, other than the figure raising his right arm. At first Nathan thinks he is pointing, but it is something else in his hand. The man has a gun. Instinctively Nathan ducks and slides down the back side of the hut, putting the structure between him and Anton. Once down, he gets his bearings and makes a dash for the car, praying the whole way he does not trip over all the stones, foundations, debris, and construction equipment scattered around this dark gray world.

29

BARRELING THROUGH THE construction fence, their car fishtails as Nathan takes a hard fast right onto the narrow road. He narrowly misses a knee-high stone wall on the opposite side, the sole purpose of which seems to be to damage a car as much as possible before it encounters a three hundred feet drop to the Atlantic Ocean. He is going fast. Too fast for a road the width of an alley, especially when visibility is just a few feet. As he increases his speed, Nathan feels like a fish in muddy water being chased by a predator, the danger of hitting something, or getting lost, only slightly less scary than what is behind.

"Slow down," Audrey is wide-eyed, more confused than scared by Nathan's abrupt entry into the car. She thought he looked spooked, and now regrets having chosen the passenger seat. Feeling weak from the long day, she thought she might have a nap on the way back to Dingle; Nathan's frantic demand for keys and sudden stomp on the gas pedal clearly punctuating this would not happen.

"They're right behind!" Nathan exclaims adamantly.

She looks behind, trying to see through swirls of fog they cut through. "There's no one chasing us," she reassures. Audrey lets him focus on the road, at least what they can see of it. They are at Dunbeg, the foot of Mount Eagle, heading east away way from Dingle. She has driven this road several times, and knows it can be treacherous even in good conditions. This speed, in thick fog, is simply suicide. She denies her instinct to brace a hand against the dashboard, wondering instead if Nathan has any idea of the bends, cliff faces, and vertical drops to the ocean he is hurtling them towards.

"Where are we going?" she tries to sound reasonable, calm. The car bumps a low stone wall, scraping the front left as the road suddenly veers right. The lane is conservatively wide enough for one: if they meet anyone at this speed, in this visibility, they would be doomed.

"Don't they believe in signs?" he asks back, cursing the predicament, heart racing from shadows of light he thinks he can see in the rear view mirror.

"Slow the fuck down!" Audrey screams, trying a different tack. Nothing happens. A few lights up the hill to the right announce Fahan, a gathering of farms barely deserving a name. Up ahead, she remembers, the road takes a sharp right, avoiding a crease in the land. She decides, for her own sake, she had better let him scare himself out of this, "All right, if we're doing this then you better be ready for a sharp left."

Nathan sends the car skidding when his lights end at a sheer cliff face rising up from a washed-out section of road. Even with her warning, he is unprepared for the suddenness of the turn or how narrowly he misses running high speed into a wall of stone. The fold of earth continues up the mountainside, causing a natural collection point for water that the road builders must have been overly optimistic about, or simply had no other choice. The car lurches and complains as he swings it left through the water and stones of this makeshift riverbed. The road beyond hugs the coast, marking a vertical midway point between the sea below and the peak of Mount Eagle above. On this whole southern side of the peninsula the slope falls steeply away to the sea, but it is especially dramatic here as he races on toward the southwestern tip of Slea Head.

Around the bend where the Blasket Islands would be visible, the fog is somehow even thicker, and Audrey is losing patience. She searches her memory for hazards ahead, remembering the land changes shape, less brutal and more sensual but equally treacherous. Collected lights announce a small village, probably Dunquin. Audrey looks back, gauging how long she can see the lights of the town to determine how far back anyone chasing them would need to be before she sees them. A few seconds are all; still no one. "You know, you could just pull in somewhere and if anyone is chasing us they would go right by. You couldn't ask for better cover," she tries to reason, then adding for good measure, "by the way, if we live I'm going to kill you."

"If he's leaving clues, why would he be trying to kill me?" Nathan remains focused on the road, but as he begins to register what he saw, what he is doing now, and somehow this floated to the top of major issues.

"Who?"

"Anton."

"You're being paranoid."

"Paranoid?!" he looks at Audrey, who now cannot help but grab the dashboard.

"Keep your damn eyes where you're driving," she chides, "or just pull over!"

Nathan returns attention to his few feet of road, slowing down.

He realizes he is exhausted from concentrating, hands clenched and unblinking eyes. The effort of the chase seems to have been worth it, as there is no sign of his pursuers.

The fog finally thins, with visibility expanding to a quarter mile. They follow a shallower incline north past Clogher Head before turning back inland. The road is no wider than before, and they do not even bother suggesting a center dividing line, probably saving a bundle in paint. This inland road, at least, lacks the sheer drop-off into the Atlantic. Here the asphalt path feels less hewn out of rock and more sunken, depressed from the weight of so many centuries of travel. Even layer after layer of modern black surface cannot lift it to grade level.

In a final burst of fear-induced adrenaline Nathan pulls the car over. Audrey watches in confused relief as he jumps out, opens the back door, picks up the bundled stone and begins running through a grassy field and up a hill, back into the thicker fog stratifying above the level of the car.

Audrey gets out, walking in the same direction. She assumes he would not get far, and in a few moments is proven correct as she sees him just ahead struggling under the stone's weight. "Stop," she cautions, "I don't want you running off a cliff carrying a heavy stone," smirking a bit at the image.

Conceding to fatigue, Nathan drops to his knees. He bows his head, wanting to lie down, but thinking twice about the wet ground. Searching his memory, thinking back and starting to realize, he looks up at Audrey who now hovers over him with a concerned look. "What the fuck was that?" he manages.

"It's all right; just shadows in the fog. Shadows often complicate judgment."

"I saw them. They were all around us."

"Nathan," she lowers her voice, trying to sound soothing, "there was no one there. There wasn't anyone chasing us."

He searches for a moment and shakes his head, repeating, pleading with her to remember it the same way, "But I *saw* them."

She puts a hand on his shoulder, encouraging him to stand up. He sighs heavily and still clutching the stone lets her lead him back to the car, feet sinking into the wet grassy field. Nearby a few curious sheep with blue paint marks on dirty white coats huddle, watching as they pass. Audrey leads Nathan across the street and around the small car to the passenger side, where he deposits the stone in the back, and then slumps down heavily in the front seat. Audrey takes over the driver position, and with a slow look behind pulls out to continue in the direction they had been heading, at least saving Nathan the humiliation of turning the car around.

They pass through Teeravane, then a few more miles before she slows down. The white sign, barely visible as they pass, reads "*Baile An Fheirtéaraigh*". Ballyferriter. There are two or three pubs along the main street, each of which have seem to drawn a healthy contingent of locals and tourists alike, sheltering them from the weather. Audrey stops at the first one, a long Gaelic name in gold letters on black under wavering lights.

"Let's just get a drink, calm down," she suggests, turning off the engine. Inside the familiar warmth and din of chatter, punctuated by laughter and loud cursing, begin to work their magic, soothing Nathan's nerves until he himself begins to question what he saw. He even begins to feel abashed, putting their lives in danger in a run from nothing. They talk sincerely, earnestly, as Audrey tries to figure out what exactly he saw. He is thankful for her not dismissing him outright, which is what he expected.

"Maybe the place is haunted," she lightens the mood without changing subject, "We could go back and burn some sage or something."

"Well, burning sage isn't going to cleanse my pants," he says appreciatively.

Audrey points at the picture of small church-like structure on the wall, a local landmark in stone built around the time of the beehive huts they had just left, but very different in shape. Next to it is a model of a small boat, looking the invert of the other. "Curious; one keeps water out from below and the other from above with the same shape."

He looks at the pair. "Probably had more to do with gravity and compressive forces. Gaudi would figure out structure by hanging wire and strings with weights attached, forming a rough upside-down model of the building. The wires and strings would naturally fall into parabolic curves and catenaries under tension, finding a balance. When he would then turn it back over," Nathan gestures more animatedly than usual, a combination of beer, hunger and talking about something he knows, "it would form a system of pure compression arches: a natural way to figure out structure of a building, and a method people probably understood a long time ago. We tend to forget as technology develops."

"Can't you just appreciate it for looking cool?" she asks.

"I do appreciate it. I just thought you would appreciate it even more if you knew the complexity of it."

"No. Not so much," she responds.

Nathan laughs and relaxes. He looks around the room, soaking in the comradery, the beautiful social living room of the village that makes a good pub. Families with small children, farmers, tourists, even a hard-core drunk or two. Scanning the tables, the faces, people by the door, he is suddenly struck by an apparition returning. His mood alters, his muscles tighten and he grabs Audrey's arm tightly. "Do you see him this time?" he asks. Near the entrance, throwing a nod and smile in their direction like an old expected friend, stands Anton Eischen.

"Perhaps I owe you an apology. He's looking rather friendly though," she observes, "maybe you saw him, but imagined the gun?"

Meeting officially for the first time after so many years, Nathan ignores the proper pleasantries as Anton walks up and gives him a big bear hug. His arms dangle under the tight embrace, forcing a half-hearted "Good to see you Anton."

"Good to see me?" Anton declares, turning towards Audrey, "you believe this guy? We haven't seen each other in decades and all I get is a 'good to see you'?"

"He's a bit shell-shocked," Audrey explains, "we've had a long day. So, how did you find us?"

"Yeah, how did you find us old pal?" Nathan's question comes out cynical, trying to mask his anger. He whispers to Audrey, "I told you he was chasing us."

"After Audrey called, I waited hours. I figured something was wrong, so I sent out my eyes and ears. Here you showed up," Anton shrugs.

Nathan takes a quick glance around the room, imagining which locals might be in Anton's network, then turns to Audrey, "You called?" he asks, feeling betrayed.

"My orders. I called from the car while you were 'under attack'."

"Under attack?" Anton shows a look of concern, "what do you mean under attack?"

"Nathan here thought he saw you out at the site, bringing reinforcements," Audrey explains.

"I can assure it wasn't me," Anton puts a reassuring hand on Nathan's shoulder, "No need to pretend, since Audrey here called me from the site when you found it, excited. Such a good little employee. You don't look as celebratory as I imagined. A job well done, I have to say."

"I saw you at the site," Nathan contests, speaking to Anton but throwing Audrey an accusatory glance.

"No, I wasn't," Anton reiterates, shaking his head, "but it is good to see you now. Sorry about all the cloak and dagger, but I needed you to put your heart into this," Anton gets the attention of the publican and orders a beer. There is an awkward silence among them until he receives it, pays, and takes a long sip.

"You're lying," Nathan accuses, thinking of nothing better to say.

Anton shakes his head again, sets the beer glass down on the bar, and grabs Nathan's shoulders with both hands. "No, I'm not, and I'm very proud of you." He picks up the glass again, and downs half in a single gulp. He turns to Audrey, "Now, if you don't mind, I'll take what I hired you to retrieve and be on my way. You will be paid well, as promised."

Audrey looks at Nathan and then back at Anton. "You did not hire me. I work for the same man who hired you. If anything, I was sent here to supervise you."

"Fine," he answers, "we'll deliver the package together." Anton then turns to Nathan and adds, "As for you, you proved yourself to me. You will be getting more calls."

"I don't want your castoffs," Nathan replies.

"Tell me you didn't have fun," Anton finishes the rest of his beer in a second gulp. "You need to decide who you are, if this works, what you can do. By the way, did you say hi to my uncle?"

Nathan remembers the thing in Chorin. "Yeah, I put that together. By the way, I think he's mostly dead."

"That's a shame. I'll have to send some flowers." Anton turns to Audrey, "Shall we?" and gestures to the door.

Audrey throws Nathan an apologetic glance, "Take the car. I'll see you again in Dingle before we leave." She brushes his chest with her shoulder as she steps past.

"Why don't you move the stones while I catch up with my old friend here, okay sweetheart?" Anton asks Audrey, staring directly in Nathan's eyes. Nathan visibly bristles when he uses the term 'sweetheart'.

Audrey continues to walk to the door, not looking back. Anton leans in, very close to Nathan, giving him a smile like he is about to tell him something very confidential. All at once, Nathan feels a warm sharp heat in his belly, so sudden and piercing he lets out an involuntary yelp, barely drowned in the cacophony of bar crowd. He looks down to see Anton removing an impossibly long knife from his stomach. It keeps going, in slow motion, until the bloody tip clings momentarily to his shirt and then the whole thing disappears under Anton's jacket. With a slight push of a hand on Nathan's shoulder, Anton backs him down onto the empty bar stool behind him.

In shock, Nathan covers the hole with his hands. There is less blood than he imagined, but enough to deepen his shock. He looks up at Anton and simply asks, "Why?"

"You know what it can do. What you've absorbed should keep you alive a couple days; two at least. I bet the surface is already healing, so at least you won't bleed out, but I made sure it's deep. You can take your chance at a hospital, or you can be on a plane."

"Why?" Nathan repeats.

"I need you to follow us, and I need you to believe." Anton looks at him more intently than before. "I need you to take my place."

Whatever dangerous, psychotic tendencies Nathan thinks about himself, Anton is way beyond. There are people who try to look different because, generally, they are otherwise quite normal. Then there are others who have to take great pains to look normal, because deep down there is something very different, very wrong, and deeply disturbing. Anton is, and perhaps always has been, the latter. In his shock, Nathan turns towards the bar and with some effort asks for another beer.

"You sure, you don't look so good," the man behind the bar queries.

Nathan lays the money down, and catches his breath. He looks back, but Anton has disappeared, not that it matters right now; he knows where Anton will be going next. He would catch up with him one way or another. Or he would flee, go to a hospital and his life in Chicago, and try to forget about all this. His beer shows up and Nathan takes a bloody hand from his belly, wipes it as well as he can on his jeans, and shakily lifts the glass to his mouth. He pictures a cartoon where he drinks liquid and it immediately starts pouring out of the hole in his stomach.

A very old, very craggy-faced drunkard next to him leans over to offer his understanding. "Son," he says in a weak-voiced brogue, "there's nothin' so bad a few pints and a good sleep won't cure. *Croi follain agus gob fliuch*–a healthy heart and a wet mouth!" The man grins and stares at Nathan. "It's usually a simple question, me boy! You choose to live, or you choose to die?"

So often the voice of clarity, the voice of reason, comes from the least reasonable-looking person, making it easy to dismiss. Although his situation is a bit direr than the simply heartbroken man his new companion takes him for, a fresh set of eyes may be what he needs. He thinks he should call Jo back in Chicago. He searches his addled brain for someone, anyone, until he lands on the only choice.

"Do you have a cell phone, a 'handy' or whatever you call it?" he asks the old man, expecting a confused look, but instead getting a nod and a futuristic looking Nokia retrieved from his tweed overcoat. Nathan searches his own jacket pocket for a card. As he finds it and sets it on the bar, the neighboring old man notices a bloody thumbprint left on the white cardboard, and decides to distance himself. Nathan dials the numbers and hopes it is not too late in the evening. Thankfully the ringing stops, a voice greeting him on the other end. "Hello, Mrs. O'Malley?" he asks, "Nathan Bang. I need to get in touch with your son." The telephone crackles, a time and place. Straight down to business, so unlike any other conversation he has had with the woman.

"Where?" Nathan repeats, making sure he heard correctly.

30

AWAKE. SO VERY AWAKE at such a dismal hour. Nathan looks around his room, discerning what he can in the darkness. It is still too unfamiliar to navigate in the dark, and one wrong move with his injury would be most unpleasant. He reaches down to feel the rough skin, still amazed at how quickly his body has healed itself. It does not feel like a normal scar, however, and he wonders if this truly is from the stone; some radiation or microbial parasite. He stares at the ceiling and hopes whatever power he has absorbed, whatever is residual, will hurry up and heal the spongy liquid feeling of massive damage underneath the scar.

Madness is a blue-orange feeling, swirling and mixing and at times distinctly striped. Plaid perhaps, but not as geometrical; geometry is order, and what Nathan feels is anything but. He thinks of the ancient stories, architects who were blinded or killed after completing a design. The work itself could be handled piecemeal, a different contractor doing isolated parts. But what does one do about the person who has seen the big picture, and knows how it all fits together? It is an occupational hazard in the realm of secrets, and Nathan fears he has now entered. An unsettling feeling to know you probably will be dead if you do not continue a job, and that once the job is complete you may be killed anyway. *How did I get myself into this?* He answers the question almost before it is fully asked. Pride. Desperation. Loneliness. Sadness. Money. And so his mind continues to swirl in blue ebbs and orange flows of forlorn emotion.

The relics, as they reassemble, gain a life and gravity of their own. Instability, Nathan knows, is the same. It is like the way people are drawn to worship an idol, or the way a town forms: there is first just one thing, often a small thing like a spring or a crossing of roads or rivers. Then there is a trading post. Then a few houses gather, then a pub and a church (usually together), and so on until it is a too big crime-ridden frenzy that needs to eat and shit like a huge beast. This object he has uncovered; things happen in its presence, and its gravity well could be like a neutron star. It may have nothing to do with its actual power; more often it is the madness it inspires, and the excuse it provides our minds to do the things our inner voices urge. Nathan foresees nothing good coming from these tablets. There is a reason it has been hidden so long.

Light arrives at his window. He had given himself until morning, enough time to decide if the wound is fatal, and if so what he wants to do with his time left. Nathan decides it is not, but, just in case, he is glad he is going to church. He squints, light pouring into the room. It is a stupidly bright, tauntingly nice Sunday morning.

He hears a knock at the lower door. Unable to remember how he got home, he hopes at least he was able to lock the door. The answer comes with the sound of the heavy door swinging open and Audrey's voice calling his name up the stairs.

"Shit," Nathan says aloud.

The knock repeats as a quieter rap on his room. She says his name again, simultaneously opening the door. Nathan still does not answer, opting instead to work up his most disgusted look and throwing it her way.

"Oh my God, What happened?" she ignores the look and comes to his bed. Audrey is dressed in tight jeans, a low neck top, and short sleeves, confirming that it really is a beautiful day. Nathan, on the other hand, is still in muddy jeans from yesterday's job site, thick wool socks and an unbuttoned dress shirt over a bloody tee.

"Our mutual friend," Nathan gestures to his belly, "you think he didn't drug us? It's worse than it looks," he reaches out a hand, "help me up."

"Are you sure?" she asks, grabbing him under his right shoulder.

Nathan achieves a sitting position against the pillows. He looks pale and feels worse from blood loss or beer intake, probably both. Trying his look of disgust again, he asks, "Why should I trust you?"

"Have I ever lied to you?" she questions back.

"Repeatedly."

"Well, Anton left already, an early flight this morning," she states.

"I thought you were going with him?"

"He ditched. I woke up and he was gone, the stones with him."

"Oh great, you're sleeping with him?"

"No, it's not like that, and none of your business anyway." Her look of disgust is far more convincing. She assesses his wound, "This looks strange and kinda chalky. How did you make it back and up the stairs, anyway?"

"I honestly don't remember."

"Are you going home now?"

"Not yet," Nathan takes a chance, "I think I need to follow

Anton." Why the hell not, he has nothing to lose.

"He said you might," she looks at him with concern, "I was surprised he left me behind, since I could help you."

"He wants me to follow him. Anton just doesn't want it to look that way to his employer, so of course he's going to leave you here to help me."

"So we go after him? He's heading straight for Mr. Moyne. If you think you can fly, and we get you cleaned up enough to make it through security, we should only be half a day behind."

"We need to get some leverage first," Nathan says.

"What kind of leverage," she furrows her brow, "and for what?"

"I have someone to help us. Help me get dressed?" he looks at her and manages a wink, the combination of question and gesture coming out only slightly creepier than he meant.

* * *

They sit in an old stone church; a beautiful building, even with its ill-proportioned square steeple. It has been a long time since Nathan has been in a church, other than as a professional at a grand opening. He finds this one comforting in its presence and tradition, a smell of must and incense. The splendor always masks darkness, he knows. He would not be surprised if the Church had something to do with these relics, at least on the periphery. Then again, almost everything in this country is somehow on the edge of the Church.

Everything in this world seems to have their deeper, dangerous edges, Nathan considers. The dark places you are afraid to look, but cannot help to. Mostly you can overlook this part of the world and just go on with your life. But sometimes it is there in front of you, demanding you peer in. Nathan thinks he has looked into this darkness a few times, but has always been able to retract himself from its claws. He is looking deeper now than ever before, he thinks, and that is when the madness comes. Churches, to Nathan, are bright shiny things like a beautiful girl in a g-string. Churches have a habit of bringing about his most depraved thoughts, the one place it could not possibly be worse to think about them. The priest walks past and glances at him. *HE KNOWS*, Nathan thinks.

The O'Malley boy enters from the side aisle, dips his hand into holy water aside the door and crosses himself before approaching Nathan. He looks smaller than Nathan remembers, perhaps due to the volume of space here, or maybe because they are not alone this time, yet his wide-armed stance and lack of a perceivable neck make him an intimidating presence. Arriving at the end of his pew, O'Malley genuflects, then shuffles sideways down the one behind. Kneeling directly behind, Nathan can feel him close, elbows an inch from his back atop the wood bench and breath on the back of his neck. There is silence until O'Malley finishes his prayers.

Nathan coughs, instinctively checking his hand for blood.

"Dia dhuit," O'Malley finally says. *God be with you.*

Nathan has heard the proper response before. "Dia's Mhuire dhuit," he replies. *God and Mary be with you.*

"What's she doing here?" O'Malley motions his head towards Audrey.

"She's helping me," Nathan is forced to talk over his shoulder, unable to fully turn around.

"What exactly do you need, and what's in it for me?" O'Malley gets to the point.

"I need help to retrieve something, and then I need you to get it, and us, out of the country," Nathan says before adding the caveat, "today."

"I don't work Sundays, and if I were to sully the Lord's Day there must be something very good in it for me."

"I can help you track down Anton Eischen. I'm sure he owes your mother rent."

"It's paid in advance, directly from your employer Mr. Moyne."

"How about I keep the lease on my apartment," Nathan offers.

"Did you even read what you signed?" O'Malley grins and furrows his brow, "you will be with us in money if not body for quite some time. Again, I believe your employer will pick that up. We have an understanding that neither of us would want to jeopardize. Why do you have it in for Anton anyway, I thought he was your friend? All three of you working for the same man and all."

"Let's just say I have a score to settle. Plus, what kind of friend drugs you?" Nathan is not quite sure, with all that happened, why that bothers him more than the stabbing. Perhaps he is just projecting the stabbing onto that event, since it is less difficult to explain.

"You think he drugged you?" O'Malley lowers his head again, as if in prayer, "That was me, but I had me orders."

"What?" Audrey finally chimes in looking cross, "whose orders?"

"Am I speaking to her?" O'Malley directs the question back to Nathan. "You tell me what you need, and then we'll talk price."

"First I need to know, how did Anton get them out? Wouldn't the stones send off alarms as historical pieces?" Nathan asks.

"How do you think? Let's just say it is not by accident that you both found yourselves renting from me Ma."

"What, in your professional opinion," Nathan did not mean this sarcastically, though he realizes how it sounds as soon as it leaves his mouth, "will he do next? Will he hand them over to his employer or keep them for himself?"

"His employer is someone you wouldn't cross," O'Malley

answers.

"What if he is planning on retiring?" Nathan says, noticing a surprised look from Audrey.

"Hmm," O'Malley ponders, "that may change things."

Nathan thinks for a moment, finally deciding to go with it. "I might need the same service."

"So it's transport you need?"

"And retrieval," Nathan reminds him.

"What is it you need 'retrieved'?"

"There is a stone with rough edges, built into the wall of a small church. There is a picture of it at the pub in Ballyferriter, so it must be near. It said 'Kilmalkedar' or something like that," Nathan explains. Audrey gives him another look of surprise. "Same edges, same size, same odd tone compared to the stones around it from what little I could see. Let's just hope the back side was out, or it's worn clean over the years." He turns back to O'Malley, "I need help removing it. And I need to get it, and us, out of here today."

"You're shittin' me," O'Malley gives him the same look. "You want me to ransack a church, and not just any church but possibly the most important church site on Dingle? And on fucking Sunday?!" His voice gets just loud enough to cause a few people nearby to stare.

"This is crazy" Audrey says, "you're done. You don't need to do any more with this."

"Yes, I do," Nathan answers, "Anton made sure of that."

"This better not be the Cross, Alphabet Stone or Ogham stone or anything like that, or it will really cost you," O'Malley intervenes, shaking his head.

"It's not; anyone else would never notice it. If you can make one just like it to replace it, no one will know." They sit quietly for few moments while the organist plays a pre-service hymn. Nathan was not a fan of organ, other than its stepped forms. He finds its sound detracts from the beauty of the architecture.

"All right," O'Malley says, "Sunday will cost you extra, though." He looks at them both, "So payment. How much can you get?"

Nathan turns to Audrey, who looks back in resignation. "I can get you 20,000; if the stone is verified as genuine." She turns to Nathan, "And you?"

"I can get maybe 10,000."

"Are we talking Euros or Dollars?" O'Malley asks.

"Dollars," Nathan says, Audrey nodding in agreement.

"Too bad. Tell you what, as someone I like and my Ma has become attached to, I'll make you a deal. I'll take your 30,000 but you owe me a favor. I know where you live, and it's good to have friends everywhere," he finally acknowledges Audrey, "especially with your training." O'Malley gives her a wink. "I'll get your little rock, and I'll get it transported and through Customs in Canada but not the US. And I'll even work on the Lord's Day, may He forgive me. But I WILL call some day." O'Malley spits loudly into his open palm and extends it to Nathan, "Deal?"

The act of spitting sends a shooting pain through his belly as he returns the gesture and takes O'Malley's burly hand, the slime between softening his rough calluses.

"We trust him?" Audrey asks Nathan.

"Have I ever lied to either of you?" O'Malley grins and begins to lean back into his pew. "Okay, after Mass we go get this bad boy. I may have to call a few friends."

Nathan looks around, feeling watched. He yawns, scanning around for reaction if anyone has been studying him. Three yawn in reaction, one just a kid. It could just be that he is talking to an O'Malley, which is suspicious enough. The organ stops, signaling

Mass is about to begin. Mrs. O'Malley comes in just in time, greeting a few similarly aged ladies on her way to join her son behind them.

Audrey nudges Nathan, telling him they should leave now to pack their bags. He gives his landlord a friendly nod as they pass by, shuffling sideways out to the aisle. As they leave the church he decides to finally give his partner Johanna a call, just in case things go wrong. While he dials, Nathan chuckles that it is a bit late for that.

31

ALONG JOURNEY can be awkward and uncomfortable sitting next to someone you have known for a short time. How much do I talk, and what if I'm quiet for too long? Can we brush elbows, or try to nap leaning against each other? At least for this plane trip, Nathan is is not alone with her; plenty of other witnesses if she tries anything funny.

So far his injury has not been disabling, simply a deep dull throbbing pain in his lower abdomen. The outward signs are almost gone, other than a need to walk slightly hunched over. He had worried most about airport security; that an x-ray machine might detect a long internal knife wound.

They left Ireland in a hurry, setting a new land speed record from the peninsula to Shannon Airport. O'Malley had assured them the stone would be waiting for them when they arrive in Canada, and they had no reason to doubt him. O'Malley and his associates were the model of efficiency, but not until their Sunday morning obligations, and Mass, were done. Nathan and Audrey packed hurriedly, met them outside the church and then followed them to the site of the ruins. A number of American tourists were milling about snapping pictures. Nathan quickly identified the stone to be removed: a nondescript piece in the ancient wall, ten feet from the ground. Satisfied it was not a high value cultural object compared to other aspects of Kilmalkedar, O'Malley found its location and integration into the wall posed serious difficulties. He snapped a few photos with his camera and sent them to a mason friend, all the while mumbling about not charging enough. With its replacement being prepared, they set about planning the stone's removal.

Nathan and Audrey were told to leave in a few moments, in order to make an early afternoon flight from Shannon. O'Malley made a phone call as his other men left. In less than ten minutes a truck with "Eire Gais" written on its side–a stylized blue flame logo translating its purpose–pulls up to the access road, and an official-looking man sets up some orange cones. Warning in place, he then drives up to announce that the site is being evacuated for a possible gas leak. As Nathan made a comment about not knowing the ancient Irish used natural gas, O'Malley told them to go and then all the other tourists would follow. They did as told, and as Nathan looked back, O'Malley was repeating the spit-in-hand handshake he had performed just a couple hours earlier. Nathan had to assume that as his indebtedness to O'Malley had just begun, someone else's just ended.

Getting a short notice flight to Canada was not a problem. Their final destination is more difficult; they would pick up a car in Halifax when they arrive this evening, drive north to the port on Prince Edward Island and then take the ferry. Audrey pointed out where they were going at the airport, but on the large scale map it barely registered as an unnamed speck in the ocean off Newfoundland. If Audrey had not been familiar with its shape, Nathan could have searched months for the meaning of the form etched on the tablet.

They have been discussing relationships for a good half hour. Actually, he has been discussing relationships, and she has been avoiding any real answers while asking questions. Nathan does not mind. Despite his pain, sleep seems futile this early in the afternoon.

Nathan follows up a question on why, despite his appreciation for exotic dancers, he has always dated his own age. "The problem with being older and having a younger, much younger, woman hitting on you is that you have probably dated her–someone exactly like her–before, and it will be a long while before she gains the experience to become anyone you haven't met. If you know what I mean."

"The sex could be hot," Audrey offers.

"Very true, or it could be awful if she hasn't figured out what she wants yet. The good thing would be, if I remember what I was like in my early twenties, she has low expectations of what a guy can or will do to please her." Nathan's mind goes to Alex, the ups and downs of their relationship. She was a woman who knew what she wanted, and most of the time he loved that about her. At the end, it all went cold and distant, and he had no idea what to do. He remembers the guilt of wanting something bad to happen to her, to save him the pain of confronting his feelings. When the bad did happen, it was nothing like he had imagined.

"What about me?"

"I have the feeling you know exactly what you want, and there is no way you expect me to live up to it." Nathan feels uncomfortable again, this time with her directness. Having all these passengers around makes it safe to talk about things like this.

"You have high expectations of me," she turns and looks out the window.

"Come on, you're probably used to guys lusting after you."

"Sure, but it doesn't matter. It only matters who I lust after, right?" Nathan honestly does not know how it works. He had heard of some women he thought were amazing–funny, smart, successful, beautiful–who were lonely and very rarely asked out. He assumed it was an urban myth, as he never actually met one. "Doesn't work that way. . ." she trails off.

"How did you get into the service, or more importantly how did you get out?" Nathan asks, knowing that if he touched on something she was really interested in, he may get a break from talking.

"I joined to get away from home. When we get there, you might figure out why," she smiles, "it is a paradise of sorts, but to a young woman with a taste for adventure it was a prison. I needed to find a way out, so I joined. I was damn good at it, too."

"I've seen you in action," Nathan concurs.

"I rose up through the enlisted ranks. I was recruited to the JTF-2, Joint Task Force, Special Forces; anti-terrorist, special ops. I was in a group of the first few women, even seeing some action. Maybe someday . . ." she gives a wan smile, realizing how pat and evasive the phrase sounds. "The military is funny in that when you reach a certain level and screw up, you are usually dismissed rather than sent back down through the ranks. They may give you the option, but I've never known anyone to take it. Too proud."

"Can I ask what you screwed up?" Nathan is truly curious.

"No," she cuts him off. Audrey knows she must pull out a biggie in order to change the subject. She is not quite sure if she is ready to sit through the answer, but it was time. "How did you get into architecture?"

Asking an architect about architecture is usually only interesting if the person asking is also an architect. Architects themselves, in general because they sense a mystique around their profession cultivated in books and movies for not really doing anything, do not understand this.

"I was always good at a lot of things, but never great at any one thing: math, science, art, history, psychology. Architecture is a good fit, since you need to be good at a big range of things, except for some reason we are not expected to know how to spell. I guess that's one of our charming quirks, made up for by having nice handwriting. Of course everything is on computers now," he pauses, trying not to ramble or digress.

"You seem to know your history."

"I love the fact that it's extremely practical and extremely conceptual at the same time. The cerebral, the visceral and the spiritual."

"The what now?"

"If it is not thought about, it's just a building. With thought and meaning it moves to the realm of architecture, yet it is still a practical object. There is a basic need of shelter. For example, consider a helmet. What is it made for? Filled with a head, it is given its prime meaning. But what happens when you place, say, an apple inside? Architecture deals with all those thoughts of ideal versus improvised, idea versus experience. That and it's always different, as this past week proved."

"It sounds like you love it, like musicians and music. I suppose without the drugs at least," she attempts humor, and another change in subject. "It's funny how excited and full of life you sound when talking about architecture, but how melancholy you sound when talking relationships," she points out.

"Melancholy is the feeling du jour; it makes troubles incredibly meaningful, and success of others irrelevant." His answer is at first flippant, but he begins to ponder it further. "I think I am melancholy about my profession, also, but not necessarily the idea of it. I think, when you've imagined enough other lives, you write. When you imagine your own life, you act. But I've only imagined . . . and so I've done nothing."

"You think you've done nothing?" Audrey asks, truly curious.

"Sure I can draw, paint, engineer but all I've ever really wanted to do was play music, which I have never shown any talent for. I've spent my life always trying to square the circle, over-thinking things simply to be on the cutting edge. Of course this weakness as a human being is also what made me good at what I do. Johanna, my partner," he interjects, realizing he has not talked about her to Audrey before, "is the people person, which is why her name is first." He realizes he has been far too lost in the worlds in his head, at the cost of the world around. He is on this plane, chasing this fantastic myth because when he finally gets a glimpse of a world like the one in his head, how desperate he is to believe.

Unsure of what to say, afraid of sounding patronizing by trying to comfort him, Audrey instead simply turns and stares quietly out the window.

They change planes in Boston. The sun is just beginning to set, early evening, and Nathan finally feels like he can sleep. He awakes later with the sound of the seat belt notice coming on, making their descent, preparing to land. Clouds stream by outside his window; wisps of white and gray barely noticing their passage. A break in the cover reveals the coastal edge of Canada stretching out before them, a great river that divides the land beyond. He stares at the bare ocean, amazed that people had made this crossing in small boats with no knowledge of what lay ahead. Why did they come this way? Why so far? The fear, cold and hunger they must have felt. Nathan stretches his legs, uncomfortable from the flight but feeling no right to complain about traveling so far in such little time on cushioned seats with two hot meals and drink service.

32

July 9, Ferry to Cap-aux-Meules, Iles de la Madeleine

*F*UCKING FERRY, NATHAN silently complains, impatient with the behemoth's slow rolling progress. He leans over the rail, taking in the salty wind and feeling its spray on his face, distracting himself from swells of anger. He and Audrey are well into the five-hour sea trip from the port of Soulis on Prince Edward Island to Cap-aux-Meules on the archipelago of Iles de la Madeleine, the Magdalen Islands. Other than some mild seasickness, and the sense of having no idea where he is in the world, Nathan feels far better since landing in Halifax. Anton may have been right about the stones, he thinks, but he is still a complete asshole. He is out there now, expecting Nathan to arrive weak and in need.

At the airport he pondered a direct flight to Chicago, barely a three-hour jaunt. He realizes now, as weak as he felt getting off the plane, those additional three hours may have killed him. Having spent time with the Kilmalkedar Stone he feels stronger, his energy and anger renewed.

O'Malley had come through, the package somehow in the trunk of the rental car when they picked it up at the airport. Nathan had asked Audrey to set it in the back seat with him, hoping it would do whatever it does to speed his recovery. He slept most of the ride north until Highway 16 and the bridge to Prince Edward Island. He awoke as they passed through a sleeping Charlottetown, barely enough time to make the 2:00 am ferry from Soulis. Now approaching their destination, Nathan feels some anxiety; he will be firmly on their turf. Ireland seemed neutral and Berlin was his. When they land, he guesses, he may not even speak the language.

Darkness of the eastern sky is changing fast. Nathan had come out of main cabin to watch the sunrise, leaving Audrey behind. In contrast to his miraculous recovery, she has lost all energy. She supposed she had been fighting some bug off and on since Berlin, at times feeling normal and other times completely drained and nauseous. The stress of the plane ride had likely given the virus a chance to take hold.

He opens the door and returns to the main waiting area. All of their bags, and the stone, were still in the car below. He at first did not feel comfortable leaving it unattended, but Audrey had convinced him it was perfectly safe. The bigger deal they made about it, she warned, the more likely to cause a problem. She is sitting alone in the half-full cabin, curled up sideways across two seats, a blanket thrown over her legs and chest.

Nathan sits down in a deck chair next to her. "So what's this place like?" he asks.

"I wouldn't say its normal. Or rather, as normal as any very isolated small town might be. Actually, it never really was a normal place: back in the 1500's when it was 'discovered' by Cartier he wrote of its great trees, fine meadows, and fields of wheat, and that it all looked like it had been planted by man's hand. My grandfather would tell stories, as all grandfathers do, about how mystical our home is. You're supposed to believe such stuff when you're a kid, but I didn't. As I got older, though . . . I don't know, I haven't been back in a while."

"Think you'll know anyone there?"

"Definitely, though I may not be recognized. There's only about 13,000 people total, not counting tourists. Seven villages, with people living scattered between," she answers.

"A big long island, so what do you do there?" he wishes he had the internet, or anything. They had just arrived at the port in time to get on the ferry, so although he had grabbed some literature, he spent what time he could sleeping while it was still dark.

"There are about a dozen islands, six of them connected by long thin sand dunes, so it's really an archipelago. Mostly fishing and tourism."

Another place without a gentleman's club for a thousand miles, Nathan thinks. At least Dingle had pubs. He hopes for the best and asks "They speak English, right?"

"There's an Irish community on Grosse-Ile, and Scottish nearby, but they can barely understand each other's accents. As you might guess from the place names, it is mostly non-English."

"Fucking French," he mumbles, hoping his time in Paris twenty years ago would come back to help him.

"Acadian," Audrey corrects.

"Fucking Acadian, then." Nathan corrects himself. "What's an Acadian, anyway? Some kind of dyslexic Canadian?"

"Clever," She patronizes. "This whole area was Acadia, a separate region from Quebec. There was a lot more blending here with the Mi'kmaq natives. The British expelled a lot of us in the 1700s, many who went to your state of Louisiana became known as Cajuns. But my family has always been here, on the Archipelago, since they came over."

"Came over from where?"

"France," she admits.

"So I was right the first time. So, what do I call you? You call it Ile-de-la-Madeleine, you call it the Magdalen Islands, you call it the Archipelago, so what are you people who come from here called?"

"I'm a Madelinot."

"And growing up here?" he pries.

"Like any small town. Everyone knows you, knows your business. There were some escapes, parts of the islands that you could truly be alone, but usually you felt both smothered yet really isolated. I suppose now with the internet you can connect to people outside in ways I couldn't as a kid." She pauses, wistfully adding, "But I was safe here. No one has to lock their doors, or for that matter take their keys out of their cars unless they worry about locking them in by accident. It was idyllic in hindsight, but you don't appreciate it until you leave."

"It shaped you," he nods his head, thinking of his own childhood.

"I always feel more comfortable near an edge. You probably know the same thing in Chicago, with Lake Michigan there. It's comforting the city cannot expand that way, and at night the feel of the blackness is really calming."

"Anything I should know about the people, the culture?"

"The people here are welcoming, but very private, very conservative."

"Like 'American conservative' or actual-conservative conservative?" he asks, not knowing if she would understand the distinction.

"Just conservative, not in the political sense." She coughs a bit and closes her eyes, signifying the end of the discussion.

Nathan closes his eyes, also. He can feel the sway of the ship and hear the chatter of others around them. It is French, he knows, but wonders if there is some kind of accent. Audrey did not seem to have an accent, even what most Americans consider a Canadian accent. He supposes years in the service may have rid her of any regionalism. It would be interesting if it resurfaces as she returns to the place of her youth.

"Want to talk about our relationship?" Audrey asks suddenly, catching Nathan completely off guard.

"Oh please. First, we don't have one, and second no man wants to 'talk about the relationship.' It's too abstract a notion. Is there something we should be doing that we are not? Do you have a question? Is there something I can do for you? Those are all fine ways to make a relationship better. As soon as you want to talk about the relationship, you are heading into a territory our brains are not wired for. And god help us if it devolves into an argument, then we have no chance of winning even if we are right."

"Sorry, just asking." The brief power nap seems to have rejuvenated her.

"Be more specific next time." He had thought about Alex on the plane, a relationship he had never grieved. But what about Natalia? Audrey's intimation that she was dead–burned in that spate of revenge in Berlin so many years ago–has still not fully registered in his brain. He was sure she had not been there; it was just her house, and she probably used the opportunity to disappear. That was a relationship he had mourned, even obsessed over for a while. Nathan had thought he had actually spent too much time mourning, but what if she was innocent and dead and he truly had not mourned enough? Or felt guilty enough? "I want someone who is generally happy, optimistic even when I am not, supportive, and for balance occasionally needy," Nathan offers suddenly, without hinting at the deeper darker thoughts behind his struggle. "At least for things I can provide," he qualifies.

"Doesn't sound too bad," Audrey says.

"I've found it to be quite rare," he assures. "Why are we talking about this?"

"It's actually not in your file, and I'm curious."

"Starting to care?" Nathan inquires.

"Never mind," she shakes her head, brushing him off. "Let's go look, we should be getting close." They step back out of the cabin together. They are close; a long string of land undulates gently from left to right on the horizon before them culminating in sheer cliff faces.

"There's the port, Cap-aux-Meules," she points, and then to her right at the jutting green-topped cliffs stepping down the coast, "and that's Havre-aux-Maisons."

Nathan is amazed, an overwhelming feeling of déjà vu. It could be a mirror image across the ocean, this archipelago and the peninsula they had just left the day before. If the sun was not in the wrong place, and the others who joined them at the bow of the ferry were not speaking French, he would have thought they had flown in a circle and returned to Slea Head. Perhaps he would not feel so out of place after all, he hopes.

"I know what you're thinking," Audrey looks at him sternly, "but you will have to trust me that this is not like any place you have been before."

33

522, in the Bay north of Dingle Peninsula

W AVES ROCK THEM as they approach shore, a young boy daydreaming while his two older brothers paddle. The currach has its sail down on this eerily calm day, and is riding low in the water, something their father will see from a distance and be happy about; the sign of a good catch. There always seems to be a good catch when Ciaran is along. Unlike his younger brother, Ciaran is the favored help by his father and older brothers on these trips, sometimes even arguing over him. The youngest brother seems to balance Ciaran's good luck by being outright cursed, usually returning with no fish but plenty of storms and rough water. In true irony, and again unlike his little brother who would live on a boat if he could, Ciaran absolutely hates the sea.

This feeling of déjà vu, however, intrigues him. He has seen this before; this boat with no sail, his two brothers, and the familiar land ahead. It was a vision, but something is different. The land is not quite right, or it should not be his brothers in the boat, or the smell of fish is too strong. As one of his brothers turns to give him a disapproving look for not paying adequate attention to the rudder, Ciaran shakes the feeling and focuses again on getting ashore. He is often accused of daydreaming, especially by his brothers. It is greater than déjà vu, more than prescience. He has learned to keep it to himself or sometimes share it with his mother. Every once in a while, if his visions have to do with fish or the weather, Ciaran will also share them with his father, but only then. He had also once–but only once–become so moved and obsessed by a particular recurring dream he traveled quite far to deliver a message to the only person he thought may be able to help. In a sense it did not matter if he was believed or not. Usually the simple act of telling someone, like a confession, unburdened him.

The young boy looks up at the ruins on the promontory looming above the shore, the old fort of *Cathair Cun Rí*. Ciaran was born in the shadow of history, near a place his mother describes as an intersection of energy lines that come from all directions. He thinks it a special place, but his father says it has only made him brash and petulant. His mother is certain he has a Gift. Her belief in these energy lines, of a greater underlying 'I' imbuing all things with life that can be tapped into, have filled Ciaran's mind with thoughts that he may be greater than he actually is. A little fantasy, he thinks, a little belief, never hurt anyone. Besides, people did treat him differently because his visions so often come true. Not always right away, and while that drew some people to him it also scared many away. After some hard lessons, some lost friends, and accusations of being not quite right, he learned to be quiet, and also sometimes dread falling asleep for what he may learn.

It was not always like that; as a small boy the dreams were fun, and he could not wait to have them. He would see such fantastic things, strange lands and creatures, things in the sky, structures so much larger than even the *Cathair Cun Rí*. But then the Vision came; a bright light that only left Darkness. Perhaps not only Darkness; with it, as though coming from a force as powerful, was also a glimpse of true beauty that wrenched his heart. It would have dropped him to the ground had he been standing. Was this the God that the Christians speak of? He liked to think it was his first sight of the gods of his ancestors, the gods he had been born a child of, but he had doubts. Even his devoted mother laments that their gods had been driven underground long ago; immortal but fading. Possessing the power Ciaran experienced, they would not have been so conquered.

He also saw a long journey, far beyond his island home. This vision kept repeating, night after night, never changing. Ciaran told his younger brother about all the things he had seen, as he often has, in the hope once purged he would be allowed to dream something else. It did not work. This message was quite obviously for someone, and he began to consider the possibilities in desperation. He began to dread going to sleep at night, partly from the power of the images, but also out of weariness of the same thing over and over and over.

And so he took the opportunity, while his family had made the pilgrimage during the harvest festival, to find a man of the new God. A monastery was being established near *Ard Fhearta*, a place where men gathered to learn and work and pray together. Ciaran slipped away, and explore if the message he had been given was meant for someone here.

The monastery was an amazing place, so large and expanding in every direction. They grew many of the provisions themselves. Everything he could imagine was there. A few of the men seemed to not have to work at all, spending time writing in books and painting pictures. He sensed the life had its own hardships, but there was something very appealing to a labor-weary young boy with an eager mind.

One man took him aside, introducing himself only as the Abbot, but carrying enough authority in his eyes that Ciaran nervously told him he might have a message. The Abbot sat down with him, further intrigued with the young boy. He told the Abbot of the Journey, of the Seekers departing. This journey was very important, both for the sake of the trip itself as well as its cargo.

What cargo? the Abbot naturally asked.

Ciaran was not quite sure. All he knew of it was that its essence must be hidden, its pieces scattered. The Abbot asked what that meant, but he honestly did not know. In his vision the world was getting too large, and such power made men crazy. It was never meant for more than one person at a time.

Where is this? Where did it come from? Ciaran knew none of these answers, but immediately he felt the weight lift, the message delivered. For the first time in a long time, he looked forward to going to sleep.

He assured the Abbot that despite many years, and being given up for lost, most would return from this Journey. He did not see the others lost at sea, but rather as staying behind. Ciaran had heard of outposts these monks have created, scattering themselves for whatever reason to isolated outcroppings of the world. Of course, he supposed his own home may be considered on the edge of the world. But to be totally disconnected from your family, your people, seemed horrible. Over time you would even lose your connection to the beauty of your homeland, eventually even yourself, as everyone you know moves on without you.

The Abbot offered a personal tour, which must have been quite an honor according to the stares Ciaran received from the other inhabitants of the monastery. Ciaran was even able to see what some of the men were writing on pieces of parchment. He had often wished a better way of capturing the wonderful stories he had heard as a child. He did not understand the symbols the monks were writing, but they were quite unlike the Ogham stones around his home which he had learned to read. He thinks, however, that though the signs and symbols on the stones are difficult, they will last a lot longer than the thin paper the men were painting on. The Abbot assured him that the stories they were writing would last forever, and if Ciaran would join them, perhaps he could be a part of that.

His dream progressed that night, related but far more gentle, even idyllic. Ciaran had a vision of arriving at an island, like home but strange people come to visit and he is not sure if should hide. He has a duty, protecting something unseen, unknowable even to him. Coming to terms this is where he would live his life, where he would stay, would be a much more difficult crossing than the one across an ocean; not as dangerous to life, but to his soul and humanity. Ciaran took the message that perhaps his destiny is to become a part of this brotherhood, perhaps move on to one of the outposts.

Later that Spring, Ciaran had given much more thought about joining the monastery. The seas were particularly rough, and the wonders of what he had seen kept gnawing at him. He is not sure if he can change his belief to One God, but there was an invitation, an opportunity, and were not his gifts being wasted here? When he had left the Abbot after his tour, he gave a half-hearted promise to return and join them, already afraid of what his father and mother, even his brothers, would say. He felt, still feels, a stronger responsibility to his family. Ciaran feels the guilt of pursuing something so selfish will be overwhelming.

Yet Ciaran is afraid he has a bigger part to play, his Vision suggesting it may be inevitable. The known future is troubling, far more than the unknown. He had fantasized a very different life, more like his father's, than he would admit. There is even a girl, just a friend now, who makes him feel like a better person when she is around. Except for the sea he could be like his father and be very happy, raising a family and working the land.

As they approach the shore he notices a man, not his father, standing with his mother. Whatever hesitation Ciaran was feeling now seems moot, the pressure to decide his own path between the old gods and the New just a few boat lengths ahead. The Abbot to whom he had delivered his message is standing there, beckoning him to a new life.

34

July 9, Iles de la Madeleine, Quebec

THE RAMP CLATTERS as they drive off, dodging a final swarm of pedestrians and bicycle riders evacuating the ferry as if were on fire and sinking. It was not, of course, though Nathan thinks it would make the day more interesting. *No one appreciates a good ferry fire.* The air is warm, far warmer than he expected, arriving on a strong wind across the harbor. The smell of sea and fish is heady, shrieks of gulls deafening; the sounds and aroma of a real working harbor. Up ahead, just before the dock's outer edge, a man and woman stand in the middle of the road.

"Do you know these people?" Nathan asks.

"No. No one knows we were coming," Audrey leans forward to get a better look.

As they slowly approach the couple in the road, the man extends his hand in a gesture to stop. He peers in the window and speaks French to Nathan, whose blank expression forces the man to rephrase his question in English. At that moment, Nathan swears he can sense a wave cross the island, a rippling announcement identifying him as Outsider. He had that feeling once before in a gay club notorious as a pick-up bar. It was like he had the word "straight" written across his forehead which left him torn; relieved for not being hit on, but sad that not a single person showed any interest whatsoever.

"You are expected at Mr. Moyne's?" the man's inflection phrases a question, even though Nathan understands it as the command it was meant to be. "You can park ze car over zer and come with us," he gestures at a small lot just beyond the fence.

"Can't we just follow you?" Nathan does not feel comfortable leaving the car, and its contents, unattended in a strange place. He considers it funny that this is his first concern, rather than getting in a car with strangers in a strange land. Events of the past week have inured him to such a proposition.

"You'll need to come with us, and wear blindfolds," the man looks stern, but a waver in his voice suggests he is unsure.

"Really? I mean, come on. This island isn't that big, and she's from here," Nathan points to Audrey, regretting that he may have offered too much information.

"Which island?" the man's voice brightens, an unrestrained smile reshaping his countenance.

"Stop it, we're not here to chitchat," the unknown woman, still looking serious, steps forward to chide her companion.

"I find more information, might be useful," the man complains.

"You were chatting her up, you perv," the woman fires back. Nathan and Audrey exchange a quick look as the other two both take a few steps away and assume defensive postures toward each other. They continue to argue for a few moments in French, after which the man comes back to Nathan's window.

"Follow us please," the man says, and walks dejectedly ahead to catch up with the woman. They get into a small white Ford, their brake lights flash on, followed by the man waving his arm out the window that they are ready to leave.

Nathan looks again at Audrey, who shrugs her shoulders. "Why not," she says, and they take off after the little Ford.

At first concerned Audrey does not know more, he next considers she set this up. Then Nathan realizes another possibility. "You think Moyne knows we have another piece?"

"Doubtful, or they would have taken it," she reasons, "I suppose it depends on how he knew we were coming here." She throws Nathan a disapproving look. "O'Malley?"

"Do we let him know?"

"Not yet," she replies, and then turns her gaze back out the window. Nathan wonders if this place has changed much since she left it. She has a wistful look that is either nostalgia or sadness in not recognizing her home. The village of Cap-aux-Meules, which congregates around its harbor, exudes the half-asleep yet half-frantic activity of many fishing villages in morning. There are a number of utilitarian buildings around docks and small garages scattered beyond the more regular homes and businesses lining the main road. Even along this major street–a curving two-lane road following the edge of the island before turning inland–the small clapboard and shingle houses are arranged more haphazardly than usual. This could be Greenland, or Alaska, Nathan thinks, but the homes have a distinct style; painted in bright colors, with tight wood siding or shingle shakes surrounding deep-set windows and steep-pitched roofs. Nathan sees a simple and complex beauty, reminiscent of both a French village and a frontier town.

Within moments they are at the outskirts of the village. In his rear view mirror, the ferry they arrived on is the largest structure in sight, looming over the modest town like a foreign giant. They pass a sign announcing "Étang-du-Nord, 6 km". Rolling hills appear soft and warm green ahead in early morning light, highlighting the middle of the island. They follow the white car as it snakes alone through the valley between.

Fucking time change. Nathan is tired as hell, still recovering from his own injuries, and helping Audrey as she grows weaker. He assumes they are speeding towards some arranged destination; hopefully a nice soft bed and not something more sinister. These relics he helped find have been sitting for centuries, so why such a hurry now?

He tries to enjoy the drive for now. *Live in the moment*, Nathan thinks. The countryside is beautiful, and, unlike the three official colors for homes in Ireland, the small wood houses they pass are painted in bright shades of deep red, fuchsia, tangerine, vermilion, and lavender. As they reach the center of the island they are still within view of the sea; Nathan senses it would be impossible to find a spot on this long narrow group of islands where the ocean would be out of sight. Everywhere a constant vision of beauty, and for many who lost loved ones a reminder of merciless power all around.

The main road veers left as they continue on a narrow lane due west, towards the opposite coast from which they arrived. Within minutes the density of houses increase into the village of Étang-du-Nord, nestled between sea and rounded presence of a large hill. Red cliffs rise up from frothing water and continue north for miles, flaring up here and there as if the ocean had pushed them up in fits of rage.

The white car pulls into a street parking space in front of one of the larger, commercial-looking buildings in the center of town. There is an open spot directly behind which Nathan pulls into. The woman approaches. "Elevator to the second floor," she says, directing Nathan and Audrey to a side door separate from the ground floor shop. The man seems to have had his speaking privileges revoked, as he does not even bother to get out of the car.

Nathan and Audrey enter the small lobby area and are surprised to see an elevator but no stair. He presses the button, doors opening with a welcoming ding. Inside, the choices are '1' and '2'. Nathan presses '2' as directed.

"What's wrong?" Audrey asks, reading a look of curiosity on Nathan's face as the elevator makes its ascent.

"I counted the stories from the outside, and there seems to be one missing," he answers, "but, come on," Nathan scoffs, "that may work in a fifty or eighty story building where no one would notice. But in a three-story building? Really?"

"Maybe the building doesn't need access to the top floor, or they find the number three unlucky."

"Well, it was the second floor that we just skipped. The timing is off. The '2' we are going to is the third floor, and I don't think it's because they follow European standards. But your other point might be valid, you know, like a lot of hotels skip the thirteenth floor. There is a lot of superstition in buildings." The elevator dings, the doors open, and they step out into a long hallway. The hallway appears longer than one would guess from the outside length of the building. "Look down this hallway, it's a bunch of offices so you would expect the same number of rooms each side. Notice how none of the doors across the hall line up with each other?"

"So?"

"It's quite logical. Bad spirits can only travel in straight lines, so if you offset the doors it prevents them from infecting other rooms,"

"Now you're just making shit up."

"I'm serious; a professor covered that in design class."

"You think maybe your professor was messing with young impressionable minds?"

Nathan shrugs his shoulders, "As valid as other design

reasoning, like using numerical sequences or so-called sacred ratios. And what's wrong with designing for the dead as much as the living?"

They ponder the hodgepodge of anonymous doors stretching before them, unsure which one is their destination. A short, bald-headed man leans out of the last door at the end of the long hallway and with a smile shouts "down here, please."

"Awfully polite," Nathan speaks softly to Audrey, "but is he going to pay us, or kill us?"

"It's probably best to hope for one and expect the other," she counsels. It is a long walk, and none of the other doors they pass have glass or signs describing their purpose. They reach the end and enter through the open door. Nathan sees a desk with a man sitting facing them. Fresh glare from a window behind momentarily obscures their host's features.

A man grabs Nathan from behind, angling his arms up behind his back and locking him in a painful hold. Audrey spins, finding the other short, bald-headed guard who had gestured them in and puts him in a similar hold. The two pair hovers before their host in a stalemate.

The man at the desk speaks first. "It's alright, let him go," he commands, and both comply. Both Nathan and the other guard rub their arms to shake out twisted muscles. "You understand my concern," the man gestures with both arms, palms up, "you showing up uninvited to my little corner of the world. It was not part of the deal. However it is a pleasure, and maybe not an unexpected surprise, to see you here. Nice to finally meet you, Nathan," he glances at Audrey, "you two together now?"

"No," Audrey scoffs.

"I am Daniel Moyne," he says, the raspy voice and gaunt face now visible confirm Nathan's initial vision of the man. Fifties, maybe sixties, and long-time smoker. The room reeks of nicotine. "You've proven your resourcefulness, maybe even some loyalty. As long as you're here, I may have another job for your specific talents."

"Have we finished the previous job?" Nathan asks. "Has Anton delivered the pieces?"

"They will be here soon."

"Well, if he's back, you probably don't need me."

"Let's just say I'm impressed with your speed and results," Moyne smiles, a pained expression forced to the surface by some conscious will.

"Where is he?" Nathan cuts to his primary question.

"After we get this done," Moyne responds. "You're not in a hurry to get anywhere else, are you?" The question has a tinge of menace to it, and Nathan remembers his big project, the biggest of his career, that now lay in ashes along a lake in Wisconsin. He actually had not thought about it for a week, and now that he has, he feels an incredible urge to return.

"You don't have any children, do you Nathan?" Moyne asks, shaking him from his thoughts.

"No."

"I've found, for others anyway, that when you've had a child you have already entered into a long-term project, and so you become much less afraid to start other long-term projects."

"I'm not afraid," Nathan snorts, "I've done plenty of long-term projects."

"Sure you are, you're very afraid," Moyne counters, "and the amount of time I refer to is beyond your comprehension. What I am referring to crosses generations, hundreds of years."

Nathan waits for him to finish as a coughing fit momentarily incapacitates the man behind the desk. *If anyone should be afraid of long-term projects,* Nathan thinks, *this man should be. He does not sound long for this world.*

"There is something on these islands," Moyne continues, a bit raspier than before as he recovers his breath, "I know it is here. It's related to the relics we've uncovered, related to Saint Brendan's Crossing. He left something here on his way back, I am more sure of it now than ever. I was born here, grew up with stories handed down by my grandfather and his grandfather before."

"You mean the story of a Fountain of Youth?" Nathan appreciates the look on Moyne's face as he beats him to the punch line. "Like Cortez couldn't find it in Florida or wherever because Brendan beat him to it?"

"You mean Ponce de Leon," Audrey corrects, "Cortez was searching for the lost City of Gold."

Nathan quips, "Now, a lost city might fall under my expertise."

Moyne smiles again, causing Nathan to flinch. "You might be looking for both," he gets his punch line after all, "Somewhere here, I am certain, there is a hidden village that is guarding something very precious."

"You are out your mind," Audrey takes a step forward, "I grew up on these islands. Do you know anywhere that is hidden, or for that matter, any secrets that can be kept for more than ten minutes around here?"

"I know," Moyne waves a hand in mock disdain, "it sounds impossible." He then slams that hand on the table, a sudden crack of sound jolting everyone else in the room. "But it is here. I'm not the first to look for it here, but I will be the one who finds it!"

"Okay," Nathan says slowly, "maybe you could start by telling us where you have looked." It comes out like a parent talking to a child in mid tantrum, and he immediately regrets the tone. To cover he adds, "Who else has been looking?"

"I have spent years. And I have been on all the islands, even the uninhabited ones. Many have looked before me, starting with Prince Henry Sinclair in 1398. He landed in Nova Scotia, but I think this is where he meant to come."

"And you base this on . . .?" again more sarcastic then he means. To Nathan's relief, Moyne does not seem to be picking up on it.

"The first piece I found was here. Well, I didn't really find it myself," he corrects, "it was handed down to me by my grandfather. I loved the stories that he told me about it, and I vowed I would pass them along. I was not so lucky, however." Moyne stands up, his thin frame rising maybe five feet at most. "Then I found another," he moves over to a map on the wall and points to the east side of the middle island, "right about here." He returns slowly to his chair, the simple act of pointing seemingly tiring him out. "The same markings, all that, and with it were some teeth and bone fragments. They were from an alligator."

"I don't suppose they were indigenous around here?" Nathan raises an eyebrow.

"I had the bones carbon-dated, and they were only from the 500's. So I put the two pieces together, and they lined up, the markings continuing across. I thought maybe I really found something of historical value, so I had a friend take a look at it, without telling him where it came from, or mentioning the alligator. He thought it might be Ogham script, which lead me to Ireland, to Anton, and eventually you."

"Could he read the script?" Nathan asks.

"No," Moyne says, "which is for the best, since I could continue in private. I learned a bit myself, I was able to translate bits and pieces, such as "Sons of" and eventually "Ardfert". As I learned more I thought maybe it was a grave marker. But the word "Life" appeared, along with the word "Death." And then Anton came along, referred to me by a friend. He said he might be able to help, for a price. And now," he physically shakes from the excitement, "I have four pieces, and there is a connection proved: Florida, where the Fountain of Youth was rumored to be, here, and Ireland from where Brendan made his legendary voyage."

"So what exactly am I looking for? I have a job back in Chicago and a partner getting impatient with my absence." Nathan's own impatience is growing.

"As I said, look for a Village and I'll take care of the rest. You seem adept at knowing if something is out of place, even if it is out in the open, and that is what I need."

"Literally a village, or some kind of secret organization? Because if it's the latter I would say you already have your own thing going, though you seem a bit understaffed for a secret society."

"Not too much secret here; people just know me as a Collector. They don't pay too much attention if I'm poking around, since I do that a lot."

"Won't they notice a stranger like me? And what about this building's secret floor?" Nathan asks.

"I hire people from time to time, not too unusual if they know you're working for me. And as for that floor, I said you were adept," Moyne says with a more natural grin of avoidance.

"Well, as long as I'm here, and you seem to be between me and Anton . . ." Nathan shrugs acceptance.

"Good. We took the liberty of finding you a room," Moyne oddly gestures at the map, "but I will assume two rooms. Most things were booked, so you will have to stay with the Carmes, at Maison de Marie, just a short drive south to Havre-Aubert." Nathan does not understand the gesture, unaware of what or where a 'Havre-Aubert' is.

Audrey groans in response. "What's wrong?" Nathan asks quietly aside. Audrey simply shakes her head.

"And as for you young lady, your mother is waiting to see you," Moyne interrupts.

"How does she know I'm here? Wait," she rolls her eyes, "what am I saying, of course she knows."

"And there's supposed to be a big secret here?" Nathan hints at the impossibility.

"There are secrets everywhere," Audrey whispers, and then louder after a deep breath, "some are just kept out in the open so long no one notices. Especially in a place like this where everyone learns to talk around it."

Audrey and Nathan turn to go, the guards politely opening the door. As they pass through Moyne coughs again, shorter this time, and then in his rasp calls after them, "Enjoy your stay!" Nathan detects a return of sarcasm in his voice, what is left of it. They walk down the long corridor to the elevator in silence, afraid of how their voices may carry in the space.

Even after the elevator doors close Nathan speaks in a hushed tone, "What if we're literally looking for a hidden house, maybe even a whole village? You think it could be possible even if really, really improbable?"

"Like you said, this island isn't that big, and I'm from here."

"Well it all seems like, underneath it all, it's all quite crunchy with a meaning he isn't sharing with us. We cross the ocean to a surreal French-speaking Crayola-colored version of Ireland, like it just broke off and drifted away, yet you know what really made me curious in there?"

"What?" she asks on cue.

"That for being his right-hand man, Moyne didn't really seem to know you."

35

July 9, Havre-Aubert, Iles de la Madeleine

THE RESTAURANT FEELS like a converted living room, which it is; a foodie version of renting out the spare room to overnight guests during tourist season. Nathan and Audrey arrive together, and as she is embraced with hugs and kisses on each cheek, he is greeted in English with a firm handshake. Word does travel fast. Though smiles were all around, his is a standoffish greeting reserved for Outsiders. It feels like an insult.

Located down the road from their bed and breakfast in the historic La Grave district–a collection of harbor front shops Nathan can only describe as 'cute'–Audrey picked the restaurant to avoid eating at their lodging house. They would even have breakfast elsewhere, she informed him, which to Nathan loses a major component of the bed and breakfast combination. He knows there is something much deeper here, but his attitude has taken a foul turn that only a good night's sleep may fix.

They are led to a light corner of the dark room, a small table for two near a window with an extraordinary view of the ocean. They are seated adjacent, rather than across from each other, as the table is tucked directly into the corner. Other couples dining nearby are local, Nathan thinks, as they are paying far more attention to each other than the beautiful surroundings. It is a quiet, warm, candle-lit atmosphere, with guests leaning towards each other in hushed tones of intimacy. The romance is not lost on Nathan, who is at once hopeful and suspicious of Audrey's motives for choosing this place.

As their host greets them in English, Nathan gets the sense that this would be the place to stay should he ever return. Not that the owners of Maison de Marie, where he and Audrey checked in a few hours earlier, are inhospitable; they are just odd. Claude and Marie–the home's namesake–were sitting in a small dining room with the local parish priest when he and Audrey arrived. They immediately stopped talking and just stared as Claude slowly moved up to greet them, closing the double glass doors behind him separating the dining room from the makeshift lobby. There were no guests other than Nathan and Audrey, despite two additional empty rooms. Nathan did not think it unusual until just now, when the restaurant host described how busy this tourist season is and that they have turned people away, being booked to capacity through October.

"So what exactly is wrong with the place we're staying," Nathan asks Audrey as the host leaves.

"It's not your normal B & B. The Maison de Marie exists solely as an overflow spot for people from the island who have nowhere else to stay."

"Like a college student coming home, but mom and dad have converted their room into an office?"

"It's more serious than that: any college student would find a place to stay, or camp out. It's hard to explain," Audrey pauses as the waiter returns with wine.

"On the house," the waiter bows with a flourish. Audrey offers a 'merci' and focuses on the glass, her fingers turning it methodically at the stem.

"Well, the priest seems to like them fine. He was still there when we left," Nathan offers hopefully.

Audrey gives him a wan smile and opens the menu. It is concise, basically just a description of what will be served rather than offering choices. Mussels are the main course. She closes it again and, placing it back on the table in front her, gazes far out to sea through the window.

"It's beautiful here," Nathan misreads her wistful look, "why leave?"

"You've never lived on an island have you?" she replies. "Even in the Bahamas you would last maybe two weeks, maximum, before going bonkers. Plus, it's not as idyllic, bright, and cheery as it seems. There is a great beauty, a great sense of life, but you know how all things are in balance. You don't have to dig far before you get to great darkness, great . . . I don't know, 'weirdness'."

"Where did you grow up?"

She shifts her gaze slightly. "You can almost see it from here," she points, what would be around the corner from where they are sitting, "Entry Island is English-speaking, hence my secondary French and not vice versa."

"Will we go out there?" he asks.

"I don't think so, it's not connected to the main group and there's no reason. It's a treeless, small, green rock; a few small settlements huddled on the far corners. We're talking severe isolation, especially for a teenager in wintertime." She takes a sip from her glass. "When my grandfather was a child, in the winter of 1910, the telegraph cable snapped and the sea was impassable by boat. Everyone here was cut off. They had to seal a wooden molasses barrel with messages inside and send it off into the pack ice. It was a week before the Nova Scotians found it and sent an icebreaker to help. It was probably even more isolated in the early days; people here survived for hundreds of years with little outside contact. Yet, now if the Internet goes down for a few hours people would go nuts. It's interesting as population and density grows, we feel the need to be more connected."

"It's superficial, though," she analyzes her words, "it's not like you're calling more people on the phone or meeting more people in person. I think the more people, the faster things happen and the harder it is to keep up. We are just trying to figure out what the hell is going on, while actually retreating more into our own little safe zones."

"Head in the sand, tail in the air?" Nathan echoes.

"I've seen it from here to Panama to Islamabad," she grabs her napkin as the waiter brings bread.

"So, back to Moyne–why the cold reception to you?" he rephrases his earlier query.

"He knows me, but I haven't worked for him that long. I think a lot of people work for him. Besides, he did mention my mother."

"I don't know, that guy we met with doesn't seem genuine. I have no doubt there is a real Moyne, or even someone else pulling Moyne's strings, but that guy wasn't it." Nathan looks at her, "I mean, you're the expert at these kinds of things, interrogation and all that. What did you think?"

"Sounds like a conspiracy theory," Audrey says, mouth full of bread. "You know why he chose you?" she asks, diverting his line of questioning.

"My fearlessness and lightning-fast reflexes?" he quips, then answering, "I assume I was Anton's only referral."

"Okay, more generally, do you know why he chose someone like Anton or you? People trust you, Nathan," Audrey answers her question, "you could walk into someone's fenced and guarded yard, and after proclaiming "It's okay, I'm an architect and by the way I love what you've done here" even a hardened mob boss sets down his gun, serves you iced tea and spills his life history. It's one of those side benefits no one speaks of. Like doctors get to see people naked."

"Yeah, I don't think doctors enjoy it."

"Most people think in language, in words, which are secondary representations of the world. You and Anton seem able to think, when and if you do think, in the closest direct images of reality. You know what I said about the stones. Moyne, despite that cough you heard, thinks he is immortal. He's fucking nuts. He is part of a long tradition, of father passing down to son one of those stones we found and all the stories that go along with it. They believe when they get all the parts together, it will tell them the location of the "Fountain", whatever it may be–a structure, a place where natural electromagnetic forces converge or some virus exists, maybe a recipe for a magic potion." She raises an eyebrow at this last thought. "Anyway, I think he he's finally gone off the edge, which is why he treated me only like a local. He is the last of a long line, with no child to pass his story down to. There is a pressure he cannot cope with, and he compensates by convincing himself he is immortal and will not let his forefathers down by fulfilling the prophecy and living forever. Moyne is desperate, and that will make him very unpredictable, and very dangerous."

"So we work for him, that's a good solution," Nathan says, ripping off another piece of bread. He feels a bit sorry for the old man. The lies people tell to make themselves stand out and feel special, even if it is just a private lie.

"If you want to find Anton, and finish what you've started here, then yes," she affirms.

When Nathan was at the Farm there was one lesson that really stuck. His university education, his time in Paris, his visual memory which he thinks Audrey was referring to, was something practical. He was not just auditing a class for others. Most, if not all, of his classmates were disciplined thinkers who could investigate and anticipate problems in a regimented way. On a flat percentage basis they were more successful at training exercises, but they were more often caught by the variable that seemed unassociated to everything else. Nathan still had a discipline, but not in the same way. His lateral thinking and connections drew praise, privately, from his instructors even if they did not like his methods. Nathan's observations here, of Moyne and Audrey, were starting to coalesce into something. At this moment he is just too tired to fit all the pieces together, but his gut feeling is that neither of them are central figures.

Audrey shifts in her seat next to him, her short skirt riding up. He tries to avoid looking down at her legs but cannot help it, rewarded with a glimpse of her panties. He quickly looks up to a disapproving glance as their entrees arrive. The choice of skirt, the coy motion, is unexpected of her, Nathan thinks, like she is reverting to a younger more reckless girl. Perhaps it is a revelation of who she was, the girl she used to be when she was stuck in this place and looking for any kind of thrill or a way out.

The mussels are delicious, bathed in a Pied-de-Vent sauce. They eat in silence, listening to conversations in French all around which he cannot understand but appreciates their soothing lyrical notes. He rests a moment, stares out the window at the eastern sky darkening opposite the sunset. Below their window, the wind-blown marram grass sits atop fragile sand dunes extending up the coast, a sand bar that continues north and east linking all the islands together save Audrey's home. That one is standing out there alone, detached and isolated.

36

July 9, Havre-Aubert, Iles de la Madeleine

NATHAN LIES DOWN, exhausted body full of seafood and wine, and marvels at the scar running diagonally just left of his belly button. He rubs his finger across it, but there is no feeling whatsoever. A white chalkiness remains, and he thinks for a moment that is not normal. Then again, he should not be walking around at all, much less enjoying the sights and sounds, tastes and smells of an evening out. He also knows he should not be having these thoughts about Audrey, a forbidden glimpse more enticing than seeing her naked. *Funny how the mind works*, Nathan thinks, wipes the dust off his finger and turns the light out.

They had returned to the bed and breakfast later than planned, but still early enough to rest and reset their body clocks from Ireland. Giddy from wine and overtiredness, they stumbled into a darkened house, the only light coming from a doorway opposite the dining room. The priest was still there–or there again–having moved slightly to what must be the kitchen. Nathan and Audrey waved in apology as the trio stopped talking to observe the pair. This time Claude simply reached over to close the door, leaving Nathan and Audrey in complete darkness.

Suppressing their laughter until the top of the stairs, they felt like teenagers coming home after curfew with not only mom and dad upset, but the local priest as well. If there were other guests they may still be out, though Nathan had the feeling they were the only ones here. It seems impossible with the activity on the streets, the lights and parties occurring everywhere around them. He and Audrey said their 'goodnights' and she continued down the hallway to her room. No need to change, just undress and lay down. Turn off the light. Drifting off, half logical thoughts moving through his mind, clearing the shelves and emptying out drawers, making room.

Nathan is floating through air, clouds of leaves in great big cumulus forms born brightly on a cool wind like rootless trees wandering the sky. He lands on one, looking in wondrous acceptance that this is the way the world is. Spotting a structure below, he launches his body back into the air and maneuvers closer.

He stands on a narrow dirt road, aside a crumbling gate to a wooded chapel yard. A low, stone wall with a rusting wrought iron fence blocks his path, and the tall iron gate between old piers is closed, one side hanging lazily off its hinge. These rooted trees are impossibly tall with no low branches, like a haphazard collection of columns extending to a faded distance all gray and green and hazy. The church itself is a simple extruded triangle, a large gable structure made of alternating stone giants and huge fir trees maybe sixty or seventy feet tall. Each giant stands angled, feet on the ground reaching skyward with the top of a tree in its monstrous hands. He can see hands from the opposite side holding up the tree next to each giant, at the same precise angle, its trunk firmly in the ground near the giant's feet. The tree's dense living canopy starts very near the earth and tapers to a point at top. And so they alternate back and forth, maybe ten of each, giant-tree-giant-tree and opposite the other side. The ends of this living/dead structure are open, light from the setting sun angling through and setting the face of the giant at the near end ablaze in emotionless contrasts.

Only a few feet from where he stands, just beyond the fence, is a cemetery, its stones scattered amongst the trees. All the graves are identical except for size; pairs of stone forearms reaching out of the earth, a stone tablet clutched at an angle between their hands. These tablets, some square at the end but some tapered to look like open books, are deeply etched. All are filled with script, some with pictures, describing the life of the person buried there. They vary in height and width, a few beyond so small they must be for children.

Where the edge of woods and gravestones meet the church clearing there is a statue, a solitary woman who Nathan finds familiar. He has moved through the fence, approaching for a better look. He steps into the shadow of the statue where the sun is shaded by the head of the woman. She has an odd posture with her arms out, as if she were once dancing. Nathan knows her but not really, not in this world. The head moves down and to the side, meeting his gaze but letting the sun sneak past so quickly in a blinding crescent that Nathan needs to look away.

In his haze Nathan hears the door open, a crack of light and fresh air from the hallway invades. The door closes again. He feels the bedcover raise and Audrey slip in, her warm body melting into him and her lips soft and demanding as they find his in the dark.

37

N ATHAN WAKES UP ALONE, startled by a knock at his
door. He quickly looks around for any sign that Audrey's
visit was real. There is a second impatient knock. He
grabs a towel slung over the arm of a chair and wraps it around his
waist. "Who is it?"

"Courier," a man's voice replies.

Nathan opens the door a crack, a familiar face. The courier
from Dingle is holding another package, similar in size and
wrapping to the one he had received previously. This time the man
acknowledges Nathan by not asking for his identification, handing
over the brown paper-wrapped bundle without a word. The courier
turns to go. "Cheers," he says over his back before reaching the
stair and descending out of sight. Nathan tosses the package onto
the bed and decides to shower before tackling its contents. From its
weight and bend it feels like half a ream of paper.

When he shuts the water off, Nathan thinks he hears movement,
a rustling of papers. He peers out the bathroom door, finding
Audrey sitting on his bed with papers spread around her. "I never
knew there were so many dark corners to this place. You think you

know your own home . . . ," she trails off studying another map.

"Excuse me, how do you know that wasn't my eyes only," he chides playfully, leaning in to steal a kiss. Audrey moves away, giving him a warning look that if he came any closer she would snap his neck. "Okay," Nathan says slowly to cover his awkward retreat.

"Let's focus on this," she directs.

"Are we going to talk about last night?" he asks.

"Great meal."

"Not what I was referring to."

"Then, no," she states, turning back to the papers, "we need a game plan here."

Nathan collects himself, trying to not look hurt. "Do you think it might happen again?" he finally asks. Audrey just stares at him sternly, which he takes as being better than a flat-out "no".

"Where do we even start?" she asks, "Suddenly these islands look huge. And how do we know these people weren't looking right at it? We can't rule out all these locations just because Moyne was already there."

"We can rule out anything that's not still in use, or at least still standing as a ruin," Nathan drops the towel to see if there is a reaction. None given, he begins pulling on his boxer shorts and shirt. He makes a mental note that he is running out of clean clothes.

"How do you figure?"

"Because otherwise he would hire an archeologist, or a social anthropologist, or some other '–ist'-type person. And besides, if it isn't, I'm not going to be of any use," he pulls his pants up and finishes, "whatever 'it' is."

"A village? A building? How do you lose a building? What are we looking for?" Audrey is at the edge of being upset. Nathan thinks she must operate better with specific directions, specific orders. If she did not get any from Moyne in this case, he would have to give her focus.

"Not sure, but it may have to do with a church and a cemetery."

"Swing a cat. Why?" she looks at him suspiciously.

"Let's just say an educated guess; the best place to store for a long time, some place that is above suspicion."

"Well, let's mark down all the church sites and do a quick reconnaissance. It's as good a place to start as any."

They sit down for at least half an hour, Audrey explaining where certain pictures were taken. Moyne included an overall map of the archipelago, which they set up as a master sheet to add marks and notes. They pack up a few of their things for the journey, with a plan to be back before dinner. Audrey returns to her room, fetching a few items of her own. She reappears in his doorway carrying a rain jacket over one arm and a duffel bag in the other hand. The bag looks heavy; Nathan can only imagine what may be inside. He picks up his small digital camera from the night stand and stops with a final thought.

"What do we do with that all day?" he points to the wrapped stone tablet he had stored under the bed for the night. "Back in the car, or do we trust it here with our hosts?"

"The best way to draw attention would be to take it everywhere we go. I think we leave the thing, maybe try to hide it a bit better," Audrey looks around the room for possibilities. "It's probably too heavy for up there," she points at the armoire.

Nathan empties his suitcase to see if it will fit. It does not. They both look around again and consider under the bed. "We leave it out," he decides, "it's wrapped up. Prop it up against the wall with my suitcase and throw a shirt over. If it's gone, I think we know where it might end up, and if we're successful here we may not need that leverage with Moyne." He slides it out from beneath

301

the bed and props it angled against the wall. His suitcase and clothes form a haphazard pile around and over.

At the bottom of the stairs their three hosts fall silent, only Claude finally wishing them a good day. There is no offer of breakfast, completely ignoring the second half of what the Maison de Marie should be, but which thankfully avoids an awkwardness Nathan had been preparing for.

In the car Audrey takes the wheel, turning completely around from its parking space. A short jaunt on the narrow street leads them north and to the main road connecting the islands. Much of this modest highway appears built on sandbars as it leaves Havre-Aubert and curves gently around the big bay and back to Cap-aux-Meules, the island where they arrived by ferry.

A rise in sea level and these people will need a new road, Nathan thinks.

The plan is to travel to the farthest island and then work their way back; just survey, get an impression of these places and the islands. If anything catches the eye they can return for a more in-depth reconnaissance later.

No sooner is this plan made than they reconsider. The two churches on the east side of Cap-aux-Meules along the highway are the most visible on the islands, and they decide to get them out of the way so they can head to the west side of the island on their return. They approach Laverniére, the second largest wooden church in North America according to notes included in Nathan's packet. The wood used in its construction was retrieved from shipwrecks, and whenever the church has been repaired this same rule has applied. Everything about it dates to its founding in the 1870's and no earlier, plus Nathan assesses it is too grand, too much an attraction; there is hiding in plain sight, and then there is just asking for trouble. The next church, Saint-André according to the sign, is within view of the harbor. Although it is stone, this church is even newer, dating from the 1960's, and Nathan does not even ask Audrey stop the car.

"Oh god," Audrey mumbles, slumping in her seat as the road angles toward the harbor, covering the side of her face with a free hand.

"What?"

"My mother," she motions with her head.

"Really?" Nathan looks around curiously, "Where?"

"Not funny. She was back there on the sidewalk; she must have come over to look for me."

"Did she see you?"

"I don't think so, but you can bet she knows where we're staying."

"So we'll meet her later."

"Yeah," Audrey takes a deep breath, "I guess so."

The drive northeast is breathtaking, and Nathan relaxes to take in as much as he can. He has learned a long time ago that focusing causes him to miss too much, and with his visual memory he can recall most of what he needs from a casual observation far better. More houses in bright colors, curious square barns with a sliding roof that Audrey informs him are called "baraque". Near some of the ports there are also distinctive herring smokehouses; they pass a fantastic one in Pointe-Basse harbor on the next island Havre-aux-Maison. By the time they literally reach the end of the road in Ile de Grande-Entrée, looping back south and west around a large lagoon, Nathan feels he has a much better ability to identify something out of the ordinary, now having a baseline knowledge of what ordinary is.

They pull up to a small wood church overlooking the lagoon they just circumnavigated. Sacré-Couer looks the same vintage as

Laverniére, but has the wear of a building heavily used by the community. Like its larger cousin, it has a stormy beginning, constructed partly of wood thrown overboard from a ship in bad weather. Audrey stays by the car as Nathan walks a simple loop around the exterior, snapping a few photos before returning. "Next," he says simply.

At Old Harry, a small bay and outcropping at the connection of the two northeasterly islands, St. Peter's-by-the-Sea is another wood church of materials salvaged from surrounding waters. Nathan takes a counterclockwise jaunt, pausing longer this time to look out at the bay leading into the lagoon.

"Are all your churches made from shipwrecks?" Nathan asks when he returns to the car.

"It's the one thing we have an abundance of. This is considered the second largest marine cemetery after Sable Island, more than five hundred wrecks scattered around here," she waits for the joke about always being second. When it does not come, she continues, "Wait till you see the Irish Cemetery that's next."

She was not exaggerating. Nathan is stunned by the seven thousand graves mostly dated around 1847 they come upon at Grosse-Ile. These were refugees from the Potato Famine who were diverted here, not allowed onto the Canadian mainland due to fear of spreading the blight. The weight of so much death in so little time must have been overwhelming, magnified in such a small place. On a positive note Nathan finds there is more English spoken on these northeastern islands, perhaps a remnant of those that survived.

"What's that out there?" Nathan points out to a dark stretch of land on the horizon.

"Iles Brion," Audrey answers, "Uninhabited, a nature preserve. You can go out there when the weather's mild, but I don't believe it has ever been settled, and certainly no structures."

The long straight drive down the north dune is interrupted by the island of Pointe-aux-Loups, which has a small church serving its handful of residents. It feels less of an island and more of a rise and widening of the sandbar that continues on the other side. Nathan walks a bit further past the church, down to the small dock area. The sand here transitions to red rock cliffs rising up to guard its occupants against the swirling waters, erasing any doubt that this conglomeration of fifty buildings is truly an island in its own right.

Crossing over the bridge just past this small outcropping they soon come to the South Dune, miles and miles of white sands and blue waters. The rise in the road after a few minutes announces they are now on Havre-aux-Maison, the "Grindstone". A brief glimpse of the green rolling hills and magnificent cliffs of the eastern coast before the road turns inland reminds Nathan of the Dingle area they had left a few days back. *If the church thing doesn't work out*, he thinks, *maybe I can convince her to check out lighthouses next.*

They stop at the Church of Sainte-Madeleine, another relatively new structure. Audrey points him to the neighboring Vieux Couvent; a symmetrical, solid-looking gray brick structure with strong, vertical windows. The original chapel had been built there, she says, but any traces of it are now under the former convent and current upscale hotel.

"Really? We couldn't stay here?" Nathan complains. As a consolation prize, they take an early lunch in its restaurant before moving on. "How many left?" he asks, finishing what is really a late breakfast. The restaurant closes an hour before lunch, and the servers are eager to clear their plates as the hour of eleven approaches.

"Just two, and you're not going to be happy with the next one," she warns.

Back on Cap-aux-Meules the modern arching roof form of the

church in Fatima is striking to Nathan, but furthest yet from what he is looking for. He tells Audrey to keep driving, not even bothering to slow the car down as they pass. The road they are on will carry them through Étang-du-Nord, and eventually past Moyne's office. Continuing this way rather than backtrack to the main road, they pass more scattered homes dotting the countryside until they gradually thicken into a town. Approaching from the north makes this town look far different than the previous day.

"Just the one church left at the southern edge of the island we're staying on," Nathan looks at the map, "and one within walking distance of the B & B."

"There is one on my island," Audrey adds nervously, thinking he might want to go out there.

"Is it really old?" he asks. Audrey shakes her head no. "They all are much newer than I expected," Nathan complains, "Even the older ones have been rebuilt. I suppose attracting lightning is the downside of having a steeple out here." He stops talking to watch the one building he recognizes vividly come into view, the one they were led to yesterday. A door opens at its far end and a familiar man comes out, glancing in both directions before proceeding down the street away from them.

"Pull over," Nathan demands suddenly. Audrey obeys and parks the car nearly opposite Moyne's building. "Anton just left Moyne's place. That's him walking down the street," he points excitedly.

"Not surprising. I hate to hurt your feelings, but I bet he's hired you both to do the same job," she looks over at Nathan, "Actually, Anton was hired first."

"Do we follow him, or confront Moyne? See if we're being sent on a wild goose chase?"

"Why?"

"Why? Well okay Ms. Special Forces, how about we narrow down why we're driving all over the place," he stares at her intently, "What the hell has happened to you since we got here?"

"Fine. Let's wait to see what car he gets into, then go up and see Moyne. We can catch up to Anton later, since he's probably not leaving the islands."

They watch Eischen cross to their side of the street and get into a green four-door sedan. It is difficult to discern the exact make of the car from the back until it pulls out, a Toyota symbol coming into view. Audrey reads the license plate number, which Nathan adds to their list of notes on the back of the map.

With a quick move Anton turns into a driveway, backs out, and comes directly toward them. They both duck down, almost bumping heads in the process, to hide as he drives past and north up the road from which they just came. After a minute Audrey rises and gets out of the car. Nathan follows her out and across the street to the side door.

No guards at the door. They enter an empty lobby and press the button, wishing there was a less obvious stair to sneak up. The elevator dings quickly, still at the floor from when Anton had come down. At the top they are again faced with the Exceedingly Long Hallway, but this time it feels different, darker at the end.

"You smell that?" Audrey asks.

"What is that?" Nathan uses a hand to cover his face.

"Blood," she is certain.

She leads the way down the hall. As they approach Moyne's office, the air is almost humid with the smell. The wall opposite the office door and the end wall of the hallway are covered in blood, a thick coating that drips down the walls. The carpet is soaked, a few sets of shoe prints leading in and out visible near the edges. They look at each other, both wondering if it would be wise to add their own tracks to the mix. Curiosity is far more powerful, and they step into view of the doorway trying not to slip or touch anything.

A horrific amount of blood covers every surface of the room, glistening in the light and moving as it settles and resettles before drying. It is impossible to distinguish any one thing from the other, the coating melts each shape into the other into a single surface.

They see the two guards, propped up in lounge chairs each corner of the office, angled and facing the center of the room with their eyes open. There is nothing, not even chairs, where they look. Nathan almost misses it as he looks up, the reddish black monochrome melting everything together, until a glimmer of metal catches his eye. Attached to the middle of the ceiling, stapled there with large blade at each extremity and a sword directly center, is a third body. Moyne.

"I can't believe anything human did this," Audrey whispers, shuffling over slightly. They both need to keep moving their feet or get stuck in the congealing fluid. "There is just too much blood, way more than three people."

"Do we call this in?" Nathan asks.

"And get the hell out."

"Wait," Nathan covers his nose with his forearm, staring at the scene on the ceiling, "look at how he's arranged, his legs slightly spread, one arm straight out over his head and the other tucked in, one sword perpendicular through his midsection and the other straight through." At that moment, the mid section of Moyne's body slides down the sword holding it to the ceiling. The blades holding his legs in begin to let go, and the whole assembly comes crashing straight down with a sickening moist thud. Nathan and Audrey duck back behind the door just in time to avoid a cloud of spray from the body hitting the floor.

Nathan steps back into the opening, shoes squeaking in blood so thick it recovers his footprints. He stares up at the ceiling where the body had been affixed. The outline is clear, blood defining the edges and a few splotches in the middle where the sword and other blades had penetrated him. The shape is instantly recognizable to anyone who has ever looked at a building plan, and Nathan is amazed at the complex artistry of this given the drawing medium. "It's a North Arrow," he whispers.

38

July 10, Iles de la Madeleine

THEY CROSS THE street quickly without running, trying to avoid attention. The area is suddenly busy with shoppers and tourists, walking and smiling in the bright afternoon. It may have been just as busy before, but the adrenaline of fear makes Nathan very aware, very paranoid. When he gets to the car and has a moment to calm down, he realizes that absolutely no one has noticed; obliviousness to the carnage a just above their heads which he finds disgusting. "We need to call it in," he tells Audrey.

"I'm not risking my cell phone," she shakes her head emphatically. "We'll call from a pay phone along the way."

They sit quietly, engine off, staring at the throng of people who appeared in the brief time they were inside Moyne's building. They dodge in and out of stores, around each other on sidewalks, between cars to cross the street. It is a frenzy of consumption, shopping bags and food in hand. No one notices two figures sitting blankly in a rental car. Nathan looks over to Audrey. "You know, he may not have done it. He may have just come across it like we did."

"If he had, he couldn't have done all that alone," she agrees. "I'm more curious about the drama. Only some of that was blood,

310

the rest fake."

"How do you know?"

"I know blood. And why would Anton do that anyway?"

"It might be part of a retirement plan," Nathan offers. "I'm not getting paid now, am I?"

"Big picture," Audrey chides. "Speaking of which, did you take any photos?"

"No."

"We need to go back up there. If there was a message, a map or a plan, then we need to see it."

"Trust me when I say I remember. A picture wouldn't show it anyway. Just do what the man says and head north." He looks around, adjusting himself to the office location. "Actually, head sort of northeast-y."

"That's good, because straight north is ocean."

Turning the car around, they depart in the same direction Anton had gone earlier, though at least ten minutes behind. They travel southeast for a short while before connecting back with the highway. As they retrace their morning drive, Nathan finds the familiarity allows him to purely focus on looking for Anton's car without distraction. More importantly, he needs to find Anton to discover what happened to him: if he is going to survive, and why he needed to follow him to these islands. The pain is worsening again, his insides melting and filling with God-knows-what.

They pass over Havre-aux-Maisons and up the south dune, crossing over to the north dune before Nathan allows himself to rest; if anyone parked a car on the long flat dune it would be easily noticed. There were a lot of small side roads Anton could have ducked down, but these first two islands they have crossed were not in the direction the corpse pointed. They simply have to be traversed because that is the road. Now that they are on the north dune, heading northeast, Nathan feels back on track.

The bump of Pointe-aux-Loups yields to the longest stretch of drive before Grosse-Ile, where they had walked the Irish cemetery. It will get more complicated once they arrive; generally the right location, but a lot of ground to cover. Because the main road hugs the northern coast, they turn south inland to cover more ground. It is less than one uneventful mile before they hook back up with the main road heading due east.

A half mile past the bridge at East Cape, where the road turns south again, they see a green four-door Toyota parked in a gravel drive to a field. Audrey slows down gently, without stopping, while Nathan checks the license plate number he had written down. It is Anton's car. "It looks empty, but I don't see anyplace nearby he would have gone," Nathan notes.

Audrey stops the car on the shoulder and backs up. She puts it in park, leaving the engine run, and contorts her body to reach the duffel bag in the back seat. Returning forward Nathan sees she has put on black leather gloves and is carrying a black Glock handgun.

"I'm not taking any chances," she says reaching for the door handle. As Nathan reaches for his own door she adds, "Stay here."

He follows her movements in the side mirror, slouching down a bit in his seat in case of a shootout. Suddenly he misses Ireland, where the violence seemed quaint and civilized. Now they were back in the Wild West, where guns are the preferred way. Nathan has no problem with this, or with guns in general; he just wishes he had one of his own.

Audrey crouches low, resting against the back driver-side panel of Anton's car. Jumping up quickly to peer in the back window, she just as quickly dives down to her previous position. She holds her hand under the car for a second, then moves up to the driver-side door. She opens it and spins to look in, gun leading the way.

"Clear," she calls out.

Nathan opens the car door and walks over to join her, scanning for surprises. There are houses around but none very close, mostly a vast amount of scruffy land. If he remembers the map, this whole area is on the edge of a nature preserve. A large lagoon, surrounded on three sides by islands and sandbars with just a small outlet to the ocean near the point of Grande-Entrée, lies a few hundred yards from the road where they stand.

"You think he's hiding out here?" Nathan looks around.

"I doubt it. He didn't know we were following him. Probably ditched the car, got a ride with someone else, or had another car waiting."

"Someone walked out recently," Nathan points at some trampled grass near the car, "either two people, or one person out and back." They follow Anton's path through tall grasses out to the water's edge. On the right side the gentle coast gives way to moderate cliffs, appropriately sized for a lagoon rather than an ocean, ending at what Audrey calls the "Point du Fort". On their left is a nondescript, rather natural-looking coastline heading south all the way to the Bay of Old Harry. There are a few small islands dotting the lagoon itself.

"Anything else while we're out here?" Audrey is irritated and not looking forward to the drive back to the opposite end of the archipelago. Now that Anton has switched cars, they have no idea which way he went. They could have passed him anywhere along the road.

"Don't we have a dinner date?" Nathan tries to lighten the mood. It is still on the early side of mid-afternoon, and he would also prefer not have to make this same drive tomorrow no matter how scenic. He wants, he needs, to find Anton. *Screw the scavenger hunt*, Nathan thinks, *I need to talk to that bastard.* He scans the horizon, a pattern beginning to coalesce as his mind tries to make sense of the jumbled landscape.

"I caught a glimpse of this before," he says, waving his arm loosely in a half circle in front of him. "All these houses, they seem scattered."

"It's like that all over these islands," she points out.

"Exactly. But if you take away the newer ones, just focus on the ones with bargeboards at the gable end–the older ones from their style–there is something organizing them. It's subtle, but not exactly cardinal. You expect south, or against prevailing winds, or responding to a natural feature. These," he points, estimating for distance, "all seem to be facing out there," his finger roughly landing on an island in the lagoon.

"There's nothing out there. I've actually sailed around it a few times, lots of people have. It's just an overgrown tiny island."

"Have you ever been on it?"

"There's no place to land, the edges are all overgrown."

"Can you get me out there?"

"I'll have to get a boat. I might know someone in Old Harry," she says.

"OK, we have a plan. But first I want to get in one of those houses," Nathan points, "do you know anyone?"

"No, I don't. Why not just announce what we're doing out here," Audrey looks cross. She resigns herself to the fact they may be here for a while Not that she was in a great hurry to get back to the B & B, or her mother.

"It's probably changed owners several times from whoever built it," Nathan coaxes, "come on, it's the only way to verify that island means anything before we spend all the effort of going out there."

They get back in the car and within a few minutes are driving down the long driveway of the closest house Nathan identified. No usual signs of life are around the structure; no dogs running out to the car, or curtains moving inside. The siding is in good shape, painted within the last few years and a new roof. They stop near the side entry and close the car doors loudly, trying to get a reaction. Nathan takes a glance around the outside, noticing an old stone foundation overgrown with weeds, jutting out perpendicular from the corner of the house like an old kitchen ell.

"That was here first; probably why the house faces the way it does," he points out to Audrey. She is already at the back door, first knocking and then getting ready to force it open if there is no answer. She puts a shoulder to it, but tries the handle anyway. The door opens easily.

"I forget people still leave their doors unlocked," she shrugs, opening it wider and allowing Nathan to pass by her. "I'll stay out here, keep watch."

Within a few moments Nathan comes out. "We have to go to another one," he says briskly.

"Why?"

"Just go," he commands.

Audrey steers the car down the driveway, briefly along the road, and then back up the gravel drive about four houses over. Again no one is home, the door is unlocked, and Nathan easily steps inside while Audrey stands lookout. She mentions that going to multiple houses is better cover than just targeting one, but Nathan stays silent.

He enters the second house, a similar style but different color, stopping in the doorway. Nathan takes a few steps inside what would normally be a kitchen. "Audrey," he calls out, "you might want to come in here."

He hears her behind him, slowing as she gets closer, and without turning feels her presence as her shoulder brushes his. "The other one was just like this," he whispers.

The feeling is like being inside a tent rather than the structure that it is. The exposed dirt floor has a few areas where scrub is growing, a damp earthy smell in the air. Scattered around this ground are several large upright stones. Gravestones. Many have smaller flat stones on end outlining a rectangle where someone would be buried.

Equally scattered are life-sized statues in various sizes and positions, mostly away from where anyone peering in a window could see them. Nathan brushes his finger across the arm of one. They seem to be a rough gray stone, very good work given their thinness. A bit of a chalky residue is left on his finger, which he brushes off on his pants. The style is sort of horrific, gaunt but realistic Giacometti, scrawny figures posed in various positions: sitting on a lone chair, cooking at an antique stove, perched on a hoe tilling a nonexistent garden. They are mostly women, a couple men, and quite a few children in various poses of play. Nathan is at once fascinated and repulsed at the sick brilliance of the display. He knows more than a few museum directors who would move this scene, intact, to an exhibit space.

The 'house' itself is simply an open shell; no second floor, only exposed structure up to the roof trusses. Most of the windows are small and vertical, typical for an old farmhouse, except one large bay window looking back towards the coastline. As Nathan steps over a few gravestones to get closer he sees it is off center in the wall to capture a specific view. The window looks straight out to the small island in the lagoon.

"Well," Audrey finally utters, "this is different."

Nathan nods his head in agreement. "Kinda fucks with your expectations, doesn't it?"

39

July 10, Iles de la Madeleine

A PIERCING WAIL consumes the house, forcing Nathan
and Audrey to cover their ears. He assumes they tripped
an alarm before he pinpoints the source and realizes it is
coming from them, the statues.

"You had to touch one, didn't you?!" Audrey screams over the
sound. She nods toward the door and they both quickly leave,
closing the door behind. Once shuttered, the high-pitched scream is
surprisingly muffled by the thin structure. Not waiting to see who
shows up in response to the signal, they speed down the driveway to
the road. "Was that it?" Audrey asks, "What Moyne sent us to
find?"

"I doubt it. Anton would have been here, and I would also be
shocked if Moyne hadn't known about this, this . . . I'm not even
sure what to call it. But it doesn't matter what he knows anymore,
does it?"

She nods in resigned agreement.

"So let's go find a boat," Nathan shrugs, trying to mask his
agony from twisting his torso getting into the car when they fled.

"You have no idea how much danger we are in," Audrey

mutters, misreading his flippant response.

"I'm painfully aware," Nathan looks sullenly out his passenger side window as she drives fast, distancing themselves from the houses that were not houses. They arrive in the town of Old Harry within ten minutes, no sign of police or anyone else responding to the alarm. She turns down a rather pathetic road to a group of buildings spread out near the bay on the ocean side, rather than the lagoon side where they want to cast off. Nathan hopes they do not have to go all the way around on water to get back to the island, since it looked within easy reach from the house. They pull into a parking lot overlooking soft red cliffs, worn with layers upon layers of lines from constant pounding of the ocean.

Audrey directs him to stay with the car while she arranges for a small boat shallow enough for the lagoon waters. Nathan steps out to stretch and look over the nearby cliffs. There are numerous cars around, most people venturing around the cliff to the expanse of beach beyond. He looks back at the loose group of structures. Old Harry is not really a town at all, he decides, but just a promising name with no "there" there. He walks over to survey the reddish-ochre brushed cliffs, soft and rounded. The wind is strong, the sea air at once invigorating and making him sick to his stomach. Gulls float in place, facing into the wind until they dive towards their perch with a screech reminiscent of the one he heard in the house.

After half an hour he returns to the car. Although he did not exactly 'stay with it', the vehicle was always within sight. Now back, and no sign of Audrey anywhere, his restless nature gets the best of him and he starts to walk towards the buildings she had left for earlier.

Approaching the road that separates the parking lot from what she called the village he sees her; she is talking close, almost intimately, to someone. It appears she leans in for a kiss, or to whisper something in his ear, and Nathan can feel jealousy well up inside. The sickness quickly turns to rage when, just as she pulls her head back, the face of the man is revealed. Nathan starts to run as the man turns away and disappears behind the shed. Anton.

Audrey sees him and quickens her pace across the road, holding out her hand to stop him. "It's not what you think," she yells.

He pushes her aside, but the delay is enough to lose Anton. A moment later Nathan sees a car leaving from behind one of the sheds, pulling out some distance away and turning back to the main road. He doubles over in the middle of the road, a jab of pain coursing through his body.

"I didn't tell him you were already here," Audrey says, "I had to make it look like it was just me."

"Why? You're lying," he accuses, looking up at her, "he knows I'm coming after him. He made sure of it. He wants me here."

"He doesn't know you're here yet," she explains, "and that is the only advantage we have right now."

"But I saw," he says getting back up slowly to face her. "You're protecting him—why?!"

"I'm not,"

"You're working with him in some way, just like Dingle. You also visit him in the middle of the night?"

She slaps him, really hard. Given her training, Nathan finds it quaint and quite preferable to what she might have done. It begs another question, though. "What has happened to you?" he asks, "Since we got here, you're hardly the same person."

"I am not a child!" her voice lowers, she speaks slowly and forcefully, "Do not treat me like a child!"

"Who's treating you like a child?" he asks before it dawns on him. "It's being here. You're falling back into some earlier version of you, before you went off and became some paramilitary badass."

Nathan shakes his head. "Who are you? First you're a lean efficient mercenary with a torture fetish, and now you're wondering which one of us will take you to prom."

"Who am I?" she retorts, "If you envision yourself as some kind of freedom-loving, unattached professional playboy then you should really look at how pathetic you've become. You're a shallow, naïve, lonely and disconnected pencil-pusher."

"Pencil-pusher! Oh please. Who's been trained to simply follow orders, be the good soldier? Is that what you're doing right now, following Anton's orders? Is that all you know how to do?"

"I trained hard, served my country, had to be creative to get out of some jams! Don't you dare turn that strength into a negative," she warns.

"Well then why are you relying on me to do all the thinking here?" Nathan asks.

"You don't think! You don't make decisions!" she spits back.

"How can you even say that? It's what I do for a living," he looks incredulous.

"Not about important things. Not about real things." Her voice tones down as she becomes aware of a few tourists noticing them. "Not when it comes to your own life. Have you done any of the things you've really wanted to?"

"It's my firm. I've got the reputation."

"It's not about that; success or glamour or whatever. Besides, I've spoken to Johanna and I know about your reputation."

"What?!" Nathan's voice raises again, causing a few heads to turn their way. "You spoke to Johanna?!"

"Like I said, it's not about that. Who the fuck do you think you are? Is it really who you imagine you are, in whatever made-up world you live in?" Audrey looks to dial the argument down a notch. "This week is probably the first time in twenty years you've felt this alive."

"Oh yeah, I feel really alive right now," he says, wincing again in pain. "And if you think this about me, then really what the hell was last night about? Your terms, your way to manipulate me?"

"Easy enough if I wanted to, but it wasn't that," she looks him directly in the eye, melting him a little.

"Well, you snore, which isn't exactly covert," he attempts to recover, "and your hands are too big for your body. They're the hands of a seven foot tall man; like big Mickey Mouse hands."

"Really, my hands?!" she waves them in front of his face mockingly. "And I'll have you know that I only snore when I drink, and I never drink on a real mission."

"People are dying–does that make it a real mission yet?"

"I haven't exactly felt all that well these past few days," it pains her to admit, "and coming home is . . . you know, people see you a certain way and you tend to fall into that."

Nathan sits back down on the pavement, thankful that the few cars moving around the area see fit to give them a wide berth. The stress of the argument, combined with twisting his injury earlier, all settle in the very pit of his abdomen.

"Not what this is really about," she states, taking his change in posture as defeat, or a signal that he was done, "is you want to finish this. You're curious, or you think there is some reward. Like I said before, this is maybe the first real thing you've done in a long time."

"My job is real; I get things built," he retorts.

"But it isn't enough. In the end it's not YOUR building, it's not a lasting reflection of who you are. The ego stroke you search for isn't quite enough, is it?"

There is silence as he stews.

"Get over it," she goes on. "We will all be forgotten, even the Immortal. Why even try. Do something now, or leave someone behind who will remember you, because none of those buildings will."

"Fine," he feels done now, and Anton is probably miles away.

"Fine," she echoes.

"Fine," he repeats.

"Let's just do this and get out of here. It'll be dark soon," Audrey points out. A positive of their argument, she thinks, is that by the time they are done, the boat is ready in the small make-shift harbor of the lagoon. It is unusual for boats to launch from here, other than a few small one- or two-person crafts, and so the only available dock is in a private back yard. The small rental metal boat is just big enough for the two of them, the motor, and the duffel bag Audrey retrieves from the car.

The trip takes longer than he expects, almost an hour of solid motoring. The whine and smell of exhaust diminishes as Audrey lets off the throttle nearing the island. She turns the boat parallel to the shore, if you can call it a shore. It is heavily overgrown, tree tops dipping down to the water masking anywhere to land. The reflection of sky and trees in the late afternoon water gives a curious effect, as if the trees themselves were disembodied, rootless, floating amongst the clouds.

40

July 11, Iles de la Madeleine

NATHAN HAS BEEN here before. At first he thinks it déjà vu, a lost remnant of a dream, but then realizes they very literally have been here before; they just completed an entire loop around the island and are now back where they first arrived. The whole perimeter is the same, tree canopy and scrub down to the water's edge like a great protective buffer, obscuring any place where they could land safely and step ashore. It is beginning to look like they would have to swim for it and hope they can sneak underneath, leaving Audrey's duffel bag of goodies behind, and the boat secured as best they can.

"Any other ideas?" Audrey asks.

"Back to the side that faces the house. East," he reckons.

She turns the boat around, speeding towards the distant shore. They angle north around the curve of the island and slow down. Nathan studies its edge. "There," he points. "It's darker there, a slight line that's too straight, and the space between the trees is too regular, too symmetrical."

She aims the boat for the spot where Nathan is pointing and guns the engine. "What are you doing?!" he yells and then dives face down into the boat as branches scrape loudly over the top of him, covering his back in leaves and broken twigs. When the noise stops he peers over the top of the hull to see where they arrived. They are in a small channel of water, the sides of it held back with rotting wood piers driven into the ground. Audrey pulls the boat up to the side and throws a rope to Nathan, signaling him to go ashore and tie off.

"You took a hell of a chance making a run for it. What if I was wrong?"

"You weren't," she states.

"When people reshape nature, it leaves an indelible imprint; that's my world. Besides the straight lines under the water, signs of dredging, were subtle."

"I still should have seen it." Audrey ponders him for a second, and then shakes her head. "If you can see that kind of subtlety, what's with the strip clubs?"

"Did Johanna tell you about the clubs?" he is aghast, then defends, "Just because I can't go in a building or I don't own the home doesn't mean I don't appreciate it."

"Spoken like a true addict," Audrey says grabbing her duffel and stepping onto shore. "There's a path," she says scanning the small clearing. All around are trees and reed grasses obscuring even the edge of the island which they had passed through.

"That one looks more formal, but that one over there looks more used," he points to a trail angling off the main path.

"Stay close," she warns, and heads down the formal path.

Below their feet the ground feels too soft. They are not sinking, but it just feels wrong. Every now and then they step on a firm spot, jolting their knees and shooting a pain all over Nathan's body. The smell is damp but less salty than other places they had stopped on their way here; a microclimate of lagoon air, and rotting leaves.

This is a foreign place, he thinks, with probably as many trees here as he had seen anywhere on the islands. "I think this island is artificial; like parts of Venice, or an Irish crannog." Nathan says.

"Crannog?" Audrey asks, not bothering to turn around.

"In the small lakes of central Ireland they built small, basically individual homestead islands, used for fishing at first but also for protection. Some were still lived on up to the 17th century."

Suddenly Audrey stops, and then soon he sees it. There is a wire stretched across, and beyond it the trail is moving slightly. "It's a trap," she admits.

"I told you the other path looked better."

She glares at Nathan, then walks past him towards the fork in the path and he follows again, the rhythm of soft ground and sudden jolts of firmness worsening his injury. Nathan was thankful she did not tell him to carry the bag. Now cutting through what feels like a narrow deer trail they move slowly, sometimes sideways. Within moments he feels lost, the sameness of trees and scrub all around.

"What are we looking for?" she asks.

"The most important, prominent spot; probably whatever hill we can find if there is one, or a place around an inlet bigger than the one we came in."

Audrey drops down a couple feet as her leg breaks through the ground. Nathan reaches for her, but too late as she has already stopped. Tossing the duffel bag aside, she extracts herself from the hole her right leg had found, the ground oozing full of water and muck as she pulls it clear. "I don't know how much further we can go," she says sitting down to wipe the mud off.

"There's a rhythm I've noticed to the pilings holding this island up. Let me lead, step where I step," Nathan directs.

The trail becomes dense and overgrown, and at least twice they think they have lost it. It is getting darker, the color of twilight beginning to change the atmosphere all around them. Slow going, but within half an hour of walking the ground becomes firmer and firmer until it feels normal. Suddenly they come out through an edge of scrubby trees and find themselves faced with the ruins of a stone wall. The wall is dry laid, only about eight feet high but curving off in both directions. Ivy and grasses have taken hold of the sides and top, making it look slightly taller. The stone itself looks the same limestone from the cliffs, much softer and warmer than one would expect for a protective wall. They follow it about a hundred yards to where a portion of it has crumbled, allowing an opening they can easily scamper over.

Inside feels like a maze. Nathan climbs back up the low portion of the outer wall they had entered to get a better look. The whole area inside the circular outer wall is filled with small stone huts and alleys between. It is a tight assembly of perfect cubes and domes, even the point of a pyramid can be seen in the distance, all from the same stone as the outer wall. The cube forms are missing their roofs, which were most likely wood when this place was used. Trees provide a sheltering canopy, sometimes growing directly out of the huts, completely concealing the place unless you are already inside.

Nathan comes back down and they begin to wind their way towards the center through tight pathways. He looks inside one of the huts. It is light because of no roof, but he can imagine how the windowless single room dwelling would have felt.

"What the hell is this place?" Audrey asks in an awed voice, "I never knew this existed here. I never could have imagined."

"I can also tell you this is Irish. This is a crannog on a big scale. This outer wall was called a caher," he points back from where they had come.

"Everyone did fortification walls," she points out.

"Yeah, but circular like this, the stonework. . ." he trails off trying to drink it all in. They walk a bit further to a larger, almost triangle-shaped clearing bordered on two sides by the stone cubes and the third by the outer wall. He points through the overgrowth. "That's a dolmen, or trilith or whatever," raising a branch to reveal a stone set horizontally across two other vertical stones like a table on legs. He walks in a bit further, moving the brush around a pile of stones. "And this is definitely a cistvaen tomb; I recognized them at the houses. These flat stone slabs on end, making a box around where the body is buried. It's a bit old for the Irish immigrants who came here. Cemeteries are architecture; how we treat our dead is a great statement of the living, a reflection of our society. And it's so distilled, so pure of an opportunity to design."

"Never really saw that in your magazines."

"Well those magazines are just like porn for architects; the hottest, latest thing. They never get to the real depth."

"And you do?" she mocks, but Nathan is too far into his analysis to care or notice.

"Beyond the visual functions, these elements by their relationships to one another, and the nature of their organization, also communicate notions of domain and place, entrance and path movement, hierarchy and order. These are the literal meanings of form and space, just like language. However, there are also connotations and secondary meanings; values and symbolic content."

"Like who gets the corner office, and what it means about their status?"

"Some things never change, like who had the highest cave or the central tent." Nathan spins around three hundred sixty degrees, trying to take in everything at once. "The form-defined space dates them. This rotated grid over here is very recent, and not original to everything else." He realizes he's lost her, or she simply does not care: probably a bit of both. *When did I start babbling when I'm nervous*, he wonders, *whatever happened to quiet and deep*? Nathan decides to go on anyway, if nothing else to clarify it to himself. "There's additive, subtractive or dimensional form. These all feel subtractive, which is odd for a place like this or any place . . . except maybe Petra that was literally hewn out of rock."

Nathan walks into another one of the vine-covered shells, stepping inside and then looking up through the missing roof. The stone is dry-laid, slightly angled to shed rain and melting snow. "Primary shapes and Platonic solids: cube, pyramid, sphere, etc. Everything else is a transformation of that in a regular or irregular way. Clustered, radial, linear, centralized are the regular ways. These are all, yet none of those. They just are." His fascination gets the better of him, and he completely forgets Audrey, Anton, the dead guy pinned to the ceiling, even his footing. He steps back out and into a sinkhole. As he extricates himself, he realizes he is in the middle of a crossing between two angled walls. They are close to the middle now, and as he looks for the center and then back again, he understands the angles and their meeting.

"This is a huge pentagram inscribed in a circle." He is overwhelmed by the raw geometry, the raw purpose of it.

"Devil worshippers?" Audrey asks, coming over to help.

"The pentagram is essentially human, pointing out the four primary elements and showing a connection with them and respect for the earth. The pentagram is also a proportion, the length of the lines where they cross also a representation of the Golden Section."

"You mentioned that before."

"The Egyptians used it, and the Renaissance was all over it. But the Renaissance theories were based on more ancient Greek mathematical proportions, especially Pythagoras' theory of means.

It's why everything we are looking at here feels like one form even though they are all different; it's all based on a strict mathematical proportioning system. Very sophisticated." Nathan falls silent.

"So what's the problem?" Audrey finally asks.

"Where did all this stone come from? It's not natural to here, so why bring it in on boats?" he asks. "And if this was a real community, there should be an open space in the middle, the chapel off to the side instead of whatever that thing is," he points to a small building with a familiar upside-down boat shape within the five sided central plot, bounded by the intersection of streets. "At most, it would be on axis to one of these streets, with an open space off to the side. The only clearing I saw was the cemetery and another small harbor on the opposite side."

"But what does it tell us?"

"That whoever built this wasn't just a group of homesteaders. There is a strong hierarchy here, and only one place with symmetry: it's physical and very direct. All around is rhythm and repetition. It wasn't just a church. These people were basically worshipping something, or someone, that was right here." Nathan moves to the central spot of the pentagram, the place where all the forces and lines and volumes are coming together, drawing power or dispersing it. He looks around thoughtfully. "But this shouldn't be here: wrong time period, wrong part of the world, wrong materials."

"This is it. I mean whoever killed Moyne was trying to keep this place hidden. The trees all around have kept it masked from anyone flying over, abandoned and grown over for centuries, and we saw how hard it is to land here unless you knew what you are looking for."

"This is at least what Moyne sent us to find. But whatever was here isn't anymore." He picks up a stone, turns it over in his hand and sets it back. "As curious as it is, I don't think this is what we are looking for. This may have been it at one time, and they've moved, or it's a ruse. Moyne was pointing this way. Whoever killed him wanted us to find this place. If he had been killed as a warning, he would have been posed as a pentagram with a circle drawn around, or something more meaningful to those in the know. I'm putting my money back on Anton. He probably followed us out here."

"Why you say that?"

"Ever get the feeling you're being watched?" Nathan says.

She nods her head to the side. "Been tracking us for at least an hour," Audrey sets her duffel down, "Time to move; you're the bait." She barely moves a foot to retrieve the gun from her bag when a figure appears out of the woods at the edge of the ruined settlement. He is tall and gangly, dressed in a loose green shirt and blue jeans with tall boots covered in mud. A moment later two large men similarly dressed flank him, carrying far superior firepower.

"You two shouldn't be here," the gangly man simply states.

"We were sent here," Audrey tries the truth, hoping the name would have some weight, "by Daniel Moyne."

"I'm Daniel Moyne," he says, causing Nathan to look at Audrey in confusion, "and I certainly did not invite you here."

41

July 11, Iles de la Madeleine

NATHAN AND AUDREY sit at one end of a long wood table, the only warm-colored piece in the room. Everything else about the space–the glass, walls, furniture, ceiling and carpet, even the lighting–all compound similar hues in each other to make the space impossibly blue. It is disconcerting, surreal as anything he has seen in his life. Nathan imagines the effect is purposeful, as fitting a room as he could imagine for interrogation. Another curious thing, as far as he could tell, is that they now find themselves on the missing second floor of Moyne's building.

The low rising sun does little to change the hue of this Impossibly Blue Room. Incarcerated since arriving from the island, they had been given water but nothing else, leaving Nathan feel very hungry. He is, in fact, feeling remarkably hungry and better. Audrey on the other hand is feeling weak again, and that has frustrated his desire to escape. As resourceful as he imagines himself to be, Audrey is the expert, and has so far nixed all of his ideas.

A door opens opposite the window wall. The three men from

the island walk in, the man who introduced himself as Moyne entering last. A flush of fresh air enters with them, displacing the staleness. Nathan decides to speak first. "Look, I know this is not a game, but I have nothing to hide. I'll tell you anything you want to know," he looks at Audrey for support.

Moyne stares him down. "You will speak when spoken to, not just because I have the power, but out of respect. Do you understand?"

"Yes," Nathan replies. Audrey simply nods her head.

Their host turns his attention to Audrey for a moment. "You should have checked in when you arrived."

"We did," Audrey replies, "We met your man upstairs. I played along with your little charade."

"Unfortunately that was not my charade you stumbled into, and it seems to have led you astray, into places you should not have gone. By the way, you also did not check in with your mother, and that is simply unforgivable," the gaunt old man manages to make it sound quite menacing yet familiar. Moyne then turns his attention back to Nathan. "Now that you are here, I'm curious what you know, and more importantly who hired you."

"I was hired by you, I guess. By Moyne. Or the Moyne that was upstairs–the guy who was murdered." Nathan regrets saying one sentence too many.

Moyne lets it go. "Why are you here?" he asks.

"Anton disappeared. I was apparently his backup, which I seriously did not know until I got a call, a plane ticket, and information to follow."

"That does not answer my question. Again, why are you *here*?"

Nathan realizes he is less interested in the facts and more about who he is, what he might offer. Suddenly it feels like a job interview. "What we know of a lot of cultures is based on the structure they leave behind. Analysis might best be done by others, but if you are trying to figure out what the builder was thinking–what an object itself was meant to represent or how a builder might hide something–then someone like me is just as qualified."

"And attract less interest," Moyne nods. "In general, you've led a rather uneventful life," he opens a folder on the table his guard had brought in with him, and then closes it again.   "Your CIA connection is a little troubling, but that was a long time ago and it looks like you were even able to make that uneventful."

"That you know of," Nathan defends himself.

"I know most everything I want to," Moyne speaks gently, softly, masking an accent that seems more archaic than foreign. If his first language is French, he hides it very well. "And what I do not know, I can find out."

"Then maybe *you* can tell me who hired me?" Nathan's response arrives pointed, but sincere.

"I hired Anton. I understand you are a colleague, but I was not the one who hired you to replace him, since he was never missing from me. I am beginning to understand why someone else may have retained you to compete with my efforts, or why Anton hired you, although as a friend he could have prepared you more. Anton has proven quite capable, but simply not that creative in his work for me."

"Didn't Anton murder the 'you' upstairs? Or was that you?" Again Nathan realizes he asks one question too many.

"What murder?" Moyne's silent guard sets a newspaper down in front of Nathan and Audrey.

Audrey translates the French. *"Local Actor Jean Vatrin Dies"* the headline of a small column on page three reads, "A local actor found dead in his home, of natural causes. He *was fifty-nine, but had retired several years ago due to lung cancer."* The picture was of the Moyne they had seen upstairs.

"Natural causes!?" Nathan is flabbergasted that such a grisly scene could be sanitized into a simple death of an old man. "What about the guards?"

"It was a horrible thing that happened upstairs and I did help clean it up, but I can assure you he was not killed by me. I cannot speak for Anton. Besides, I was down in Havre-Aubert all day, collecting this." Moyne gestures, and a guard steps out the door, returning with the stone from Nathan's room. "And yes, what goes on in my building should be under my control," he waves his hands in a gesture of exasperation, "but sometimes things happen right under your nose. My grandfather used to say that instead of keeping your friends close and your enemies closer, it is much safer to just keep everyone in the dark. I am beginning to see the wisdom in his words." Moyne opens the folder again and glances through it, "How did you get the 'information' you spoke of?"

"A messenger delivered a package. Once in Ireland, and once here; the same guy," Nathan responds matter-of-factly, but his heart sank as soon as he saw the stone. Whatever leverage he had to confront Anton is now gone. "Maybe Anton hired me, to finish what he couldn't? You said yourself he has been less than creative."

"Possibly. However, Anton completed his job. He has, in fact, delivered the piece this morning. I am more concerned about what you are doing here, and what you saw out on the Island."

"What were those structures out there?" Nathan's curiosity gets the better of him, and he forgets who is questioning whom. "They looked old, but not Native American."

"These islands have a way of cleansing themselves; you no doubt noticed our churches tend to be as old as the previous lightning strike. But yes, those structures are ancient. People have been living here for a long time, and even when explorers arrived in the 1500's they noted the islands looked cared for, cultivated in a way unlike natives would. My family has also been here for a very long time, and we are now owner of the island upon which you trespassed. My grandfather impressed on me the importance of the ruins there, and that they should be protected. Think what would happen if they became public."

"Those houses with the statues inside, they also belong to you?" Nathan asks.

"I wouldn't say they belong to me, but I do help take care of them," Moyne answers, "along with quite a few others. Now, let's get back to business: you answered 'why', but what do you know?"

"I know this has something to do with a fountain of youth of some kind," Nathan answers. "The stone, the one I was sent to find, has some kind of power."

"Interesting," Moyne turns to Audrey, "what is your take on this?"

"That thing does possess some kind of energy; you can sense the vibration. It seems to help Nathan, but it does nothing for me," she responds.

"Also interesting. It is true that they do not affect everyone the same; I have unfortunately not felt its power either way, but I do believe that when they are all collected–assembled into their original whole–its power will be great."

"So your ambition is to reassemble this . . . what, tablet? Some kind of mystical quest, and then live forever?" Nathan asks him.

"Not mystical, but very human. I am the last of my family that has guarded over the original pieces that were here. I must do something to fulfill my obligation," he answers, raising his chin in a gesture of pride, "my duty"

"Or greedy, cornering something that if *anyone* else knew existed would pay outrageous sums to get their hands on, even for a moment!" Audrey shoots Nathan a look of disapproval, yet he ignores her, "Or maybe you're just afraid to die?"

"Aren't you?" Moyne retorts. "Most are content to live their lives, have children, and leave a nice headstone and a legacy of life. I am more ambitious, and at the same time not so lucky. Like you, Nathan; though you may be content to reshape things and leave your mark in stone and steel, even if it does bear someone else's name. You have to admit that with all you've seen–your own willingness to kill or die for this piece of rock–that the need to matter, the need to leave a legacy, or simply the fear of leaving this life without so much as anyone knowing you were here, is the primal drive. Even sex is just an aspect of this."

"So fear–fear of death, and not sex–is our prime motivating force? I suppose it depends on your age," Nathan responds.

"You are telling me all, yet have probably told all kinds of lies to Audrey. Death is about truth, and sex about lies. Propagation of the species as an evolutionary instinct is strong, and I believe in evolution. I simply believe the fear of not accomplishing anything– the fear of leaving this world without so much as a mark–overrides that primal drive we used to overpopulate the world. We have been successful, so we no longer need our original programming."

"Talk about overpopulation; what if people did live forever?"

"It would be horrible, but fortunately it does not work like that. Throughout history, even in the Bible, only a handful of individuals have lived so long. And even they died eventually."

"So, do you have what you want from me?" It was Nathan's turn to get to the point. He directs the question as much at Audrey as Moyne.

"I could have you killed right now. Both of you," Moyne looks at Audrey in answer.

"Add Anton in, and complete this little triangle," Nathan

elaborates defiantly.

"Death is not a triangle. Of all human endeavors, only love can fit that geometric pattern; a triumvirate of you, the other, and your hopes and dreams. I think that is where you find yourself now Nathan, is it not? Very few are equilateral by the way, they always seem to rely mostly on one of the sides more than the others. I'm sure you appreciate the geometry of it," Moyne smiles.

"Why Audrey? Doesn't she work for you?" Nathan asks, skipping over the jab.

"All guns-for-hire expect a certain amount of danger with the job, and therefore are usually untrustworthy. I don't trust Anton. I certainly don't trust you. And though I know her mother quite well, what I am doing is too important to trust our lovely friend. She has been good at her job, however, keeping tabs on Anton and now you."

"You're paranoid. You probably have other guards who watch these guards here," Nathan points at the two large silent men in the room with them.

"Just shut up, would you," Audrey warns, breaking her silence.

"You like to talk, don't you?" Moyne asks Nathan.

"I never thought so, but if it stalls my demise or gets me a job, then yes. I guess I do."

"Sophisticated wonderment, if not dignified innocence," Moyne muses. "Innocence because you may have done it all before and still do not understand the 'why', but can at least appreciate the 'what'."

Nathan shakes his head. "That was like a sentence translated from English into Japanese and then back again" he observes. "I'm hardly innocent. I just think you, your kind living in this 'underworld'–and I've met more than a couple of you in the past week or two–have a completely skewed vision of the world, on life and what it means."

"Oh, now suddenly you're an expert! Had some great epiphany, have you? There are always you others wondering what they lost in the night, but never having the urge to stay up and find out," Moyne pauses for a breath, "but you are the ones who lash out at us during the daylight, thinking that while you sleep we plot to invade your homes, your lives. It's not true. We know life, and what it means. We see it snatched away so easily, perhaps have a more transitory view of things, but we know. You just want everyone to be like you, and we in turn think everyone should be like us. It's instinct," Moyne stops, slightly red in the face from his little tirade, "and by the way, don't you think you are one of us now?"

"It has been an interesting week. I guess the old curse goes 'May you live in interesting times'."

"Is there ever a time that wasn't? All right, I hear your complaints but I would actually listen to a solution," Moyne makes a gesture of openness with his arms, showing the palms of his hands.

"Let me go. I'm good at keeping secrets and I live rather far away. You need never hear from me, or about me, again."

"What if I'm not done with you yet?" Moyne asks him.

"I depends what the job is," Nathan hopes he holds some power yet, some expertise that is needed.

"So many remember that point in their lives where they look back and say 'then my whole world collapsed'. For some, it's when they are young and experience the death of a parent. For others– Audrey here has certainly experienced it, I can see it in her eyes–it happens later as a young adult and causes them to make certain career or lifestyle choices. And for you Nathan, it happened once in Berlin, and now that moment might be happening again." He moves closer, Nathan can smell his breath. "I will not hesitate to force you. You will tell me the whole truth. You will cooperate with whatever I ask you to do. This is, as you may have guessed, the most important thing in the world to me."

Nathan is quiet, feeling put in his place. All the cockiness he had been building up suddenly vanished in that last moment. He considers his alternatives, and how much he really cares what happens to him now. Suddenly, something piques his interest. "You said Anton delivered the piece. Just one piece?" he asks.

"What do you mean by 'just one'?" Moyne moves closer again.

"No. No." Nathan quickly backpedals. "I thought maybe he had gotten hold of our piece, but it's clear that you just picked it up yourself. I'm just really hungry, not thinking straight. Can we go now or at least get some food?"

Moyne studies Nathan's face, his cold blue eyes boring in, radiating a hue cold and distant, blending and fading into just another extension of the Impossibly Blue Room.

42

July 11, Iles de la Madeleine

NATHAN'S SCREAM REVERBERATES immediately in his ears, forcing a repeated yell in frustration at his own foolishness. He was stupid for holding back information so obviously, and even more idiotic making a loud noise in such a confined area.

He is hanging, upside down his hands tied behind his back, in a black room he supposes was once a small closet or a large chimney. He decides the latter, as he remembers being hoisted up a distance. His shoulders brush the sides of the space, and when he swings himself like a pendulum from the rope tied securely around his ankles, it takes very little to not only touch the sides but also his back and front. Nathan hopes the rope is tied securely, because if it lets go he has no concept of how far he would fall before landing on his head.

Outside the small door at the bottom stands a guard, and beyond him the door from the Impossibly Blue Room out to the hallway. The elevator bypasses this floor, so there is only one exit stairway from the back side of the building, the same one they entered the evening before. Audrey is certainly still in the Room, but through her illness could easily pretend she had no knowledge of what Nathan was hiding. Even if he learns his lesson, and divulges everything, she could plead ignorance. Nathan is betting, as he hangs here, that she will not betray that Anton is still holding on to one of the stones. Blood pooling to his head, tingling, swelling. Unsure how long he may be here. Why could he not keep some information? This indiscretion was after all not between him and Moyne but rather him and Anton; Nathan needs it, especially since Moyne took his other leverage.

Everything starts to slow down. Blinking of stars fills his eyes, but he could not see anyway. *Why not just die*, he thinks, *and teach everyone a lesson? Who would really care, anyway?* Johanna's patience has almost run out. Audrey–why would she? Alex is gone. Natalia, if alive, would either hate him or not even remember. He considers that all have been no more than that surface beauty, that garden he had dreamed of, and he had provided them no more attention than whatever current project he was working on.

Nathan closes his eyes tighter to fix his last thoughts–if these were indeed to be his last thoughts–on Alex. Not working; too many fleeting thoughts of Natalia until the fresh image of Audrey begins imposing itself. He can hardly remember Alex's face, though he had looked at her for years; Audrey's face, beautiful and scarred, keeps implanting itself. He focuses harder, tightening his eyelids against distractions. It is no use. Every now and then even Johanna's image crops up, which just feels wrong.

He hears a loud pounding and steadies himself, concentrating for its source, then realizes it is the ticking of a watch that is so deafening. Nathan had forgotten he had one on, forced by Audrey to wear it. The timepiece does not have a light feature, and with hands behind his back it is useless. Despite the regular rhythm, he has no idea how long he has been in here, whether twenty minutes or twenty hours. In its own way this is worse than the plane with Audrey and her toys; at least he knew the plane would need to land.

Unable to focus on anything else, Nathan forms a plan. If he could free his hands he might be able to untie his feet, and wedging his body across the small width of the chimney let himself down quietly. If he then busts the door open, he may either hit the guard or at least have a split second of surprise to overpower him. *This could work*, he begins to imagine.

It would be heroic. It would be the best thing he has done in years. And, truly, he may not have anything to lose. This is not about being resolute and regal in the face of the firing squad; Nathan imagined that if faced with execution he would not go quietly, seeing no dignity in not putting up a fight. This is simply his shot.

The tiniest of places often provide the most space to realize who you are, and what you want to be. *Like Raskolnikov's bedroom and later his cell*, Nathan ponders, *such a small space where infinite plans could be hatched, infinite realizations discovered.* He jerks violently, trying to force some slack into the rope that is around his waist holding his tied hands up against his back. Almost every part of his body collides with one of the sidewalls in the process, leaving a lingering ache to the back of his head and left shoulder.

The guard knocks on the door.

"Fuck you!" Nathan yells out in defiance.

The tie around his ankles, it turns out, is not secure. Nathan feels it slowly slipping, loosened by his previous movements. The rope at his waist, however, also slackens and he works feverishly at his hands so he might free them and catch himself to avoid breaking his neck. He is almost there when he feels the final slip and suddenly he is weightless. Pain in his leg and head, flashes of bright light like fire pass through his eyes as he falls. No thoughts, just a feeling of flight in the dark chamber. Then a frightful noise, louder and worse than he imagined it would be. Finally, thought returns and he realizes he is at a horrible angle on the floor, his legs still above him.

The rope now completely loose, he is able to free his hands. Nathan's brain is on fire, the pain in his neck becoming more acute as he puts his hands on the floor and tries to right himself. Despite the resulting undignified fall, his earlier violent movements must have desensitized the guard, as there is no knock again to see what the sound was. Nathan hopes he may have left. Thinking it unlikely, he positions himself to open the door with the maximum force he could muster in close quarters. His feet? His shoulder? Nathan decides he could get more momentum, more force, from his legs even if it put him in a worse position to escape once the door was open. He also considers just knocking to see if the guard opens the door for him.

Nathan feels for the door and rolls onto his lower back, his shoulders against the opposite wall. The door is well-sealed, no cracks of light showing through the bottom or sides. The good news is that it is a wood door, and he actually stands a chance of busting it open. He feels for plates either side, gauging which is the hinge side and where the handle would be. There is no handle on the inside, so he guesses the height where the latch would be, and sets his feet there. Pulling them back to his head, a knee at each ear, he silently counts to three and tries to project all his strength to his legs, kicking for the bolt.

The door bursts open to a horrible brightness, blinding him. He sees a form nearby and, shuffling forward on his forearms and lower back, he kicks out again instinctually, landing one on the guard. The big man goes down, taken completely by surprise. As Nathan's eyes adjust he finds no one else is in the room. He barely gets to his feet, grabbing a chair to swing hard on the guard's head who has managed to get to one knee. They both fall down, one unconscious and Nathan from the sudden burst of adrenaline that had left his body.

Not wanting to waste any time, he forces himself back up and to the door. Turning the handle slowly, he opens it a crack and looks down the hallway. Nothing. He opens it some more and peers around the corner in the opposite direction, towards the exit stair. No one in sight, but there is a blind corner just beyond.

The next guard would not be so surprised, he thinks. He glances back at the guard he had managed to overcome and braces himself for the run, orienting to where the exit should be and where the next guard might be standing. A wave of nausea and return of flickering lights in the back of his eyes disorient him as the blood begins to return to normal gravity.

Nathan flings open the door and runs to his left. As he passes the corner that leads from the main hall he sees his next target. This guard shows no sign of surprise on his face as Nathan rushes him, unfolding his meaty arms and reaching for his sidearm. Nathan gets there a split second before he can draw, and the two go toppling down the stair, Nathan on top riding him like a sled. As they stop at the bottom landing there is no movement. Nathan had used his arms to hold the guard's head down, effectively making sure that he broke their fall at every step with his head. Nathan did not think he was dead, but the top of the man's head was rubbed down to where he could see his skull exposed.

Out the door. The air is fresh and cool, a slight mix of salt from the ocean, asphalt and burnt gasoline from the parking lot he arrives in. He begins to move unsteadily amongst the parked cars, testing the door handles as he goes. Nathan hopes one is open and would improbably also have the keys left in. So far they are all locked; he had hoped the islanders would be more trusting.

Then he sees her. Audrey is in the parking lot, equally shocked to see him. God, how beautiful she looks! He is almost to her, wanting to embrace her when he feels a stunning blow to the head, a blinding light and then blackness and interminable silence. *Shit–* Nathan fumes, realizing, *this must be death.* He floats a while in the ether. Calm, no panic. No uncertainty, no pressures, no worries, no guilt. *The peace, the beauty*, he would have tears if he had a body.

Brightness returns with a sudden sense of pain and disappointment. He opens an eye to a guard standing over him as he lay on the floor in the little room, his chimney off the Impossibly Blue Room, legs up in the air over his severely arched and twisted back. The guard asks him if he is hurt.

43

A**UDREY WATCHES CLOUDS** move past the window. Nathan stares at her, pondering the not-so-chance encounter at the bar. Their relationship smells moldy, he thinks, like an old wig on a basement floor. The feeling color is similar: fake brown tones and concrete grays with a damp shininess around the edges. Despite the hectic pace and night of passion, being with her was actually quiet at first, unlike most new relationships. In the chimney, however, it began to make a faint noise, like sheep in the distance or leaking balloons, until now it is a silent scream that fills the room. Nathan is surprised no one else can hear it.

"You gave that up pretty easily," Audrey says, her concentration broken by a patch of clear sky.

Nathan agrees he had indeed given Anton's secret up easily, for better or worse. He was additionally embarrassed, once discovering he had been locked up for less than an hour. It seemed like forever. However, when he told Moyne about the other piece, he had not lost his leverage. The gaunt old man in jeans seemed to warm to Nathan, as if the air had been cleared, or some kind of test had been passed. Perhaps it was a test; the old man may have known all along.

"That was really stupid," Audrey chides, following up her insult with admonishment.

"Why didn't you say anything?" Nathan asks. He rubs the back of his neck, the pain there and on the top of his head is rather astounding, perhaps even the source of the scream he imagines.

"Because unlike you, I know this isn't all about me. I was trying to show some benefit of doubt to keep a secret," she answers.

"I don't think this had anything to do with me, at first anyway, but we are involved now. Anton made sure it is personal, and it's something I either need to find out more about, or stop before it goes any further." He still has not told Audrey everything, he realizes. If he is keeping any secrets, he is keeping the most from her.

The door opens to the Impossibly Blue Room. Moyne enters first, swinging the wood slab wide till it holds against the back wall, allowing some yellow light of the hallway to invade the space. A parade of guards enter, carrying the various pieces of stone Nathan is now quite familiar with, their large arms struggling against the weight. He recognizes two of the tablets, but the other two are foreign yet almost identical in shape and size. It begins to make sense. If Anton had been hired and shown a picture of these, he may have recognized the piece his uncle was holding. It was probably when his dreams of an early retirement began to form.

"Here they are," Moyne says proudly. "I understand you have a score to settle with your old friend, so I do not take your lie to me personally. It may be useful, as you may be able to get closer to Anton than my men could. If he knows we are on to him, he may run. I will give *you* the chance to confront him," he offers magnanimously," but you will return the tablet to me." He waits for Nathan to nod his head in understanding, and then continues, "But for right now, perhaps you can help me fit these together."

Nathan first stares at him in disbelief, before glancing over to Audrey who is nodding her head for him to comply. *Insane or overconfident, perhaps desperate*, Nathan surmises. "Seriously, what is with you people? A little physical harm and suddenly we're best friends? Is it a hockey thing?" Nathan turns to Audrey. "You might understand: you only trust people as damaged as you are." He turns his head with some effort and pain back to Moyne, "but you?"

"I am an old man, tired and lonely. Probably as tired and lonely as the monks who traveled here searching for answers and finding this," he gestures at the tablets on the table, "or making this. I'm sure Audrey filled you in on my theory of what these stones are." He gets close to Nathan's face. "They have power, you cannot deny that. My family has always been guardian to the piece left behind here; father to son. But I am the last. There is no son, no daughter, not even a nephew or niece I trust. After hundreds of years, I am the break in the chain. It is my duty to do whatever I can to continue our legacy." Moyne sits back down. "Perhaps it is a sign from God, that it is finally time to reassemble the pieces. If it means I must live forever, than so be it."

"I thought their power didn't have an effect you," Nathan responds.

"Not individually. But together, once translated . . . That is why you are alive yet, Nathan. You can get close to Anton. You can complete this."

Nathan nods his head in understanding. "You want to live forever, but not because you're afraid of death. You have no one to mourn you." He snorts a chuckle. "Or you could name any price in the world for these things; even if it extends life just a few years, I'm sure some rich guy would pay it."

Moyne smiles, suppressing anger at Nathan's insolence. "Now, I would appreciate you and our associate here," he gestures to Audrey, "finding our mutual friend, and completing your work."

"And then I can go home? No problem? No double-cross, no 'tying up loose ends'?" Nathan asks.

"You have my word. I will finally leave these isolated islands and disappear somewhere . . . warmer." Moyne smiles again, this time in humor. "Who would believe you anyway?"

"Good point." Nathan stands to study the four pieces laid flat on the table. All four are positioned with the writing face up, and Nathan only guesses since he cannot read it, top-side-up so that all the words or symbols are in the same orientation. "Have you been able to translate?"

"Not entirely, but I have not had so many pieces to look for repetition of symbols until today."

"Wouldn't it be in ancient Irish, or Gaelic or whatever?" Audrey asks.

"The ogham alphabet," Moyne nods, "first thing I tried given my family's stories. Parts work, but others do not. It's quite exciting, since that means either parts of the ogham alphabet have been missing for a thousand years, or there was a more advanced alphabet here in the Americas than anyone thought."

Nathan looks for strings of symbols, and where they may be broken and continued on another piece. It does not occur anywhere, which is odd even if the tablet was broken quite carefully to make the roughly regular and rectangular shapes he is looking at. He squints, looking for pattern and feeling, at the overall sizes. One piece is roughly square, the other three rectangular with two approximately the same size. These two the proportion looks familiar; the Golden Section again, though the roughness of the edges makes it more an approximation. Still odd if it was Native

American, as the proportion does not figure as greatly in their culture.

The edges; there is something far more intriguing about the edges to Nathan.   Here is a pattern.   Two pieces look like they would fit together, but not in such a way that the writing would be continuous.   Actually, not in the way Moyne might expect at all. "You see these edges," Nathan runs his hand across the one to his right. "They're not broken. Those are carefully tooled even though they look rough."

"But when you match them up closely, the writing shifts from one side to the other, one piece to the next," Moyne states.

"Sacred geometry: Platonic solids, like the structures out on your island, are not just primary shapes. It's the difference between a square and a cube.   It's sacred. The edges are meant to fit perpendicular to one another. This is not some rectangular tablet, it's a cube," Nathan declares.

44

THEY EXIT TO a warm, fresh, deafening wind. It is the same door, the same parking lot from Nathan's vision, yet he feels less heroic Given his freedom, even if it is on Moyne's leash, Nathan is satisfied just to have a chance to go after Anton.

"If it's a box, he's not just missing the piece from Anton, he's missing a sixth piece," Audrey says.

"More importantly," Nathan replies, "if it's a box, aren't you curious what was in it?"

Audrey looks at him over the roof of the car. Nathan tries the handle, but she only unlocked her side. She gets in and reaches over to open his door; a quaint but annoying gesture in the electronic age. "So I've been risking my life for the fucking box the real prize came in," she mutters as he enters and sits down.

"The sixth piece, not that I'm sure it matters all that much now, could be anywhere in the world. What are the chances it's on that island where Moyne found us?"

"It matters, but it's not out there. He, and his family, have been over every inch of that island for centuries," Audrey answers.

"Where else then? These islands aren't that big, Moyne has been here his whole life and you grew up here. What chance do I have?" Nathan asks.

"It's not our task to find it. Unless–and it could be very likely–that Anton happens to know," she reminds him.

"So, call him."

Audrey looks over. "What makes you think I can just do that?

"Just take me back to the Bed and Breakfast," he responds, "I need a shower."

"You were headed in a different direction, but then went back to becoming an architect. Why?" Audrey asks, breaking the silence as they make the subtle transition driving the long sandbar south and to the southernmost island of Ile du Havre-Aubert and the Maison de Marie.

He thinks about it. The memories, the answer he comes up with, surprises him. "It was Johanna."

"Johanna," she nods, "Were you two . . . ?"

"Not like that. Not even like you," he pauses, "I used to think about her all the time, I guess sometimes in an obsessive way. Not exactly stalking, mind you, but I used to go places hoping she would be there. One time, just once, she held my hand as we walked along the street. That moment is still one of the most romantic memories I have." It actually felt good to say it out loud. "No offense," he adds snidely.

"None taken. You ever tell her?"

"No. How could I? It's way too late now anyway," Nathan fully realizes.

"Instead you're a full-grown man who doesn't know what he wants, or waited too long."

"Way to make me feel better." He thinks back to the past few weeks, months, years even. "I don't think she's been very happy with me for a while, and I certainly don't think she would approve if she knew what I was doing right now."

"Well, the ones you truly love are rarely there when you finally do prove yourself." Audrey parks the car on the road in front of the Bed and Breakfast. "Speaking of which, the Ford in front of us belongs to my mother."

Nathan's room has been ransacked, as expected. Ransacked may be an exaggeration, he thinks, since he has just an extra pair of jeans and a few shirts. It does not take long to clean up, but the principle of someone uninvited in his room–taking what he thought was the one piece of leverage, of power, he had–is galling. Annoyed and curious, he decides to face his hosts to discern how complicit they were.

At first Claude Carmes waves him off, as if he does not deserve any explanation. His wife Marie and the ever present priest look on in stoic support. Nathan insists, and Carmes finally offers that, perhaps, he had suggested Nathan's visitors go wait in his room. When Nathan suggests that, *perhaps*, he had not been expecting any visitors, Claude reminds him that it is their house and they can let anyone in, or ask anyone to leave, that they want.

"And where were you last night anyway?" the priest asks with a tone of concern and accusation only a priest can muster.

Nathan thinks, but does not ask, the same question of him. He returns to his room, undresses and showers. The hot water feels incredible, and Nathan is thankful for that brief moment before it turns cold. "Damn it!" he shouts, shutting off the water and falling to his knees in the tub. He drapes his arms across the water spout, resting his head on top, and lets the sobs of emotion, the outright cries, take over his body as cold drops fall slowly, crashing on his back.

Nathan stays like this, hunched over and on his knees on the cold porcelain, until the wave has passed. The dripping has stopped, and little is left to dry off as he steps out of the tub. He checks his face in the mirror. His eyes and nose are red and he needs a shave, but he otherwise looks normal. Actually pretty good, he thinks. When he finishes shaving, he feels around in his scalp for where he had landed on his head in the chimney. There is a bump, but surprisingly no pain as he presses on it.

A familiar voice outside draws him to the window while buttoning his shirt; Audrey is out front with a woman Nathan assumes is her mother. They exchange some heated words, and then enter their separate cars. Audrey takes off, spinning her tires on the road and almost clipping the back of her mother's car as she angles out, heading north up the road at high speed.

"Shit," Nathan mutters and quickly pulls his pants on. Slipping into some shoes, he does not bother locking the door behind before bounding down the steps to the first floor. He approaches Claude, who in Nathan's mind owes him for losing his piece of stone. "I need to borrow a car!"

"Non," Claude dismisses him again with a wave of his hand.

"It's important!" Nathan raises his voice, then calms quickly. "Besides, it's a fucking island. How far could I go?"

The priest stands up. "I was just leaving, anyway. I will take you where you want to go." All three look at him in surprise, and Nathan reluctantly follows him out the door.

"So, where we go?" the priest asks as he opens his small black Ford.

"I can't answer a lot of questions, but we need to catch up to Miss May and follow her."

"I like adventure," the priest gives him a wink.

Nathan feels slightly creeped-out as the priest hits the gas, suddenly tearing up the narrow road at eighty miles an hour. They find her within five minutes, heading north at the normal speed limit along the sandbar.

"It is easy to find someone when there is only one highway," the priest says, slowing down to match speed and keep a safe distance. Nathan also hopes that when there is only one highway, there is less suspicion seeing the same car behind you mile after mile.

They follow her through the middle island of Cap-aux-Meules and past the main port, across the bridge, and onto the neighboring island Ile du Havre-aux-Maisons. These two islands, unlike the others, are close enough to almost form a single entity. They slow, passing a sign that announces the town of Pointe Basse. As the name implies, this main village of Ile du Havre-aux-Maisons sits at a low point, surrounded by some of the most dramatic hills and cliffs on all the islands.

Suddenly the priest turns the car off the highway, and they begin to ascend a hill on a small country road. "What are you doing?" Nathan asks in panic, Audrey's car dropping out of sight.

"My church up there," he points, "at Cap Rouge. I drop you off," the priest says helpfully.

"You're fucking kidding me!" Nathan is exasperated.

"No good to swear at a priest," he smiles, "but you find Audrey in town. Easy walk, all downhill. Have nice dinner and make up." The priest stops the car on the road in front of the church.

Nathan gets out, slamming the door behind him. He hears the priest yell "*bienvenue*" in a sing-song voice behind him as he stamps off. From Cap Rouge he has a good survey of the whole island. The concentration of houses, if you can call it that, suggests most of the residents seem to live in Point Basse or west, even though the drama is out on the eastern edge facing the ocean. Ever present horizon during the day and blackness strangely comforting at night, there is a squat lighthouse barely visible at the peninsula. He remembers the odd name from the map as "Cap Alright", and wonders if is pronounced differently, or means something in French. The lighthouse is set in from the edge of the peninsula as a rather safe and boring counterpoint to the drama of the cliffs that extend north up the eastern coast. Inland, beyond the church, are some isolated stands of trees rolling over smooth green mounds.

Nathan follows a path down the hill closer to town. Red cliffs carved by wind and wave, tall pillars of red sandstone on a white sandy beach. Houses of bright blue, purple, yellow, orange and scarlet with steep roofs, some standing like sentinels too close to the edge of the sea. Nathan supposes the edge may have moved since they were built. Scattered. Houses dot all the level areas, some areas more or less dense than others, which make it difficult to tell if Pointe Basse is actually a town at all; there is no definition of where it might start or end.

He passes a group of beautiful old stone structures with long steep pitched roofs. Tan and red doors hang like beautiful ornaments, perfectly placed in the simple form. Visually beautiful, there is the strong aroma of a smokehouse: herring, he hazards to guess.

There is a great beach in Pointe Basse, nestled beside a busy harbor smothered in colorful boats; Nathan assumes they use the extra paint from their homes. He looks around, but no sign of Audrey or the car. Suddenly he has trouble remembering what color it was. All the cars are looking the same, compared to the houses and boats around here. He suddenly doubts his ability to recognize anything.

"What am I going to do now," he sits on a lone wood bench at the edge of the beach. Not a question, not even a statement. He could stay, or he could find a ride back, or start walking. He could walk to the port and get the hell out. Nathan wanted to see Anton. Now healed, it is not from need, but he is curious and pissed off, a little unbalanced, and really had nothing better to do that he could think of. And there is the possibility that Moyne may not allow him to leave if he does not finish his task.

Nathan stares at the houses nearby, their porches and entry doors face south and to the harbor as they should. But of course this is the Madeleine Islands, and amongst those lie the scattered that seemed to conform to no greater organizational power. Many have a slight east-west orientation, responding to the best orientation for sun and wind. He stands up, scanning as many details as he can see. The oldest ones–not just the historic-looking but from details and their simplicity the actual oldest ones–are facing east and slightly north. This makes no sense whatsoever, he thinks, since these should be the ones that respond the most to sun and wind patterns. Even stranger, no two of them were together, which would make sense if there was an old center of town.

It dawns on Nathan that this might be it: what better place to hide than in plain sight, like a book in a library or a stone in Ireland. Accessible but hidden, which you need when your secret is a living, working one. This must be the Village, and Moyne probably drives through it twice a day without seeing! This must be where all those people from the little island in the lagoon came to, once the population started growing and their isolation began to draw attention. Move here to a burgeoning settlement, and let others fill in. Where else could you hide once so many more people came?

Nathan moves in, walking among houses to the nearest Old One. It has been added on to, but the addition could not mask its original shape. It had been a two-room first floor, a fireplace in the middle to heat both rooms and a small sleeping loft above. As basic, and efficient, as could be. He moves to the next, and then the next after that, walking through yards and the occasional barking dog. There are few people around; a few mothers with children but no one in the houses Nathan is checking out.

Finally, at the northeastern-most house he stops. He looks in the general direction the Old Ones are facing and sees nothing. Perhaps he is reading them wrongly, and they are responding to something in one of the other three directions. Standing alone, in the middle of a field at the edge of a foreign town, Nathan worries he is projecting patterns onto nothing at all. Nathan kneels down, brushing some of the grass away from the old foundation to get a better sense of its age.

The wind dies down. Anywhere else this would be unremarkable, but here the wind is always blowing, always in your ears. Its absence is unnerving, even more noticeable than the fog rolling in. When he looks up again, Nathan sees he is now half surrounded in the darkening gray mist; twelve, maybe fifteen people total, about half women and half men in differently colored jackets. They stand quietly, motionless as statues, all focusing on Nathan. He mirrors their frozen stance, scanning the mist-concealed figures, and searching out the gaunt presence he knows should be there.

"Anton?" Nathan calls out.

There is no answer, other than the gaunt figure raising his right arm. At first Nathan thinks he is pointing, but he knows better. He has seen this vision, and it is something else in his hand. Anton is there, pointing a gun at him.

45

O N THE MIDWESTERN plains where Nathan spent most of his life, a sudden unsettling calm means a violent storm. The storms on these islands tend to grow from the constant winds; simply a slow increase until they reach their apex and then fade back to a dull roar. This dead calm puts Nathan on edge in a way like no other; in just a few short days he has become so accustomed to the consistent whistle in his ears that its absence is disturbing.

"You look well," Anton moves closer, coalescing out of the fog, "too well." His long tan shirt hangs loose from his jeans, a black beret capping his pale gaunt face. Nathan does not remember seeing anyone else wear a hat around here, probably due to the wind. Despite the recognition, or because of it, Anton's gun remains trained on Nathan. "You clever bastard–you found another piece, didn't you?"

"No," Nathan denies, for no other reason than to be a pain.

"You're a terrible liar. I was counting on you being motivated enough to find it for me." He lowers the gun, smiling as he draws nearer. "I knew you'd . . ."

Nathan hits him square in the jaw, sending Anton backwards onto the grass. A sharp sting careens down Nathan's arm from his fist. It would have been better to target neck or stomach, or kick in the groin or shins to avoid breaking your own hand, but at this moment he realizes he had never been faced with the decision before. His wave of personal satisfaction is tempered by causing himself as much pain as he had given.

"What was that for?!" Anton rubs his jaw, still lying on the ground. "I could have shot you!"

"You fucking tried to kill me!" Nathan shouts, shaking out his hand. "You're worried about accidentally shooting me after you stab and leave me for dead?!"

"I was, I am, doing you a favor," Anton slowly gets up, keeping the pistol lowered at his side. "I'm bringing you into something you never could have imagined."

"You didn't give a shit if I lived or died, as long as I served your purpose. I suppose now you want me to thank you for the motivation?"

"We're destined for great things, Nathan. You've seen it, experienced it." Anton stands very close now. "Where is it?"

"Moyne has it," Nathan shrugs. "He's looking for your piece also."

"No, no. That won't do." Anton glances around, then turns back and smiles. "Wait a minute; he sent you to get it from me?"

"I suppose he did, unless he had his goons follow me, which is more likely," Nathan shrugs again.

Anton looks concerned, but then his scowl softens. "Doesn't matter. Our friends here will protect us."

"Who are these people," Nathan surveys the dozen figures, still unmoving in the fog.

"They fancy themselves guardians," Anton leans in close to

whisper, "but they're more like parasites."

"If they're with you I believe it."

"They are, in fact, my clients," Anton reveals.

"I thought Moyne was your client," Nathan looks at the small number of normal-looking folk in windbreakers. They hardly seem able to outbid Moyne for Anton's services.

"Two clients, two pieces," Anton shrugs, "I thought it would work out well for me."

"What do you want?" Nathan asks.

"What I want, what I need, is for you to take over. I need you to replace me," Anton states.

"Why not just ask?" Nathan questions. Physical violence delivered, Nathan faces the other reason he had chased Anton this far.

"Believe it or not, you are the closest I ever had to a real friend," Anton pauses, hoping the statement will sink in. "You are the only person I trust; who I thought would be remotely qualified. You were the professor's second choice, you know, after me."

"So the ruse in Ireland was just bait?"

"Yes and no. I did get hit on the head," Anton takes off his hat and points. "More importantly, I stole things from some people you should never steal from. I can't just disappear; I have to be dead."

"Well, good luck with that," Nathan means it.

"It might have worked for me in Ireland, but I wasn't done yet. Plus I had Audrey watching over me," Anton explains.

"And Moyne just knew to call me. Great. I don't want to be your successor," Nathan reiterates.

"It's not your choice anymore," Anton explains, "you probably already have a few messages waiting for you at home. These are people you do not want to disappoint," he warns.

"And Audrey?"

"Oh yes, our Audrey," Anton smiles.

"She's working for you?"

"I wish," he says. "She is sweet, isn't she?"

"You're a fucking bastard," Nathan's jealousy rises.

"Yes I am," Anton smiles. "But you forgot 'rich' fucking bastard."

"How does Moyne not know about this place?" Nathan looks around.

"Loyalty, and paranoia. With a population this small, rumors are bound to circulate, especially with such an odd bunch. Yet here they are. I suppose everyone on these islands is a bit odd, but I believe this group cloaks it under the guise of a religion; Bible study or something that explains their get-togethers. Moyne might keep them on his radar, but has no chance of infiltrating. I'm here because they hired me. You're here because I am, and they might need you."

Nathan nods; hiding in the open. He would not have found them if their deference to some other entity greater than nature just beyond here–somewhere northeast he gauges–had not manifested itself consciously or subconsciously in the way their houses were laid out.

"The question is how did you know about this place? Did Audrey whisper it in your ear late at night?"

"A pattern of use," Nathan answers, "leaves a physical trace. These people built their homes at the same time, all facing the same direction, in a unique style."

Anton nods his head, seemingly satisfied. "I've been following you; your career, your work. It was getting to be time, and your relationship with Alex was posing a problem. Fortunately, that all worked out," Anton winks menacingly. "I was hoping to have some time where we could work together, show you the ropes, maybe even get together with Johanna. Like old times. Unfortunately that's no longer possible. It is quite a lucrative career I'm offering you, and no end of projects. Actually, saying 'no' is the hardest part; you have to be careful who you say 'no' to."

"Are you saying you had something to do with Alex?" Nathan ignores everything else.

"You were the one who broke it off," Anton shrugs. "You should feel guilty. You were an asshole."

"You know what it's like when you want something bad to happen to someone, just to save yourself the pain of being honest," Nathan shakes his head. "When it does happen, it's nothing like you imagine."

"Boo hoo. That seems to be a pattern with you. I was counting on it."

Nathan is taken aback. "You are so smug, so convinced of our own righteousness!"

"No, it's not smugness, though what I'm doing is right for me. I'm just not convinced, as you are, in everyone else's wrongness." Anton dismisses him with a wave of his hand, hoping to end the subject.

"Holy shit," Nathan realizes, "you burned down my hotel to get me here!"

"That one I can't take credit for," Anton denies the accusation. "Besides, you and I do love the same things. I may be morally flexible when it comes to people, but I could never do that to a building."

"You are fucked up," Nathan shakes his head.

"We do not change so easily," Anton counters. "You have an addictive personality Nate. You may have just become addicted to something else."

"Maybe your stunt–your stabbing me–did have a profound

effect, just not the one you wanted. But you," Nathan points, "you envy what you can't have. You miss what you don't have anymore; even criticize what you can't do. You never had the career, the respect, I have."

"But I do now!" Anton exclaims. "And respect? Your clients use you just like mine use me. I just get paid better."

"What about the sixth piece?" Nathan asks, unable to argue the point further.

"How many are there?" he seems genuinely surprised. "I guess that doesn't concern me, though I guess it has become your first job as my replacement. I would suggest you ask the Villagers here, but between you and me they don't seem to know shit."

"Monsieur Eischen, you cannot be here," a man standing in the group calls out in a thick accent. "They cannot find you here with us."

"I don't think anyone can see us in this damn fog," he says aloud, and then more softly to Nathan, "I hate fog, and fucking sheep."

Wind returns, and the fog begins to swirl and dissipate. The Villagers seem to move with it until there is only one left: an older woman in a light blue windbreaker, a hood masking her head. She gestures at the two of them to come inside.

"Don't let these Villagers fool you," Anton says to Nathan as he turns to follow. "They may be parasites, but they do know how to keep a secret. They're keeping a big one somewhere close. I can smell it; it's bigger than any I ever had to keep."

46

T HE HOUSE INTERIOR is rugged, almost inhospitable. A huge central fireplace divides a kitchen and eating area from the room where everything non-food took place. Nathan senses, as he and Anton sit alone in this latter space and at least twelve Villagers stand sequestered in the kitchen beyond, that this particular house had not seen a real family in half a century. Nathan gestures towards the group in the kitchen now pacing around, "Who are these people? Don't they have jobs?"

"Who needs a job when you have faith," Anton responds flippantly.

"Faith in what; those stones? Isn't that false idol territory?" Nathan recognizes the irony in his words, how far his thinking had turned during these weeks.

"You can't deny their power," Anton points out.

"*The power*," a Villager responds from the other room. Nathan and Anton look at each other and huddle closer.

"But look at this," Nathan points to the chalky scar on his neck. He lifts his shirt to show a similarly white, powdery mark on his abdomen where Anton had plunged the knife in. "It's probably some radioactive remnant that might have a strange healing side effect, but will eventually kill me faster."

"For some, they do just that. For some, the stones just kill; slowly and painfully, sucking the life force out. Ninety-nine percent of people, including me, they have absolutely no effect. They are selective, and it's a rare thing when they heal. It worked for my uncle, but not for me. Still, there are a lot of desperate people who would take the chance, no matter the side effects."

"So you were betting on a long shot when you stabbed me," Nathan says.

"Audrey told me about the scar on your neck: a telltale sign. It heals you," Anton says. The Villagers in the other room stop pacing and look through the doorway at Nathan, muttering in French to one another.

"And all so I would take your job?" Nathan shakes his head.

"It's not just a 'job'," Anton leans in even closer, "it will be every aspect of your life."

"You're not selling it well," Nathan leans back, reclaiming some personal space. "What makes you think I would even be qualified? I'm not exactly adept at keeping secrets."

"Of course you are. Just do what you do, but don't trust anyone. Not clients, coworkers, contractors. Not anyone."

"That's no way to live," Nathan shakes his head.

"And who do you have in your life right now that you trust?"

"I trust Johanna," Nathan says emphatically.

"But does she trust you? I wouldn't be surprised, given your antics of late, if she is considering a more stable partner."

The woman in the blue windbreaker comes into the room alone. "The stone, it heals you?" she asks Nathan.

"I guess so," he responds, and she turns around and goes back into the kitchen. There is a rise in the volume of their foreign

366

muttering, Nathan unable to perceive any meanings.

"A strange bunch," Anton comments, "but wealthy. They paid in cash, up front. Good thing you showed up to do the work for me."

"You're still an asshole," Nathan says.

"I'm serious, and I'm grateful," he pauses to look into Nathan's eyes. "You were out on the Old Island," Anton says. "What did you think?"

"There was something at the center. I wouldn't be surprised if it was the piece Moyne's family had, since they seem to own the island now. But like here, there was a secondary deference given to certain structures that people probably did not even recognize was happening. Might have been tradition, but it was unique. It felt like the whole place was carved out rather than built up, and there was a perfect geometry overlaid, a pentagram inscribed in a circle. I should have put it together back then, since an arm of the pentagram points up here."

"How do you know?"

"Spatial memory; one thing I was always better at than you," Nathan states.

"Now who's being the asshole?"

"Did you try asking them what it is?"

"I'm not exactly trustworthy," Anton admits.

The woman in the blue windbreaker comes back into the room. "You need to see the Old One," she speaks to Nathan, looking earnest.

Nathan turns to Anton in confusion. "Don't look at me," Anton shrugs, who then suddenly rises to his feet. "This is it," he declares.

"What do you mean?" Nathan stands up in response.

"You're never going to see me again. So if there's anything else you need to know . . ."

Nathan thinks a moment. "Was it worth it?"

Anton smiles. "That is probably all relative: has your life so far been worth it?"

Nathan has no answer, and he follows Anton to the door. They step outside, with the older woman in the blue windbreaker appearing suddenly to follow them out. The sun is bright and warming as it approaches the horizon, a beautiful summer evening. After walking a short distance from the house and woman, Anton stops and grabs Nathan's arm. He leans in and speaks in a lowered voice. "Didn't you notice something peculiar about the stone itself?"

"Not really, but I didn't have it long enough to study it."

"Come on Nate. Details. I looked it up, and it's not Irish."

"Why would you expect it to be? Audrey said they brought it back from here."

"Like most things about her, that's kind of true. But I had it tested, and the phosphorites in the stone are unique to the Middle East."

Nathan is unsure if he should tell Anton about his deduction, since he appears to be wiping his hands of the whole matter. "It's a box," Nathan finally admits. "The stones form a box. Perhaps ritualistic, the monks Audrey described brought it with them to carry something sacred back."

Anton thinks about it a minute. "A story Moyne described was that the Abbot, in order to calm their fears, convinced his men that if the world is flat there must be land on the other side to hold the water in. This land would be where God kept His secrets. As they first arrived, they even called the natives here the 'edge dwellers'."

"So Brendan and his monks came looking for a secret, some knowledge to take back," Nathan shrugs.

"No, I don't believe so," Anton states emphatically, squeezing

Nathan's arm tighter. "They came to hide one."

The direction of the houses point generally uphill, with little land left before cliffs dive to ocean. Nathan realizes he was not exactly correct before; reorienting himself, one of the arms of the pentagram is not pointing here to the Village but rather towards the same hills along the eastern coast of this island. Where the two cross . . . Nathan thinks it might be worth the walk. It may be nothing, or buried, but it may be something; something more important up on that hill.

Anton had barely finished his sentence when a shot rings out. There is a look of surprise on Anton's face as he reaches down, a small spot of blood that is growing larger. He tries to hold it in.

Nathan looks around for the source, seeing nothing but grass and sky. The lady in the windbreaker has not moved, completely still in fact, hands in pockets. Nathan turns back to his old classmate, his old friend, still standing with a stunned look on his face.

"That looks pretty convincing, Anton." Nathan steps around him gingerly and heads up the hill to whatever awaits, the sun beginning to set behind him.

47

A BOY STANDS before him, a child with a soul as old as this hill: *Ard Fhearta*, "the hill of miracles". The Abbot himself had been born nearby on Fenit Island, and his mentor Bishop Erc had ruled from this very spot. As this young heathen spins his tale–a vision from the god Ecne he had been so bold and erroneous to credit–the place lives up to its name once more.

The Abbot sits in his room near the center of the monastery complex. He is proud of how fast this place has grown, how hungry the locals are for his true God. This hill was a perfect choice, yet he knows part of his draw comes from the Secret Trust he had been given, and about which this lad has too much knowledge. This small stocky boy, who at times is brash and other times almost apologetic, is now daring to lecture him about the dangers of immortality. There is wisdom in this child's words, despite the irony that immortality, Everlasting Life of the soul, is a major selling point of the religion that built this monastery.

The boy Ciaran had ironically come under the guise of pilgrimage to the god Lughnasa, part of a harvest festival now going on outside these walls. His Celtic beliefs had a different sense of immortality from the Abbot's: they believe in a changing state very unlike the Christian sameness forever. Trees that once produced the Apples of Immortality have been cut down, reducing their gods to trolls and fairies growing older and smaller without actually dying: the Tuatha Dé Danann retreat below ground, humans crowding them out. Old gods, like Lughnasa, were immortal but shrinking; a horrible fate, a trap with no escape, and hardly the Everlasting Life the Abbot now understands.

As a young novice, the Abbot had been personally chosen by Bishop Erc to build a stronghold for something very precious, something Biblical; though at the edge of civilization, there was need to prepare for the world moving ever closer. The Stones of Methuselah, the box that transports a sacred relic, are hidden on this hill.

The Bishop said there was a reason ages of certain individuals in the Bible were so long: they were guardians of this Relic, a gift from God and source of significant power. Unfortunately it does not work for everyone, as it did not for the Bishop, nor the Abbot. Nor anyone else they knew, which made it all a matter of Faith. For a very, very few it aligns the body's energy–Bishop Erc had used the word 'spirit'–to help it heal itself. It was not immortality per se, but nine hundred years is more than enough. An unlucky few, however, have the opposite reaction, and energy is pulled out of them. The Stones themselves, the container of the Sacred Relic, had absorbed enough of its energy to have a similar but weaker effect. Apparently, the type of stone used for the box was special, a dense internal crystalline content from the ancient lands of Babylon, and were the only ones able to mask the full power of this sacred object. The Abbot, when he had seen the Stones, thought they looked rather normal. His life, his homeland, is surrounded by stone. What he really wanted to see was what the content, the Relic itself.

The Abbot had his doubts then, he still does. Bishop Erc told of the Sons of Milidh bringing this Relic out of the Middle East, first to Spain, and then on to Ireland. Even here too many people were closing in, and the Relic had been taken to the Community of Ailbe almost fifty years before. The Stones were brought back here so it could not be moved without the Bishop's knowledge. This young boy's vision, if it is to be believed, means that soon neither the Stones nor the Relic will be safe.

The Community of Ailbe is their furthest outpost, a long and dangerous voyage. To venture further would truly be an undertaking. He would need help, certainly a better boat than could be made here. The Abbot had heard of Roman technology, of great sailing vessels far beyond the small fishing craft he and this boy are familiar with. The Pope may be able to provide, but a suitable cover story would need to be constructed, as Bishop Erc never bothered to inform the Pope of the Relic they possess, or what they plan to do with it. Rome would certainly want it, obscuring the message and good works they have achieved here. The Abbot does not consider this a lie to the head of his Church–the popes seem to come and go, there may be a new one already for all he knows–but rather loyalty to his beloved mentor who had sworn him to secrecy.

"Immortality is only up to the gods," the boy's words shake the Abbot from his pensiveness. *Or God*, the Abbot corrects. "To live that long just leaves you disconnected from the world, though many would wage wars to possess the ability or even risk death to see if it would work for them."

This boy Ciaran shows some qualities that would make him a good monk, the Abbot decides. This vision, this message, was indeed being delivered to the correct person, but the warning is just as much for Ciaran himself. Bishop Erc had a similar ability to this boy's, and had told him about a monk that would be his next messenger, joining him on long journey. He had, however, expected a real monk, not a local child. This would certainly require more work.

"This journey was central in what I saw," Ciaran continues, "it is important in and of itself. They, these Seekers, would be looking for something, or somewhere, and when they find it the pieces must be scattered."

The Abbot asked what this cargo was, where it came from, where they would be going; anything to discern exactly how much the boy knows. *The pieces must be scattered*, this point seems reckless. The Relic is a gift from of God. The trail must not be completely obliterated. Someday, when the time is necessary, someone must follow it again.

Apparently finished, the Abbot thanks the boy for taking the chance to open up to him; it certainly could not have been easy to approach a man of power with the contents of a dream. Then again, if this is a normal occurrence for the child then it would explain his confidence, and why his addition to the Monastery would be so useful. He offers him a tour, and uses that time to convince Ciaran that in a few years, with his parent's permission, he should return and join them.

As the boy takes his leave, disappearing through the gate back into the village, the Abbot thinks it may be time to take a pilgrimage himself. Time to think. There are decisions to be made, prayers to understand what kind of Faith he should put in this message he received. He always loved the mountains to the west, near his home. If God will provide him clarity, and in his heart of hearts he already is leaning towards Belief, he would have much to plan. And perhaps, on his way back, he could stop by and recruit a certain young man with very useful visions and knowledge of the sea.

48

July 11, Iles de la Madeleine

A ROAD UNDULATES with the gently rolling hills of the island's eastern coast, gray ribbon over green lulling forms violently cut off by sheer hundred-foot cliffs meeting the ocean. Nathan stands aside this narrow roadway, Chemin des Montants, as the sun sheds its final light on his back. Warm darkness envelops all around, but it is ominously black ahead over the sea. He looks both directions along the paved surface, a pathway wide enough for two cars to pass but lacking a formal line suggesting where that may occur. No one within sight, yet Nathan feels he is not alone.

"Audrey!" he calls, "I know you're out there!" Windy silence makes him briefly self-conscious of his paranoia. "What have you done?!" he yells into the wind anyway, turning around. Still no response.

On the other side of the Chemin des Montants, at the end of a long gravel drive, stands a lone farmhouse. The house itself is unremarkable, yet the setting on the high point near a cliff, all of the islands in view, is quite extraordinary. He can barely see the small lagoon island, but the direction of the pentagram located there pointing to this spot feels right. A few of the farmhouse's windows reflect sunset, bright oranges and reds, the rest are as dark as the ocean sky in the distance.

Nathan crosses the road onto an overgrown gravel path. Like the abandoned farmhouses he explored as a child, this one exudes an aura sad yet strong, an echo of joys and miseries which took place there. It may be a projection of his feelings, his own memories, but it was one of the things that drew him to architecture: that buildings had personalities and could stir emotion. He would spend hours imagining the life and hardship that went on inside, and wonder what strong attachment existed so long after they were abandoned that the current owners could not tear them down, even after they become unusable. There must be a power, a purpose, in their ruin. Either sentiment, or warning.

It occurs to Nathan that his musings are about the life inside, not the building itself. Like Moyne with his stones, he had allowed himself to become so transfixed with the power of the shell that he had forgotten the importance of what goes on inside. There is a life to what you see, but even that life would not occur unless something was unfolding inside and all around. If he follows the path Anton is laying out for him, would he be any closer to experiencing this unfolding, or would it just be more of the same rut he has been in, but with more dangerous clients? Like it or not, he needed these past two weeks to kick him in the ass. The question is, where will it lead him to?

The driveway path is actually two tire lanes of gravel and a strip of long, flowing grass down the middle. Nathan walks down the right gravel lane, stones crunching under his feet and tall grass brushing his outstretched hand. The drive has not seen a car for a long time. It does not lead directly to the farmhouse, but rather between the house on his left and a small shed on the right. Behind the shed stands a barn, a few boards missing but otherwise in good shape, the group forming a courtyard. There is a dramatic opening between the barn and a stone wall behind the house that frames an expanse of ocean beyond.

From the end of the driveway the whole complex looks wild, overgrown. Nearing the house and its leaning front porch, he realizes the care that has been taken. Structure is leaning, but it is solid and no peeling paint. Vines grow rampant, but are carefully thinned and kept away from certain areas.

In front of the house, remnants of a stone wall poke through wild grasses. This must have been constructed with the home, Nathan surmises, since he had not seen stone fences as a matter of course elsewhere on the islands. It is low, but he can make out a curvature as it passes the house and disappears around the other side. It is dry laid, stacked and curved in a way that reminds him of a bawn: the Irish stone-fortified enclosure seen around ancient farms.

Nathan notes the proportion of everything: windows, doors, siding and trim, the size of stones, the shape of buildings and distance between them. They are perfect. An overly large misshapen stone header, a few twisted tiles set into walls, an old bench and small table angled for a view; even the odd elements fit perfectly. It all looks so deceptively simple, yet Nathan knows how very sophisticated this all is. He has seen it before, and it is something that can only occur over a long period of time. Places like this are not designed, they unfold over centuries.

Nathan thinks of Audrey, wishing he could share this. Would she care? He doubts it, but he realizes how much a part of his life she has become in such a short time; infatuation fueled by circumstance. He hopes, he wants to believe, that if someone dreams of someone else like he does her, then she must dream of him also. It is too powerful an energy to just dissipate into the ether.

He also realizes there is very little about her that he really, truly knows. Audrey has been several different people within the past two weeks. Nathan supposes everyone has multiple personalities.

There is a larger stone wall behind the house enclosing a courtyard. Small gaps in the dry-laid stone allow him to see in; mostly just leaves and vines, but it looks like there is another stone structure inside. The din of waves crashing far below masks any sounds of life. Nathan recognizes the dry-laid stonework and its proportions, a shape like the Gallarus Oratory on Dingle.

Nathan walks back to the space between the house and the shed. Everything was leading to one spot, this one place that stands apart. Not in the way that a village square or a town hall becomes a focal point for a community, but more in the way that a leper was given a place at the edge. This is an outcast's home, in the most loving way possible, left alone to fill their time with what they had around. This place speaks to him, to his soul, to the very core of his being.

Nathan turns all around, and then falls to his knees in a dizzy spell. The sun is now set, a purple red-green glow fills the west. There is a sense, an indescribable feeling, of life both real and imagined that permeates this spot; the land, the sea, the house, the details of the stone walls and ruins. Every inch is natural and man-made, cared-for and alive in absolute proportion. It is a perfect moment, a perfect place. Energy coalesces here; he can almost see the lines coming from every direction. It is that thin place where the world vibrates, a beauty so true that Nathan thinks he is going to pass out.

He manages to stand and walk a few steps to the side door. As Nathan stands there, his hand poised to knock on the wooden slab, he feels a sensation like when the wind died down earlier in the day: the pain and itch of the deep, deadly wound Anton had given him is completely gone.

49

Iles de la Madeleine

AN OLD MAN answers the door. "Welcome Nathan," he grins, his voice hoarse, then casually turns and shuffles back into the lowly lit room.

"Who are you? What is this place?" Nathan asks in rapid succession, following him inside. The figure before him is hunched, ancient, all bones and loose dry skin. He wears brown slacks and an ill-fitting shirt, though Nathan doubts any shirt would suit his gaunt frame. He is pale, very pale; if he has seen the sun in years it has left no trace.

"I'm Daniel Moyne," the old man turns and extends a wrinkled hand.

"You're the third one," Nathan responds. "I suppose I've met your son?"

"He is a descendent, and apparently has been useful for once. Unwittingly, I would guess. We let him play his little games, but his collection is being retrieved now."

"You were the one on the phone to me. You hired the actor," Nathan assumes.

"I have cleaned up the mess of others. When I realized who you might be, I led you here," he answers. "Your friend Mr. Eischen was hired by those below the hill: the Followers. I am afraid we have to appease them every so often to buy their secrecy." The old man sits down in a corner chair, gesturing for Nathan to do the same beside him. "Miss May, on the other hand, is a far more complex matter. She is not who you think."

"No one ever is," Nathan states. "Audrey and your son, grandson or whoever, will you kill them too?"

"He has no heirs, is of no use now. He will die soon enough."

"That's cold."

"That's life," the old man shrugs his shoulders. "Our sense of its passing is just different."

Nathan looks around. Open windows and strong breeze barely mask the musty air. There is a low cacophony of ticking, and as his eyes adjust he realizes the room is filled with clocks. Hundreds of them. Some are working, but most have stopped at various points in time, their hands frozen.

Moyne anticipates his observation. "Gifts from the people below the hill," he gestures towards the walls. "Over the years it has become a bit of a tradition: a new clock for each Guardian. I'm not sure if they mean it as tribute, or a cruel joke."

"You're the Guardian," Nathan nods his head.

"I was a monk," Moyne explains. "Which is not prerequisite to be Guardian, but in the past it was holy men who had access, who were tested. The Acadians here, when I arrived, just called me *moine*: 'monk'. I eventually took it for my name. I have not heard my real name in so long it has become meaningless."

"You also seem to eventually had children; that's a bit odd for a monk."

"I have lived several lives. I hoped one of my children may inherit my, or I should say 'our', ability."

379

"How long have you been here?" Nathan's heart races, anticipating the answer.

"Longer than you would believe," Moyne evades, lowering his dark eyes in remembrance. Nathan finds the reply frustrating; not that he would believe the expected answer. "So obviously you are not the first to come here," Moyne suddenly stands up, spryly for his advanced age, and Nathan again follows. "You will not be the last. Many, many others were sent away, or settled below the hill. A long time ago, before me, they had an island of their own." Moyne winks in a gesture acknowledging Nathan had been there. "Surprisingly few have tried to force their way. When it has happened, they would find nothing, and leave."

The old man leads him past a fireplace and small kitchen into the dining room. There is an old wooden table at its center. At the end wall is a set of French doors swung open to the back garden and ocean beyond. They stop in the opening, the monk leaning against its wood casing, and together look out into the walled garden. It is not the same in structure, but in faded daylight the feeling of this space is the same as Nathan's dream: a chapel, living and dead. Beautifully manicured vines cover stone walls. Statues and fountains are surrounded by flower beds. Nathan can make out a few of the flowers that are nearby, brilliant even in darkness. In full daylight, this garden would be a burst of every imaginable color. The enclosed area is not large, but every inch of it has been utilized, taken care of.

"I have much time to tend to this," Moyne explains.

Directly before them is a statue of a woman, her arms outstretched as if dancing. Something strikes Nathan as wrong, and Moyne notices. "The only wife he had who shares our gift," the old man points. "Her exposure to the Relic did some nasty things."

It takes a moment to sink in before Nathan realizes it is a corpse, and not a statue. "Why is she outside?" Nathan is surprised this would be his first question. "Isn't it," he hesitates to find the right word, "damaging?"

"She loves it so out here. I have her brought in during winter, though."

"Why not bury her after she died?"

"Oh please, that would be cruel," Moyne looks shocked, "she's not dead." He lets his words sink in. "It would be a horrible thing being buried alive in our condition."

"She's alive?!"

"Oh yes. It is quite a comfort to have a woman around the house."

"You're saying she is still alive!" Nathan shakes his head in disbelief. This is harder to understand than the old man's age, even of the healing powers he has experienced firsthand. Would this be his fate now that he has been exposed?

"And she can hear us right now, so regard what you say. I bet she is quite happy to have visitors; she never could have the visitors she wanted." Moyne winks again. "You understand, don't you?"

"Not in the slightest," Nathan whispers, staring at the nude form. He begins to recognize her less as art and more of a person, and retracts his hand from touching her. "You don't feel the need to, you know, clothe her?" he asks.

"Like I said, we do not have many visitors. Actually, we make sure we do not have any visitors. I simply did not think of it. Have I offended your modesty?"

Nathan almost laughs aloud at the question. "You obviously haven't researched me as deeply as you thought." He begins to put it all together. "The others we found in those houses, they are . . . like her?"

"Wives, husbands, children; we must care for our family,"

Moyne nods his head in confirmation. "I thought about making them useful, using them for columns or something," he smiles. "'Caryatids', is that the proper term?"

"Only for women. It's called a 'Telamon' if it's male." Nathan regrets the correction immediately. "The people below the hill, the 'Villagers' they call themselves, along with your what–great-grandson?–they take care of those in the houses?" Nathan asks.

"They have accepted that honor. The truth is most who have suffered effects were those that live below the hill. As you know, there are several stone pieces that formed a box for the Relic. People have been coming here for a long time, long before Columbus. Monks from the Community at Ailbe followed Abbot Brendan here. They were the start, the first entrusted with a piece. Ciaran, the original monk who stayed behind, was starved for companions other than the few natives who hunted here. Unfortunately, as civilization encroached, a bit of a cult grew up around the piece. Also, unfortunately, grew the side effects. They tend to be permanent, and caring for them has taken on a life of its own; a fine distraction for those below the hill. Right now they are under the direction of the priest, who I believe you met."

"I can't believe he would be in charge of anything," Nathan comments.

"He doesn't really like it here, and there's obviously something unnatural going on with him and that couple. Other than that, he is a good priest. Not my kind of priest, mind you, but there would not be any of those left."

"So they, the people followers below the hill, never knew the stones were a piece of a container, and that it held something greater. You let them believe they held the prize. But if it is not something to be used, something in fact that should be hidden, why does it need a Guardian? Why not just bury it deep, or drop it in the middle of the ocean and sail away?"

"It is a gift from God," the old man cannot comprehend such disregard.

"Like your long life."

"But I am lucky; I am ending my usefulness. I had no problem torching your little building on chance to motivate you. I would have had no problem even if people were inside. It matters so little in the long scheme of things."

"You did that!" Nathan takes it personally. "It would matter a great deal to those people, and their families."

"See? You still have that part of your humanity."

"You had that actor killed to send me a message. You could have just told me where you were."

"The message wasn't just for you. It was a warning for Mr. Eischen, which is why Miss May was delayed and did not take you there until Anton had a chance to see it. But at least I picked someone who was already dead for that message."

"So he did die of natural causes?"

"No, but he would have soon."

Nathan considers the danger he may be in. The man may look old, feeble, but he has demonstrated his reach, and his lack of mercy. "Why now? Why trust me?"

"When your own generation, then your own children and then grandchildren pass on, you lose your connection to this world, to life." Moyne lowers his head, and then raises it again. "Like Macbeth, I am beginning to not understand this life that goes on and on with no purpose. That is a very dangerous thing with the knowledge and power I have. Physically, I could be here for many more decades. Psychologically, I just do not think I can continue another year."

Nathan is torn, trying to discern what he has seen and

experienced from the delusion and fairytale that has been fed with it. "Most think the story of Brendan's Crossing is a Christian retelling of the common tales of the Celtic Otherworld. You're telling me it was real?"

"What is real, what is true," Moyne shrugs, "is a function of time. There is what I believe and what I have experienced to be true, though I seem to lose sight of those things more often lately."

"Like the reason you became a monk, a man of God, but now have no problem killing people?" Nathan asks. "Apparently, everlasting life doesn't suit you."

"It was not the Christian promise of everlasting life that turned my soul to the Church in the first place. Not the devil of temptation either, but rather a true sense of duty. Yes I seem to have failed some of that," the old man nods, "but I have fulfilled my duty to God in ways my brothers could only dream of. There is something here that is Biblical, unique in the world, and truly dangerous. Even if it would not hold the power it does, you can imagine from its historical significance what some may do to possess it."

"So, guarding this object gives you license to do whatever you need to do, and then, like Anton, when you want to quit I am suddenly the only person qualified to take over? One of you, maybe both, is going to be sorely disappointed." Nathan turns back to look over the garden. It is dark, completely black in places with intermittent moonlight as clouds blow over, incessant winds careening over the stone wall. Pale light from inside spills out, casting shadows and illuminating the garden and statues and a portion of the stone structure in the center, the one he had seen earlier shaped like an upside down boat. He squints, thinking that he saw a flicker of light from within.

"I think you only partially understand," Moyne laughs dryly. "But to be clear, I'm not the guardian of the Relic; that honor is truly rare in history. I am the guardian, or 'caretaker' to not be recursive, of the true Guardian; of the Monk named Ciaran." The old man gestures out to the stone structure in the garden. "And he is looking forward to meeting you."

50

Iles de la Madeleine

T HEY WALK SLOWLY, an old man shuffling and a young man respectfully keeping pace; two figures moving through night towards a stone structure. "I must warn," Moyne cautions. "You have personally noticed abnormal healing. Now, imagine that over so many centuries." The old man looks at Nathan to assess his understanding. "Also, you never really stop aging, so he looks . . . well, one tends to shrink, I suppose like his Celtic gods."

Nathan remains skeptical, unsure if the old man is crazy, or if he is crazy for wanting to believe. *A pile of bones with a wig on at best*, Nathan thinks. He can rationalize the effects of radiation, but Brendan and his crew would have made their crossing–if they ever made it at all–almost fifteen hundred years ago! Even Methuselah did not live that long.

"Also," Moyne adds, "he can no longer speak. He has, in fact, been unable to communicate other than tones for a very long time, well before I arrived. However, I should be able to speak for him."

"How, exactly?" Nathan asks, thinking another link in the crazy chain has been added.

"He foresaw you, as he did many things yet to come. It is all written down."

"The script on the tablets?"

"No, that is much, much older. This was written on paper and leather, but I transcribed it all onto the computer upstairs."

"Of course you did," Nathan comments.

They reach the small structure shaped like an upside-down boat, its stones dry-laid and angled to shed water from the sky rather than the sea. Moyne stops at the opening, and Nathan ducks his head inside. In the complete darkness, he is immediately overcome by the smell: foul and base, like rotting flesh, the kind of abhorrence coded into our very being. He instinctually covers his nose and mouth with his forearm, cutting the stench very little.

"You get used to it," Moyne encourages. He enters and stops behind Nathan, lighting a small lamp by the outer door. "Perhaps I should go first."

The lamp dimly illuminates a series of progressively smaller openings. The stone structure they stand in is simply an anteroom, built over a smaller, older stone house, which in turn was built over an even smaller, older, authentic-looking stone beehive hut; an original clochán here on the other side of the ocean.

With Moyne leading the way they duck through the other two openings in rapid succession. Once inside Nathan is barely able to stand, his neck hunched down trying to avoid whatever might be coating the curved ceiling. A small lamp, similar to the one Moyne carries, flickers and casts opposing shadows on a squat wooden table at the far side of the room. There are few other simple furnishings in the room: a small plank wood chair, a similar table, and a very low, small platform that has a few blankets strewn across.

It takes Nathan a few moments to realize that the blankets are not as haphazard as they would first seem. There is something there: white, chalky, almost translucent in some places, about the size of a large hairless cat. He moves closer, wondering if this is the cruel joke Moyne has planned, and any moment a hatchet would come down on his spine. It looks like a porcelain doll that has been split and roughed up, vaguely human but otherworldly. There is a nose and mouth, two eyes that are shut. What were once arms are fused to the torso. One arm still covering his nose, Nathan uses the other to lift the blanket back, wondering if there are legs.

The head moves a bit, and the tiny curled thing emits a screech that makes Nathan's eyes water. *The damn thing is alive!* he panics. Nathan runs out, hunching through low doors, and throws up in the beautiful garden.

He returns slowly, more carefully this time, trying to keep his eyes on Moyne. "What the fuck is this?" Nathan whispers.

"This is Ciaran," Moyne gestures to the figure, "You have no idea what an honor it is for you to be here."

"He's been here, alive, this whole time?" Nathan manages, his voice shaky. "If it–sorry, he–is who you say, that would make him over a thousand years old," he shakes his head. Nathan summons his courage and kneels down next to Ciaran to get a closer look. The head turns slightly with its whole body. He can see movement behind the closed eyelids, and Nathan wonders if the thing can see through them.

"Whatever he had to say, he said a long time ago," there is sadness, tiredness apparent in Moyne's voice. "Whatever new knowledge he might have, whatever golden truths, wisdom, or answers, are locked in there. Though sometimes I hope he cannot think at all anymore, I know better: he is, unfortunately, quite lucid."

"Why me? What am I doing here?" Nathan asks.

"You are very lucky," Moyne replies.

"Am I?" Nathan doubts. He turns to Moyne momentarily, but

quickly turns his attention back to the tiny creature on its rough bed. "Even if there is a scientific explanation, he should not be alive. How could this be real?"

"That is something he, and I, do not know."

"He must know if there is a God, if there is an afterlife," Nathan concludes.

"Living longer does not yield any greater answers. It is our irony that only those who die know if true immortality exists," Moyne replies. "In his writings, he thought he died the very first winter he was here, but that his body was trapped. I hope his soul really did move on that winter. Trapped so long in a body like that would sap its energy, leaving nothing to feed on other than the soul. He may have given up his immortality by living for so long."

Nathan can no longer take his eyes off the withered figure. He wants to touch it, but considers how rude that may be. The porcelain doll analogy works for the color and effect but is otherwise deceiving; close up his shape is craggily and pitted like a small deformed tree, its outer layer dusty and white. The cartilage of ears and nose are long gone, leaving simple pits. It makes small sounds, moves ever so slightly, and intermittently emits an odor that forces Nathan to lean backwards and run back out to the garden.

"He described himself as a different kind of undead," Moyne continues, "where there is always tomorrow to accomplish something, so nothing ever happens. It wears the soul, living so long," he repeats, "to the point that he fears there will be nothing left to move on."

"So a Holy Man, because he has accepted a duty from God, is banished."

"He has sacrificed much," Moyne nods.

Nathan agrees, the physical evidence before him. "But the things he must have seen," he turns back to Moyne, "all the things you experience and gain from living so long."

"He has never left here. He never dare. He searched for a long time for someone to replace him, but there was no one really. He found others, like me, but has outlived even their usefulness." Moyne hesitates, "Now there is you."

"Now wait just a minute," Nathan shakes his head vehemently. "No way in hell I'm staying here."

"What would you have me say, that you are special and it has all come to this moment? It is more by chance, rather than grand plan."

"That's awfully fatalistic for a man of God," Nathan comments.

"I've lived a long time. All plans are imperfect; people make sure of that. I used to believe in God's greater plan, but neither I nor anyone else has insight into what it fully may be. I used to believe that God was the source of all, but I have seen the energies that criss-cross this earth, and perhaps God is the source of these, but they seem to move of their own will. I used to believe Truth, like Beauty, is in the eye of the beholder. But I have learned that neither are; that both are from the same unknown source," Moyne looks over at the Ciaran on the bed, "and both are a function of time. It is our ability to see, to interpret, that not only allows us to learn but also mess it all up. It is not fatalism, it is experience."

"It's fantastic, nothing short of immortality," Nathan asserts.

"Yet you see what it does. You want immortality to experience life, but you become less and less human as your connection withers. It becomes tedious. Every day just seems a journey to night, every night an island of calm before the next journey. There is of course figural immortality, those who are remembered by all through the ages, yet that usually occurs through an untimely death such as our great martyrs. All things in this world must end. Even this universe will end someday. Only God is truly immortal."

"I don't think anyone expects forever to actually mean forever.

Immortality is relative."

"It is. But it is also not as sexy as vampire movies make it out to be. It is not eternal youth. Here on earth it is ugly, and draining."

"Then maybe the goal is just to be remembered, and then hope for the afterlife."

"That is more human. When people sacrifice themselves in war or for their children it is because they believe they will achieve something greater, that they left their mark or allowed someone else to leave theirs. They hope someone may remember them. The question then becomes does it matter in this world, or does it only matter how we live in the eyes of our God? As I said, to such philosophy we offer no more than anyone in this world has ever known."

"He must have a special relationship with this world, with God," Nathan asserts, looking for more.

The Ciaran-thing on the bed emits a low sound, moving the loose end of his arms. It catches Nathan by surprise, glancing at Moyne for reassurance. The old monk takes a deep breath, and closes his eyes.

"The years have made me more of a pantheistic monotheist, for lack of a better term: one God that grows. What other purpose for everyone to be so different, so unique? I am looking out from my eyes, and you experience it as you looking out of your eyes at me. Why tragedies in the world? Why bad, why good? It only seems to mean something if you learn, and the only way God could really learn is to become a part of it all. God grows with every soul that joins, a parent learning from its children," Moyne continues to stand in his trance before opening his eyes adding, "remember that Ciaran grew up believing in the pantheon of Celtic gods before he converted."

"You have come here looking for something," Moyne relapses

into his trance. "You seek the meaning of your own life, even if you have no interest in questioning the greater meaning of life in general. That," he warns, "is something you need to answer for yourself. You also seek the source: the underlying source of how we relate to one another. You have searched your whole life for this source in order to capture it, recreate it at will, in the hope of finding some power through it."

There is a pause as Moyne continues to stand there, speaking for the ancient one. Nathan raises his eyebrows in a gesture to go on, that the monk has his full attention.

"You have had glimpses because you searched for beauty, but you were too preoccupied with surface beauty to see its relation to deeper life. They are of the same source."

"As a monk, I assume you mean God?" Nathan interjects.

"A gift from God, but not God itself. I have struggled with that, since my Celtic upbringing would see them the same. You have some strong connection to it, which is what allowed you to find your way here. It is why you were able to not just extrapolate a few parts, but also account for the unexpected."

"It is reassuring that my addiction has a purpose," Nathan quips.

"It does not. It has led you away from understanding. You have focused on the idiosyncrasies, which may keep things interesting but is a minor part. You should have been looking for the elements that connect us all. A unity of mind. This power is what draws you, I can sense you saw it before you came in. That is why we have met. But for me, so many centuries ago, it was something different."

"Your search was for something else," Nathan concludes. "Hope? Truth?"

"Hope? Hope is a world where truth actually means something. I had tried the truth, and I rarely succeeded. Perhaps it was me, I did not inspire; lies are usually far more inspirational, and how can a simple truth compete with that?"

"Humans are funny creatures, fueled more by outrage and righteous indignation than by joy or love," Nathan feels hesitant about what he can offer, but assumes anyone out of touch for a few centuries may have missed something. "The more outrage and righteous, the more they can declare their Christianity and patriotism, both of which are based on the opposite. And because they then do nothing other than make a declaration, nothing happens and their anger is fueled even more. All the while, they are told to ignore those who may point out the hypocrisy, saying the majority is against them, even if they are using their own vast media sources to spread the message."

"So it has always been," the monk affirms. "It is comforting to feel misunderstood; that makes it the other person's problem and not your own. Anger motivates, anger sells, in ways even sex could not. This is not new to any time in history."

"But the world is just too big," Nathan justifies, "people focus on what they can. It is hard to think it all the way through. Extremism is easier,"

"Extremism is considered a value by the foolish, the Godless. But the immortality you seek, the lot in life I have been dealt, is also extremism. It is not human."

"You seem to have retained some of your humanity," Nathan offers. "You seem to be aware of what is going on."

"All the things of which we have been speaking of have gone on since I was a child. I am not aware, as much as remembering what it was once like and has continued to be. You just have better heat and plumbing, more convenient ways to get your food. It makes your captivity more bearable."

"My captivity?" Nathan is confused by the direction the monk is taking.

"The monk in me still thinks in biblical terms. Adam and Eve's metaphorical sin was in creating civilization itself; becoming captive to the rules and manners of a society, and once that knowledge is gained, the ability to break those rules."

"Isn't free will necessary for the vision of God you described?"

"Of course it is necessary. Free will allows us to question, to learn and to grow. However, it too is a function of time. Change–true innovation–cannot occur with one person living so long. Despite how certain fundamental things stay the same, species adapt and change their way of thinking. Individuals are less flexible. For all my experience and knowledge I am a man out of time, of no relevance or use to this world other than to point out the obvious, which no one wants to hear. The simple fact is I have not really done anything in all this time I have had."

"And so you stayed in hiding, afraid to try. How convenient," Nathan shakes his head. "And now you want me to do the same."

"It all seems so important to you now, what so-and-so did, this or that political party, or transgression. I've seen it, and in 100, 500 years it will mean nothing, or maybe be a footnote if it is truly remarkable. The world goes on, life moves on. This duty requires you to stay outside of that."

"I have to believe what we do matters," Nathan insists.

"Spoken like the truly living," the old monk replies, opening his eyes. "I could go on about my observations of the world over the centuries. It may be funny to say, but we just do not have the time. What is it you really want to know?"

Nathan does not need to think about this, though it pains him to say the words aloud. "Have I ever killed anyone?"

"We all have, directly or indirectly. But you ask about someone in particular, someone who was close." Moyne searches his memory. "Yes, you have. But probably not who you think." He pauses then asks, "But is that what you really want to know?"

Nathan thinks a bit longer, about the questions he already asked and the very human limits of the old monks. He is truly afraid to ask what is expected of him, and is not sure if he would heed the answer. He finally decides that there is only one truly pressing, truly relevant question. "Can I see it?"

51

Iles de la Madeleine

A LOW SCREECH breaks the silence. Nodding in affirmation, Moyne moves deftly from wall to wall around the room, touching various stones before returning to Nathan's side near the low platform upon which the ancient monk is lying. He presses a low panel at its corner, causing a large section to open to the side.

"Seriously. You're hiding it under the bed," Nathan scoffs.

"There are safeguards if anyone uninvited tries to enter. The relic needs to be as close to him as possible," Moyne explains, struggling to straighten himself. Once upright, he points for Nathan to reach into the dark space.

Nathan shuffles on his knees the few feet to center himself at the opening, nervous about reaching his bare hands into the unknown void. With a deep breath, he closes his eyes and reaches in with a single hand, expecting the worst. Just a couple feet in, Nathan touches something solid. He extends his other hand and feels around to find the edges. The object is round, cold to the touch, about the size of a human head. Nathan cups his hands either side just under its curvature and with a slight lift begins to pull it out.

"Not too far," Moyne warns, taking a few steps backward.

As it reaches the edge of the platform, Nathan gets his first glance; a perfect, metallic, almost mercury-looking sphere. Deep black silver in color, constantly changing and swirling in the dim light, it is ornately carved in symbols like those Nathan remembers on the stones. Interspersed are small carvings, hieroglyphics, which he does not remember seeing preiously. He sets it back on the floor just at the edge of the opening, steadying it with one hand so as to not roll away.

"A gift, or a fluke, of the universe," Moyne says from behind him, "it emits radiation, or an electromagnetic field of some kind. Unlike the protecting stones that form the box, this will kill most people."

"Thanks for warning me," Nathan responds. It is beautiful, hypnotic. Nathan believes he would have reached in even knowing the potential danger.

"Yet for very few it has the opposite effect," Moyne continues, "It does not grant immortality; I'm dying, and the end is near for the Ancient One. He has to stay very near to it."

"It's beautiful."

"Those who care for it are destined to not find their immortality elsewhere. Only one can care for it at a time, and they could also die very slowly and painfully. You are tied to it, cannot leave it, enduring centuries alone."

"Why not destroy it then, or just bury it? The loss cannot be worthwhile: it's just an object," Nathan says.

They both look at him, Nathan swearing he can tell a look of confusion in the craggily body of the ancient monk. "We did not expect that blatant hypocrisy," Moyne admonishes. He closes his eyes again as Ciaran emits a series of almost inaudible sounds. "At first it was mine to protect. It is Biblical, something fundamentally wrong with destroying it. Even if hid well, all bottomless pits tend to have a bottom. To be honest, we tried, but there was nothing that could destroy it: both stone and steel shatter. When the technology did become possible, after I saw the atom bomb in the 1940's, I feared that whatever force this thing possesses could destroy the world. Launch it into space and send it into the sun, perhaps, but perhaps it would burn the sun out. Send it back into the abyss, and someday some one or thing may find it that should not. No, it is a burden to be watched over."

Moyne takes another step back, sitting down on a chair near the entry. "Your friend Audrey was willing to kill for it, even though she does not want to live the life she has. Your friend Anton, and my own descendent, were ironically willing to die to possess its power." Moyne looks intently at Nathan. "Even you: last week you did not know it existed, and now you stare obsessed."

"There's obviously a radius of effect. Why not stay at a respectable distance?" Nathan questions.

"The alternative is worse; you saw them. Our wives, our husbands, our children. Once a certain amount is absorbed, there is no going back," Moyne explains. "You may already be there."

Nathan's glare never leaves the object at his knees. "When did it come?"

"How should he know?" Moyne asks in return, "That was way before his time."

Nathan finally turns to address Moyne. "If it is safe here, why not keep the Stones also?"

"They were only assembled to move it. The same aspect of the Stones that absorbs energy also protects those who might move it. Also, the Stones have been useful in finding and testing possible guardians, like me," he sets his palm on his chest. "It is rare in those that they heal. Rarer still is what you are doing right now, holding the Source. Even I cannot touch it."

Nathan stares again at the sphere, turning it around. A rhythmic resonance captivates him. "There must be something on here, some great Truth."

"If there is anything to be learned from living so long, it is that truth tends to be brief, and everything else merely commentary."

"Your life has been anything but brief."

"Yet the defining moments were but instances. All this time, going on and on, has seemed to water down any of my real accomplishments."

"So I should do something fantastic, something great, and then kill myself" Nathan says, "go out in a blaze of glory and all that? What about the sanctity of life?"

"I was not suggesting that. You may create something, and then think you could never do better, yet you never know if God has something more planned. It may not be greater, but it may be more important."

"So what is left for you, and for him?" Nathan queries.

"Every truth has a limit at which it stops being true."

"Him I can understand," Nathan looks up from the sphere to see Ciaran looking at it in the same hypnotized fashion, "but you, Moyne, you have some time left."

"And I will need it; he will die soon. I do hope I notice when it happens."

"'This is the way the world ends, not with a bang but a whimper.'" Nathan recites quietly.

"You are not a Holy Man, but you may be a good choice. There are times in history we cherish our past, times when we would tear it all down for the future. You, and your career, set you in between. It is a good place to be, the world where real things get done. I have lived a long time, and have never been there."

"Yet you've had children, you've had a life. You don't seem crushed under the weight of duty," Nathan points out, "you simply seem depressed."

"Despite how unique we think we believe ourselves to be, our big questions and big fears are the same. These questions I cannot answer, and the fears I know all too well."

"That you will be forgotten, having never existed at all?"

"We will all be forgotten in this world. Your genealogies, your pictures and video, in a thousand years will be lost. In a million years we may look like the cavemen do to us. Our scratching may be meaningless, if they survive us at all."

"That's dark," Nathan remarks.

"There are no immovable objects that can resist an unstoppable force. This world, this galaxy; at some point all the energy of life we know will dissipate. Sometimes, in my weaker moments, I think even the Almighty may not be mighty enough."

"But it doesn't really matter, does it? It only matters to those who think like we do. In a million years, who cares what they think of us. When the sun is gone, we will all be gone, so it's all good. We only matter to each other, and perhaps to God if you believe."

"I did not expect you to be so optimistic," Moyne comments. "Either our research is wrong, or you have made some fundamental changes." He directs Nathan to put the sphere back. Nathan does so with some reluctance, reaching into the void more comfortably this time. The panel closes, and Moyne reverses his movements around the room, resetting the protective measures. More than just an alarm, like the Mona Lisa if there is a break-in, both Ciaran and the Object would descend to safety until help arrives, or the perpetrators give up or die of old age.

Moyne nods to himself, nodding in satisfaction. "You needed a challenge, the love of someone, before you would feel comfortable accepting this."

"I may have passed your tests, but that is no guarantee I would ever stay here with you," Nathan charges.

"The offer is near immortality, and on your terms. You can live your regular life, and then come back; a choice I did not have. It was purely out of duty that I stayed, so many times tempted to leave." The old monk looks very tired once more. "Given my situation, that seemed like suicide, and we know how God views suicide."

"What would it matter if my soul, my memory, withers as his has? You're asking me to gamble: that I should take your offer of staying long on this earth, even if it means losing the chance for Everlasting Life. Go with the immortality you can prove, eh?"

Moyne gestures it is time to leave. For an awkward moment Nathan is unsure how to address ancient Ciaran, the poor doomed monk marooned so many centuries ago. He finally just bows slightly, as an unseen sign of respect, and quickly ducks out the set of doors. They return through the garden to the house, the clocks inside still ticking a time no one heeds.

"You straddle a line between darkness and greatness, never knowing when you will cross it either way. But cross it you will," Moyne warns, showing him to the door. "Despite all the words spoken on his behalf, there is that other simple reality he has come across in his very long life: that even if Truth is brief and everything else is just commentary, sometimes the commentary is necessary. The Truth is that you will be back. You will be back, because unless something drastic changes, your fear is as strong a force as the ancient monk's devotion was. You will come, and you will serve your term here or elsewhere. You will do it in secret, alone. In the meantime, if you are smart, you will live your life as best and as fully as you can."

52

AUDREY ADJUSTS HER binoculars impatiently. *Why is he just standing there?* She knew she had been followed; she was counting on it. She needed Nathan to think he was the hunter, that she did not want him to find Anton. Waiting for him to return, she ponders how different things worked out from her original plan. It seems like she had been waiting forever when he finally moves again, walking slowly across the road, not bothering to look either way, and coming through the field towards her. Everything is working out perfectly.

There is not much cover in the low scrub of this island, but she has dealt with worse conditions and tougher adversaries. Audrey stays very still, at a respectable distance, as Nathan passes blindly following his previous path. Once his back is visible, she moves quickly and quietly to a spot behind him, and begins to close the gap. Nathan stops, feeling more than hearing the presence behind him.

"Give it to me," Audrey demands.

"I have nothing," he assures her.

"Like I believe you, of all people, could resist something so

402

beautiful."

"You've seen it?" Nathan turns to confront her.

"So it *is* there," she confirms with a smile.

"You can put it down, you're not scaring me," he lies, focusing on her gun.

"Go back and get it," she commands.

"Or what, your boss will be disappointed? Not my problem. Besides, I couldn't get it if I wanted to," Nathan tells the truth and thinks about turning and continuing on, curious if she would actually shoot him in the back, or if she had some code of honor that forbade such a thing. "Do you even know what 'it' is?" he decides to ask.

"First of all, I am the boss," she states smugly. "Secondly, I could care less what 'it' is; I already know about how large it could be, based on its box. I know you could carry it."

"You're really missing the whole point," Nathan admonishes. "Where is your intel? I thought you would be more prepared."

"Back to the house," she motions with the gun impatiently.

"I've paid for enough lap dances to know someone at work," Nathan points out. "There was no 'mutual employer'. You hired Anton, but he wasn't quite working out as hoped. You convinced the local to get rid of him, feeding the cover story about the importance of local history, plus who could resist a woman like you? Then you felt regret, or pity, or uncertainty? When he wasn't dead, you nursed him back to health."

"Pure necessity," she interjects, "the stone he went to retrieve that night was not the right one. Somehow he found the one fake, of all the fucking stones in Ireland"

"By that time I had shown up, called in by Anton's instructions to Moyne, to retrieve the same piece. You saw some promise; I was more successful than Anton, as I always have been. First I lead you right to a piece that Anton must have known about, making you more suspicious of him. I know you didn't kill the old man in Chorin, but you would have, just to steal his piece. Then you torture me, to verify I'm not playing you. In Dingle you drug and strip me to deflect suspicion towards Anton, yet later let me see you with him. The same time, you are seducing Anton, to get him to bring the pieces here while you see if I have any other surprises. And I delivered."

"Yes, you did."

"We get back here, but instead of feeling more certain because you're on your home turf, you seem less in control. I start to wonder why. We're getting close: Family, the Source, all of that. You hire an actor to impersonate Moyne, who is either your partner or your competitor, it really doesn't matter. He acknowledged you, but not really as either one of those."

"My father. Not that he would care, even if he knew. All he's ever cared about is himself."

"Yet you were with me, so you didn't kill the actor and stage that little scene. Did your father lie to us?"

"That may have been my mother and her little cult; she's quite a piece of work, too. And if she thought you played some part in their little drama, she would have left you a clue, and a warning to me. You'll have to ask her. I'm sure she will want to know what you saw in the house. With you, I may have finally delivered something they could not have done themselves."

"Looking for mommy and daddy's approval, are we?" Nathan taunts. "That is the whole point, isn't it? I figure it's one of three possibilities: either do something to finally prove to your parents you belong in their little club, do something that will exact your revenge for them loving these damn objects more than their little girl, or if all else fails sell the information to get back into good standing with your former military commanders in the JTF2. How am I doing?"

They arrive at the familiar old wood-sided house. Nathan wants to ask if the earlier scene with Anton was real or staged, but is equally reluctant to know. Audrey directs him to open the door, an empty room, an empty house, waiting for them.

"You're here because of your friend," she reiterates, closing the door behind and moving around to his side in the middle of the room. "I'm here because of my father, my real father, who never even knew I existed. It's too bad, since part of his insanity is that he believes he is the last of his line. My mother always insisted another man, one of the Villagers, was my father. I only found out this year, a medical emergency with my fake father, that I left the military for to donate a kidney. Surprise! Not a match for DNA! Not that I could tell him; my mother made sure he would never believe me. It is now up to me, to carry on somehow. My responsibility." *I am the one pulling all the strings*, Audrey reminds herself, *I am the constant.* "You were pretty close," she continues, sitting down in the chair, the gun still trained on Nathan. "Anton and I were working more closely together than you described. He led me to believe you possessed skills he did not."

"I do."

"I was using both of you. If you haven't noticed, those damn Stones make me sick, which is one of the reasons my mother never let me into the fold."

"How did you know I would be, for lack of a better term, 'Stone-Postitive'? Someone the Monks would let in?"

"I didn't," she shrugs. "I would like to say I had a feeling, but I was prepared to be doing this a lot longer. Frankly, I had nothing to lose."

"You could have trusted me. I probably wouldn't have believed you, but I would have helped."

"You had to stay pure, and find it on your own, or you would have smelled as bad to the Monk as any of the Villagers."

The smell: Nathan is reminded of the stone hut and the terrible, sad thing inside. "You know the ancient thing that's still alive up there. Your mother, her people, must know what's really in that house."

"You believed his stories? The old man on the hill is quite senile, you know. Dangerous, but senile."

Nathan is not quite sure what to say, what might free him or what might get him killed. He is feeling a bit invincible, a man with nothing to lose. "The prize you're looking for isn't an object, it's a person. You've seen how I've healed; now imagine that a thousand-fold. There is someone up there who has been on this island for almost fifteen hundred years; since he landed here as part of St. Brendan's crew. Imagine if you made that public," he ponders the sensation for a moment, also realizing no one would ever believe it.

"How gullible are you?" Audrey confirms.

"I thought that's what you believed in, why you're here," Nathan rationalizes. "Anton was like me, which means I was destined to make the same mistakes. The pictures I found in his room were so typical for an architect. They were the same kind I would take; buildings and sculptures, empty street scenes at just the right hour."

"Sounds boring," she says.

"To most people, because there is one thing usually missing," he explains, "*people*. We assumed that we were looking for an ancient object. If we were supposed to be looking for a person, and not an object, we would both have missed it."

"That's all crap. You yourself said there was something in that box. And you give Anton too little credit; despite his limitations, he knew what he was doing. In the end, he tried to play the hero."

"Anton a hero? How do you figure that?"

"You need to find a way to deliver whatever is up there, and I don't mean this bullshit about an immortal monk."

"I can't. You know that."

"You will."

"Maybe I brought a bit of help."

"That senile old man on the hill? I think I can handle him."

"No, someone a bit more ruthless for fun and profit. You would be surprised how many connections O'Malley has right here in your old home town," Nathan lies, trying to divert her attention long enough to make a plan.

At that moment the front door opens, surprising them both; Nathan thinking maybe O'Malley magically did sense his need, and Audrey for a moment believing Nathan was telling the truth. Instead, the woman in the light blue windbreaker enters. "What are you doing?" she demands, glaring at Audrey.

"Nathan," Audrey introduces, "this is my mother."

"Of course," Nathan responds, "your mother would be one of the parasites."

"We are not parasites," Audrey's mother corrects, "we have been here almost as long as the Relic. We're here because of what the monks brought, and we have supported the Guardians and kept their secrets. The Ones on the hill are always changing, and they should value our aid. Instead, they barely tolerate us, because we have acquired knowledge, and because we know the real prize is there." She leans in close to Nathan; he can see blankness in her grayish blue eyes; the same as Audrey's eyes but without the fire. "Did you see it?"

"Yes."

She leans back and smiles. "Few have ever returned. Those who have eventually never left," she nods.

"All these centuries, and you people have never really understood what this is about," Nathan shakes his head.

"Who are you to lecture us?" the mother demands. She points at Audrey, "You're as bad as this poor excuse for a child!"

"Get out! Now!" Audrey yells.

The woman in the blue windbreaker shakes her head, and with a look of disgust at Audrey steps through still open house door, slamming it behind.

"Don't take it personally. It was never about you. It was about my father, and my mother, and that thing that was always so much more important than me." Audrey moves to the door. "If you're not going to help me . . ."

"I can't help you," Nathan regrets.

"Then you can feel what its like," she threatens. "Forgive me if this feels familiar to you."

She grabs a bottle on the counter and smashes it against the wall. Keeping the gun on him and her back to the door, she pulls out a lighter with her free hand. She flips open the top, getting a flame on her first try. Audrey then throws it down to the liquid stain on the wall and curtains. She pauses until satisfied the growing conflagration is established. A final look and she backs out, closing the door behind her.

Nathan rushes to the door, finding it is locked. The curtains are engulfed immediately, flames licking at the ceiling and blocking the windows as a possible exit. He knows these types of homes: the old wood structure will go up quickly, the fire spreading in every direction through the concealed spaces between floors. He scrambles to the kitchen, hoping she did not have the foresight to lock the back door. He pulls on the handle. It is an old plank door like the one at front; it would break his shoulder before he would damage the door itself. The smoke is beginning to affect him, and the glow from the front room reinforces his opinion that he must get of the kitchen, or he will not escape at all. The window is small, the old glass looking that if it breaks it will leave deadly shards, but he thinks this is his best option until he spots the thin security bars beyond.

Nathan looks around for a knife, and finding one in a wood block on the counter, he uses the dull side of the thickest knife to frantically work the pin up out of the door hinge. The first one at top comes easy, as does the second middle one. As the door shifts weight he needs to rebalance it with his shoulder in order to get the bottom pin out. It finally comes free, the blade bending and breaking as he screams at it to move. Throwing the door back from the hinge side, he steps out the back, doubled over and coughing. The flames can be seen on the second floor, a thick blackish-gray cloud beginning to fill the sky above. Nathan collects himself and staggers around the side, pausing as he nears the edge of the front porch.

Audrey is still there near the steps, facing her mother. For once she looks sad, defeated. He moves to step between them, to dramatically confront her with his escape, as a single shot rings out. Audrey slumps down, leaving him close enough to tug his leg on her way down. "She never would understand," the woman in the blue windbreaker explains. It is not remorse, nor lament, but simply resignation.

A car arrives, gravel crunching until it stops nearby. Moyne– not the Monk from the hill but the interrogator, and Audrey's father if he would believe her–gets out, walks over to her mother, and takes the gun out of her hand. He puts his arm around her carefully, almost lovingly, leading her to the passenger door of the car. She looks back before closing the door and driving away. They would not go far; they would find a way to avoid responsibility, as they had for centuries.

No speeches, no drama; Audrey is just gone. Nathan remains behind, holding her head in his lap and stroking her cheek even as his sadness confounds him; he had never felt this bad for Natalia, or even Alex. Yet Audrey was someone he hardly knew, and after the torture, being used, and attempted murder, he assumes anything he did know about her was probably a lie. Nathan knows he should not feel anything but relief, but still wants to scream. Perhaps she had potential, and denial is stronger than logic. Perhaps he had turned a corner in his life, and she was supposed to be in that future.

A deep pain returns. Nathan reaches down to his abdomen and feels a warm stickiness. He raises his hand to where he can see it, and studies the blood dripping from between his fingers.

"Shit, not again," he grumbles, a casualty of being too close to the target, and once again facing the decision if he is dead or not.

53

July 14, Iles de la Madeleine

"YOU LEAVE, *TOUT DE SUITE*," the words come in a thick accent. Nathan looks over his shoulder to find the priest, the one who delivered him here, with a look of sadness and concern on his face. He did not hear the car pull up over the now roaring fire, nor could he remember how long he had been kneeling here, holding on to Audrey's lifeless body.

"Call an ambulance," Nathan begs.

The priest shakes his head, confirming it is too late, or more likely indicating that he does not want to get involved. "I take *you*," he says, "but we must go."

"What about last rites, all that stuff?" Nathan asks.

"*Non*," again the priest shakes his head, "not for her."

"Why not?!" he cries. "What kind of priest are you?"

"An honest one," the black-clad figure motions emphatically for Nathan to get in the car. "I am certain her death will serve purpose: for Moyne, the Villagers. Perhaps even for me."

"They're the ones who killed her," Nathan contests, setting Audrey down gently. He stands up with some effort, the feel of blood that had pooled in his lap now running thickly down his thigh.

"The dead are very adaptable to causes." The priest opens the door for Nathan and motions again for him to come. Nathan does as he is told. As he gets closer the priest suddenly holds out his open hand in a gesture to stop. "Wait," he cautions, "there is a blanket in the back." He opens the back door and reaches in, reemerging with a dark green tartan grid blanket, its fringed edges flapping in the wind. "Please no blood in the car."

"Where are we going?" Nathan asks accepting the blanket and draping it casually over the passenger seat, as if he simply had a wet swimming suit.

"To port; ferry leaves in an hour."

"I can't just leave! Besides, don't I look a bit suspicious?" Nathan tugs on his bloody shirt.

"I will speak to Captain, *no*? You will be down below, where they are used to such things." The priest starts the car and shifts into gear. "You need to get off these islands for a while, at least until Moyne are forgotten you, or dead." He raises his index finger to Nathan's face. "They did not expect I would help you, or that you could leave so quickly without them knowing–it is a small island after all."

Driving away, Nathan's thoughts return to Audrey, her body barely visible as it recedes in his side mirror. A mix of sadness, anger, and surprise overwhelms him. "Was anything about her real?" he mutters.

"Assume it was all a lie. Unless it hurt your feelings, then it was probably true," the priest smiles at Nathan, a response far too flippant for the moment. "She had the effect on you she had calculated; there really is nothing more alluring than a civilized criminal."

"But I didn't know. I still don't know if she was a criminal. No matter what, there was no need to end her life."

"*Oui.* Death is never the answer. Unless, of course, when it is," the priest philosophizes, his eyes on the road ahead. "Your friend, she simply underestimated their power. Power itself does not corrupt, but it does tend to attract the corruptible," the priest looks over at Nathan to make sure he understands the distinction. "You have been offered power. You will need to ask yourself why you would accept it. If it is for the wrong reasons, you will be no better."

They drive down the narrow road, its houses appearing less colorful than before despite the bright sunshine. Nathan feels disconnected, just a pair of eyes watching the flashing lights of a fire truck approach them, the scream of its siren piercing the air through his open window, then fading as it passes.

"She wasn't like them. I could never be like them," he reiterates quietly.

"You are already picking your memories of her. You certainly have a distorted image of yourself, as we all do. People fit their memories to their biases, not the other way around. It is why some remember good times under a certain leader, even if it was terrible."

"I'm not very political, for one thing, and my memories are very clear," Nathan responds.

"*Non,*" the priest counters with a chuckle, goading him on, "of course you are, everyone is, and of course they are not."

"They are," Nathan contends, confused as to which question he is answering. "Besides, politics are predictable: we have two parties, basically the same but with opposite weaknesses: the problem with Republicans is that they do the opposite of what they promise, and the problem with Democrats is that they do what they promise. And quit trying to change the subject; she's dead."

"Oh, get used to it," the priest chides. "You will see many more die before you. That is simply how it will be, and you must find a way to cope."

Nathan scoffs at the unexpected, almost crass tone of the priest. "So that's it? How exactly should I get used to it then?"

The priest thinks a moment. "*Rituel*. It is ritual, then, one thing I understand well," the priest gestures in the air again with his index finger. "Order, balance, harmony tend to come through ritual. You speak of the difference between two: your two parties, Audrey and her parents, you and Audrey, the Monk and the Villagers, living and dying. Dichotomies are useful or misleading, not true or false. They are simplifying models for organizing thought, not ways of the world. Ritual is a more stable way of resolving ever-changing circumstances" he nods as if all has been solved.

"What the fuck are you talking about?" Nathan asks.

"Aeschylus said 'Men search out God and in the searching find him'. To always search is a ritual of sorts, a way to cope rather than just accept what you have been given," the priest slaps the steering wheel emphatically with both hands, jarring Nathan. "I believe that will be your answer over the many years to come."

"Maybe that is the problem; the search supposedly ended with Christ, . So much of what has happened to me, what happened to her, in the past few weeks have had to do with religion."

"Not all of it bad, *no*? And do you really believe it left us nothing else to search for?" the priest shrugs. "Besides, do not confuse being religious with being sectarian. I preach to those in the Village, but I know it is just a cover. Their true devotion lies elsewhere."

"You don't sound disappointed," Nathan judges. Thinking of his first meeting with the man sitting next to him at the Carmes house, he wants to ask what their relationship is; as sordid as his imagination leads? "You actually seem to be making the most of it," he finally adds, impressed by his own tact.

"Life is a party; either pay the cover charge, relax, come in and have a drink, or you pretend you have something better to do," he shrugs again. "It does not make me a bad priest."

"There does, indeed, seem to be an inverse ratio between the willingness to judge others, and the ability to judge yourself," Nathan assesses. The pain below his rib is subsiding. He is tired of banter, of listening carefully through the priest's accent to understand his words let alone their meaning. Yet, the distraction has worked. Nathan has seen this man several times and discussion did not seem to be a strong suit; this has been for his benefit, and he is quietly thankful.

They cross the bridge to Cap-aux-Meules, the island he arrived on. Nathan had not taken this journey to find the meaning of life–he had the same chance of success pondering it at home with a cheap bottle of scotch–but rather it was the meaning of himself he had needed to search for. Removing the safety net of family and whatever friends he had left, of those that expect you to be a certain person, had given him opportunity. Whether or not he had any success may take longer to discern.

"The Monk," the priest begins again, "what he offers is hope, *fantaisie*. It is unreal, something impossible in a too real world. Despite the horror of what his Guardian says he has become, he is of the same source that everything of importance comes from."

"I thought it was a fluke," Nathan responds.

"*Chance*? I do not believe in such a thing."

"The monk said people do not change; that's why he is useless, obsolete, 'a man out of time'."

"In his first life, his normal life, he is certain to change. After that . . . well, you see the same patterns repeat themselves over and over and wonder what the point is."

"But times change. He saw the Dark Ages, the Renaissance, the

Industrial Revolution . . ."

"He did not see shit on these islands. And even if he had, he would have been an observer, and not a participant. Knowledge may accrue, but creativity is more . . . slippery. You would be different" the priest looks over to Nathan. "Souls are like my church: some solid and practical like the stone, and some radiant like the stained glass. They are all needed in their different ways."

"The monk said something like that. But isn't your church made of wood, and prone to fire?"

"*Oui*, but I am trying to make a point. How people relate to each other and the divine is always based in the need to live in your own time. There is a danger, an insurmountable loneliness and loss of humanity, if you do not."

"Are you trying to talk me into coming back here, or out of it?" Nathan wonders, the town coming into view. "Besides, think of the great cathedrals that would never have been built if those generations had demanded they be completed in their lifetime. We no longer have that bigger vision." The more they talk, the less faith Nathan has in the priest's credentials; not that he had much to begin with. It is refreshing that someone who is supposed to have answers is grasping at them as much as Nathan. He had known men in positions of authority who would speak with certainty, often to cover their own doubts; only someone as uncertain of themselves and their philosophy could preach such definitudes. What would happen when is alone again, what would he think about on the ferry?

"Do what you can while you can," the priest looks over as they wait to turn at an intersection. "Life is such a gift, and can be so fragile even when, like the Monk, it is not so fragile at all."

"That sounds very un-priest-like," Nathan is certain.

"You followed a path you did not have to. Even if your friend was pulling your strings, she never had to chase you: you made a choice. The same thing that ruined her belief, made you believe."

A large white ship appears in the distance, overwhelming the small port.

"If the bleeding is done, there is a clean shirt and jacket in the trunk," the priest offers. "You were very lucky to be so close to the Source. When you come back, you will be good as new."

"I'm not so sure I'll be back. These out-of-the-way places have too much excitement for a simple city boy like me."

"I was not aware you had a choice," he parks the car and looks sternly at Nathan. "God has decided, *no*? You will be back."

"Now that sounds like a priest," Nathan sighs.

54

Chicago

NATHAN HAD LEFT at a time when his world was flat. He returns rounded, battered and bruised; as many good lessons tend to leave you. Fate had come looking for him since, like most people, he had no intention of seeking it out. Sitting at his table, alone at home, he flips the large kitchen knife back and forth between his hands, watching the reflection of light as it catches one eye then the other, a blinding miniature sun leaving ghost images in his vision. Nathan reaches out, takes the bottle of Jameson and douses the blade. The brown liquid pours across its sharp edge and into a glass strategically placed below. He downs a big gulp from the now-filled tumbler and then slides the wood-handled knife carefully but with some pressure across his forearm. A rush of pain and fleeting ecstasy causes him to gasp, his heart racing. He watches in fascination as blood begins to draw up, suppressing a desire to grab the flap of skin and pull it up revealing the beautiful landscape below.

"Shit," he exclaims as blood runs down the side of his arm onto the table. Raising the bleeding appendage up, he holds his other hand underneath to catch any drops while he runs to get a towel.

He has done this a few times, as a test, convincing himself it is not becoming a problem.

Johanna may disagree. Reliable, good friend Johanna; she had taken him in on his return, no questions asked. Nathan had driven all the way back from Canada, stopping once to stock up on food and a case of water. Missing his luggage, he had also bought a disposable cell phone and had called Johanna several times, getting back up to speed on what had been happening, but not offering much in return; he was not sure what to say, or what she would believe. When he arrived in Chicago, he went directly to her house. He must have looked a fright when she opened the door. She assumed he had been mugged in Tijuana, or some other nefarious event befitting his character.

She insisted he shower and shave before doing anything, and he happily obliged. A woman's house just has more mirrors, and he was finally able to check his back and see what other damage had been done, and how freakish it looks. Though the entry wound from the bullet was just below his rib on the right side, the exit wound was higher, just below his shoulder blade, ricocheting inside his body. If he had not intervened, he thought, the shot was probably aimed somewhere far less fatal to Audrey than where it had gone. He had changed its direction. He had killed her.

Then sleep. He laid down for a nap after the shower but did not wake up until noon the next day. When he stepped out her door, stepped foot in Chicago again, all he could do was stand there. He had been in a different world. He wandered the streets for a day, a sort of culture shock of his spirit. Nathan was noticing things, noticing people, in ways he never had before. He sat in one spot, watching these people, observing them, trying to somehow capture their essence, which is so different than the way he could capture the essence of a building or landscape. He could not draw them, could not even write them, and eventually gave up. For now, that time he sits watching just melts into a vibration, and people become notes he crumples into his pocket. He is still unsure whether it is a permanent change or a temporary high, whether he is happier now or before. *It is rare when people realize they are happy*, he counseled himself while observing the singles and couples and families who had suddenly invaded his reality, *they tend to only remember when they* were *happy*.

He stayed a couple more nights with Johanna and her family, thankful for the friend and partner she has always been, and soaking up the sound of a house full of life. Johanna talked little about business. Just being there he saw in her, for the first time in a long time, the woman who had been his friend first. His two weeks away had progressed at a different rate than time had unfolded here, yet what he was feeling were years and decades of constructed walls coming down. And for once Nathan felt if she peered behind those walls, that it would not be hiding a thickly unmaintained circuitous pathway to hell.

Nathan hinted at some referral work coming from Anton, which led into a series of remembered stories over the dinner table, sometimes hilariously verging on inappropriate for children and husband. He made his meeting with Anton sound casual, as if they had run into each other on vacation, and Anton was looking for a career change. When she asked what kind of work it might be, he was unsure how to answer. There had apparently been a few inquiries, mostly at the office; cryptic messages left when the caller was informed Nathan was out. So far they have respected his privacy at home. There had not been any contact from the monk, or anyone from the islands, though he had not expected any; their sense of time was on a completely different scale.

Nathan had always wanted was his own piece of immortality.

Meeting that monk, that thing the monk had become, he considers that life would not really begin until he gives up that notion. Anton offered a thrilling, potentially deadly obscurity. The Monk is a similar reflection in an opposingly warped mirror. Presented with two paths, Nathan decides it might be better to go off-road, if he has a choice at all.

There is a picture on his table, within reach of his outstretched and still bleeding arm, of him and Alex in a cheesy autumn outdoor portrait she had forced him to do. They look happy, he thinks, and she was certainly beautiful. What attracts his attention are the trees in the photo, their branches bowed in silent sorrow, gazing down wistfully at the burden they have lost now lying peacefully on the grass surrounding the two smiling figures in a posed embrace. Burdens are often missed once they are lifted, and the realization occurs how much these obstacles are needed.

It was time to visit Alex's grave. It was time to contact a friend who might know what really happened to Natalia. It was time to mourn, forgive himself, and move on. He was not just likely to do things differently from this moment; he really has no idea how he could continue the same way he had. The winds of change are usually no match for mountains of stubbornness and single-mindedness; they can only hope to blow around and bring a fresh breeze here and there, erosion taking a much longer time. Nathan knows that real changes are usually subtle and slow, except when they are not, and an earthquake of vast proportions suddenly occurs. He is testing, not wanting to deceive himself. This cut will be the last, he swears, before he is convinced.

Whiskey and loss of blood are having their effect. Nathan smiles through the haze, a memory from long ago: as a young boy, as many boys do, he had begun digging a hole in the backyard. He simply started digging as a primal, instinctual need. He did not know what other boys think–if there will be treasure, fire, antiquities–but he knew in his mind that if he just dug a little further he would find the top of a pyramid, even bigger than the ones he had seen on television. It would imbue him with some mystical strength and wisdom, and of course make him very famous for discovering this ancient mystical culture of America. Of course he had to give up his dig–his father was very clear about the stupid hole he almost ran his lawnmower into–and strength and wisdom would have to wait. After all these years he had finally started digging again. It would not be a fabulous misplaced pyramid, and it would not make him famous: it is exactly the opposite of that.

The phone rings. His answering machine is apparently turned off, as it continues seven or eight times, Nathan happily counting along but unsure if he had started with the first ring. Some of these people are real bastards, and he might be in as much danger for not taking a job as for accepting it. Whatever happens, Nathan decides, it would be on his terms, and they may not like how it turns out. He would have to be smart, smarter than Anton.

Nathan knows he will return to the islands sooner rather than later, admitting it will be out of fear, but hoping one day it will be for some greater motivation. His little life here, his little dramas, are no match for a fate that has chosen him. It is reassuring, and scary as hell. Time is suddenly a friend, but only to the extent that he respects it. He is not invincible, as the blood on his arm proves.

The bleeding has stopped, the scab looking reddish brown. He would not forget; there were several other reminders not quite so normal. Nathan stands up a bit unsteadily, wraps his arm with a bandage and pulls his sleeve down. It is reassuring, if not humbling, to scar like everyone else.

www.ingramcontent.com/pod-product-compliance
Lightning Source LLC
Chambersburg PA
CBHW051541250626
47157CB00001B/144